The Dead Sit Round
in a Ring

The Dead Sit Round in a Ring

DAVID LAWRENCE

Thomas Dunne Books
St. Martin's Minotaur ⚏ New York

THOMAS DUNNE BOOKS.
An imprint of St. Martin's Press.

www.minotaurbooks.com

ISBN 0-312-32710-2

First published in Great Britain by Michael Joseph

First U.S. Edition: May 2004

10 9 8 7 6 5 4 3 2 1

To John and Michelle

Thanks to:
Rob Bastable for tactics and hardware
Emilija Leskovar for idioms and childcare

The Dead Sit Round
in a Ring

1

Four people sitting in a ring.

Two women and two men. The women and one of the men perched on chairs, the second man on a small upright sofa. All looking inwards, all leaning slightly forward as if staring at something that lay at the centre of the ring.

All of them dead.

They had been dead for a while, but DS Stella Mooney couldn't be sure exactly how long. Forensics would make a calculation based on insect infestation, rectal temperature, the degree to which blood had puddled in the joints. Corpse cabbala.

The women were wearing skirts and Stella could see lacerations and raw scabbing on their legs. It was rodent activity. She always remembered to be aware of that, because her first suspicious death had involved a stiff that was a few days old, and the smell had been pretty bad, and she'd been making a good job of hanging on to her lunch and pretending it was all in a day's work while forensics did what they do. Then she'd crouched down to bag a near-empty bottle of Famous Grouse next to where the stiff was lying, and his trouser leg had suddenly boiled up and a rat had run out across his shoe, and she'd lost the battle with her lunch.

*

The scene-of-crime officer had prepared an uncontaminated path from the street door to the living room of the flat: to the little group sitting there like figures from another age; like a council meeting in some prehistoric bunker. Stella reflected that if they'd been sitting side by side, it would have looked more natural: an audience of some kind. They'd all sat down to watch *Who Wants to be a Millionaire?* and had died of envy. Had died of want.

The women were in their late sixties or early seventies, so far as she could tell. It wasn't an easy guess because death had done things to them over the past few days. It had pumped them up and made them up – a light sheen of colour in some places; in others livid stripes and shadows. Stella knew that death was all about change: about complexion; about weight gain; about masks.

One of the women was tall, half a head above the woman next to her. The men looked to be at either end of middle age: one in his early forties, a full head of hair, heavier than the other, who was sixty-something, bald to the crown of his head and carried crepe and wattle round his neck and jowls. The tall woman had lost an eye. To some scavenger, Stella thought; some little feaster at death's table. The woman peered obsessively at the world she had just left with a dull blue eye on one side and a bad penny on the other.

Forensics were sectioning the room and taking samples: three figures in white disposables, going on hands and knees, their heads hooded, their feet covered. They might have been followers of some obscure religion, shrouded as a gesture of respect, hands ghostly in latex. They bagged shreds and leavings, hair and dust, scraps of detritus. Relics.

The scene-of-crime officer was DC Andy Greegan. He was stocky and had sandy hair and a Scots accent to go with the looks. He walked forward as the video man backed off to get a different angle. 'Just us and the landlady, boss,' Greegan said. 'The diced carrots by the door – that was her. Nice of her to get clear of the immediate area before she lost it. Puke apart, it's a pretty good scene.'

As they spoke, they wagged their hands in front of their faces like royalty waving to a crowd. The room was full of flies: big bastards, green-backed, blue-backed; they flew with a low, persistent drone. Close your eyes and it could have been plainsong from a further room.

'No evidence of trauma?' Stella asked. 'No violence done to the bodies?'

'No external evidence.'

'You're thinking . . . what: Kool-Aid cocktail with a touch of cyanide?'

'Some sort of poison, yeah.'

'Group suicide.' Stella looked again at the forensic team on all fours like supplicants. 'Cult thing . . .'

'Have to be, wouldn't it, boss?' As he said this, Greegan was looking at the stuff on the wall. 'Spook-ee. I've never seen this before. Anything like this.'

'Where is she?'

'The landlady? Outside in a car.'

'Our car?'

'Her car.'

The stuff on the wall was posters mostly. The light of the world. A dove. A heart shedding gouts of blood.

3

Christ with children: *'Suffer them to come unto me'*. Christ with the disciples. Christ crucified, nails ripping his wrists, head hung, the crown of thorns jammed down on his brow, his ribcage sprung like a bowsprit.

This last was not a painting but a wooden crucifix fashioned from polished oak and all of two feet high. On the other side of the cross, more posters: The risen Christ. Christ in glory. Christ the lamb. Christ ascending to heaven, a long spiral of angels at his back.

Flies were swarming on the crucifix as if they knew. Stella thought of how there must have been flies at Golgotha, given the geography, given the heat, given the blood and the stench, given that fear and pain will make a man foul himself. There must have been a mob of flies. A great black singing halo of flies.

DC Pete Harriman was back from a tour of the building, knocking on doors: there were two other flats in the house and an attic bedsitter. Stella looked at him as he entered the room. He shook his head: no one in.

'The landlady,' Stella asked him. 'She ready to talk to us?'

'Can't shut her up. She's on fast-forward.'

'Name?'

'Mary Something.' He looked at his notebook. 'Callaghan.'

'Okay,' Stella said. 'Find someone to drive her to the nick. I'll be down in about fifteen minutes. Get a statement; something for me to read. Something for me to hold in my hand. Let her take her time.'

Harriman looked across at the group of dead people: the way they all seemed to have stalled on a breath that was waiting to be exhaled. Then he glanced at the posters on the wall. 'Does look a bit like a prayer meeting, doesn't it?' Stella followed his gaze, but didn't answer. 'People like that . . . What makes them decide it's time to die?'

'You don't know it was that.'

'They had a vision, I expect.'

Stella half-smiled. 'You've closed the case, Pete, have you?'

'Members of a cult,' Harriman assured her.

'What cult?'

'The sort of cult where they sit round in small groups waiting for a sign.'

'Waiting for death.'

It's not Golgotha, but the flies can be a real problem. They get in your mouth and in your eyes and you know exactly where they've been.

The smell is a problem too, rich and heavy and corrupt, but you can put a smear of strong decongestant on your upper lip to take away the worst of it. Those are the outward manifestations of death. There's something in the air, though, more unsettling than bluebottles or dark, crusty odours. It's death itself and it's made up of all sorts of things that are difficult to put your finger on.

Mostly, Stella thought, it's the way corpses have of being still. Just as their eyes have emptied of seeing, so their bodies have emptied of gesture. It's more than heaviness or immobility. Something's missing. The ghost in the machine has taken a walk.

When forensics had finished, someone opened the windows and a medical team arrived with kick-down gurneys and body-bags. Rigor mortis had come and gone, so they didn't have to break any bones. The bodies were sticky with their own fluids. The team handled each corpse carefully, aware of the danger of puncture-and-spillage.

'Ask about the PM,' Stella told Harriman. 'Last I heard, they were backed up.'

Two bedrooms, a bathroom, a kitchen, the room where the dead sat round in a ring.

Stella went into the bedrooms and flicked through the wardrobes and the drawers. She wore latex gloves and a paper coverall with a hood: everyone sheds hairs all the time, sifting down as we nod or shake or scratch. The bedrooms were for the women. In fact, it was easy to see that the women lived there and the men didn't. If the bedrooms hadn't told the tale, the bathroom would have: not just the lack of a razor or a bottle of Lynx; there was a lightness about the room, a fragrance. No heavy hand.

In the kitchen was a table with four chairs. On the table were the remains of a meal along with a bottle of Chilean Merlot and four wine glasses, one still half-full. It took less than a minute for forensics to dub it 'the last supper'.

An accident, a fight, a fire, each collects its little group of watchers, gathered on the far side of the street, perhaps, or gazing from windows. A billow of smoke will draw them, or the sound of metal on metal. The sight of an ambulance and two police cars in a quiet street in Kensal Green.

Fifteen or twenty people stood outside the house. They were motionless and they were silent, more or less.

Now and then a muttered question or a piece of amateur guesswork. Blue-striped police tape marked a boundary: a line where the humdrum world gave way to a place of dark, uncontrollable images. It excited them; they wanted to peer into that place, but they didn't want to go there.

Except one man. He walked through the scattered group of onlookers as if he had a job to do and got to the door of the house as Stella was emerging. She recognized him at once for what he was and he smiled at her as if they might be old friends: not that they knew one another.

He said, 'I gather it's a group suicide. Religious thing, yeah? I wonder if –'

'No,' Stella said, 'there'll be a statement later.'

'I don't want a statement, just confirmation.'

'What's your name?' Stella asked.

'John Delaney.'

'Which paper?'

'No paper. Freelance. Can you confirm how many people –'

'You're causing an obstruction, Mr Delaney, and I'm asking you to step back behind the police line –'

'Sure, okay. Someone said it was four dead –'

'– which is indicated by the blue and white tape'

'– and there's evidence of some sort of fundamentalist –'

'– or I'll be more than happy to have you arrested.'

Delaney held up both his hands and backed off towards the police tape. 'Just trying to get the story right.'

'Yeah?' Stella smiled without warmth. 'Why not make it up? It's what you guys usually do.'

'Statement when?' Delaney asked, still back-pedalling.

'Eventually.'

'And you would be –'

'Detective Sergeant Mooney.'

'So I speak to you if I want more information.'

'There'll be a –'

'Statement. I heard you. But if I want more information . . .'

This time his persistence brought just a hint of humour to Stella's smile. She said, 'Fuck off, Delaney,' ducked under the tape and headed for her car.

Andy Greegan caught up with her. He said, 'The landlady's in casualty, boss. Keeled over in the interview room.'

'Where?' Stella asked.

'Charing Cross.'

'Good,' Stella said. 'Well, that's bloody wonderful. That's a great start.'

It was late summer, a summer of rain; even now there was a hint of rain in the air and the room seemed cold. The video man and the stills man had finished, having looked at death from all angles. The forensic officers had their collection of glassine envelopes, their detritus, their stains and parings.

DC Greegan looked round carefully, like a goodwife making sure things were in order. Flies still buzzed in corners and made airborne scribbles over the wooden crucifix. The figure on the cross gave him a sorry, sideways look.

2

Mary Callaghan was wired to an ECG monitor and they'd put a cannula into a vein on the back of her hand. She was paper-white apart from the down of hair on her upper lip, which was a faint beige. Stella looked in to the A&E cubicle and was waved away by a teenage nurse.

Pete Harriman was one floor up on a flat roof overlooking the car park, smoking a cigarette. Stella had seen him as she parked her car in one of the disabled bays. He said, 'She's still talking.'

'Not to us.'

'She'll be fine. They said she's absolutely fine.'

'I'll bet she is. Despite the fact that she looks like shit. Who drove her to the nick?'

'I did.' Harriman dropped his cigarette and trod on it, then took another out of the pack. The breeze on the roof lifted his dark hair into a coxcomb and tugged the smoke from his mouth as he exhaled. He wore a suede jacket and blue jeans and, on his own time, a thin hoop earring; dark like a gypsy.

'She didn't seem in shock at all?' Stella suggested. 'Pale, sweats, trembling, light-headed?'

'Said she felt wobbly. No surprise there. Anyone would, walking in on a bunch of week-old corpses.'

'Week old?'

'I'm guessing.'

'Don't guess.'

'Okay, boss.'

Stella sighed. 'Then what? After she felt wobbly . . .'

'Got to the nick; I started to take a statement, someone turned off the lights.'

'Did she damage herself?'

'She was sitting down at the time. Went sideways out of the chair, must have taken a few bruises.'

'Didn't hit her head, or –'

'Nothing like that.'

'You're supposed to be able to recognize the signs of shock, Pete.'

'I might have if she'd stopped talking for half a second. As far as I could see, she was running on high-octane fuel.'

'Yeah,' Stella observed, 'it's one of the signs.'

Stella went back down to A&E and showed her warrant card to the teenage nurse, who handed her on to a charge nurse whose ID plate read 'Liam Cotter'. Liam suggested Mary Callaghan be given twenty-four hours. He said, 'More people die from shock than from the trauma that causes it,' and Stella could see the sentence in italics, as if she were reading the textbook in question.

She said, 'I just need a couple of minutes. A couple of questions.'

'I'd sooner not.'

'It's important.'

Liam had been writing on the admissions board with a marker pen; now he turned back to the task. Maybe Stella would cease to be there if he couldn't see her. She waited, not speaking. After a moment he said, 'I'll be timing you.'

Mary Callaghan got a rent cheque every month from one of the women, Caroline Deever. Her name was on the agreement. Mary thought the other woman must be Caroline's sister, but she wasn't sure. It was an agreement for a two-person occupancy. She didn't know the men. Stella picked these facts out of a long, seamless stream-of-consciousness that had to do with God, death, religious fanaticism, the problems of owning a rental, the capriciousness of tenants and the cost of replacing furniture into which the dead had leaked.

She sat propped up on the A&E gurney, her monitor beeping, the hospital gown pulled across her scrawny tits, and offered her view of the world at no charge. Mary was feeling a lot better.

AMIP stands for Area Major Investigation Pool. They are the murder squad. People watch TV and movies and see a murder take place, then see the hero-cop set about solving it. He'll be a detective inspector. His sidekick will be a detective sergeant. And he's on the case no matter where the killing takes place; he's on the case no matter how often murders occur.

That's not how it happens.

The local guys take the triple-nine call. They establish that a murder has been committed. Unless the cuckolded husband is standing over the bodies of his cheating wife and her lover with the dripping butcher's knife in his hand, their next move is to contact the AMIP coordination centre in west London. A detective inspector will be briefed. He'll put together a team: mostly, if he can, people he's worked with before. This will be set up within an hour or so; later, the team moves in on the local nick, requisitioning offices, or a police house, and working from there. The DI will visit the scene of crime. After that, he (could be 'she') will be pretty much office-bound along with other members of the team: an investigation coordinator, an office manager, an accounts manager (as the case proceeds, *everyone* bitches about the budget), an exhibits officer, the scene-of-crime officer, a couple of civilian indexers.

Admin: there's a lot of admin.

And from time to time, the squad might call on people who are not day-to-day members of the team: forensic scientists, the divisional intelligence officer for the area, a police surgeon, a profiler. Even, sometimes, a psychic: more used than spoken of.

But the near-to-the-knuckle work, the dirty work, is done by streetwise detective sergeants and detective constables. People like Stella Mooney.

The AMIP squad had set up in a police house near Notting Hill nick, alongside the flats at half a million and rising, the cars at thirty grand, the organic butchers, the pubs with window boxes. It was the side of Stella's patch closest to Notting Hill Gate and Holland Park Avenue. Estate agents' offices flanked antique shops and chic little stores selling food in foreign languages.

The houses on the south side of the Avenue started at a couple of million. Go north and you soon hit the Saints and people dealing openly in the street. Further north and a couple of miles west, things were tougher, more competitive, better organized. Up there, your status symbols were a Beamer and an Ingram MAC10 spray-and-pray machine pistol.

Despite these differences, Stella still worked both sides of the street. Last year, the squad had set up close to Wormwood Scrubs, where a black hooker had been found knifed. Her three-year-old child had been in the flat with the body for two days before she was found. Six weeks later, Stella and her DI, Michael Sorley, had stood at Heathrow and watched a plane take off for Jamaica. On board was the Yardie who had killed her for her stash. The fact that he was an 'illegal' made things easier, because he was wanted at home for three other killings; this fact took him off Sorley's hands and off the hands of the DPP, which is why Sorley was grinning as the 747 nosed up into the sunset.

A couple of months before that, a day trader with a house in Norland Square, another in Wiltshire and a Mach 2 Porsche had been found hanging from a tree in Holland Park. At first sight, you had to make it suicide; however, the post-mortem showed the cause of death to be a blow to the head that had crushed the skull in a long, flat line just about where he parted his hair It's a fair bet that taking such a blow would have left him gloomy and upset, perhaps even prone to suicide, but it was difficult to see how he'd managed to string himself up.

Stella wanted a man called Randall Sinclair for it. Her guess was that Sinclair was supplying the trader with cocaine and also sleeping with the trader's wife. It was a good guess, but the squad couldn't get close to proving it. They closed the case on the coroner's verdict of person or persons unknown. Later, Stella heard that Sinclair had taken up both the wife and the Porsche.

Stella worked both sides of the street, and worked them well, but she knew the poor side better than the rich: knew it from having lived there. She had grown up on a west London estate, one of only three kids from her school to go to university.

She became a copper because she fell in love with a copper: a casual romance that somehow became a marriage and after a couple of years became an amicable divorce. She'd joined the Met on graduate entry and was pretty fast track to DS, via a stint in uniform. She was on course for DI if she wanted the job, but was holding back. DIs were managers – paper pushers – and Stella preferred her coppering to be done at the sharp end. A DI never went out on the collar. A DI would always leave the questioning of suspects to the detective sergeants because a year off the streets and you lose your feel for who's lying and who isn't, lose your feel for the fault lines, the whiff of corruption, the rhythm of interrogation.

Stella felt at home with all that. But there were risks attached and she had found them; or they had found her; and she still carried the scars.

Everything was bagged and labelled. The purpose of a murder inquiry is to bring order out of chaos, and a lot of that is done by stealth: things in the right place, things in the proper order, things catalogued and listed and entered on a computer system.

Stella was sifting through the bagged and labelled contents of the pockets of the dead, along with DC Paul

Lester and DC Susan Chapman. Sue was in her early thirties and had a wild perm; if she ever switched to uniform, the perm would have to go. Paul was the exhibits officer. Anything relevant to the crime, including the murder weapon, was his to have and hold. Sue was the team's lynchpin, the computer operative; she coordinated the entire operation from first to last. Every scrap of information from the triple-nine call onwards: witness statements, pathology reports, court proceedings, the jury verdict and the sentence; or the moment when the case hit a wall and the file closed, unsolved.

And along the way, everything had to be papered; everything. Reports had to be filed on every move the team made. Each officer wrote reports on each undertaking at each stage of the investigation. No exceptions. Paper.

They had the contents of pockets and handbags, together with the relevant contents of the flat: wallets, keys, small change, letters, chequebooks, credit cards, a driving licence, photographs, unpaid bills – everything. Everything they could want. No problem about identifying the two women and the older man. They were Caroline, Joanna and Conrad Deever: brother and sisters.

Forensics had found little on the younger man apart from six hundred pounds and change, a room key, a mobile phone and a fat crop of maggots. In fact the younger man was a very big puzzle, because when the initial forensic report came next morning, it stated that there were four sets of fingerprints on the wine glasses on the table, but none of them belonged to him. One other thing distinguished him from his dead fellows.

The pre-post-mortem examination concluded that the two women and the older man had almost certainly died from barbiturate poisoning. The police doctor's guess was that the drug was self-administered. The younger man was a different case altogether. There was a puncture wound between his third and fourth ribs, small to be sure, but the purple, puckered rip in his flesh was plain to see.

He had died from a stab wound to the heart.

Stella passed the information to Sue Chapman for logging and shared the problem with Mike Sorley.

'So what's our guess?' Sorley asked. 'The old dears killed him, then topped themselves?'

Like Sorley, Stella didn't think so; but she couldn't offer an alternative theory.

'And none of the prints are his?' Sorley asked.

'Not his. What we've got is four glasses, three wine drinkers and him.'

'And a missing person.'

'Well, a person missing, yes. Whoever was drinking from the fourth glass.'

'Maybe he killed the Mystery Man.'

'Maybe. It's pretty clear that he was known to the others. Well, some of them, at least. We'll try finding him through them.'

'These are positive IDs, are they, Stella?'

'The women, sure. It's pretty obvious who the women are. In fact, the landlady made a positive ID of one of them: Caroline Deever. The other is her sister: they lived together.'

'Sister's name?'

'Joanna.'

'Which one was Caroline?'

'The taller one. We're looking for evidence of the men – letters, photographs, you know . . .' She paused. 'Here's an odd thing about the younger man: he was carrying six hundred in cash.'

'People do.'

'Not distressed gentlefolk.'

'Then he's a builder or a crook.'

'What do you mean – *or*?'

Sorley smiled. 'So we could PM the women.'

'Thought we'd leave them all in one piece for a while. Tough to ask someone to ID the dear departed if they've been trepanned and unzipped.'

Sorley nodded. 'What are we doing about that? Finding a relative, a friend, someone connected?'

'We're following leads from the flat; plus the press have got the story, and TV.'

'Four dead in cult suicide,' Sorley observed.

'It makes a good story.'

'And what's our story?'

'We're still making it up.'

'Good.' Sorley smiled and looked down at the papers on his desk, which meant, Get on with it.

The two women looked serious and engrossed, heads slightly bent, a tenseness about them as if they were both grappling with the same thought. The men looked vaguer, somehow, less concerned. The photographs had been retouched to get rid of most of the discoloration. Caroline Deever had been given a new eye. Stella wondered whether the priest realized that he was looking at people who had been several days dead. He glanced, said 'No' and handed the photo back. Stella smiled and returned it to him.

'People often say "No" too quickly. Sorry. I'd like you to look for longer.'

The priest held the photo for another five seconds, then said 'No' again. He added, 'These people are dead.'

'As I said, they were found –'

'I mean they're dead in these photos. They were dead when the pictures were taken.'

'Yes.'

It was dark and cool. There was a broad patch of shifting, buttery light where racked candles burned in front of a shrine to Our Lady – which was how Stella still thought of her despite years of having her back firmly turned on the Church. The priest stared at the photos, one in either hand. 'God forgive them,' he said. Then, as if wanting to make clear that they were never his responsibility, never his to save, added, 'They didn't worship here.'

'You don't know them?'

'No, I don't.'

Stella took the photographs back and gave him another that showed the decorated wall: the posters, the crucifix. He shrugged, then looked up at her: So?

'A cult,' she suggested. 'Fundamentalist . . .'

'Ah,' he said. 'The mad minister, the corrupt clergyman.'

'It's just a theory,' Stella observed. 'We're not fixed on it.'

'But the press people are.' Stella let the veiled accusation hang in the air. 'You expect me to say that people come to Christ in different ways.'

'This lot came as a package tour,' Stella said, and instantly regretted it. To her surprise, the priest smiled.

He said, 'There are more loony-tune, self-asserting, self-worshipping, self-interested splinter groups than you might guess. And what they most often preach is self-sacrifice, which means they want your money. But some of the cult leaders, if that's the right way to describe them, also want power. And power's a dangerous thing: it can get out of hand. It can get out of *their* hands.'

'What would you call them?'

'Sorry?'

'You said, "if that's the right way to describe them".'

'Oh, yes. Well, I'd call them crooks at best. Sociopaths at worst.'

'Jesus Christ was a bit of a sociopath, wasn't that what they said about him?'

The priest smiled again, this time sadly. 'Don't tell me you're a lapsed Catholic, Detective Sergeant.'

'Have you got any thoughts – about where I might look? Local crooks and sociopaths, for example?'

'Not really. This is London. There's the usual sprinkle of nonconformists and fringe groups. Seventh-Day Adventists, Mormons –' he paused – 'Baptists,' then laughed at his own joke. 'I suppose there are bound to be groups called something like the First Church of Christ in Terminal Agony, but I don't know who they are.'

They were sitting in a pew by the altar, but off to one side and close to a confessional. Too close for comfort,

Stella thought. Her eye flicked over part of a frieze depicting the Stations of the Cross, which put her in mind of the heavy, low droning of the flies in the murder house.

As if it had just occurred to him, the priest said, 'You've tried other faiths, I suppose?'

Stella wasn't quite sure whether he meant officially, or as a failed Christian. She put the photos back in her pocket and said, 'No one seems to know them.'

'Well, not everyone feels the need of a church when they worship.'

Stella gave him her card and made the standard remark: 'If you think of anything.'

She made her way to the aisle and almost turned to the altar, almost dipped her knee, and probably would have if the priest hadn't been watching. Like you don't walk under a ladder; like you throw spilled salt over your shoulder to blind the devil.

A couple of days later, a squad DC called Steve Sheppard called on Mary Callaghan to get some back-up on the identities. He asked if she would be willing to take another look at the bodies: maybe she'd recognize more than Caroline Deever. She talked all the way to the morgue, but fell silent as they walked into the cadaver room, where she had nothing at all to say.

Caroline, she told Sheppard as they got back to street level. She knew Caroline: she'd met her a couple of times when there had been some problem about the flat: a smell in the drains, a damp patch on the wall. She had never met the sister. She rarely found herself on friendly terms with her tenants because they lived in different worlds. That was what she said: different worlds. Sheppard drove her back to Hampstead.

Henry Deever was more help. He turned up at Notting Hill nick two days later, wearing a business suit and a worried frown.

3

In the AMIP squad room, he'd been known as the Third Man. The pinboard was crammed with SOC photos, among them shots of the four dead taken from different angles. Someone had doctored one of the ten-by-eights so that a white silhouette with a red question mark over its head sat in with the group: the person whose unidentified fingerprints were on the unfinished glass of wine. Every morning someone came up with a new face for the Third Man: a cut-out from a newspaper or a magazine. He was Tom Cruise or the Prince of Wales or Liam Gallagher. On one occasion, he was Jesus Christ, which struck Stella as more than usually witty.

When someone pointed out that the Third Man could just as easily have been a woman, Sue Chapman doctored the collage with the face of Madonna, a grace note to the original joke.

Henry Deever was a lot less exotic than any of his stand-ins, but he had the advantage of being the right person. He was in his mid-fifties and stick thin, with a careful parting in his pepper-and-salt hair. His eyes were pale blue and seemed out of focus, as if they had a film of wet over the iris. Stella couldn't help thinking of Caroline Deever: her dark eye-socket.

Henry sat opposite Stella and Pete Harriman in interview room 3 and skinned one thumb with the nail of the other. Stella started the tape and told him that in his own time would be good.

'Caroline,' he said, 'and Joanna and Conrad made the decision between them. They asked me to go with them, but I couldn't. I don't know why Caroline went. I can't understand why she did that.' He spoke in a low, flat, mechanical tone.

'Your sisters and your brother,' Stella said, giving confirmation to the tape.

'Jo was ill. She heard about a month ago. It was what our mother died of.'

Stella waited, but he didn't offer more. In the end she said, 'Cancer.'

'Yes.'

'She was having treatment?'

'No,' Henry said. 'The hospital wanted to help her, they offered to help her, but they couldn't cure her. They told her that. Inoperable.' He closed his eyes a moment. 'Isn't that a terrible word? Imagine hearing that said to you.'

'But Caroline was well.'

'Jo and Conrad, they started things . . . It was mostly them . . .'

'Conrad was ill too?'

'Angina. He'd had it for years, but it seemed to get worse every day. I'm eight years younger, you see.' He said it as if apologizing for his own good health. 'Eight years younger than the youngest of them. Conrad was tired, he told me. Bone tired, he said. That was the way he put it: bone tired. He couldn't walk far, couldn't do much, couldn't get up a flight of stairs without stopping all the time. They made this decision. It was after Jo was

23

diagnosed. I can't understand why Caroline agreed to go.'

'Did you ask her?'

'In a way. Not really. They telephoned and said would I go over. We had something to eat. Then they told me what they'd decided.'

'And asked you –'

'To go with them.'

'And you said no.'

A blood bead had sprung up on Henry's thumb where he'd been scraping at it. He licked it off, nodding as he did so.

'What did you say to them?'

'I said no.'

'I mean, about the fact that they had decided to kill themselves.'

'Oh. Well, yes, I tried to talk them out of it, of course. But they seemed to have made up their minds.'

'What did you say?'

'I *pleaded* with them.' Henry suddenly seemed to see that fervour was needed; sincerity. Stella thought it was quite likely that his feelings were genuine: he just wasn't used to letting them show. 'Obviously, I didn't want them to –'

He turned his head away and stopped speaking. Stella gave him a couple of minutes, then asked, 'You didn't think there was anything you could do? Anything you should have done?'

Henry looked back towards her, his mouth slack with suppressed weeping. 'What?'

'Reported it.'

'Who to?'

'Us.'

Henry looked at Stella, then at Pete Harriman. He seemed puzzled. 'To you? Why? You didn't know them.'

It was genuine, Stella realized. When she had said 'us' Henry thought she'd meant herself and Harriman: a couple of strangers. What business of theirs?

She asked, 'The posters on the wall, the crucifix . . .' Henry nodded as if agreeing with something as yet unsaid. 'You were all churchgoers, was that it?'

Pete Harriman suppressed a smile: *churchgoers*.

'All believers,' Henry said. 'It's a personal thing, really, isn't it?'

Someone brought in coffee. Henry Deever set his styrofoam cup down amid the torn scraps of thumb-skin that freckled the interview table and looked at the photograph Harriman had just handed him. He said, 'The problem was, he turned up at the door. Just turned up.'

'Which door?' Stella asked.

'The door to the flat. He asked us to help him, but he didn't say what he wanted. We let him in.'

'He needed help, all right,' Stella observed. 'He'd been stabbed in the heart.'

What Henry said next went down in AMIP-5 legend: 'He certainly looked unwell.'

'Did anyone phone for an ambulance?'

'I expect we would have. He died, though. We helped him on to the sofa, he was sitting there, he didn't seem able to say much, and after a minute or two, he died.'

'A minute or two?'

'Moment or two.'

'You didn't think it might be a police matter?'

'We thought about what best to do. It seemed he'd had a heart attack or something.'

'No one made any attempt to revive him?'

Henry looked at Stella, puzzled. 'He was dead.'

'Heart massage or something?'

Henry shook his head impatiently, as if his message wasn't getting through. 'He was dead.'

'So what decision was made?'

'They thought they'd go ahead. What difference could it make? It seemed . . .'

He paused, as if deciding whether or not to confide something that Stella might not understand. 'In fact, it seemed like an omen, if you know what I mean.'

'A sign.'

Henry looked pleased. 'A sign, yes.'

'And you left.'

'And I left.'

'Why have you come to us now?'

'I saw it in the paper,' Henry said. 'I started to get frightened.'

Stella asked him, 'What did you think would happen – when they were found?'

'I know. I know I should have gone back. It's up to me to make arrangements and so forth. The thing is . . .' Henry shrugged and gave a little smile, as if Stella ought to know what he meant.

'Go on.'

'I'm married. There's a wife. I don't know what she'll say. I just don't.'

Stella could see that, to Henry, it was a perfectly good excuse. She switched off the tape and told him he could go. Pete Harriman led him through the maze of corridors to the street door of the nick.

Henry said, 'I think I know why Caroline went with them.' Harriman looked at him. Henry said, 'It would have been very lonely for her.'

Henry Deever had 'seen it in the paper' and so had most other people, including Stella. John Delaney's article was the one she read twice, not so much because she was specifically mentioned as having no comment, but for the confident picture it built of a dangerous fundamentalist cult whose disciples were encouraged to top themselves in order to get closer to Christ.

It was, she thought, a nifty piece of fiction; skilful, too, because Delaney had been careful to set up the idea of such a cult without falling into the trap of saying that the Deevers had been members. 'Maybe' and 'could be' were all over the piece, but hidden neatly between the lines.

She picked up a late edition of the *Standard* as she and Harriman walked back from the nick to the squad room. It was dusk and a light, sticky rain was falling.

'We can ask for post-mortems now,' Stella said. 'Tell DI Sorley.'

Harriman nodded. 'Just the Deevers, right?'

'All four.'

'We don't know who the other guy is yet. You don't mind his rellies having to identify bits and pieces?'

'We need to push on,' Stella said. Then, 'Sam Burgess'll put him back together again. More or less.'

Neither spoke for a while, an uneasy silence. Stella glanced at the headlines as they walked. Finally Harriman

27

said, 'Assisting three suicides and failure to report a suspicious death, surely.' He meant Henry Deever.

'For Christ's sake,' Stella said. 'What would have been the point?'

'Sorley might have other thoughts.'

'Sorley's got an eye for budgets. Waste of money bringing Deever to trial. Anyway . . . poor bastard.'

A low-spec Ford went up towards Ladbroke Grove carrying a sound system loud enough to bend girders. The ground throbbed under their feet.

Stella said, 'You heard what he said: that the guy turned up at the door of the flat, not the street –'

'Not the street door, yes; it means he lived in the house. Don't worry. Steve Sheppard and a forensic team are already down there.'

'And if he lived in the house, then Mary –'

'– Callaghan must have known him, yes.'

Stella punched him on the arm. 'Will you stop doing that.'

She logged the interview, checked her messages, left a note on Sorley's desk recommending that Henry Deever be called back for a caution, then scooped up the day's reports from her desk and took them to the pub directly opposite the nick where she ordered a vodka.

She needed that space; just half an hour.

The vodka had to be poured into a shot glass full of ice cubes right to the top: a meaty drink; it had started as an affectation and recently become a habit. When she got home, George would be there, they'd talk, maybe watch an hour of TV; he liked companionable evenings and so did she. The half hour was for herself, no one around, no one talking. The vodka was sometimes chased by another; if she was stopped she'd show her warrant card: simple as that.

She put the reports on the bar and glanced at the topics. Her drink arrived and she raised it so that it wetted her lips, then hesitated a moment, relishing the coldness and the first delicious sting of the vodka, then drank half. The heat and the little kick in the head as it went down produced a tiny shudder: a barely perceptible quake across the yoke of her back. In the same moment, she realized that someone was reading over her shoulder.

John Delaney pulled back a little and turned to order a beer, as if that had been his intention all along.

Stella said, 'You know how to take a risk, don't you?'

'Deever, Deever and Deever,' he said. 'Caroline, Joanna and Conrad; and someone called John Smith.'

John Smith was the same as John Doe: a no one. And the identities of the women would have been easy enough: ask the neighbours, check the electoral roll. But how did Delaney know about *Conrad* Deever? He was tempting her to ask, but Stella decided to let it ride: maybe she'd get more if she didn't push.

'DS Stella Mooney, thirty-one,' she remarked. 'Why do journos always put in the age?'

'It gives the reader a picture. I could have put slim, attractive, dark-haired, blue-eyed detective sergeant Stella Mooney, five feet nine, looks good in Calvin Klein jeans and Armani jacket, but you might think I was at it.'

Stella snorted. 'Gap jeans, Armani I wish, and five feet ten,' she said. She didn't think of herself as slim and attractive: more as someone who could stand to lose a pound or two and could never get her hair right. 'How did you know where to find me?'

'Lots of coppers drink in here. It's just a step from the nick.'

'What do you want, Delaney?'

'You said I could get in touch if I wanted –'

'– more information. Bollocks. *You* said it. I said nothing. Anyway, it seems you've made your mind up. They were Jesus freaks.'

Delaney eased on to the bar stool next to Stella's and poured his Budvar into a glass. He caught her smile and laughed at himself. 'You're right: drinking from the bottle is *so* last millennium.'

'Delaney,' she said, 'where are you from?'

'London. The Irish connection was three generations ago.' He was tall, so he let his shoulders sag to avoid looking down at her. Brown hair with a curl in it, and good, flat planes to cheeks that were dusted with a two-day stubble. He was the one wearing the Armani jacket, she realized. It made his earlier remark all the more irritating.

Stella knocked off the second half of her vodka and gathered her papers.

Delaney said, 'Buy you another . . .'

'I'm driving.'

'So: you get stopped, show your warrant card. Simple.'

'You've got a cynical view of the police, Delaney.'

'You're right. What are you drinking?'

'I told you – no.'

She made to leave and he tried to stop her with a story. 'I've been writing a series of pieces on cults. I got back from America a month ago. They breed a lot of Bible-carrying crazies over there.'

She wondered whether to tell him he was wrong, that the Deevers' suicide pact was a Deevers affair. Maybe they expected to skip purgatory and go straight to heaven, their sins washed from them by the Blood of the Lamb, but that wasn't their motive: their motive was getting out before the pain and humiliation started and they were too weak to do anything but endure it.

'Jonestown was the ultimate,' Delaney was still talking, 'but there are others, lots, thousands, all run by cynical bastards who like the idea of getting rich and fucking the prettier disciples. But they're very persuasive, they are *amazingly* persuasive, and you almost wonder why you're not handing over your life savings and putting on a white robe and stumbling down the steps to the baptism tank yourself.'

'It sounds personal.'

Delaney gave a little start, barely perceptible, and took a swallow of Budvar. He said, 'I'm not the first to want to nail these scumbags.'

'Yeah, but it sounded –'

'It's a good story.'

'I can hear it.'

'But it would benefit from a few more details.'

'I can't talk about the case, Delaney, you know that.'

'Some do.'

'Not me.'

'I don't want anything that's prejudicial or might harm –'

Stella said, 'I have to go.'

'– I don't really work on news pieces unless they have

a bearing on what I'm doing. It's more think-pieces, long articles, maybe a book.'

'Talk to me when it's over.'

'When will that be?'

'Who knows?'

'Right,' Delaney said, 'so AMIP have taken a look, and they're still looking. Which means it's not just four nutters holding hands and knocking back the pills for Jesus. It's murder. Someone assisted.'

'Keep guessing,' Stella said. 'And it's Stella Mooney, thirty-four. I know you guys like to get these things right.'

She drove to Hampstead before going home, though it wasn't exactly on her way. Stella lived with George Paterson in what some people liked to call north Fulham but was really the badlands of west Kensington. Stella had been on her way home just a week ago after a very late shift when SO19 had abseiled down the West Kensington Estate tower blocks on a drugs raid. She had stopped to watch until a uniform told her to piss off. She went. Showing rank wouldn't have been showing class. People were looking out from pubs and pizza places and the doorways of game arcades, all of them thinking, Stella guessed, 'Shit! There goes my score.'

She and George had been burgled twice in six months, not a bad average since they lived in a garden flat close to a rehab centre. Chelsea was a street mile and three hundred thousand pounds away.

Mary Callaghan was wearing a hunted look. She gave the photo back to Stella without really looking at it.

'Jonathan Smith. I did know him. I knew him when I saw him in the room. I didn't want to get involved.'

'He was a tenant,' Stella said. They were in Mary's living room: expensive bad taste on all sides. Stella was standing, Mary sitting. It was done by waiting until the punter sat, but not sitting yourself. It meant they couldn't get up again without feeling awkward and you could look down on them as if by chance.

'Just one room. A bedsit. Had its own shower and a bit of a kitchen.'

One room: a bed, a shower, a kitchen. Stella wondered briefly about the square footage and what Mary charged in rent. 'You identified Caroline Deever.'

'I'd met her more often.' Stella just looked at Mary until she changed her mind. 'Well, I knew him, of course I did, but we had only met the once: when I showed him the room.'

Stella suddenly heard Delaney saying, John Smith. So not John Doe, then; not just A.N. Other. He was using it as a *name*. 'Jonathan Smith,' Stella said.

'That's right.'

'Not John.'

'No.'

'Not John Smith.'

'I don't know. Jonathan, John . . .'

'Jon is short for Jonathan,' Stella observed. 'You just spell it without the aitch.'

Mary sighed. 'It was just going to be a short let. He said as much.'

'Which is why you asked for cash, and why he didn't have a rent book, and why you wouldn't have been declaring the income.'

'I hadn't got round to it. I was going to. I was going to get round to it next week. I'd made a note.'

She took Stella to the door, through a hallway decorated with job-lot watercolours and beaded lampshades, hurrying alongside her and looking anxiously at Stella like a dog hoping to be taken for a walk. As she opened the door she said, 'My husband's a magistrate.'

Stella laughed: genuine amusement. 'Of course he is. Natch.'

Mary came out on to the step. She asked, 'Will anything happen?'

The fine rain seemed to collect in a cloud round the porch light. Stella spoke without looking back. She said, 'I've made a note.'

George was preparing a meal when she got home. She fetched a glass and poured herself some of the wine he'd opened, then perched on a stool to watch him cook. He was older than Stella and, she considered, wiser. Dark, wavy hair, some of it tipped with grey. He wasn't tall, but he was muscular across the chest, the result of years spent handling small boats in a heavy chop, though he'd stopped sailing a while ago. He had a lean face and good bones and a faint cleft to his chin that she particularly liked; it marked him out.

He was a boat designer and good with his hands, so cooking might have been a special skill, but he cooked as galley cooks cooked: top of the stove. He'd made a salad, put some potatoes on to boil, and there were two swordfish steaks laid out ready for the pan. While she talked, he made a salad dressing and brushed the pan with oil. Stella checked the dressing and began to make changes.

'So you let them both go.'

'Go where?'

'You know what I –'

'Yeah, well, it's up to uniform. Would be.' The changes were making things worse. She poured the dressing down the sink and started over. George didn't mind: he would never boast about his salad dressing. 'Deever couldn't see what he'd done wrong; and, if I think about it, I don't suppose Mary could either.'

'Tax fraud.'

'George, there are multi-millionaires in this country who pay tax on an annual income of five grand. Don't ask me to shop Mary Callaghan for pocketing a couple of hundred quid when I've got better things to do.'

'No . . . I just don't like landladies. Bad memories.'

The oil was smoking, so he slipped the fish into the pan. Stella liked it, the sound of something sizzling in a skillet: comforting, like ice cracking as you pour on vodka, or music playing when you wake to sunshine late on Sunday morning. Sounds of home.

Over dinner she told George about the way the case was moving. They were on their second bottle of wine and she felt comfortably muzzy. He said, 'Would I do that? If some doctor said no way back, would I wait, or do it myself?'

'Don't talk about it,' Stella said.

'What would you do?'

'Wait for a cure.'

'There isn't a cure.'

'Is this a fantasy?'

'Of course.'

'Right. Then there's a cure. Fantasy cure.'

'It's my fantasy. There's no cure.'

Stella took another sip of wine: a tip-you-over sip. She said, 'In that case, I'd kill us both.' She paused. 'You first.'

Later, in bed, he asked her to marry him. It was the fiftieth time he'd asked. The hundredth. The thousandth. And it was no joke. She slid across and covered his mouth with hers, to keep him quiet, and he made love to her like someone who could never get enough.

They loved one another, but it wasn't an even match.

She lay awake listening to the night noises: sirens, the bass-line from a party two streets away, planes dropping into the Heathrow corridor.

How did he know? Delaney: how did he know about Conrad Deever? And how did he know about Jon Smith? Who was talking to him?

After a while she slept. At three, she woke. Always at three, because that was the deepest, darkest hour of the night. In London, of course, there's always light in the sky: the sodium glow from streetlights, the collective glow from the lamps of the city's insomniacs, the lights from store windows. In London, you can hear songbirds at all hours. For Stella, the deep darkness of three a.m. was a darkness of the mind.

It was always a dream that woke her and the dream was always the same and there was no escaping it.

4

The four sitting in a ring were now four laid out side by side. All in all, human beings are a sorry sight naked. Old human beings are worse. Old dead human beings look like nothing on earth.

Stella went to post-mortems because Mike Sorley wouldn't and he could pull rank. When Stella had first come on to the team at AMIP-5, the case in hand had been a machete murder. One of the DCs had shown her the post-mortem blad: stage-by-stage photos. She had gone through, wincing, then passed them to Sorley, who had pushed them back across the desk. 'Christ! Don't show me those!'

She soon found out that DI Sorley didn't do gore. During her first PM, about a month after becoming a detective, Stella walked the foggy line between fainting and faking. It got a little easier each time, but watching that fine-art butchery, that dark red gardening, was never routine. Stella often found herself reassembling the dead meat into the walking, talking thing it once was. She thought about that person's everyday stuff, because even villains and bastards and gang warriors had everyday stuff like cleaning teeth, deciding what to wear, eating a meal. Especially eating a meal, because stomach contents were often high on the list of clues.

Bizarrely, she sometimes thought of them making love. It was something she would have liked to get out of her mind, but when the Y-incision was made and the scalpel tracked down to the pubis your eye followed. In the business of human affairs, it's tough to ignore the most usual source of pleasure; the most usual source of pain. Until a latex-gloved hand takes out the heart and weighs it, that is. Then other thoughts take over.

Stella had seen the PMs on all the cases her team had investigated. All except one. That was the Bonnelli case. The Bonnelli case had almost finished Stella off. Some people would say that she was probably still recovering from it, but they would be wrong; she would never recover, not entirely, and the two people who knew this were Stella herself and Anne Beaumont. Anne was Stella's shrink and no one knew about her. No one. Not even George Paterson, and Stella had been living with George for more than five years.

Anne was Stella's dark secret. She was the only person who knew about the three a.m. dream.

'– except this one,' Sam Burgess was saying, 'your odd man out.' Sam was wearing scrub greens, a white rubber apron, wellingtons, latex gloves; his mask was pushed down around his neck. The apron was mired with gore and frosted with particles made by the trepanning saw.

He had filleted them and assessed them, delved in among their gizzards and their brain-pans, taken swabs from their mouths and nostrils, their vaginas and rectums, their ears, between their toes, under their fingernails, and at no time had anything resembling a soul slipped past, pale in the halogen glare, beating for escape and sight of the sky.

'He's your odd man out because all the others died of

barbiturate poisoning and he died because someone first doped him, then inserted a thin probe between the third and fourth ribs and into the heart.'

'So three suicides and a murder,' Stella said. It wasn't really a question, but she wanted Sam Burgess to draw his own conclusions.

Sam had been a pathologist for almost twenty-five years and had seen everything and heard everything, and certainly knew enough to never second guess a violent death. He leaned up against the steel table which bore the eviscerated body of Mr Odd Man Out and looked at the preliminary lab reports. He seemed perfectly at ease in his working clothes. He was short and neat and had a white, monastic fringe; the wrinkles on his forehead went a long way back. You might have expected a cleric's clipped tone, but what you got was a Knightsbridge drawl. Sam liked to work to music; there was a mini-system and speakers on a far bench. Today, the music was Mahler: the Ninth Symphony.

'Well, I might have said he could have done it himself if it hadn't been for the trace of Rohypnol in his blood.'

'Rohypnol. Roofie. That's the date-rape drug.'

'Used for that, certainly. Used for other things, though. Works wonders for the terminally ill. They forget they're dying. Hope I can get some when it's my turn.'

'So this guy didn't know he was dying, either.'

'Didn't know he'd been killed.'

'You mean he dropped dead on the spot?' It didn't fit with Henry Deever's story of a man turning up at the door.

'Well, I was speaking figuratively. I mean, yes, in theory he should have died almost at once. But the mind's a powerful thing: if he'd been drugged and didn't know he'd been stabbed in the heart, he could have stayed alive for a bit – no shock factor, that's crucial. More people die of shock than from the trauma that causes it.'

Stella raised her eyebrows. 'Is that right?' Clearly, it was a favoured statistic among medics.

'Also, the probe didn't gash the heart. It punctured the right ventricle and came out cleanly. To some extent, the wound might have been self-sealing for a while: leaking but not pouring; and the right ventricle is the less important of the two.'

'He could have got up, walked around.'

'Wouldn't have got far on his morning jog. But yes, it's feasible.'

'Death within –?'

'He wasn't all that fit: good covering of fat, below average musculature. But given the nature of the wound and him not actually realizing that he was walking dead . . .' Sam shrugged and looked over his shoulder at the wide-open corpse, as if hoping for a hint. 'Five or ten minutes? With a bit of exertion to cause a breach of the heart.'

The phrase went straight into Stella's very own black museum: *a breach of the heart.*

'Okay, could it be this –' devil's advocate now – 'three of them OD on painkillers, but this guy doses himself with Roofie then stabs himself through the –'

Sam stood aside as a mortuary assistant approached with needle and twine. 'You mean, they all committed suicide, but he chose a different method to the others?'

'Yes.'

'If he stabbed himself before the Rohypnol became

effective, it wouldn't exactly take the edge off things, would it? And if he waited until it kicked in, he'd have forgotten what it was he intended to do.'

'Okay.' Stella watched the big, cobbler's stitches going into the abdomen of Jonathan Smith. 'So we have three suicides and a murder.'

'I suppose it's possible that the barbiturate victims were forced to overdose.'

'But you don't think so?'

'No, I don't. No sign of coercion anywhere – bruising, minor lesions, nothing. You'd expect to find biochemical evidence of stress, but there isn't any.' He laughed. 'They all seem to have been pretty relaxed, really.'

Stella nodded. 'What do you get from Odd Man's wound, Sam?'

'Ah, yes, another reason why it couldn't have been the man himself: professional job, no question.'

'Medical knowledge?'

'No more than anyone might have who was good at killing people.'

'I really meant, have you seen it before?'

'Not quite like this. Not this combo: flunitrazepam and a probe.'

'What does it make you think of?' Stella wondered.

'I don't know.' Sam fell silent for a moment or two. 'Execution?'

'That's what I thought. Execution.'

Sam walked with her, shouldering aside the overlapping slap-flaps and out through the lab, with its stainless steel sinks and white light and bottled spare parts. Stella wondered if he was going to accompany her down the street in his gory greens: your man with the off-cuts and offal; your family butcher.

He stopped where the steps to his underworld ended and the realm of the living began. He was thinking about the suicides. 'I don't blame them,' he told her. 'One with a sclerotic artery, the other with a tumour the size of a grapefruit up her arse.'

'What about the third one? The tall woman?'

'Clean as a whistle,' Sam said. 'But then unhappy thoughts don't show up.'

He turned and went back. Stella glanced after him for a moment, at the plain concrete steps, the low-wattage bulb behind a steel mesh casing, at Sam turning the corner into the shadows.

She walked towards her car, hanging her head first to one side, then the other, using her finger-ends to flick at her scalp and round her ears. It was silly, but she could never shake the feeling that crumbs from the trepanning had spun off the saw and got into her hair.

She sat behind the wheel and put the radio on while she made some notes: things that were fresh in her mind. Rohypnol. A thin probe. Grapefruit. As she wrote, she realized that something was nagging at the back of her mind: not something she'd heard or something she'd seen; a thought that hadn't quite surfaced. Whatever it was, it made her uneasy. She tried to find it by making her mind go back: her arrival, the autopsies, leaving with Sam just now. It almost surfaced, then sank before she could grab it.

She drove back to Notting Hill at walking pace, one of a thousand caught in a series of inch-by-inch tailbacks.

It had rained while Stella was below ground, but now the sun had broken through and London was steaming.

Rohypnol. A probe. Execution.

Then she saw herself looking back as Sam disappeared into the shadows: the dim bulb behind metal mesh, plain concrete steps leading to an underground room; and the thought surfaced again and this time came clear.

Secret Police.

5

The AMIP squad room had Jon Smith's picture up everywhere: the new centre of their inquiry; the murder victim. Careful makeover had failed to remove all the darkness from his face or take out the puffiness round the jawline. He looked like a suntanned man in desperate need of a dentist.

Mike Sorley was asking questions, getting answers, making suggestions. Sorley was overweight, but hadn't compensated for the fact by restocking his wardrobe; his gut hid his belt buckle. Male pattern baldness had eroded his pepper-and-salt widow's peak to a tuft. He was asking more questions than his officers had answers for.

It was about ten o'clock, so people were eating and smoking and drinking coffee; some were doing all three pretty much simultaneously. Everyone smoked except Sue Chapman and one of the civilian indexers, though their secondary inhalation factor was about a pack a day. Stella had given up, but didn't yet consider herself a non-smoker. The desks were littered with styrofoam cups, open packs of Marlboro Lights, Twix bars, half-eaten bags of salt and vinegar crisps. Everyone liked salt and vinegar. It was an AMIP-5 convention. You probably couldn't even get a bag-man's job if you favoured cheese and onion.

'Jonathan Smith,' Sorley said, 'is going to pop up where?'

Steve Sheppard looked down a list that Sue Chapman had given him. 'Faxes to every nick in London, posted on the database, missing persons being looked at, possibility of a spot on *Crimewatch*, but I don't think that's going to be necessary.' Sheppard was the youngest on the team by three years, sharp, just married, out for promotion. He was skinny and looked as though he got by on four hours' sleep a night. Stella liked him for that.

'We lifted his fingerprints?'

'Being checked, boss.'

'It's been three days.'

'I'm on to it,' Sheppard said. 'They take their time.'

'Execution-style killing,' Sorley said. 'Temporary address. Going under an aka and a six-hundred-quid wedge in his pocket. This guy's got to have connections.'

And so he had. In fact, three arrived almost at once: a positive fingerprint, an agitated fax from SO10, a call from a nick in Bethnal Green.

The fingerprint was in first. It identified James Arthur Stone, aged forty-three. Stone had served four terms in jail, the longest for aggravated assault. The photograph that came with the positive print made the dead man look thinner, but not much fitter. It gave three aka names, an address in Walthamstow and a list of known associates. Stella saw that among them was the name Tanner and her pulse rate rose a notch.

The Tanners were a family: blood relatives but also partners in crime. Their operational area started in Paddington–Marylebone–Maida Vale, then swung up to the Kensals, dropped into Notting Hill and pushed west to Harlesden and Stonebridge. They weren't exclusive, and a lot of their business was import–export, but when it came to guns, drugs and girls, their business plan involved a pretty large spread. Not Shepherd's Bush. They were pushing at the borders, but some heavy-duty people were pushing right back.

The Tanner family had its own tree, full of bad fruit. Denis and Hugo Tanner were brothers, both now in their mid-fifties. Hugo got his name from a liking for designer labels, with a particular weakness for Hugo Boss. Denis had a wife called Carrie; Hugo a wife called Norma. Carrie and Norma liked the good life. They liked big houses, here and in the Costas, they liked nice clothes, they liked jewellery, they liked Mercedes Benz. They liked it and they got it.

The brothers had several children: three were girls, two of whom liked what their mothers liked. The third, Hugo's child, had turned her back on the family and gone to Australia to work with animals. Hugo put it down to bad blood. There were two sons, Stevie and Maurice, both now in their thirties. Stevie was Denis's son; mostly, he ran the girls; mostly, Maurice handled the drugs; but there was crossover, and both Denis and Hugo oversaw the operations. Maurice was away, doing three years for GBH, so Stevie and Hugo were covering for him. The only exclusivity in family business was that Denis did guns, because he really liked guns.

The Tanners didn't use flighty euphemisms: they weren't 'traders' or 'insurance executives' or 'commercial operatives', they were gangsters. That's what they liked to be called; that's how they thought of themselves. Gangsters. Outlaws. They conducted a running war with the police and, for both organizations, it was a bit like being behind the lines. There were skirmishes and full-on battles; there were guerrilla tactics; there were victories and defeats and truces and constant two-way surveillance.

When Stella had lived on the Harefield Estate, it had been the Tanner brothers' little empire: their beginning. The drugs, the whores, the wrecked lives had been down to Denis and Hugo – and the sons had come on fast. Stella's view of the Tanners was uncomplicated: they were the enemy. She had seen the damage they could do. She didn't work in drugs or vice, so, although she despised them, she had never looked across the trenches at them. Now here they were, known associates of her murder victim.

She highlighted the name and passed the report to DC Paul Lester. 'Let's look at them,' she said. 'But keep your distance.'

Stella made a call to Bethnal Green and discovered that they had Jimmy Stone on a restraining order that kept him at least a mile from the high-rise block where his wife and daughter lived. The story from a uniformed sergeant there was that Stone and his family hadn't lived in Walthamstow for over a year, and since they'd come to Bethnal Green there had been four triple-nine call-outs by Patricia Stone, which had led to a probation order being issued against Jimmy, along with the RO. The theory was that Patsy Stone had found a new friend and someone had told Jimmy what was going on. The sergeant gave Stella Patsy's address. He said, 'Watch your back, okay?'

The SO10 contact was rank to rank: the AMIP

superintendent, Geoff Meakin, got a follow-up call from Superintendent Mark Palmer, who simply informed him that there was a problem, and would Meakin let him know when would be a good time for an SO10 officer to make contact. No explanation and certainly no list of known associates, though when Meakin passed his notes on to Mike Sorley, they agreed that SO10 must be among Stone's associates, though obviously not 'known'. Sorley gave Stella sight of Meakin's notes and asked her to speak to whoever Serious Crimes were going to send over.

Suddenly, there was a smell of sulphur in the air.

Stella made the call, fixed a time, then made a second call to let the station inspector at Bethnal Green know she and Pete Harriman would be on his patch.

They drove over in slanting rain and a whipping wind.

'The end of summer,' Harriman observed, peering out of the side window. 'I wouldn't mind moving to Spain.'

'To do what?'

'Buy a bar.'

'Everyone thinks they'll buy a bar,' Stella said.

'Some do.'

'Yeah, and they come home broke.'

Harriman hunched further over towards the misted window. He sounded sullen. 'It rains all the fucking time, doesn't it? They ought to find a new name – not summer, something else.' He paused. 'The rainy season,' he said, and started to laugh.

Patsy Stone was perfect in all respects: Barbie hair, liverish lip gloss, tight cleavage, Lycra pedal pushers, kitten heels. She was late thirties and in full retreat from forty. When she opened the door and saw Stella and Pete Harriman, little lines of disgust gathered at the corners of her mouth.

She said, 'They've been, they've told me. There's lots of others can identify him. He's got a mother, he's got a sister. I don't have to, neither does Pauline.'

'I'm not after you for that,' Stella told her. 'It's your decision.'

Patsy kept them on the doorstep. 'He was living in bedsits. What he didn't take with him, I chucked out. There's nothing of his here. Nothing left. Not even a bad smell.'

'We're investigating his murder,' Stella said. 'We're talking to everyone. Even people who knew him really well.'

Patsy smiled at the joke, but didn't invite them in. Harriman was standing to the left of Stella and a pace back. He leaned forward and said, 'It's raining out here.' There was an edge to his voice. Patsy turned and walked away down the hall, leaving the door open. The Lycra was electric blue and tight as a drumskin. Stella and Harriman followed her to a room off the hallway; when they entered, Patsy was already sitting on a sofa aggressively watching an afternoon talk show. She had a drink which she topped up: lots of this, not too much of that.

Stella said, 'It's a case of who he knew, who he hung out with, who he worked for, what he was doing.' A pause. 'Why he was killed.'

'Look, he had form, right? You're more likely to know who he went round with than I am.'

Harriman asked, 'Did he see Pauline at all?'

'The restraining order said no closer than a mile.'

'But did he see her?'

'She's fourteen. She's got her friends.'

'So the answer's no.'

'That was the way we liked it.'

Stella asked, 'When was it – the last time you *did* see him?'

Patsy stood up, crossed her arms to take hold of the hem of her top on either side and pulled it up to her neck. Her breasts bobbed out amid a froth of black lace. She turned, showing Stella and Harriman her back: a scar ran from just under her neck to three inches below her bra strap.

'When he done this,' she said.

Harriman stared. He said, 'What was that?'

'Kitchen knife.'

'Why your back?' He meant, why not your face?

Patsy turned round and looked at him, her top still raised, and gave a short laugh. 'I was running away,' she said. 'What the fuck do you think?'

As they were walking back to the door, Patsy asked, 'Someone'll go to see his mother, I expect? And his sister?'

'Yes,' Stella nodded.

'Will it be you?'

'I don't think so.'

'Whoever it is, ask them to say I won't be at the funeral, yeah? But I'll be along later to piss on his grave.'

Concrete catwalks and a lift that doubled as a toilet took them back to their car. Stella went round to the passenger door and got in. She said to Harriman, 'You can drive. I'm bloody sick of London traffic.'

To get to the Deever sisters' front door, Jimmy Stone had left his bedsitter, walked out to a half-landing and gone down three flights of stairs, which must have been an epic journey to a man whose heart had been punctured by what Sam Burgess's report had called 'a thin metal probe'. There was something about the word 'probe' that made Stella wince: it sounded like the tool for the job all right.

Forensics had come back with a haul: Jimmy's personal belongings, the usual things, but also a laptop computer and some items that were far from usual. Sue Chapman was sitting at the laptop and sifting through files and folders.

'It's just the murderabilia,' she said, 'and a record of sales. Also he's on the internet, so I guess he sold online.'

The murderabilia.

Stella had cleared a table and was laying it out: Jimmy Stone's little sideline. Killers' collectables; keepsakes from the land of the dead. She picked up a sheet from a 'Lion' exercise book, on which was a handwritten poem, then passed it to Sue, pointing at the signature.

'Know who that is?'

'It'll be in his catalogue. I could find it if you give me –'

'Reggie Kray,' Stella said, 'the well-known philosopher and poet. That was how he described himself during his last few years.'

Sue scrolled down. 'Here it is,' she said, 'priced at a hundred and fifty. I wish he'd listed these alphabetically.' She started to make a new list, keying in the items as Stella laid them out on the table.

- A letter from Myra Hindley to Ian Brady, written from prison.

- A scene-of-crime photograph of the Manson killings.
- A ballpoint pen sketch by John Wayne Gacy, one of America's worst.
- A half-brick and the plate from a light switch taken from Fred West's house.
- A board game called 'Serial Killer'.
- A police mug shot of O.J. Simpson.
- O.J. Simpson's autograph.
- Off-screen stills from the O.J. trial.
- A copy of the pathologist's report on 'Dark' Annie Chapman, Jack the Ripper's second victim.
- A copy of the letter sent by the Ripper to George Lusk.
- Dennis Nilsen's handprint: right hand, the hand that did the business.
- A collector's set of 'serial killer' cards.
- An account of Ruth Ellis's execution as told by the hangman, Albert Pierrepoint.
- And signatures: dozens of signatures, photographs of killers autographed by the men and women in question. Men, mostly. Almost a hundred per cent men.

Every item authenticated and carrying its written provenance. Murderabilia.

Stella picked up the house brick and the switch-plate. 'I doubt this,' she said. 'The West house was reduced to rubble and the rubble was pulverized: for just this reason. Ghouls and profiteers.'

'Who the hell buys this stuff?' Sue wondered.

'Sick people. Thrill-seekers. In the US there are even agents for it; will be here soon, I expect. They write to killers, visit them in prison, make a relationship with them, especially serial killers, then ask for whatever they can sell. Handprints, bloodstains, drawings, letters, signed pictures, articles of clothing, tape recordings. Then they market them over the internet. Jimmy Stone will have a website.'

'Some of the stuff is official: documents, autopsy reports . . .'

'Come from cops, from coroner's clerks, from path lab assistants. A chain of profit going back to the death itself. Back to the moment when one person murdered another. We call it a clue, or a piece of evidence; others think of it as merchandise.'

'I don't get it. What's the point?'

'It puts them closer to the killer,' Stella said. 'Closer to the act of murder itself.'

She was still holding the brick. She wondered what power it was supposed to contain, what echoes of screams, what memory of blood. Her hand tingled as if from a mild electric shock. She put it down too hard and Sue looked up at the noise.

Stella's face was flushed; she said, 'Walls have ears, yeah?' and laughed. Laughed it off.

Nothing else from the bedsit gave Stella any leads; the murderabilia was Jimmy's stock, the laptop his business tool; apart from that, he lived light. A few clothes in the closet, razor and foam in the bathroom, crocks in the kitchen, wank mags by the bed. A cheap notebook, a pen. Bottles of Scotch, bottles of beer.

Everything had been through forensics and back to Paul Lester's exhibits room. Stella leafed through the notebook, finding mostly the names of horses. She wondered if the six-hundred-pound roll in Jimmy's pocket had been the result of a tip and made a mental note to send someone to the local bookies' shops with the PM mug shot.

There were several phone numbers. Stella rang them and got a pizza-delivery place, a cinema box office, an escort agency and a woman who happened to be passing a call box in Fulham.

There were someone's initials, JP, and a date for the future – of which, Stella reflected, Jimmy Stone had none.

She was halfway down her vodka when John Delaney came into the pub. He took the stool next to hers and said, 'Just touching base.'

Stella drank off her shot of vodka and stood up. She said, 'I've got some questions for you, Delaney. Another time, though.'

'I spoke to Mary Callaghan,' he said. 'That's how.'

She smiled. 'That's what I thought.'

'I spoke to Mary and she told me about Jonathan Smith and, yes, I did pay her for the information. That's how it works.'

'I ought to be somewhere else,' Stella said. 'And I know how things work.'

'Stay and have a drink.'

'No.'

'Look,' he said, 'there's something you ought to understand about me. I'm not a red-top tabloid vulture and I'm not looking for a headline. I write long investigative pieces that sometimes make a difference to people's lives. I won't say I'm a crusading journalist because people always laugh, as if it were a contradiction in terms. Let's say I write exposés, that sounds just sensational enough.

I thought the Deevers might be relevant to a piece I've got planned. Cults, suicides, mind control, kids hijacked and kept from their families, big money going to clever and manipulative and evil men, lives ruined. Maybe I was wrong, but the Deevers still look like religious nuts to me, so they might provide a footnote. And no, I'm not indifferent to the fact that they're dead. It's a human tragedy and that's my subject.'

Stella nodded. 'Okay. But there's not much I can give you that you don't already know, so what are you doing here?'

'Came to buy you a drink.'

'Sorry?'

'I came in the hope of finding you here and to buy you a drink if you'd let me. I came yesterday and the day before, but no luck.'

Stella laughed. 'Are you coming on to me?'

'That's right.'

She said, 'I have to be somewhere. I'm late.'

'Okay,' Delaney said. 'Another time.'

She walked out of the pub, then turned round at once to go back for the reports she'd left on the bar. Delaney was at the door holding them out to her. He smiled and gave a little bow as he handed them over.

She drove down Kensington Gore towards Knightsbridge, watching the digits tick over on the dashboard clock. Every minute in the tailback was a minute lost with Anne Beaumont.

Okay, Delaney, she thought, but it doesn't tell me how you knew about Conrad Deever. You can't have got that from Mary Callaghan. Her other thought was, Why did

I say I had to be somewhere? Why make an excuse? Why not just say, 'I'm spoken for, I'm with someone'?

Good questions to ask your shrink. Except when Stella saw Anne Beaumont there was only one topic for discussion.

6

The three a.m. dream was a peepshow. No introduction, no little narrative to bring her to the moment, just Stella stooping and pushing open the brass flap of the letterbox and peering through.

'Tell me from the beginning,' Anne said, because although she'd heard it a hundred times before, she knew that's what Stella wanted to do.

Judith Bonnelli's body had been found by her husband when he returned from the pub. She had been stabbed twenty-seven times. The TV was still on and the children, a boy of five and a girl of three, were in their beds and asleep.

It hadn't been difficult to discover that the marriage wasn't a happy one. And no one could really say for certain that Luca Bonnelli had still been in the pub at closing time. There wasn't enough to charge him, but everyone had him in the frame. Stella had taken him down to the nick for questioning. She thought he'd cave in before morning. The idea was to keep at him all night: Stella and a DC called Tom Maynard.

He kept asking about the kids; he was worried about the kids. Stella told him not to worry, the kids were being looked after by his sister.

Dawn came up, but it was perpetual night in the windowless interview room. Stella was a smoker at that time – a little more than a year ago it was, and her throat was raw with the cigarettes she'd got through since midnight: the best part of a pack. Luca talked a lot, but really only had two things to say: 'I didn't kill her' and 'What about the children?'

Stella put him through it again and again, made him tell the story again, and each time he would cry when he talked about finding her, how she'd been lying just inside the door, so that he'd had to shove to get in. He cried when he remembered the blood, the gashes to her arms and face, the way her dead eyes stared him down.

Stella had seen it before, especially in domestic killings – the murderer in shock, the agony of 'no way back', the terror of 'what next?' – and she knew it was genuine. She asked him just as she'd asked him a hundred times that night, 'Where were you? Who can vouch for you?'

The answer was always the same, 'In the pub. Playing pool with the guys.'

'What guys?'

'Some guys. I only know their first names.'

'Where do they live?'

'I don't know.'

'So, Luca. It was about eleven-fifteen. You got home and found Judith –'

'I told you.'

'Tell me again.'

And then a couple of 'the guys' had been found by a DC following likely leads. One was watching TV sports with a six-pack at five a.m., the other had to be kicked awake by his wife. They'd both said that yes, Luca had been there playing pool. Getting in the last round. Definitely.

But Stella hadn't been sure. How come no one else remembered: the bar staff, other punters? She asked her DI to get a superintendent's authority for an extension of custody.

'Are the kids all right?' Luca wanted to know. 'Who's with the kids?'

Stella needed to talk to the kids anyway, so she phoned social services to arrange for a careworker to meet her at the house. This was somewhere close to seven in the morning.

It was an unscheduled call. She went alone, at the end of her shift. The careworker never turned up. No one answered the bell, which seemed odd. It was early and, in any case, Maria Bonnelli had agreed to stay in the house with the children.

Stella rang the bell a few more times, then lifted the letterbox and peered in.

Her cry was the sound of someone who has just witnessed the unbearable: the cry of someone waking from a nightmare; except that Stella was waking to a nightmare.

She had seen the children's feet where they slowly twisted and turned below the banister. She stooped further and could see their little bodies still in their night clothes, but she couldn't see their faces. It wasn't until she took a house brick to a window and climbed in and went through the living room into the hall that she saw their faces.

She spent a long time looking up. Not moving. Then she called in.

She couldn't touch the children: couldn't touch the

washing-line rope and bring them down. Not that she didn't want to or couldn't bear to – the SOC officer would need things to be just as they were. The video man. The stills man. The forensic team.

She went halfway up the stairs until she was close enough to reach them and went through the routine of checking for vital signs, as if it made a difference. Their appearance made it clear they had been dead for hours. Then she went down and sat on the floor of the hallway to wait for the team.

She sat there, waiting, looking up.

After that, she'd been fine. The team arrived, she was busy, she had things to do. It only took a day to find Maria Bonnelli holed up in a flat over a drinking club run by an old boyfriend. All she would say when Stella cautioned her was, 'Fucking bitch. She's dead. She's dead now, that fucking bitch.'

It was a family affair.

Stella was fine. She was fine for the rest of that week and fine for the committal hearing and fine when she finished her reports and signed off. Then she got up one morning, said goodbye to George, got into the car, drove through her west London patch to the A40, the North Circular, the M1, and stayed on the road until she finally had to stop for fuel at Scotch Corner. After that, she drove up through the Lowlands of Scotland and on to Wester Ross, which was as far as she could drive, as far north as she could manage, even on the scalding charge of adrenalin that was pumping through her system.

She slept in the car, found a hotel when she woke, and stayed there for six days while the nation looked for her.

She thought she was dreaming everything. She thought she was having a terrible dream about dead babies.

Even though she scarcely left her room, someone at the hotel recognized her and phoned in. George came up to drive her home.

She said, 'I'm not dreaming, am I?', and he held her while she asked him questions that he couldn't answer.

They got as far south as Newcastle when she asked him to find a hospital. At first, he thought she simply meant 'a place where they'll look after me, a place where they'll know what's wrong'. Then he looked across at her face, dead white, and she said, 'I'm bleeding, George.'

She had guessed that she might be pregnant, but had been waiting to find out for sure. But she knew, really: she felt different, she felt new. She had been carrying the child for six weeks when she had broken the window in Luca Bonnelli's house and walked through to the hallway and looked up.

Stella took two months off on full pay, then went back. They asked her if she was all right and she said she was fine.

Three days later, she was looking at the melted face of a man who had been sprayed with petrol and torched by some local boys who thought he looked like a Romanian beggar. They were wrong. He was an Albanian beggar and he died of his injuries the same day.

It was a high-profile, high-pressure race murder with the press and the politicos making waves. Everyone waited for Stella to fold under the pressure, but she didn't do that. Since then, she'd been on four cases, none of them pleasant. The Deevers and Jimmy Stone was the fifth. She'd been fine. But everyone knew that it was just a matter of time before someone called in a suspicious death and the body was that of a child. Stella knew it, too.

But, no, she was fine – and everyone could see that. Except they didn't know how often she would think of those two little bodies twisting in the overhang of the stair, and how often she would think of her own child and wonder whether the shock had killed it –

More people die of shock . . .

– whether her being a cop had killed her baby.

In London, the end of summer has a smell to it: damp leaves, exhaust smoke under rain, the last few warm days raising a hint of rot.

Anne Beaumont was forty but looked younger, helped by the cool complexion, strawberry-blonde hair and high cheekbones of Anglo-Saxon stock. She moved with a light step, crossing behind Stella's chair to close the skylight. Her consulting room was at the top of her house: a large loft that looked across to Marble Arch. Dusk was coming in and a low mist was rising. On the far side of the park, lights swayed like the lights of ships.

'You can't tell George about it?' Anne said. It was an old question, but she asked it again from time to time.

'I don't know why.' Stella's eyes were fixed on nothing. 'He knows about it, of course he does – knows it happened.'

'But not that you think about it so much. Not about the dream.'

'No. Not about the dream.'

The dream was just like the reality, except for one thing. In the dream, there were three victims: the Bonnelli children and Stella's baby. Each time she looked through the letterbox, she hoped for deliverance, but it was always the same; and each time, she felt guilty because she was hoping for two dead children – two would be okay, two would be fine – not three. But each time, it was there: her tiny corpse. And the worst thing, the unbearable thing, was that she knew the child. She recognized it. She had given it a name.

'Why did you do that?' Anne asked her. The same questions, the same answers, like a ritual.

'It was in the dream,' Stella said. 'I didn't do it consciously: I didn't mean to. I found the name in the dream.'

'Boy or girl?' Anne asked.

Stella shook her head.

'What did you call it?'

She shook her head. They were questions she would never answer.

7

The SO10 officer was a DS: rank to rank, like they'd said. His name was Alun Ward. He was short and slim, but there was more than a hint of muscle under the chinos and denim jacket; he was losing his dark hair from the crown, so he'd cut it close to the skull and wore a compensatory stubble. There were two bedrooms in the house AMIP-5 had taken over: the cataloguers were in one, the other was bare. Stella and Ward carried chairs in; Stella went back for two coffees like the caring hostess.

Ward said, 'Jimmy is a Stone we'd like left unturned,' thereby losing Stella's sympathy at a stroke.

'You'll need to tell me why.'

'He's one of ours.'

'He's the victim of a murder that we're investigating, and he's got two pages of form. He's anyone's. I'll need more than that.'

Ward shook his head. 'We'd be happier if you just closed the case. He was a scumbag. No one minds that he's dead.'

'I mind,' Stella said.

'No you don't.'

'Are you telling me what I think? Or telling me *what* to think . . . ?'

'The reason it's me talking to you,' Ward said, 'is because the higher it goes the more visible it gets. You can talk to your DI and he can talk to his Senior Investigating

Officer and that's okay because it's internal. But if it's two-way traffic at senior level, everyone wants to know what's going on. We've got something at stake here.'

'Some*one*,' Stella suggested and Ward shrugged. 'Jimmy Stone was an informant. It's on his record. Obviously, he was informing for whoever it is you don't want to talk about . . . Look, Christ, let's not play Twenty Questions. If you've come here to ask a favour you must be authorized to share something.'

Ward drank his coffee in three gulps as if he were getting set to leave. 'His name's Diver. Code name. Deep cover, yeah? So Deep-C. So Diver.'

Stella laughed. Who the hell had worried that out? Bunch of kids.

'Jimmy Stone was giving Diver information. He had certain contacts. He didn't know all that much, but he could be useful. Introductions, preparing the ground, making our man look genuine: thin end of the wedge.'

A pattern assembled itself in Stella's mind: *click-click-click*; things coming together. 'Certain contacts . . . You mean people with an unhealthy interest in Lee Harvey Oswald's nail-clippings. Ward looked at her, then away. 'People with a weakness for autopsy reports and the mug shots of serial killers.'

Ward said nothing for a while. He got up and walked to the window: making a decision.

Stella said, 'We found his stock and the computer catalogue. We found his website, too. "Murder One"; not very original.'

She thought, He'll need to phone in, clear it with his boss before he admits the connection. But Ward surprised her by saying, 'Sickos. Yeah.'

'You're right, they are. But it's not illegal.'

'No.'

'So it's not that – not the murderabilia. It's something else. It just happens that the people in question are the sort of people who like that stuff.'

'Are you expecting to wear me down, darling? Because it's not going to happen.'

Stella smiled broadly. She said, 'Darling? Did you just call me darling?'

'What can you give –'

'Don't do that. Okay?'

'What can you give me here? How far can you go?'

'We won't compromise your man,' Stella said. 'Just tell us where he is and we'll stay away.'

'No chance,' Ward told her. 'Easiest thing – keep us informed and we'll let you know if you're getting too warm. How does that sound?'

Stella knew what deep cover meant: it meant living the same life as the people you're out to collar. They're drug dealers? – you deal drugs, you sell crack and scag for real, you drive a brand new Beamer, you carry a gun. They're pimps? – you run girls. They're arms dealers? – you run guns. You do it for real. You put your life on the line every day: no warrant card, no back-up, no prejudicial briefing; the less you know about the people you're mixing with, the less likely you are to give yourself away. You act like them, think like them, in some cases you run a severe risk of becoming them.

She said, 'Yeah. Okay. We'll keep you up to date.'

Ward smiled and left without saying goodbye. Stella had the feeling that somehow he'd got what he'd come for, and at minimal cost.

*

She sat on the usual bar stool and drank the usual drink. The idea was to leave the vodka to chill on the ice for a full minute: it gave her time to scan the topic notes on any reports she was taking home with her, or to read the *Evening Standard* headlines. The Deevers were no longer news – famous for fifteen paragraphs.

She drank slowly and looked over her shoulder a couple of times as if expecting someone.

She opened her front door to silence, although the light in the kitchen was on to fool burglars. It was a gesture. Nothing fools burglars. George was having dinner with a potential client.

Stella put the radio on, then switched it off. She opened the fridge and ate some slices of ham and a piece of cheesecake as she stood there. She put the television on, then switched it off.

She spread the day's reports out on a low table and flicked through them, quickly reaching the conclusion that the only positive lead they had was that Jimmy Stone sold murderabilia to people who were connected to an SO10 deep-cover officer with the bad-joke name of Diver, who was currently living in Apache territory. She had written her own report to Mike Sorley and got a memo back with a completely contradictory message along the lines of 'Walk on eggshells, but take no crap'.

'He was a scumbag,' Alun Ward had said. 'No one minds that he's dead.'

'I mind,' Stella had told him. But she didn't, not all that much. What she minded was that someone had killed him and she didn't know who.

*

You walk past Stella's flat, past the lit window of her living room, then continue down to the North End Road and the tall shadows of the West Ken Estate tower blocks. You turn right, heading for Fulham Broadway, passing the half-and-half shop, a couple of arcades with their gimcrack window displays, a pawnbroker, a white-tile cubicle selling five sorts of fast food . . .

Now you cross the road, edging between backed-up vehicles, the long, noxious plumes of exhaust shot through with iridescent green and red and blue by the all-nite neon in the Best Bet Bedding Centre. Trash still in the gutter from the morning street market: cola cans and bad fruit. An ambulance hemmed in on a junction, whooping and wailing.

Finally, you come to this side street: a long perspective of terraced houses, most split, upper from lower, to make box-room apartments. Anonymous street, anonymous people. You walk past the lit rooms, the drawn curtains, the same TV show playing. There are cars parked on both sides, making the street a one-vehicle thoroughfare. Halfway down, a four-track and a snub-nosed economy car are headlamp to headlamp in a Mexican stand-off. The four-track has bull bars and its driver has a heavy way with the horn, but the snub-nose is further down the street and damn well knows its rights. A man walking his dog has stopped to watch the contest. They are outside a house with peeling paint and wet-rot windowsills. You can see a number of houses like that in the street – they're the rentals.

In the upper apartment of the rental, Ivo Perić was drinking whisky and watching TV while he waited for a delivery. There was nothing sinister or deliberate about his proximity to Stella's flat: it was just one of those things. He had ordered a pizza and a girl, and was hoping that they wouldn't turn up at the same time, but life's like that, and as the pizza-delivery bike was buzzing down the street the girl was finding a parking place.

Perić was hungry, so he ate a slice of pizza while the girl took her clothes off; then he finished his whisky and handed her a black drawstring bag. 'This next.'

She looked at the bag and shook her head, then glanced towards the door. Perić said, 'Put it on.' His voice was low and soft as if he were soothing a cat; it terrified her. She put the bag over her head and he helped her to pull the drawstring. She could breathe through the cotton, but not easily, and she was as good as blind. Perić looked at her as she stood there waiting for what was next. She had a good body, a little thick in the waist, perhaps, but she was young. What he needed from her was on display, the bag cancelled the rest.

She left an hour later, walking a crooked line to her car, knocking into a passer by.

The television was on; it had never been switched off. Perić poured himself another whisky and took a bite of cold pizza. He lit a cigarette, slender fingers snapping the wheel on the lighter. His hair was dull blond and pushed back from his forehead. A narrow face, hard-edged, the skin tight to the jaw and dusted with sandy stubble, but his blue eyes were oddly prominent. He watched a little of the news broadcast, but there was nothing about the death of Jimmy Stone. Perić had been astonished by the man's endurance: he had killed him, had found the space between the ribs, tickled the probe in, then gone straight to the heart. How could he have survived that, walked down three flights of stairs, gone to seek help? It was a good reminder: you have to be sure; you have to kill them twice.

The reminder sent him to his closet, where he pushed aside the racked clothes and removed three items. One was a packet that came in layers like a Christmas surprise: first a cardboard sleeve, then a length of green plastic-fibre cloth, then cream-coloured waxed paper, then a fifteen-pound block of Semtex.

Semtex was his first choice: pretty much harmless, easy to handle, only needs a blasting cap and a length of detonating cord to set it off. This little package had come from the Czech Republic via rump Yugoslavia. He put it on the floor and turned to the second item, a twelve-gauge riot shotgun with a revolving cylinder that pumped out twelve shots in less than three seconds. The manufacturer called it 'the Street Sweeper'. With its folding stock retracted it measured a fraction over twenty-five inches and fitted nicely under a long coat. It was an eccentric weapon, but he'd used it a lot in Bosnia: in Srebrenica and Goražde. The third package, wrapped in wash-leather, was a Militech 9110 combat magnum, an 11mm weapon that left the workshop complete with laser sight and recoil compensators.

Perić set the guns down next to the Semtex, then rearranged them all slightly, like a fussy housewife. They made the perfect combination. Something for back-up, something for covering fire, something for maximum impact.

Perić was a man in waiting. He might have a job to

do, or things might come to nothing. He was hoping for action because he was a man of action, but, in the meantime, he was happy to eat pizza and drink whisky and fuck girls, all on expenses. He was happy to spend his mornings sleeping and his evenings watching TV. After the girl had gone; after the pizza was eaten. Between times, he liked to walk the streets of London: part of the throng in Piccadilly or strolling with the strollers in parks. It made him feel powerful because he was anonymous; among all those people he was a well-kept secret. No one knew his face or what he'd done. He would stand in the Virgin Megastore choosing a CD or feed the last of his lunchtime sandwich to the pigeons in Holland Park and think of the gun and the gift-wrapped Semtex back in his room, and he'd grin, like a man who has just remembered a pleasant moment or is thinking of someone fondly. Then he'd walk all the way back to his flat, wired, snapping his fingers, his heels ticking on the paving.

Wired and ticking. As if he were the bomb.

Stella removed her make-up, poured herself a vodka and took it to bed. Getting between the sheets produced an immediate sexual itch, as if going to bed early could only mean one thing. She reflected that George wouldn't be home for another couple of hours and, anyway, would probably be outside a couple of bottles of wine; then she realized that somehow that wasn't the point: what she was feeling hadn't got anything to do with a specific man, or men in general; it was just desire, like something in the air, something in the blood.

She reached down and slipped a hand between her

legs, but let it stay there motionless, liking the fact that there was no urgency in what she felt; it was hers, it wasn't a response. After a moment, she picked up an all-purpose remote control and found the news on the TV that sat on a narrow table at the foot of the bed.

There were children sitting by parched waterholes in Africa, the ice cap was falling into the sea, loggers were bringing down the last of the rainforest, small wars raged like bushfires; and four men had been shot shitless with automatic weapons while they were playing poker in a shebeen on the Notting Hill–Shepherd's Bush border.

Stella looked for connections in the news the way politicians looked for advantage. The shebeen blood-letting was something that could easily have come her way. It had 'gang killing' written all over it. Which indicated territory. Which indicated drugs. Which is what Metropolitan policing really is about.

It means going up against a well-organized industry with an annual turnover of fifty billion pounds. It means guerrilla warfare with gangs who run girls, run guns, run 'illegals', run kiddie-porn; who use kidnap and torture as everyday methods of persuasion. It means an average of thirty Yardie-related street slayings every year. It means rival groups who operate almost as nation states.

It means everyone carries guns except the cops.

Stella watched the SIO on the Shepherd's Bush killing making the usual statement. She would have given good odds that he already knew who the killers were – they'd be the same killers as last time and the time before that. She channel-hopped for a couple of minutes, then went to sleep with her drink in her hand.

When the phone rang, she came awake with a start and some of the vodka shipped on to the bedclothes. Alun Ward had to say his name twice and then say 'SO10' because her head was still fogged with the dream she'd been having. The TV screen was filled with naked flesh and the sound track seemed to be of someone running uphill.

'It's almost eleven.'

'Yeah, I'm sorry; I like to say things while they're on my mind.'

'So: what *is* on your mind?'

In the background were music, laughter, voices raised to be heard. A copper's second office: the pub. Stella could smell the beer and smoke.

'Better idea than you reporting in and us letting you know if you're in the danger zone.'

'Which is?'

'Stay out of zones altogether. Do what I asked before. Let Jimmy Stone be.'

'Is your mind the only mind at work on this?'

'I'm here with my DI.'

'Put him on.'

'He's getting a drink in,' Ward told her. 'Last orders.'

'You've got a good man there,' Stella observed.

'He's a treasure.' Ward laughed, then let a silence in.

Stella joined the silence. A voice came out of the background mush that sounded like a fight starting up; then she realized it was rap, some riled-up ranter wanting people to kill each other or fuck each other or fuck themselves. She gave it a count of five, then asked, 'It's not just Diver, is it? Not just a man at risk.'

'That's what it is.'

No, Stella thought; no it's not. She said, 'I don't suppose you popped Jimmy Stone yourself, DS Ward. You're not my prime suspect, are you?'

First, he laughed; then there was a little blank pause which Stella knew was Ward taking a drink. He said, 'Stay zone-free. You'd be doing me a favour.'

'What – forget there's been a murder?'

'Of course not. You have to go through the motions. Do the minimum. We're protecting an eighteen-month operation here, and an undercover officer. One less Jimmy Stone in the world: does that matter to you?'

'You've got your business to do,' Stella said, 'and I've got mine.'

'Of course you have. Look, what I'm saying . . . Don't push too hard. Do the minimum, sign off.'

'I can't help you,' she said. 'But I will report in: as we agreed.'

He sighed. 'This could come from a higher source.'

'No, I don't think so. If not initially, then probably not at all. Unless your SIO knows less than you.' Which, thought Stella, is beginning to sound like the case.

Ward fell silent again, and Stella put the phone down on his silence. In the soft-porn movie a woman with a perfect body straddled a man with perfect hair and trampolined up and down. They gasped and grimaced and whined 'Yes-yes-yes' in unison. The vodka had soaked in, so Stella topped and tailed the duvet, then put the TV off, switched out the light, and lay in the dark with her eyes open.

Her dream had been a muddled, brightly coloured affair that involved small animals and a walk on a pebble beach that she seemed to remember from childhood.

She made a mental note of it for Anne Beaumont then closed her eyes, wondering whether she might sleep and revisit the beach and the animals: she'd liked the look of them.

It was too early for that other dream.

8

The world's a market and there were customers queueing at Jimmy Stone's murderabilia website. For the sake of good business, DC Sue Chapman was minding the shop. Stella was eating a prawn and lettuce sandwich and looking over Sue's shoulder as she logged on to Jimmy's email.

'It'll hot up later when America comes on line.' Sue clicked on 'Connect' and turned to face Stella. 'I'm sort of assuming that enquiries from the States aren't relevant. What about Europe?'

'Make a note of them,' Stella said. 'America, too. Just don't expect any foreign trips.'

'These are sick people,' Sue observed. 'They put in special requests. There's a guy who keeps coming back about Myra Hindley. Is there mayo in that?'

'Low fat.'

'No such thing as low fat.'

'What does he want, Myra's friend?'

'Underwear.'

'That's ridiculous. How would he know it was authentic: Cash's woven name tapes?'

'I'll send him a pair of my knickers,' Sue suggested, 'and ask him to make the cheque out to bearer.'

Stella was reading through the new mailings. 'Nothing useful, though?'

'They're pretty much of a muchness. Just a bunch of

people with gruesome shopping lists. The emails read like messages from strangers: nothing to suggest that Jimmy knew any of them.'

'They give addresses: where to mail the stuff?'

'Oh, yeah.'

'What are you doing about that?'

'Sorry sold out: more merchandise on the way.'

'Keep them hooked.'

'They are hooked. There's even a trade-in factor.'

'Your Nilsen toenail for a Charlie Manson scribble?'

'Sort of thing, yeah.'

'But no one local? No one anywhere near the scene?'

'No, boss.'

Squad officers were still collating the results of a house-to-house and checking known associates, but the murderabilia site struck Stella as the best bet simply because everything else about Jimmy Stone was unremarkable. A small-time operator; a petty criminal. Such people get killed, of course, but not in the way Jimmy had been killed. Even planned hits were often carried out by whoever happened to be handy and needed some pocket money. Not long before, a key witness in a murder case – a villain on an amnesty deal – had been taken out as he sat in his brand new Saab convertible waiting for his wife to leave the hairdresser's. The killer wasn't a pro: he was a bouncer with a couple of convictions for aggravated assault. Someone gave him five hundred pounds and a 9mm Glock. He'd rapped on the window of the mark's car, holding a copy of the A–Z and wearing a puzzled look. The witness had got the window halfway down before a frothy soup of brain and arterial blood washed the dove-grey leather interior. After the killing, the bouncer had returned the Glock because he'd had to pay a deposit on it.

Jimmy's death wasn't like that: someone's sideline. Stella's problem was trying to figure out why a small-time waster like Jimmy Stone should earn the attention of a technician.

There were twenty fix-it notes on her desk and another eight messages on her voicemail: the day-to-day stuff of a murder investigation. Everything gets papered. Murder is all about priorities and paper. One of the notes was from DI Mike Sorley. Stella found him in his office staring out at the weather on the streets; grey rain on a grey backdrop.

He asked, 'Are you married?'

'No.'

'I am.' He laughed without smiling. Stella was expecting more, but he turned away from the rain and said, 'I have to talk to the press. Usual thing.' He shook a cigarette out of a pack open on his desk and lit up quickly, inhaling hard. When he breathed out, there was no smoke: it had been soaked up by the spongy root and branch of his lungs. 'Are we getting anywhere?'

'We were. Things have slowed down. We're still trying the website: to see if we can make a connection.'

'So you'd like Jimmy Stone kept out of the papers . . .'

'His customers aren't going to apply to a dead letterbox.'

'It's not a close secret, though, is it? Some people had to be told. The wife, those of his known contacts that we've spoken to.'

'Sure. But let's play it down.'

Sorley nodded.

Stella opened her mouth to mention Alun Ward's late-night call, then closed it again. Some instinct at work. In the same moment, Andy Greegan knocked and put his head round the door. 'Henry Deever's climbed out on to the roof of his house. Uniform thought we might be interested. They've got a counsellor down there and the emergency services. Do you want someone to go?'

Sorley shrugged. He said, 'We've finished with him now, haven't we?'

Stella parked on the civilian side of the police tape. Because the rain had stopped, a small crowd had gathered at both ends of the street. Stella shoved through and held up her warrant card to the PC standing there. He glanced at it, then turned his attention back to the drama. He looked up just as everyone else was looking up. Henry Deever was easy to find, sitting astride the ridge of his house like a weathervane waiting for a change in the wind. There was a turntable ladder ready to be cranked up, but no one would start the mechanism until Henry was in agreement. Say the right thing, do the right thing, get the sad bastard down alive.

As Stella approached, she could see the counsellor at a small mansarded window high in the loft, leaning out and talking to Henry over his shoulder. He looked like Mr Punch asking the children where the baby had gone. As if they were part of the same entertainment, neighbours were also leaning out, two or three to a window. The audience at the far end of the street had started a slow handclap.

Directly opposite Henry Deever's house, along with

the turntable ladder, were a patrol car, a police Land Rover and the personnel that went with them. Two women stood slightly to one side, a WPC nearby. The women stared up and spoke in whispers. They were dry-eyed, but looked like roadside survivors of an accident. A doctor sat in his car with the door open and used his mobile phone to reschedule appointments. Stella found the uniform in charge leaning up against a parked car and drinking coffee from a styrofoam cup. Inspector Howard Duncan. He was lanky and narrow-shouldered and there was a half-smile on his lips that made it seem as if he might soon laugh out loud. Stella told him who she was.

'You've finished with him, though . . .?'

It was what Mike Sorley had said.

'He's not a suspect, if that's what you mean. Or a witness.'

'Just curiosity then, is it?'

'I'm hoping you'll get him down.'

'He's a good man.' Duncan nodded up towards the roof and for a moment Stella thought he was talking about Henry Deever. 'The negotiator bloke. Counsellor. I've worked with him before.'

'Do we know what he wants?' Stella asked. To make things clear, she said, 'Deever.'

'Oh, yes. He wants to die. Seems to be sold on the idea.'

'How long has he been up there?'

'About an hour.'

'Is that a good sign or bad?' Stella was no expert in jumpers.

'According to Our Man at the Window, there's no

80

second guess to this kind of stuff. I'd tend to agree with that. Three years back, I spent half the night sitting slap in the middle of a back street in Acton with a guy who'd doused himself in petrol and was playing with a Zippo. We talked about everything under the sun: women, movies, cars. He was a Crystal Palace supporter. I told him if I was a Palace supporter, I'd top myself, too. He laughed.'

With no traffic in the street, the counsellor's voice was just audible as a low, mellifluous murmur. Henry Deever shifted his position a little, moving towards the drop. Stella and Duncan talked without taking their eyes from the roof. The clouds broke and they had to raise their hands to shade their eyes. The first sun in a week. At the end of the road, the onlookers were still putting up a desultory handclap. Duncan raised his voice slightly to reach the driver of the patrol car.

'Offer those jokers a threat, will you? It's not a fucking variety show.'

Except that's just what it was. Street theatre.

'What was his problem? The man in Acton.'

'Usual. Wife buggered off having got custody of the kiddies. Good job she did: he used to smack them around. People are bloody weird. When they're with him they're a pain in the arse, when they leave they're a hole in the heart.'

The mention of a wife made Stella ask about Henry's and Duncan pointed briefly towards the two women. 'The one in blue. The other one's a neighbour.'

Mrs Henry Deever had a blue quilted coat round her shoulders. She wore no make-up and her hair was cut in a girlish fringe. Stella thought she was speaking rapidly to the friend at her side, but then realized that her teeth were chattering, as if she had a fever.

'What happened?' Stella asked. 'The man in Acton . . .'

'He told me his life story, I told him mine, we promised ourselves a pint and a curry in happier times, we watched the dawn come up, he set fire to himself. Woomph! Took my eyebrows off.'

The counsellor disappeared and Duncan immediately took out his mobile. Seconds later, it rang. He listened for a moment, then said, 'He's seen you.'

The counsellor met her just inside the front door, shook her hand in irritation and said, 'Matthew Lippman. I tried to turn him off you, but he's insistent. It's not good; it breaks the continuity. I wish he hadn't seen you.' Which meant, I wish you hadn't turned up.

'You were making good progress,' Stella suggested.

Lippman said, 'No, not really. But he's still on the roof, so I haven't failed either. What worries me is he said he wanted a last word with you. I don't like the sound of that. Last word.'

'What do I do?' Stella asked. 'What do I say?'

'Talk positive.' They were going upstairs and Lippman had lowered his voice; he was a fat man and the stairs were taxing him, but he was setting a fast pace. Between the softness of voice and the gasping for breath, Stella could barely make out the words. 'Don't talk about whether or not he intends to jump.'

'Does he?' Lippman looked exasperated. Stella said, 'You don't know.'

'That's right. I don't think he knows, either.'

'Any tips?'

'Just recently his sisters and –'

'Yeah, I know, it's my case.'

'Okay, right, well that's why he's up there. Says he feels guilty.'

They were at the door of the upper bedroom. Lippman put out a hand and braced himself against the wall. He was looking at the floor and breathing hard.

'If he says he wants to come in?'

'I'll be right here by the door, watching you. Give me a thumbs-up, I'll get them to start the ladder.'

'Not back through the window?'

'I've had three go over because of that. Getting out is easier than getting in.'

Stella went to the window and looked out. She could see the street scene but she couldn't see Deever. Looking up from down below was fine; looking out from up above was disorientating. His voice came from a few feet back. She knew he was there, but it startled her all the same.

'Detective Sergeant Mooney.'

She craned round, getting a slice of sky with some wind-pushed cloud and a flash of sunlight. She didn't know whether to call him Henry or Mr Deever.

'How can I help?' she asked.

'Because you were there.' He said it as if he'd been in the middle of an explanation. 'You were there at the house. You saw them, you were with them. Before they were taken off. I thought you might be able to say something.'

'Say something . . .'

'To my wife.'

'Why don't you talk to her? She'd understand. Why don't you tell her –'

'No. No, there's no time for that. It's past time for that. But she deserves an explanation. Just, I'm not the person to do it . . .'

'She's your wife,' Stella said.

'We were never close.'

'Your wife . . .'

'Yes. It's not quite like family, though, is it?'

Stella couldn't think of a word to say.

'Since you were there,' Deever said again, 'since you *saw* . . .'

He stopped speaking and shifted his position. Stella's head swam and she felt a fizz of apprehension, bubbles in the blood. Either the ridge was cutting him or he was bracing himself for a push. He settled again, and she tried to read his look.

'I should have gone with them. It was wrong of me. They asked me to go.'

Stella tried to think of a way of turning the conversation. She was alternating between looking up at Deever with the sun behind him, and resting her eyes by looking down. Down was a long way.

'Will you help me?'

For a moment, she thought he'd had a change of heart, then she realized he was still asking her to offer his apologies. Make his peace. As she turned to him, the sun went in and suddenly she could see him plainly, perched on the ridge tiles like a boy on the branch of a tree, his face quite composed, his eyes on her, waiting for her promise.

'Will you help me?'

It was one of those fork-in-the-road-buried-treasure language games. There had to be a right answer, but Stella couldn't think of it. Say no, and he jumps out of desperation, agree and he jumps because everything's taken care of. She was tongue-tied.

The cloud slid by and she was dazzled again. Deever said, 'Oh, well,' in a resigned tone of voice. 'Oh, well,' like someone turning to an unwelcome chore.

Somewhere, just behind the haze of sunlight, Stella saw a large bird, wings spread, as if about to gather itself and land on the roof right next to where Henry was sitting. It seemed to hover a moment, touch down, then change its mind and swoop into space. Leaning out, she felt the rush as it passed her: a rattle of wind, the noise a kite makes when the breeze first catches it. Something struck her shoulder, a heavy blow, making her grab the window frame.

Screams rose from the street. Stella saw the last of Henry Deever as he turned once in the air, a complete somersault, and landed on his back. It seemed to take a long time before his body came to rest.

9

Sue Chapman had printed out three of Jimmy Stone's emails and left them on Stella's desk with a note paper-clipped to them: *These look handy.*

Stella read through the greetings, the misspellings, the casual obscenities. The orders for items from Jimmy's black boutique. Either these three knew Jimmy pretty well or they were frequent customers and had an email relationship with him. Tough to tell: emails are like chatlines: people will say anything.

Mack. Ferdie. Billy Whizz.

Among Jimmy's files was a client list. Sue had pulled off addresses for the three. Hounslow. Paddington. The last address was a gift: Harefield Estate. Home ground. Stella would have known, anyway. She knew Billy Whizz.

Imagine you're being stalked: you go to the police; they give you some advice, some basic techniques: try not to go places on your own, vary your routine, give someone you trust your schedule.

Stella sat alone at the bar in her usual place, at the usual time. Why not? It was her local. She reflected that she had never bothered to tell George about the stop-off between work and home, the time out, the vodka shots. She bowed her head to read the reports and a fold of hair fell across her cheek. She pushed it back, noticing that it felt greasy. She had sweated for Henry Deever.

'So it's a clean sweep,' Delaney said, taking the next bar stool; reading her thoughts. 'All the dead Deevers.' He was wearing a long black leather coat, rain beads freckling the shoulder-yoke. The rain had set in again. He put a clear plastic Muji folder down on the bar and ordered a beer. When she didn't reply, he added: 'He jumped off a building in –'

'I was there.'

'Oh . . .' He seemed faintly disappointed, as if he'd been scooped. 'What happened?'

'He jumped off a building. You got it right.'

'While the balance of his mind was disturbed.'

'Well,' Stella conceded, 'balance did seem to be a problem.'

'Lack of balance,' Delaney suggested.

'Over-balance.'

Why am I doing it? she wondered; and, *Poor Henry Deever.* But she smiled at Delaney's smile and took the top off her vodka. This was her rationale: John Delaney knows things he shouldn't know and I want to find out how he got the information. If he wants to flirt with me, that's fine; he's off guard. The Muji folder contained some sheets that had come off a colour printer, but the plastic clouded them.

He asked her about Henry and she told him. She told him, too, about the man who had talked till dawn then torched himself. There wasn't anything in it for Delaney; even Henry was old news and, anyway, Henry's pathetic little one-man show was a two-para job at best. She mentioned how the sun had transformed Henry into a big black bird, and how his clothes had made that shuffle-snap in the wind as he went past.

Delaney drank his beer and listened and noticed that a tiny patch of sweat beads had gathered at her temple while she was telling the story. The way she told it was eerie-funny, and he wondered if she knew she had a small talent for that.

Thinking of his article, Delaney asked: 'I don't suppose he said that Jesus made him do it?'

'He didn't. But don't let that stop you.'

He pretended to wince. 'Are you hungry at all?'

Listen, I live with someone. I've lived with this person for five years. We're not married, but we might as well be. So I'm sorry, but I'm not in the market for dalliance, flings, one-night stands, or even one of those mythical 'friendly affairs where no one gets hurt', so maybe one of us ought to start drinking in another pub.

But it wasn't what she said. She said, 'Things to do; sorry.'

When his mobile phone went, he moved away to take the call, putting his back to her. His back in the black Gestapo coat. Stella laid her hand flat on the Muji folder and pressed, bringing the clear plastic down to the sheets that lay inside. A logo sprang up: an eyeball pierced by a knife; next to it the name of the website: Relix. This wasn't just a list, like Jimmy Stone's, it was a catalogue with sexy copy, a sales pitch.

The night before they tied him to the chair and put the bull's-eye target over his heart, Gary Gilmore wrote some letters . . .

There was a reserve price, unstated, and bids were invited. Stella moved her hand to the bottom of the folder and pressed.

The Boston Strangler shows up at your front door. Who is he today – the mailman, the plumber, the guy come to fix the waste disposal? You're a trusting kind of girl: you let him in. Your neat apartment. Your tidy bedroom. Just imagine what the place will look like when he leaves. Imagine what the police photographs will show . . .

She drank off the last of her vodka as Delaney returned to the bar. I'm giving him some rope, she said to herself. Enough to hang himself: maybe that'll show up on a murderabilia website.

'What in hell is that?' George asked her. She had walked into their bedroom, naked from the shower. She followed his gaze to her shoulder, then crossed to the wardrobe and stood in front of the mirror. The whole boss of her shoulder was blue-black with a dull yellow corona. She had been aware of the pain for a while, but only as something at the back of her mind.

She told him about Henry: much as she had told Delaney. 'He caught me as he went down. Must have been his foot.'

'Why didn't you mention it?'

'I would have.'

'Just another day coppering . . .'

He had come to stand behind her and she smiled at his reflection. 'Just another day.'

He leaned forward and kissed the back of her shoulder, where the bruise had spread like a port-wine stain, then slipped his arms under hers and cradled her breasts. Five years sets up little routines: the way you kiss, the way you touch, what happens next. Stella on all fours, George kneeling up behind her. She looked at him over her shoulder and the bedside light flashed in the mirror.

Henry Deever passing her unseen, the blow to her shoulder, the sound of a kite in the wind.

10

Mack was Colin McKenzie. Ferdie was Barry Ferdinand. Stella checked with the local nicks to make sure they weren't treading on any toes, then took Pete Harriman with her to make the calls.

Ferdie lived in a low block near Paddington Green. He opened the door dressed in a towel, looked at them and made an involuntary half-turn, the body language for *run*. Then he remembered that he hadn't done anything . . . well, nothing much; and not that particular week. He backed down the short hallway into the living room, then pointed to a room off that.

'Can I put some clothes on?' He was fleshy and smooth-skinned, somewhere between twenty-five and thirty-five, though his shaved head made it difficult to tell. There was a roll of fat just under the nape of his neck, waxy and damp.

'Why not?' Pete Harriman said. 'I'll come with you.'

'Whatever.'

As they moved into the bedroom, a woman's voice said, 'Jesus *Christ!*'

Ferdie came back after a minute or two wearing track-suit bottoms and a T-shirt. Stella noticed that Pete Harriman took a touch longer to emerge. She gave Ferdie a picture of Jimmy Stone. Dead Jimmy Stone. They'd applied to the family for something that showed Jimmy in a better light, but it seemed that, in life, Jimmy hadn't been eager to have his photo taken.

Ferdie said, 'Jimmy Stone, yeah.' Then he took a closer look. The expression on his face told Stella everything, but they went through the motions. Ferdie wasn't a collector, he was a dealer. 'It's legal,' he told them. 'There's no law against it.'

'We know,' Harriman said. 'We know about the law.'

Ferdie had been around Jimmy Stone for years but they weren't close. As for the day in question, he'd been in Amsterdam doing a bit of business: big Nazi trade, if they really wanted to know. SS flashes, daggers, items said to be from the camps: hair, teeth, bone; fragments of striped cloth, spectacles, odd shoes.

'Kids' shoes,' Ferdie said. 'They go well. Funny.'

Stella told him they'd check. In fact, they'd double check. But in her mind she was already crossing Ferdie off the list. As they were leaving, Pete Harriman advised Ferdie that he was a scumbag.

'Free market economy,' Ferdie told them as he kicked the door shut.

Colin McKenzie said he'd never seen Jimmy Stone and he never expected to. Stella could see the logic in that, since Mack was blind. His status as a murder suspect was further reduced by the fact that he had come to the door of his narrow, beaten-up terraced house in a wheelchair. Stella didn't bother to tell him that Jimmy was dead. They went in to a deep odour of cooking oil and piss. Each wall bore a line of grease, like a rank dado rail, where Mack had used his hand to judge distance and direction.

Unlike Ferdie, Mack was a collector. His murderabilia was displayed in a long case in the shape of a square U that ran along the back wall of his sitting room and part-way down two sides. It was mahogany and glass and looked incongruous beside the gimcrack furniture and the worn carpets. He knew where everything was, he told them that several times; he also mentioned that it wasn't against the law to own such a collection. Stella and Pete told him that yes, they knew about the law.

There were a couple of questions Stella had to ask. First was: 'How do you email Jimmy Stone to leave an order?'

'I don't. My old girl does that for me.'

'Old girl?'

'My mother.'

'Your mother orders up post-mortem shots and scene-of-crime photos . . .'

'Yeah.'

'She doesn't mind?'

'Mind what?'

Stella passed a hand over her eyes. People knock you out. People take your breath away.

She asked the second question. It wasn't a murder inquiry question, but she needed to know. 'Why do you want this stuff? You're blind. What's it for?'

'I can hold it.'

Stella remembered how the brick said to be from Fred West's house had delivered a tingle to her fingers, a tiny electrical pulse, and her face flushed.

'You'd be surprised,' said Mack.

*

It was early evening and a big, dark sky was building over the grey cliffs and canyons of the Harefield Estate, near-black cumulo-nimbus coming in shelf by shelf; a sick yellow lay between the cloud cover and what seemed the horizon, but was really a long bend of the Thames. The colour combination made Stella remember the throb in her shoulder. She and Harriman sat in the car a short way off the estate feeder roads and had a pointless argument: pointless because Stella outranked Harriman and could do as she chose.

'It's not an option,' Harriman said. 'It never is.'

Stella was proposing to go to see Billy Whizz on her own. 'I grew up on this estate. I know the people. I don't want it to be more of a provocation than necessary.'

In some ways, Harefield was like many inner-city estates. You learned fast and experience came at a cost: the eight-year-old muggers, the ten-year-old dealers, the twelve-year-old rapists, the twenty-five-year-old grandmothers. The name was one of those sick planning-office fancies, like 'Broadwater Farm', like 'Blackbird Leys', places that sound idyllic, but look like poured concrete hell and smell like a cross between a shebeen and a shithouse. They are less like city states than tiny principalities, each with its own ruling elite, their borders distinct and heavily guarded. They have their own laws and law enforcement, their own economic systems. You can get anything you want on Harefield if you have the asking price: a rock of crack, a brick of hash, a key of scag, a moody car, a fistful of credit cards, a crate of mobile phones, a truckload of stereos, black-market white goods, MAC10s, AK47s, MP5s, VCRs, TVs, DVDs, CDs, PCs, just make a list.

'When did you leave?' Harriman asked.

'When I went to university.'

Not so much leave, she thought, as tunnel out. *University.* The majority of kids didn't see much education between exclusions and bunking off. Stella often wondered what had made her an exception. She'd had the same sort of life as the rest: absent father, depressed mother, government money, but the difference in her was as indefinable and as obvious as talent.

'Fond feelings?' Harriman was trying to read her silence.

'I hate the place,' she said. 'I fucking hate it, I'd bring in the wrecking ball, I'd nuke it off the map,' and the choke in her voice was startling.

There was a little dead moment in the car, like a breath taken but not yet exhaled. Finally, Harriman asked, 'Look, what do you think Sorley would say to me if this Billy decided to give you a smack? What's his real name, anyway?'

The code of nicknames . . .

Most people had another name, not just villains, but anyone who was part of a group: a park football side, a darts team, a pool team, or just a bunch of kids hanging out together. Street names. Just as drugs are scag, brown, charlie, nose-candy, blow, spliff, rock. Billy's real name was Neil Pinto, but he liked speed, which is otherwise known as Billy Whizz.

'Look, boss, going in there and asking Billy questions about Jimmy Stone is a provocation in itself. Turning up in an unmarked car and a pair of 501s isn't going to make the difference. If it was up to me, I'd put in a call for back-up. ARV crew, maybe.' Stella's look told him that it wasn't: it wasn't up to him. As an afterthought, Harriman asked, 'Have you got people in there?'

'Not any more.'

Stella's mother had remarried and moved to Manchester eleven years before. Now and then, motivated by a combination of guilt and curiosity, Stella phoned and they spoke to each other like acquaintances who meet in the street and can't quite remember each other's name. There were times when Stella thought that her childhood was a story someone had told her.

She started the car. 'I expect you're right,' she said. 'Let's try to keep it low profile.'

'Model of tact,' Harriman assured her.

'Even if provoked.'

He was silent on that one.

The Harefield buffer zone was a third of an acre of balding grass littered with cigarette butts, syringes, condoms, KFC cartons, cider bottles, lager cans, supermarket bags, a sofa and a burned-out Nissan Sunny. In the middle of all this was a children's play area. The sofa wasn't a throw-out; old folk liked to sit there when they felt brave enough and the weather was good. They could gaze out at a seamless ribbon of traffic moving under a blue haze. The ruthless geometry of the blocks was interrupted, here and there, by dark blotches where a window should have been. Fire damage.

Stella had the address. She took Harriman through the back-doubles, a neo-brutalist maze of stairwells and concrete walkways, each logo-tagged in prime colours, each giving off a warm, rank smell that was all too human. A smell that brought everything back: kids on the balconies in high summer, fifty sound systems going, minor wars breaking out everywhere, a whiff of Moroccan gold on the breeze. For Stella Mooney, things could have gone either way.

The flats were a dullard's design template: a front door, a window alongside to shed light into the hall. Few of the original windows were in place, and few of the original doors. They'd been kicked in, wrenched out, knocked down, even, on occasion, blown up. Of the new doors and windows, a few were reinforced, sometimes because the occupants were frightened of what lay outside, more often because they wanted to protect what lay inside.

Billy Whizz's front door had a steel skim and his window was barred. There was a bell, though. Harriman hung back a little while Stella pressed the button. It produced an unlikely, suburban gonging. After a couple of minutes of non-stop ding-dong, Billy's face showed up at the window. He stared at Stella, who stared back: mutual recognition, mutual loathing. Most people on the estate who knew Stella regarded her that way. She had gone over to the enemy.

Billy opened the door and stood in the frame of the threshold like a sentry in a sentry box. Stella said, 'You want to do this on the doorstep, Billy?'

'Unless you've got a search warrant.'

'It wouldn't take long to get one. I could be back in an hour with a full crew and a hydraulic hammer. I'd like that. Haven't tossed a place in months.'

Billy turned and walked down the hallway towards the living room. Stella followed. She was halfway there when Billy turned fast and ran at her, putting the speed and impetus of his run into a shoulder charge that took her on her bruised side and shunted her off against the wall. She went down in a clatter of limbs, giving a yell of pain as her head whacked the skirting board. Billy went full length over her outflung foot, hit the edge of the open front door full-face, got to his feet again and was gone.

Stella heard Harriman's shout and the sound of feet slapping concrete. She lifted herself on to her hands and knees. Her cranium was singing, a long, high note that started up in either ear and circled like a crown of sound. She shook her head; pain crowded in from all directions and the note grew even more shrill, so she stayed motionless for a while, then got into a crouch, then straightened up. Either she swayed or the tower block did. She thought it must be her. She leaned against the wall for a moment, then walked slowly into the flat, located Billy's bathroom, and threw up into the sink. She wasn't thinking fast or straight, but the sink had been a conscious decision because she had caught sight of the lavatory as she went in and, frankly, it wasn't an option. After waiting a few minutes to see what would happen next, she walked into the living room, careful step by step, and sat down.

Things went in and out of focus. With her head tilted back she could see the tops of three of the other blocks. Rain hit the window like gravel. The sky outside was now almost uniformly plum-purple, with just a few ragged patches of violet, a queasy, electric colour like nothing else in nature. Stella closed her eyes. When she opened them, a downpour was hammering the glass and the tops of the towers were blurred by rainfall. She remembered how she had sometimes fantasized, on days like this, that the upper floors stood above the weather in a warm climate of chubby white clouds and glancing sunlight.

Little Stella Mooney, her homework spread out on the kitchen table, the TV blaring, her mind searching for a getaway.

Billy Whizz would have been faster without the broken nose, without the blood flowing across his upper lip and over his mouth, especially with his mouth wide open and hauling in breath. Breath and a spray of blood. He cuffed it away and licked it away but it kept coming.

'Bitch!' he was saying. 'Fucking-copper-bitch-shit!'

Billy had come almost to ground level, running the walkways like an old hand. Harriman was fit, but, for him, the estate was a foreign country, with its concrete back-routes, its slab-built byways. As Billy vaulted the low wall on the last walkway and set out across the scabbed grass, Harriman was thirty yards back and losing ground.

The architect who designed Harefield was a man with a bleak sense of humour. It wasn't enough of a joke to build drab, grey hutches stacked one atop the other all the way to the sky; not enough to pour an admix of indifference and tight-fistedness into the roughcast; no, he wanted some play areas for the bad boys, somewhere for the deals to go down, for the muggers to meet. So he constructed a couple of subways that went straight from the estate to the outside world. The tunnels were there, in theory, so that the elderly could get from their doors to the shops without having to cross the four-lane road on the eastern side, the four-lane speedtrack. The elderly never used it and never had. They might be old, but they weren't necessarily ready to die. Billy Whizz headed straight for it. Harriman went in behind him, gaining a little, as the slap-slap-slap of Billy's sneakers echoed off the brickwork. Then he heard the echo fuddle and stop.

Although her eyes were open, she came to with a start, as if she had been sleeping, and looked round. A moment's puzzlement was followed by alarm.

'Oh, *Christ!*'

She snapped open her mobile: her first thought was to get some help out to Harriman. *Officer in pursuit of suspect, needs assistance.* She nominated Harefield and the surrounding area, but that was the best she could do. She almost called an ambulance, but got to her feet and registered that she felt better, apart from the fact that her ears were still ringing: a thin, jazzy note with the drum of the rain as backbeat.

She looked round, taking in Billy's flat for the first time. It was a statement. Billy was clearly a minimalist. A mattress covered by a cheap throw, cushions at the back, a low table, a state-of-the-art TV and sound system with speakers the size of wardrobes; the last two items might as well have had 'ramraided' stamped across them in red. That was it apart from a clutter of fast-food cartons, beer cans, videos and discarded clothing.

He went out fast, Stella thought. He knew he was in trouble. It was true she didn't have a warrant, but she'd get one. It only took some sharp-minded brief to worry out the fact that a search had been made without licence and Billy would be showing her a finger as he sauntered from the court. She would make an official search later; the unofficial search could start now.

She tossed the room, trying to leave no trace, and came up with nothing apart from some pornographic videos and a small stash of grass. The bathroom was thick with the smell of her own puke. Working carefully, she rifled the matchwood cupboard and got nothing, though she wondered what in hell Billy wanted with the talcum powder that was, disappointingly, just talcum powder. Bad feet, maybe. She shut the door on the reek and went back to the living room. As she moved towards the door of Jimmy's bedroom, someone on the other side made an identical movement.

There was a curve in the tunnel where it went under the highway; you could hear the sound of vehicles overhead like the wind in roadside wires. Harriman came round the curve and into sight of three men standing shoulder to shoulder across the width of the tunnel. Billy Whizz stood behind them and a little way back, breathing hard and cuffing blood off his chin. They were a joke, really: laughable photofits with their shaved heads and tattoos, their sleeveless denim and big sneakers. One of them had a Staffordshire bull terrier on a lead and, in the other hand, a lock knife.

Laugh that off.

Three ways to go, Harriman thought. First way: leg it. Not a good idea, since you have to remember that most of the men on Harefield are feral; it's in their blood to chase anything that turns its back on them and runs. Second way: pretend they're not there; muscle through. All in all, he couldn't see them agreeing to that. Third way: announce that you are a police officer in pursuit of a suspect, that any attempt to hinder you will make them guilty of an offence, and that to step aside would be the wiser option. Try as he might, Harriman couldn't bring himself to believe that sweet reason played much of a role in their lives.

The man with the dog smiled, showing four lost teeth. Harriman felt a little rush of fear that raced to his gut and curdled there. He thought of a fourth way and decided that since he was already dead, he might as well do that. He walked up to Dog Man as if he were going to walk right through him, or over him, and stopped close, so close that he could feel the guy's beer belly pressing up against him. Hairs rose on the dog's ruff and along the line of its spine. Its growl was rocks in a mixer.

Harriman said, 'It's simple. You're going to have to kill me, because unless I'm dead I'll find you and I'll make absolutely fucking certain that your tariff is sky-high; I'll fit you up for every unsolved I've got in hand, and I'll be putting cash in pockets to make sure you get a serious smacking on the first of each month.'

Dog Man had dog-breath. He stared without blinking. Harriman was trying to keep the man's knife-hand in the corner of his eye.

Billy Whizz said, 'Bastard filth,' and laughed, sputtering blood.

Stella was making decisions of her own. The noise had stopped; in fact she had only heard it once, and was wondering whether the crack on her head and the ringing in her ears were the cause. She could leave and call for back-up for herself; she could call for back-up and stay where she was; she could do what she most wanted and continue her search while no other officer was around to complicate the issue.

The door was closed but not locked. She kicked it, hard, and waited. There was no response. After a brief while she opened it an inch, then kicked again, sending it back on its hinges. The kick sent a fizz to her head that almost toppled her; she swayed and put out a hand to the door jamb, closing her eyes for a moment, then went into the room.

The unmade bed had a litter of junk round it that Stella didn't want to look at. Put this in an art gallery, she thought, and you're a bright new prospect with a fine line in irony; put it in a bedroom in Harefield and you're a sleazebag sicko. Opportunity is everything.

Billy kept his clothes in a mirrored closet. Stella watched herself approaching it and wondered why she seemed slightly blurred, like the rain-soaked towers. The cheap wood had bowed and she had to tug hard to get the doors open, and when she did she was looking at exactly what she had hoped to find. A few clothes on wire hangers, two pairs of sneakers, a baseball bat and a lot of drugs, shelves full of drugs, a drugs warehouse. Either Billy Whizz was the biggest operator in west London or he was holding stuff for every dealer on Harefield.

Stella made a little stock check, taking care to leave things as they were. Everything from scag to uppers, from E to H, from heaven to hell. She closed the doors and reached for her phone. There was just time to catch a glimpse of something in the mirrored doors, something

airborne, before it landed on her back, screaming, teeth
bared.

Dog Man said, 'I'll have you, filth.'

'Better get started,' Harriman told him. 'You won't
get another chance like this.'

'I'll fucking have you.'

'It's now or never,' Harriman advised.

He was fighting to keep the tremble out of his legs,
out of his voice, but he knew he was in with a chance
because he wasn't dead. Because Dog Man was talking.
He decided to push slightly. Very slightly. Looking past
Dog Man, he said, 'What difference does it make, Billy?
Now or later? She'll have been on the radio by now –
back-up all over the place.'

The mention of another officer, or perhaps it was the
reference to back-up, seemed to bring some urgency to
the stand-off. The man furthest from Harriman looked
over his shoulder and said, 'Are they in your gaff?' Billy
looked miserable. The man put his head back and closed
his eyes for a moment; his fists were clenched; then he
said, 'Piss off, Billy.'

Harriman stood belly to belly with Dog Man while
the sound of Billy's sneakers smack-smacking against the
tunnel floor faded. When it was just wheels overhead
and the hollow rumble of rain at the tunnel mouth, the
three men broke ranks and moved on; they might have
been sentries walking the perimeter.

Harriman didn't turn to watch them go. It wasn't what
I played for, he thought; on the other hand, I'm not dead.
After a moment, he felt the discomfort he must have
been masking and walked to the side of the tunnel where

he let go a long stream of piss against a lurid lime-and-orange graffiti tag that might have read '*Dread*', or '*Dude*', or '*Dead*'.

It was like trying to shake the devil off your back.

Stella was twisting and turning and clawing, her own screams tangling with the screams of whatever was attacking her. An imp, a demon. She whirled round the room, hearing her jacket tear as teeth went in, feeling a long line of pain as a set of claws raked her neck. There was a hot, sour smell: something like damp dog, but worse, more visceral. It was a genital smell. In its fury, the beast was rutting her back. She flung a hand over her shoulder and caught a muscled arm, thick with fur. As if by way of reply, a hand snarled into her hair and ripped.

Stella turned, shrieking, and in turning passed the mirror and was able to glimpse what was on her back, arms wrapped round, fangs showing. Her knees buckled and for a moment the lights went out. Maybe it was that, the moment of unconsciousness, that saved her from worse injury, because she was already moving at speed when she stumbled and went backwards, hard and fast, a dead weight against the wall. The creature fell off and the release brought her back to herself. She got to the door and through, and slammed it.

11

The invading army consisted of a patrol car, two armed response units, back-up from AMIP-5, an ambulance and an animal handler.

The Barbary ape was taken to an RSPCA holding centre; Stella to A&E, where she was given tetanus shots together with treatment for bite marks on her back and parallel tears on her neck made by the creature's clawing fingers. Her scalp throbbed where a handful of hair had come out by the roots. It didn't show as a bald patch, but the crown of her head was matted with blood.

The animal handler's name was Russell Norton. He was on the police computer under 'Ancillary'. He'd worked in zoos and circuses, at veterinary surgeries and as a wrangler for TV companies. He wore jeans and Caterpillar boots, and his long hair was tied back: the roadie look. Norton had gone down to the hospital because the trauma consultant who had first seen Stella was eager for specialist knowledge, but there wasn't much to tell: 'Treat it like a dog bite . . .' He was able to say that the RSPCA had instituted a routine test for rabies. They were making it a priority and the results would be through to Stella's GP very soon.

'That's great,' said Stella grimly. 'That's just wonderful.'

'They're peaceful beasts under the right circumstances,' Norton said, 'living in a colony, looking after their young, foraging for food. Not apes at all, of course. Short-tailed monkeys.'

A senior house officer was threading a needle. He needed to put a stitch to either end of the bite on Stella's back, two or three inches below the nape of her neck, but was being hampered by her bra strap. He looked across at Norton. 'Do you mind?'

Norton left the cubicle and Stella sat bare-breasted while the stitches went in. Some butterfly tape completed the job. The claw gashes on her neck only needed tape-dressing. Both wounds had been bathed in antiseptic. Afterwards, with the blood dried to a brown only a little darker than her hair and with her polo sweater hiding the marks on her neck, she looked just fine. Apart from the paleness in her face; apart from the way she put the flats of her hands over her ears.

The SHO wrote her a scrip for antibiotics and told her to look out for signs of shock, because more people died of shock than –

Stella promised she would. Norton gave her a lift back to AMIP-5. He drove slowly because rain was gusting over the road in squalls and they looked out through a blurry wash even with the wipers going at speed. Stella thought back three hours to Harriman saying, 'If it was up to me I'd put in call for back-up.' Good thinking, Pete. Smart guy. Right on the money.

'*Macaca sylvanus*. Short-tailed monkeys,' Norton said, 'not apes at all. This one most likely came in a dog cage with a dose of tranquillizer. Imported from Paris.'

Stella had heard about it, but hadn't seen it: not until this close encounter. She said as much.

'Yeah, you're the first casualty I've come across,' Norton told her. He sounded as if he might jot her name in a casebook. 'They're brought into France from Algeria mostly: a few from Gibraltar, perhaps. Yeah, they're big in France. No reports of them in Britain.' He paused. 'Well, not until now.'

The rainwater on the windscreen was catching the light from streetlamps, water and sodium washing back and forth, a lurid swill. It hurt her eyes, so she looked away to the side. Pedestrians were bent into the wind, or scooted along with the blow to their backs. Her head was still singing a song of its own, thin and shrill.

Kids bought them and traded in them. In Gibraltar or Algeria, they cost maybe fifty pounds. Sold on to the foot soldiers of the Parisian estates, they could fetch ten times that, fifteen times. It was the kind of fast-thinking that puts the bad guys a step ahead of the good. The law takes away your pit bull, your cross-bred mastiff, you look around for a substitute. Barbary apes. The mother will nurse the baby for a year. That's the time to kill her and take your investment. You might have to kill the father, too, because Barbary apes are pretty democratic in domestic matters.

The Parisian kids put Pampers on the babies, and when the babies mature the kids walk their adolescent apes on a leash. They're a fashion accessory, also a weapon of choice. Sometimes the owners stage monkey-fights in tower block basements or on waste ground, so the creatures can also be money-spinners. They have strong limbs and they can bite through leather. When they attack, their method is to throw themselves at their enemy's head. Stella knew that.

'You say they're peaceful,' she said, 'in the wild.'

'Yeah.' The rain was tropical now; Norton was peering through the torrent like a sailor looking for harbour. 'A few people get bitten by the apes on Gibraltar, but then there's a high visitor incidence. Some people are bound to piss them off. Odd thing,' he said with a laugh, 'more women get bitten than men. Pretty much a seventy–thirty split.'

Stella laughed back at him. 'Well, let's face facts, women do ask for it.'

The ringing in her head was melding with the sound of rain: wispy, now, like a Pan pipe. Her wounds had begun to throb and sting as the local anaesthetic wore off, and her scalp was raw. They pulled up at a set of traffic lights and she watched a man's umbrella turn inside out with a whiplash crack. On her left, a metallic silver BMW Z3 sports edged up on the pedestrians and revved an aggressive 'No quarter'.

'So they're pretty docile apart from the occasional sexist outburst. What makes them . . .' She couldn't think of a term.

'Useful attack beasts?'

'Yes.'

'Do with them as the world did to their owners. Treat them badly. If it works for people,' Norton observed, 'it's bound to work for monkeys.'

The AMIP-5 house had a shower that the all-nighters used. Stella got Norton to drop her off in the street. She found a chemist's and bought shampoo and shower gel. As she walked the hundred yards back, the rain soaked her matted hair, releasing trickles of blood that grew weaker and pinker as they dripped from her chin.

She went through the ops room saying, 'I'm all right, I'm fine,' and people heard the warning in her voice. She got into the shower and washed the rest of the blood out of her hair and, although she was dislodging the wound dressing, washed her back again and again, because she imagined she could still detect the dark, rank smell of rut.

She dried herself with a hand towel, then sat on the lavatory seat with her head in her hands, but that was no defence against the ringing in her ears: the simple, one-note, non-stop music of tinnitus.

'They'll pick him up,' Harriman said.

Stella nodded. She was looking through the list of drugs found in Billy's flat; enough to keep west London bright-eyed for a week. The list also contained items of murderabilia – not displayed, but carefully packed away along with a price list. A complete set of photographs of Peter Sutcliffe's victims, including a SOC shot of the third body, together with snaps of Sutcliffe at the wheel of a Clark Transport lorry and Sutcliffe and Sonia on their wedding day: all this was on offer for a hundred and fifty pounds. At thirteen of Sutcliffe's victims dead and seven traumatized for life, that worked out, Stella reckoned, at eleven fifty a murder with the rest thrown in as makeweight.

A shot of Albert Fish in the electric chair was a snip at thirty pounds.

'The drugs squad say thank you,' Harriman told her. 'You've put Harefield products off the market for a month. Others aren't so happy. Muggings and burglaries will likely go off the graph with dealers needing readies for new stock.' He smiled. 'One door opens, another door closes. Oh, and they say there's no question of Billy Whizz being a dealer. So he was a warehouse for sure.'

It was a dealer's insurance. Even if the drugs squad turned up mob-handed at dawn with the hydraulic enforcer and the dogs, and you have to dump whatever stash you're carrying for short-term selling, you can still draw on your warehouse stock and deal the next day. The idea is to pick a warehouse manager who never deals, so runs a rock-bottom risk of being raided. Of course, he'll almost certainly be a user, and there's always the possibility that he'll dip into your stuff, but it's not that high a risk since your next move would be to nail him to his own front door. Basically, you're looking for a low-level creep who can be trusted. Billy Whizz, he's your man.

'I want to know when they pull him,' Stella said. 'Night or day.'

Harriman was standing behind her as she sat at her desk sifting through letters, Post-it notes, memos, reports. Her hair was still damp from the shower, and the overhead light shed a glisten on a scarlet patch of scalp about an inch in circumference. He said, 'Why not go home, boss?'

'I'm fine.'

'It's going on seven.'

'Things to do.'

There was no one else in the room. Harriman said, 'Stella, for Christ's sake, go home.'

*

George didn't know what she meant until she bowed her head to show him the lumpy scabbing there, then stripped her polo sweater. He re-dressed the wound on her back. It had seeped slightly. The stitches looked like barbs.

'Did they give you anything to take?'

'Terramycin.'

He went away and returned with a glass of water. She found the pills in her bag and swallowed a couple. They stood in the bedroom, close but not touching, Stella with her water and pills, George with his gauze and scissors, and talked about her day like characters at a Surrealists' cocktail party.

'When will you know?' George asked. He was worried about rabies.

'I spoke to this guy Norton,' she said, 'who didn't seem to think there was much risk. It's likely that the thing had been raised in captivity. Almost certain.'

The bite in her shoulder, the scratches on her neck, the bruise on her shoulder were all to the left side. 'Gives me a side free to lie on,' she observed, then backed up to the bed and lay down and was asleep at once.

George watched her for a while, watched over her, then went downstairs and poured himself a drink. He hated it. He'd never told her just how much he hated it: police work, police risks.

After an hour he went upstairs to check on her. Maybe she'd want something to eat. He found her sitting on the side of the bed with her hands over her ears.

'It won't stop,' she said.

12

Ivo Perić was at the place where boredom turns to anger. Just so many pizzas, just so many whores. Maybe it was time for beefsteak and a chocolate dessert in a Chelsea restaurant; maybe it was time for a girl who hadn't been used until she was soggy. He made a brief call on his mobile phone. The message hadn't changed: stay still until we need you. If we need you.

He cleaned the Street Sweeper, though it didn't need cleaning. He checked the wrapping on the Semtex. He went out for a run, cutting through the backstreets to Hammersmith Bridge and along the towpath for a couple of miles. He came back and watched a football match on TV. It wasn't enough. He changed out of his warm-ups and into jeans and T-shirt without bothering to shower. There was a coat he liked to wear when he was feeling lean and on the make: soft brown leather, boxy shoulders, knee length, with a slight drape. It had a scarlet lining and a narrow wallet-pocket under the lapel where he kept his knife. Anyone could have told him the coat was ten years out of date.

He'd been keeping himself to himself – trips to the mini-mart and trips to the movies, places where single people go without being looked at or sought out. Not enough fun, he thought. Perić's people didn't want him to be looked at and they certainly didn't want him to be sought out. But London's a big city, Perić thought, big and busy and hard-nosed. Easy to be cold-shouldered in London, easy to be one in a crowd. When Margaret Thatcher said 'There's no such thing as society,' London was listening.

He went to a bar called Shadows that had once been a useful Fulham boozer. Now it was rich kids with nice jobs and fast cars, multicoloured cocktails and clubbers' music loud enough to make the punters have to lean into each other's faces and shout. As Perić looked round, it seemed to him that everyone was laughing. He sat at the bar and ordered a Mexican beer and a selection of Thai hors d'oeuvres; it was just the place for that sort of thing.

The girls looked loose-limbed and fresh.

Billy Whizz needed somewhere to become anonymous, so he went up west. Get off the patch, that was the best move. An area that took in Piccadilly to Cambridge Circus, with Soho and Chinatown to either side, offered the city equivalent of hiding a tree in a wood. His idea was to play a few arcades, building on the fifty quid in his pocket until he had enough to allow him to stay away for a few days. He was a good man on the machines.

He wasn't sure where to go. He knew the law would catch up to him unless he dropped out altogether – stood on the M1 approach road with his thumb out and never came back. Though maybe he could stay in London after all, drift a little further east, a little further south.

The pain from his broken nose was like a steel brace clamping his head. A big purple bruise had spread across his face like warpaint, and his teeth felt loose.

He dropped the fifty in less than an hour and emerged to a light rainfall. The streets hadn't had time to dry since the last shower. In Leicester Square he sat on a bench outside a neon-splashed sex shop and made a call on his mobile. When Dog Man picked up, a wave of pub noise came across before he said, 'Yeah?'

Leicester Square was filled with tourists, buskers, kids on rollerblades, hawkers. Billy spoke in the soft, guarded tones of the mobile-phone generation, able to tune in the call and tune out the rest.

'It's Billy.'

'Billy, Billy, Billy . . .' Dog Man let the name hang until it squirmed. 'People are well fucked off with you, mate.'

'There's no fucking way they knew about the stuff.'

'No?'

'No fucking way.'

'What the fuck did they want, then, Billy?'

'I don't fucking know, do I?'

A group of Swedes stopped right next to him and spread out a street map as if they were airing laundry. Raindrops rattled the London postal districts.

'I'm in it, Gazza. I'm fucking in it. What can you do for me?'

Dog Man's name was Gary, so he was Gazza by right. 'I lost a fair bit of gear, Billy. I lost a lot of fucking product. Other people lost more.'

'Yeah, right, and I lost my fucking commission. I lost my fucking minder's fee, didn't I? I'm sitting in Leicester fucking Square in the fucking rain. I don't know what the fuck to do.'

His nose was blocked with dried blood and snapped

cartilage. I sound like someone with a hare lip, he thought. I sound like some fucking dummy.

'Come on, Gazza, help us out. Did I ever let you down?'

Dog Man laughed. 'Let me down? Where's my stash, Billy? Where's my fucking scag, mate?'

'I'm in a fucking hole, Gazza. I'm fucked.'

'You're an arsehole, Billy. No one's happy about this, you know that, do you?'

'What can you do for us, Gazza?'

'You ought to go north, Billy. Manchester, Newcastle.' He might as well have said Budapest.

'I can manage here, Gazza. Work out what the fuck to do.'

'What is it – money?'

'Be handy, yeah.'

'Stay there,' Dog Man told him. 'Stay there, Billy, and don't fucking move.'

The girl was with a couple of friends, but that was all right. Blondie. She had corn-coloured hair, so Perić had decided to call her Blondie. The bar had filled up and she was sitting close enough to touch. He could smell her perfume, but he would have liked to be able to catch a scent that lay deeper than that, *her* smell, what you smelled when she warmed up.

The friends were a man and a woman, clearly together. Perić didn't mind whether they made a foursome or whether he and Blondie struck off on their own straight away. He knew that she was conscious of him. On a couple of occasions, as she shifted on her bar stool, her knee had almost tapped his. He toyed with his glass –

vodka, now – and caught her eye in the bar mirror, just as he'd planned. When she broke the look, he smiled knowingly.

Play game, Blondie. Nice stuff. You'll do for sure.

Two vodkas later, the other woman picked up her bag and made for the far side of the bar, where a batwing door carried the silhouette of Marilyn Monroe holding down her billowing skirt. Blondie was laughing at something, and the laugh faded as Perić leaned across and said, 'I will buy you drink.'

She looked at the other woman's man and they exchanged a smile. Perić said, 'What do you want? Whisky?'

'I'm fine, thanks.'

'Please. I can buy your friends something.'

'We're okay. Really.'

She was more than half turned away from him; the conversation was taking place in the mirror.

'What is it?' He was pointing at her drink.

'We were just thinking of leaving, you know?'

'No, you see, I ask what is it because I don't know. I never see drink like this.'

'Oh . . . Crystal Sunset. Prosecca and blood orange.'

'Blood orange.' Perić seemed pleased. '*Blood* orange.'

She laughed, despite herself. Perić called the barman over and ordered four Crystal Sunsets. Blondie sighed. Her mirror image showed a downturned mouth. The man with her swivelled to look across to the women's room.

Perić said, 'I was thinking to get some food. Do you know place near here?'

'There are lots of places.'

'Place you like.'

She didn't reply. The other woman came back, looked at the row of drinks and felt the silence inside the circling blare of music and voices. She glanced at Perić, then at the man, and last at Blondie. Perić picked up his Crystal Sunset and drank off half of it.

'Good,' he said. 'Blood orange.'

Blondie leaned over and put her mouth close to her friend's ear. The friend nodded okay. She took her bag in one hand, the man in the other, and walked a mazy line to the outside door, weaving round groups and tables. They left without looking back. Perić pushed Blondie's drink across to her, but she didn't take it.

'Polish?' she asked.

'No.'

'Czech?'

'No.'

'Yugoslav?'

Perić gave a little frown, then laughed. 'There is no Yugoslav, not as you mean. That is over.' He paused to drink the rest of his fizz and orange. 'Serb.'

'Ah, yes, right.'

'What – "ah, yes, right"?'

She reached out and took the lapel of his leather coat between her finger and thumb. 'This coat,' she said. 'You had to be from some fucking peasant backwater.'

He watched her as she threaded her way towards the door. He was breathing hard, like a spent runner, and the points of his jaw were locked. There was a terrible impulse in him to movement and violence. Without knowing he was doing it, he got down from his stool and took two long strides towards her retreating back, his hand going to the slim pocket under his lapel, then checked himself suddenly, standing flat-footed in the middle of the crowded bar, because –

Not her. Not here. Not now.

– but his eyes felt hot, as if they were filling with blood.

Billy Whizz was running options.

Disappear for six months, maybe a year. After a while, the cops would forget to come looking. He could spend months going from squat to squat. He wouldn't be able to go back to Harefield, of course, but there were other areas of operation. Or else, get on to that brief who'd done the business last time out when Billy was selling prescription drugs to clubbers. You could get them off the old fucks who wandered round Harefield with their rubber-tipped sticks and their stupid hats: doctors over-prescribed, the old fucks copped some pocket money, the clubbers would swallow anything at ten quid a pop and their own adrenalin supplied the high. Fifty hours' community service and some blah-blah from the magistrate: piece of piss. Maybe the brief could find some clever route to go. The flat wasn't in Billy's name, after all; it was down to some geezer his mother had shacked up with three years ago. Now she was gone and the geezer was gone and Billy sat in the rain considering whether 'some geezer' was a workable defence.

He didn't see them coming. He didn't see them at all until they sat down, one either side of him. They were laughing.

One of them said, 'Billy . . . Not enough sense to get in out of the rain.'

*

Blondie had been right, the area was stiff with restaurants and the restaurants were full of people. Perić walked fast, passing the windows without looking in. He was talking to himself, a low monotone that rose and fell in rhythm with his anger. He could have flagged a taxi, but he wanted to walk, wanted to barge into the wind that had got up behind the rain and soaked his trousers below the knee. Below the knee-length coat that only a hick would wear.

May she have a bad accident. May she be scarred. May she have a bad accident but live to see her scars every day in the mirror.

The Thai hors d'oeuvres had been minimalist and the vodka had put a real edge on his appetite. He crossed the road to the Golden Fry, skipping between a cab and a bright red panel van, forcing the van to slap on its brakes. A voice yelled something and Perić stabbed his middle finger into the air, a language spoken fluently by all.

The Golden Fry hot cabinet was stocked with items that seemed as if they might be about to hatch. Batter-pods. First there would be a crack or two in the surface and a small seepage of fat, then something pale and blind would nudge the crust, seeking the milky light and the stale warmth. It would inch out, pushing with its slick, slippy shoulders at first, then breaking through and coming in a rush. Something already equipped with hair and teeth.

The Golden Fry and its mutant takeaway.

Perić paid up and left. As he walked, he delved into the bag and broke off a bite-sized piece. It was hot and he juggled the fragment round his teeth, blowing out steam.

The bright red panel van had turned and parked, two wheels up on the kerb. He should have seen it, should have read what it meant, should have remembered the shriek of brakes and the angry yell, his finger lofted: *Fuck you!*; but he was past before the set of signals that meant 'danger' registered and he turned too late to avoid the door as it opened, slamming into his back and sending him face forward on the pavement.

The bag split and his deep-fry scattered into the road. He back-pedalled fast, going on heels and elbows, but not fast enough to save him from taking a kick on the thigh. There were three of them, two scrambling out of the cab, the man who had booted him already shaping up for a second kick. Perić rolled over twice, taking himself out of that man's line of approach, then bunny-hopped to his feet. The driver and the third man were coming at him fast. They might have been triplets: overweight, scabby stubble, T-shirts and loggers' boots, studs in their lower lips, hoops through their eyebrows. Triplets or clones.

The driver threw a punch that caught Perić high on the shoulder. They were shouting at him, but he couldn't hear much of what they were saying because he was closed off to everything except what to do and how to do it.

He went across the road in the face of a car and a motorcycle that was overtaking on the inside. The car stopped, the bike went round him in a wash of spray. By the time he hit the opposite pavement, he was sprinting hard. The street was crowded. They saw a man being chased by three clones with murder on their minds. No one stood between them, or yelled out, or made a phone call; no one wanted to touch this; it can come off on your hands.

Perić ran wide to get round some garbage sacks and took a side street that led to the river. The idea was not to outrun the men, but to put distance between him and them, room to manoeuvre. Beyond the terrace, the street petered out into workshops, then lock-ups, then an alley that opened up to darkness. There were no people or vehicles, but Perić could hear the sound of running feet. He took the alley and found it ended in a raised pavement sloping down to the river.

The panel-van men were about thirty yards back, no more. He ran down the pavement in the direction of the slope and came on to the towpath at a low point, where there was not much between the river and the bank. A high tide had left a clutter of detritus, bottles, rope, driftwood.

Perić made a sharp turn and started along the towpath as if doubling back, but at the lower level. That way, he fell into the shadow of the raised pavement. He had picked up a piece of wood about the same length and heft as a baseball bat. He'd also picked up a bottle. As the panel-van men hit the path, Perić lobbed the bottle up in the air so that it smashed on the ground, giving them a pointer. He ran hard for the count of twenty, then found a gap in the shrub land that bordered the path.

The men came up, running in a loose bunch, one slightly adrift. As they passed, Perić stepped out and swung his chunk of driftwood at the straggler, taking him on the side of the head. There was a sound like iron on iron, dull and flat. The man stalled, as if all his energy had been siphoned off. He went another ten feet on rubber legs, then sat down hard.

The second man heard something and turned, but saw only his friend seeming to lose his footing: no one else on the path. He'd catch up. And a moment later, that's exactly what appeared to happen: footsteps coming up fast, the sound of someone breathing hard. Then the sky lit up for an instant and the breath left his lungs. He was still running, but he couldn't see and he couldn't hear; and then he was running on air.

The first man slowed down when he heard the splash. He looked sideways towards the river because it didn't occur to him to look back. There was something in the water, but no sound. Then he saw Perić as you see someone in the moment that you turn a corner and walk straight into him. He flung up an arm and the knife took him just below the wrist, cutting to the bone. He kicked out, but Perić was round him, circling left against the right-hander.

Perić knew how to do this. It was Bosnia.

He saw Van Man's knees buckle and knew that shock had set in. He must have gone through veins at the wrist – there'd be a strong blood flow, so he didn't want to make contact. He moved in, feinting, and moved out again, a little war dance, a little attack two-step, and Van Man danced with him, going back, going forth, going left, going right, but not seeing the move that was for real as Perić dropped a shoulder and moved in close, drawing the knife across in a quick arc.

The blade sliced Van Man's cheek from the point of his jaw upwards, nicking open his left nostril. He said,

'Ooooh,' as if he had just been given some dreadful news, then went down on his back.

Perić moved in behind him, grabbed his hair and lifted. Just the same. Just like Bosnia. Cutting a throat was easy, no specialist knowledge required. And if you had a little time to spare, the 'Serbian necktie', perhaps: the throat slit and the tongue then yanked down and out through the slash to loll on the neck. But not today, not this time. There was other work to be done and he'd stepped out of line. Now he would have to go to earth.

He yanked Van Man's head back and spat in his face. Then he cut him across the eyes.

Stella rang the bell, but nobody came. There was something in the air, something like a bad smell or a scary noise, but it was neither of those things; it was a feeling. She remembered something she'd read: the Bible, was it?

I have felt the draught from the wing of the Angel of Death.

She crouched down and raised the letterbox. As in a movie shown on a small screen, everything she saw was cut to a rectangle. Their heads and upper bodies were out of shot, and the lower steps were obscured, but the torsos and legs of the children were in view, the cartoon-character pyjamas, the chubby feet, the little hands hanging limply at either side. Then she was inside and looking up, and if it wasn't true that her heart had stopped beating, she hoped that it soon would.

When she heard the phone she knew exactly what was happening.

I'm dreaming and the phone is going to wake me up.

But she couldn't find her way out of that house; she couldn't stop looking up; and the children were still there, their heads cocked towards her, their faces solemn and unnaturally dark.

George woke her, rolling over in bed with the phone in his hand. He said, 'Jesus! It's three o'clock!', but she knew what time it was.

13

Billy Whizz smoked as if he were on the attack, drawing deep, snatching the cigarette from his mouth, exhaling hard.

Stella said, 'They grassed you up, Billy. Someone grassed you up.'

'Yeah? Who would that be?'

'Friends. Good friends.'

There was a pause while Billy thought about this. Finally he said, 'I was minding that stuff. I wasn't dealing it.'

'Thanks for not saying you had no idea how it got there.'

'What?'

'Who were you minding it for?'

'Don't fucking start.'

'The same ones that grassed you up, Billy?'

Another pause. Billy was shifting ground again. 'Is there anything you can do? Is there anything we can do, here?'

'A deal?'

'Yeah, some sort of –'

'A deal, Billy? Is that what you're talking about?'

'Depends, doesn't it?'

'It does, yes. It depends on what you've got to offer. It depends on what I want. Someone ought to look at your nose, Billy. That's a bad break.'

*

It was almost five o'clock. Harriman was in the room, but he wasn't talking. Stella was working well, she'd found the right pace.

Everyone else was home in bed, including Mike Sorley. Sergeants questioned suspects. Sergeants put the questions and listened to the answers: listened for the hollow note, the off-key response. They were attuned to it. They shared the street with the pushers and the grifters, with the pimps, the twoccers and the muggers, the GBH men, the conmen, the dog men, the van men.

Q&A: a certain rhythm, a certain pulse.

Billy lit another cigarette, dragging deep while the match was still in place, then letting smoke roll out of his nose and half-open mouth.

'You want to see a doctor?' Stella asked.

'Yeah.'

'But first you want to do a deal.'

'I can give you some names. I can't be a witness.'

'Not a lot of use in that, Billy.'

'You'll know who to look for. They're hoolies,' he said, as if this were the first piece of information that might secure him three years in an open prison and early parole.

'We already know who to look for. And where to find them.' She was lying, but it sounded good. 'What we need is a case against them.'

'I can't. I'd be fucking dead.'

'All hoolies?'

'Most of them, yeah.'

'Same club?'

'Nah, some here, some there.'

Hoolies: it was short for hooligans. You can classify

hoolies in different ways: football fans, neo-Nazis, xeno-phobes, psychopaths. They like to think of themselves as patriots, as young warriors. They like football, but even more they like fighting, and even more than that they like fighting foreigners. On both sides, people die. It's a blood feud, a cross-border invasion with national flags flying. In France, Germany, Holland and Belgium town centres are laid waste. In Greece and Turkey there's blood on the streets. Cities mobilize riot police and water cannon. They load their rounds of rubber bullets. Tele-vision newsreels show young men with shaved heads and beer bellies, their faces smeared with red, white and blue warpaint, pouring mob-handed across the foreign cobbles.

And sometimes, of course, the flags are lowered; some-times the young warriors come home bearing their dead, because other countries have hoolies of their own.

'What do you think you're looking at here, Billy? Seven years? Ten?'

'I was just holding the stuff. Warehouse.'

'Who's going to believe that?'

'On my life.'

'Jimmy Stone's a friend of yours, isn't he, Billy?'

A startled look, but not a guilty look. 'Jimmy? Jimmy's not in this.'

'So who is?'

'I can tell you stuff, but I can't go to court. I can't go public.'

'There are methods –'

'No, listen, don't talk about witness protection or anything like that. I've been pulled. They gave me up. If

I walk out of here, they'll know. If there's a deal, it's a deal where I speak to you but I don't speak to any fucking judge.'

'Try me. No promises.'

'No promises, no fucking names.'

Stella looked towards the wall-mounted cassette recorder, gave it a beat, then looked back at Billy. 'I'm sure that a court would take your cooperation into account when considering sentence. This information could be given in confidence if you felt your safety might be at risk.' She spoke slowly and clearly as if presenting evidence.

Billy gave a name. Then two more. Then a further five. Suppliers and dealers back along the chain as far as he could go. Or as far as he was willing to go.

Harriman went to the desk, brought back the personal organizer that Billy had lifted during a thieving expedition to Covent Garden and copied down the mobile phone numbers that Billy linked to the names he'd given. This couldn't have been done without Billy since the organizer gave only nicknames: the numbers were for Dino and Fishbelly, for Spank and Harry Alfa. It wasn't code, it was who they were to each other. Stella wondered how many of them knew Billy Whizz's real name.

They took a break for coffee and the bathroom. Stella locked the cubicle door, unbuckled her belt, shoved everything down past her knees. When she sat down, her head swam. The jangle was there in her ears, a distant bell, closer and louder if she brought it to mind. Her clothes reeked of tobacco smoke and she felt nauseous.

*

She switched the tape back on, gave the resume time, then said, 'Tell me more about Jimmy Stone.'

'I said: Jimmy's not in this.'

'I know. It wasn't just drugs we found at your flat, Billy.'

'What?'

Stella gave a short list, including the Sutcliffe material.

'It's not –'

'Don't say it's not illegal, Billy, because I've heard that before. I know. I know it's not. I also know you bought it from Jimmy Stone by email. That's your connection to Jimmy. That's why I think you might be able to give me some information about Jimmy.'

'What do you want to know?'

'Well – first things first – who killed him?'

Billy's face went slack. He was looking Stella straight in the eye, but not to send a message. He said what any innocent person might say: 'Jimmy's dead?'

Stella gave the date and asked Billy where he was at the time.

'You're not saying I killed Jimmy Stone?'

'Where were you, Billy?'

'Fuck knows.' It was a good answer.

Okay, she said to herself. It wasn't you. But then she hadn't thought it was. Billy might kill someone, but not with a probe between the ribs.

'Tell me about the murderabilia.'

'Good business. Lot of interest.'

'The hoolies – do they buy it?'

'They like it, yeah.'

'How did you take delivery?'

'Go round to Jimmy's. Or he'd bring it to my place. Or the pub.'

'Who were his friends?' Billy shrugged. 'I need to know.'

'Hoolies, you know. He was into that. Used to travel with them. Liked a ruck.'

'Anyone in particular?'

'Bloke called Raymond. Him and Jimmy used to hang out together.'

'Who's Raymond?'

'I don't know him. He'd be in the pub sometimes. Or round Jimmy's when I went there. You know, we'd have some drinks, do some business.'

'Business?'

'He liked brown.'

Billy stopped short, then sighed acknowledging the mistake. 'It's not my stuff,' he said. 'I don't deal. I told you that.' He paused. 'I used to take a bit off the top sometimes.'

'Let's go back to Jimmy Stone.'

But it was clear that Billy didn't have much to say about Jimmy Stone. Stella told the tape that she was ending the interview. Billy asked, 'What now?'

'Well, Billy, now someone else wants to talk to you. DS Patmore. Drugs squad.'

'You're drugs squad.'

'No, I'm not.'

'Not drugs . . .'

'No. I'm investigating the murder of Jimmy Stone. Your stash isn't really of much interest to me. I expect DS Patmore's got one or two things to say about it.'

Stella watched as a cloud passed over Billy's sun.

'I just did a fucking deal with you.'

Stella shook her head. 'If Serious Crimes act on the information you gave me, they might be willing to put in a word for you. The fact is, Billy, it's not my case.'

Billy stood up, knocking his chair back. Harriman took a couple of steps forward.

Stella said, 'You bastard, Billy. There are twelve-year-old crackheads on Harefield. They mug each other for their mobile phones, then sell them to stallholders on the North End Road market to fund the next rock.'

Billy sat down and knuckled his eyes. He yawned and thumbed a cigarette out of his pack. 'Yeah,' he said. 'Well . . . you know kids.'

She worked a full morning clearing back-paperwork and writing a guarded progress report to Alun Ward saying that there was, in fact, little progress, but that Billy Whizz had been arrested on drugs handling charges.

Paper, more paper, everything papered.

She didn't include a tape of her interview with Billy, just a mention of the fact that Billy knew Jimmy and bought murderabilia from him, but hadn't been a 'close associate' of Jimmy's, and had been eliminated as a suspect. She thought 'close associate' a nice touch of officialese.

Ward was getting information on a need to know basis; if she followed leads and they came to anything, then she would mention it. Information she hadn't yet acted on was, she considered, none of his damn business.

A Post-it note was stuck to her VDU, asking her to call John Delaney and giving phone, fax, email, mobile and pager. Stella knew that Andy Greegan had taken the call because he always wrote messages in capitals, a meticulousness that informed his scene-of-crime activities. She made a mental note: *Delaney spoke to Andy. So do they speak at other times, perhaps, off the record?* She didn't return the call, but she slipped the Post-it note into her address book.

Paul Lester was on his way out to chase down a few more names on the known associates list for Jimmy Stone. It was a routine job and took up time, but it had to be done, although Stella suspected that Lester was making work for himself. AMIP investigations are good news for sergeants and lower ranks – they get automatic overtime and it's great money. Upwards of sergeant and you're putting in the time because, listen, it's your job and the job has to get done. Paul Lester had the full complement of wife, kids and mortgage, and O/T was a way of staying ahead of the game. Also, his clothes weren't the standard husband-and-father gear. He was tall and good-looking in an offbeat sort of way; and he liked to dress the part.

He dropped more paper on to Stella's desk. 'The Tanners,' he said; and when Stella looked up: 'Nothing.'

'You're sure?'

'Jimmy might have done a job or two for them. Most of the pond life in west London have done a turn for the Tanners.'

'Okay.' She shrugged, disappointed.

Lester had worked with Stella before. He knew she had grown up on Harefield and he'd heard her talk about the Tanners. He said, 'Yeah . . . Well, I'm sorry, boss, but I can't make a connection.'

'Doesn't mean it isn't there.'

'Sure. I'll keep looking.' He opened the door and looked at her over his shoulder. 'Are you okay?'

'People keep asking me that.'

'And?'

'I'm fine. I'm great. Piss off. Come back with something useful.'

The squad room was warm, but the early hours had been cold and Stella was wearing a roll-neck over a T-shirt and a jacket over that. The roll-neck was chosen, in part, to hide the three parallel stripes on her neck. She took off the sweater and put the jacket back on. The welts were still raw; they tugged when she turned her head. For the first time that day, she thought about the rabies test.

The tinnitus was a constant. What was happening in her ears, now, was a high monotone but with something new: a faint background slush. It was as if Stella had suddenly become attuned to something that was normally beyond human pitch: supersonic dog-whistles, or the tangled skeins of music flowing on radio waves from transmitter to receiver. The slush was something akin to the sound of surf on a distant beach. She stuck a finger in either ear and scoured. The noises grew louder. She closed her eyes and slowly lowered her forehead to her desk.

Sue Chapman knocked on Sorley's door and sidled in. He had set up in a tiny lobby off the main room: the sort of space estate agents might call a study. He was on the phone, so she didn't say anything, just left the door open so that Sorley had a clear view of Stella's work-station.

He finished his call and went out. Stella was lying with her face amid her paperwork, her arms hanging straight down. She was snoring slightly, her breath leaving a dampness on the report she'd written for SO10.

Sorley went back to his office and dialled her extension, seeing her head snap up, the look of disorientation slowly clearing. She washed her face with her hands, then lifted the phone.

'This is your leader,' Sorley told her. 'Go home to bed.'

She went to the pub. It was before twelve and the place was clean and abandoned, with the residue of last night's smoke pushing up under a low ceiling of carpet shampoo and air freshener. The barman gave a little start, as if surprised to see her, then feinted at the vodka optic. Stella asked for a lime-and-soda. She took out the Post-it note and called Delaney's mobile number. His voice came on asking her to leave a message.

When the barman brought her lime-and-soda, she said, 'And a vodka.'

Once the first was down, she felt better and oddly reckless, as if sitting in the boozer before real business had begun and drinking out of turn was just the thing to be doing. She thought she might stay through lunch and on into the afternoon, waiting for the equivalent moment, when the place emptied out and only the rock-hard drinkers could be found, each with nothing more demanding to do than press on deeper into drunkenness.

Delaney arrived just as she was starting her third. She was on a stool at the crook of the bar, where she always sat if she could, and he took the stool next to hers, just as he had before.

He said, 'What the hell was that?'

Stella raised a hand to her neck. She had forgotten to put the roll-neck back on. Now she remembered the barman's reaction, his moment of wide-eyed surprise.

'Hostile monkey,' she said.

Delaney opened his mouth to make a joke, but stopped short. Stella told him about the fashion for Barbary apes and how they limpet on and what their scream sounds like if you're getting it at close quarters. She told him about the bite on her back and how the *fucking* thing had ripped out a handful of her *fucking* hair and she was waiting for a *rabies* test, for Christ's sake, and even helped him to speculate on where Billy Whizz had bought his ape, before she realized how much she had said and concluded that she must be slightly drunk. Slightly drunk and very tired. Slightly drunk and very tired and growing increasingly desperate about the ringing-singing in her head.

'Are you all right?' he asked.

'Why?'

'You don't sound all right.'

'How do I sound?'

'You sound shaky.'

'I didn't get much sleep.'

'I'm not surprised. Rabies, for God's sake.'

'No, not that, not the monkey bite. I was interrogating a suspect.'

'The Deever case?'

'In a manner of speaking.'

'You know who the mystery man is.'

'Maybe,' she said, then shook her head as if denying what she'd said. She knew she was being indiscreet; more, she knew she was being coy. Put it down to bite-trauma, she thought. Put it down to all-night interrogations and mid-morning shots of Absolut.

'You know who he is,' Delaney said, 'and so do I.'

Stella remembered the sheets from a murderabilia website that Delaney had been carrying in the Muji folder.

Sure you know. Of course you know. But who told you?

She turned to him to ask just that question and saw that he was surrounded by a blue-black outline, like cross-hatching on a pencil sketch, that the outline was spreading; that his face was receding; that the room had grown utterly silent; that he seemed suspended in space, the outline leaching from him like an aura.

She thought, *John Delaney, Master of the Dark Arts.* Then Delaney caught her as she fell sideways into his lap, his arm tightening round her, his free hand cradling her head to keep it from harm.

She was out for less than thirty seconds and came to lying full length on the pub carpet with Delaney kneeling beside her.

She said, 'Oh, shit,' and sat up. An old-fashioned bell alarm clock was going off in her head. The barman was on the phone. 'What's he doing?'

'Calling an ambulance,' Delaney told her.

'Don't,' she said; then, louder, 'Don't. No ambulance.'

The barman spoke a moment, then hung up.

Delaney said, 'You're not right.'

'I'm fine. I'll be okay. I've had a couple of drinks.'

'It's not drink. You went over like a tree in a gale. If you won't let him call an ambulance, let me take you to Casualty.'

'For Christ's sake, Delaney, I'll be fine.'

She tucked her heels underneath and put out a hand to push herself upright; somehow, this left her lying flat on her face.

'Okay,' she said. 'You take me.'

They went to the hospital that had stitched her bite and, like Stella, the SHO was back on duty. He shone an ophthalmoscope in her eyes and tested her reflexes and asked her if she'd been throwing up. Finally, he said, 'You took a blow to the head. Maybe you should have a scan: danger of embolism.'

Stella told him about the ringing in her ears. 'Tinnitus,' he said. 'Drives people crazy. Well . . . can do.'

'I thought I could have my ears syringed.'

'No. Could even make it worse.'

'So what do we do about it?'

'Nothing. Nothing you can do. Well, some people opt to have a little transmitter inserted beneath the skin at the back of the ear. The idea is that it emits a note at the same wavelength as your tinnitus, thereby cancelling it out.'

'Does it work?'

'Not usually. If the wavelength is slightly off, it means you've got tinnitus twice: once naturally, once artificially.'

'Yeah? Well, thanks for telling me.'

She took off her T-shirt and bra and he re-dressed the wound on her back. 'Rest,' he told her. 'Take things easy for a few days. You need a note?' She shook her head.

'Okay. I'm going to give you a referral to Radiology for an MRI scan.'

'When?'

'Now.'

'No, I mean when do I have the scan?'

'Now.'

'You saw something when you looked in my eyes.'

'No, I didn't, so I know you haven't got a subdural haematoma of any significance, but you passed out and you feel bad, so let's not take chances. The MRI is fast and accurate.'

'What happens?' Her tone of voice meant, No messing with my head, okay?

'It puts a magnetic field across the brain. The field is modified by the brain's hydrogen ions. A computer image shows any change of status. Tells us everything we want to know.'

Not everything, Stella thought. It doesn't tell us about good and evil, or where love comes from, or why Henry Deever jumped off the roof.

Delaney walked with her through a mile or so of corridors.

She said, 'Go away, for Christ's sake.'

'If you pass out again?'

'I'm in the right place for it.'

'I could call someone. Your husband.'

'I haven't got a husband.' It was all she said on the subject. In any case, George was at a meeting in Southampton, setting up for a trip he was about to take to a boat show in Seattle: two commissions in view; nice money.

'I could call the police.'

'Here I am.' She laughed, then gave a little stumble. His hand went out to her.

'Oh, look,' he said, as they reached Radiology, 'they have old copies of *Hello!* And I thought I might be bored . . .'

Stella went to the reception desk with her note. They sent her through almost at once. Delaney took from his inside pocket a thin sheaf of papers, on top of which was a picture of Jimmy Stone. The papers were murderabilia catalogues, along with some research notes for a new feature.

Among the notes was a contact address for someone called Zuhra Hadžić. Not an address, a *location*. The next three pages contained the details he'd scribbled down when he'd first met Zuhra. It was because of her that he'd contacted Stella at AMIP-5. She was an odd coincidence; something he ought to share. But he could save it for another time: another opportunity.

I haven't got a husband. But he guessed she had someone and the thought rattled him.

What is it? he wondered. You meet a thousand people and just one of them makes you itch. It wasn't looks, or a turn of phrase, or mannerisms. Maybe it was all of those – something like *style*.

He thought, I can cope with this as long as I'm in control.

He used the page with Zuhra Hadžić's details on it to jot down some references to Barbary apes, reckoning there might be a story there somewhere. Then he picked up a back issue of a Sunday supplement and enjoyed an article that reviewed conspiracy theories about the death of Diana, Princess of Wales.

Stella was back in fifteen minutes. They walked back down the mile of corridors.

'Clean bill of health,' she said. Then, remembering, 'Except I haven't had the rabies test results, yet.'

'Did you know,' he asked her, 'that the Princess of Wales was murdered by Mossad acting on instructions from MI6, who, in turn, got their orders direct from the Queen of England?'

Stella shrugged. 'Sure. Everyone knows that.'

They came off Shepherd's Bush roundabout and started up towards Notting Hill Gate. She said, 'You can drop me by the nick. I'm parked there.'

'Or I could drive you home.'

Something was nagging at her; the same feeling you get when you remember that something's upsetting your day but can't call it to mind. As she got out of the car, Delaney gave her his card: phone, fax, mobile, email, pager.

'You like to stay in touch,' she observed.

'Yes,' he said, 'I would. I would like that.'

George got back around eight and found her asleep on the couch. He asked her whether she'd eaten and how she was feeling.

I've got this fucking noise in my head that makes people kill themselves; I'm waiting to find out if the monkey has

rabies; I did three large vodkas before midday, passed out, had
a brain scan. How was your day?

She said, 'I'm fine. Shall we order something in?'

In bed, he held her in the hoop of his arm, his hand
resting just below her breast as if he were checking her
heartbeat. They listened to the sound of rain slanting
against the window.

'Seattle will be almost two weeks,' he told her. 'Two
weeks, is that okay?'

'Come back with the commissions.'

'What do you want?'

'Metallic silver BMW Z3 that goes vrrmmm-vrrmmm-
vrrmmm.'

'Keep an eye out for FedEx.'

She reached up and kissed him, and felt the breath
catch in her throat.

When she woke, the bedside lamp was still on and his
arm still round her. She eased out and he turned in
his sleep, giving a little sigh; a little moan. She got up
and went to the window, looking out at the street through
the sodium-orange rain-spangles, and in that moment
she remembered what had been fretting at the back of
her mind.

You know who he is, Delaney had said, *and so do I.*

And *you* called *me*, she thought. Which means you
know something I don't.

She switched off the bedroom light and went downstairs to make the call. His voice answered on both land-
line and mobile. She left a message: 'It's me. I think
you've got something to tell me. You'd better call.'

As she put the phone down, she realized what she'd said.

It's me.

14

They were doing notes in the squad room: coffee and cigarettes and chocolate bars. DC Steve Sheppard with his fist in a bag of salt and vinegar, DC Paul Lester coming in with a box of Danish. Everyone had a copy of the interview tape Stella had made with Billy.

Andy Greegan was reading through a fax from a friend on another AMIP team: the same patch but a different bit of business – on the towpath near Hammersmith Bridge. One man blinded, one in ITC with cranial trauma, a third dead in the water, his body washed up by Chiswick Eyot. The man with the knife-cut across the eyes had got back to the street, walking against the traffic flow with his hands flapping and a curtain of blood covering his face and chest. You could hear his howls over the sound of car horns from the backed-up traffic.

A red panel van had been parked illegally in the Fulham Palace Road. It was carrying two hundred videos, part of a consignment that had been ram-raided in Brentford two nights before. The current theory was villains falling out: three chancers taking more than their share.

Andy read the main details out loud.

'Fucking good luck,' Steve Sheppard said. 'Let them kill each other. We could issue guns.'

Sorley had Stella's report in front of him. 'This Neil

Pinto,' he said. 'Billy Whizz. There's no way he fits the frame?'

'I don't think so,' Stella said. 'Nothing to put him at the scene. And you didn't see the look on his face when I told him Jimmy was dead. Tough to fake that.'

'Has he got an alibi?' Sorley wondered.

'Billy could find people to lie for him,' Pete Harriman observed.

'Maybe, maybe not,' Andy Greegan said. 'His mates turned him in, don't forget.'

'We ought to look for likely motive,' Stella said, 'as a matter of course; but I don't fancy Billy for it, I really don't.'

'Because of the MO,' Sorley guessed.

'Exactly.'

Sue Chapman laughed. 'To find the right place for the probe, you'd've had to count the ribs. Too much maths for Billy.'

'So what have we got?' Sorley asked.

'The murderabilia website's still taking orders.' Sue held up a list of hits. 'Nothing very useful, though. We're looking for anyone who seems to know Jimmy at all well, but most of the site visitors are sickos from round the globe. Fewer and fewer hits each day, of course, because we're not supplying the goods.'

Paul Lester cracked a can of Coke. 'We're well placed for that, come to think of it. Autopsy reports, signed confessions, candid snaps of strip searches.'

'I'll update the site,' Sue told him.

'So we've got the website and hoolies,' Sorley said. 'And this guy Raymond.'

'We've got as far as we can go with known associates,' Stella said. 'Jimmy wasn't exactly a loner, but there don't seem to be links with any particular firm. We're still checking.'

'So he was freelance,' Sorley suggested.

'Probably. Had some form, but small stuff. Handling stolen goods, theft, living off immoral earnings. Nothing big time, nothing connected. Frankly, it's difficult to see why anyone would kill him.'

'Immoral earnings?' Harriman looked across at Stella. 'Not Patsy . . .'

'You guessed it.'

'Jesus. When did this come in?'

'Sue has been collating a potted history of Jimmy Stone. He was a chancer, all right.'

'Who's Patsy?' Sorley was thinking back through the reports.

'His wife,' Stella said. 'Jimmy used to fly-post phone boxes in the area. There was also an ad in the local press – "Hot massage. Your place only".'

'Married love,' Sorley observed. Stella noticed the downturned mouth, as if he'd bitten on something sour. He said, 'So this Raymond . . .'

'We're looking at it,' Stella said. 'We're looking at the whole hoolie thing: talking to uniform, talking to football-club liaison officers in west London.'

'Nothing from the new house-to-house?' Sorley wondered. A second trawl had been set up to catch people who'd been missed first time around, especially after it was discovered that Jimmy Stone had lived upstairs from the Deever sisters. But whatever evil had occurred, the wise monkeys in the surrounding streets hadn't seen it or heard it, and certainly weren't prepared to speak of it.

Sorley lit up a cigarette and made a new contribution to the tobacco fog that was damping the windows. 'Some bastard killed him. Someone knows something.'

Stella said, 'It would be a hell of a lot easier for us if we could give Jimmy Stone to the press. Press and TV.'

'SO10 won't have it,' Sorley told her. 'Definitely something delicate going on.'

Stella thought back to Alun Ward's late-night call: *Go through the motions. Do the minimum.*

Is your mind the only mind at work on this?

I'm here with my DI.

Put him on.

He's getting a drink in . . .

I don't think so.

Stella went on her own to see Mick Armitage. Mick was a 'chis'; that's *Covert Human Intelligence Source.* Used to be called snouts. You have to paper them: a report to your inspector to say the meeting's going to take place; a second report once you've met. Reports are seen by a lot of people; which is why chissies all have nicknames. You don't want your information source revealed to just anyone. He's your invisible friend.

Stella called Mick Armitage Jesse after Jesse James, because he always wore cowboy boots. In her reports, he was Jesse. When she made mention of him to colleagues, he was Jesse. He called her Stella: a straight interloper in a world of doubles.

On her way, she called Delaney's land-line and mobile again. They both asked her to leave a message.

Why hadn't she given Delaney up at the briefing? Why hadn't she said, 'There's a journalist who's been dogging me; he seems to know about Jimmy Stone. Maybe we should have him in, issue a few threats, find out what he knows?'

Well, because someone in the team was talking out of turn and she needed to know who. That's what she told herself. She parked up in Norland Square for a moment and called her GP for news of the rabies test. He told her tomorrow for sure.

Mick Armitage had been on the payroll for a couple of years. He worked for Stella, but he worked for other officers in other outfits, which was handy for Mick because he could sometimes sell the same information three or four times and, since everyone had a different name for him, he could stay happily incognito. Mick didn't do it for the money, though. He did it partly for the favours it put in the bank and partly because he liked working both ends against the middle. In another life, and with other opportunities, Mick would have made a great career among the subtler, more lethal crooks in big business.

Mick did some good deals in Notting Hill, but home was Shepherd's Bush. He spoke the language and he liked the climate: diesel-sleet and fast-food humidity. They had set up a meet in a pub on the west side of Shepherd's Bush Green. Stella walked through the Green, going between the thick scatter of dog shit and the burger cartons; between junkies and drunks, deep in their bags and blankets, and pre-teen fashion-victims who were still learning their trade.

Down the fringe of one pathway grew two small clumps of some unnameable flower, their dark heads heavy with cadmium. The sun glinted off pools of broken glass. It was a late summer's afternoon in the Bush and the rain was holding off.

The pub was a barn-sized space split by a horseshoe bar. Two jumbo screens were showing sports; on one side American football, on the other ice hockey. The seamless, high-pitched bellow of the commentators collided over the bar in an hysterical macaronic backwash. In deference to the US football/hockey axis, Mick was drinking Miller Lites with shots of Southern Comfort on the side.

The football players tucked down over the grid. 'Fucking stupid game,' he observed. 'They all wear full Kevlar body armour and every twenty seconds they all fall over and the play stops. Load of poofs.'

Stella bought him another round, bought herself a tomato juice, and they moved to a table by the door, where the traffic noise overlaid the sports. Mick picked up the shot glass and emptied it into the beer. He had LOVE tattooed across the first and second knuckles of his left hand and HATE on the right. A swallow was flying a rising curve on his neck, just above a dotted line with the legend CUT HERE. His denim sleeveless showed arms that bore Celtic bands, a red rose, a dragon's head breathing fire, a bloody dagger, a tiger's eye, SS flashes and a snake that spat from his bicep then wound round the elbow to the wrist. Under the loose-fit combats, on his thighs, from knee to crotch, were black-and-red vines that grew flowers with baby faces. He carried a death's head on his chest, centrepiece of a frieze that included Samurai warriors and bats out of hell. And, like a front-line trooper, he bore the union flag on his back. In all things, Mick was a traditionalist. The tattoos on the inside of his lower lip and on his dick both said SUCK THIS.

The skin art had the odd effect of making him ageless. If your body's your canvas, you keep it primed. Mick's day was sleep–workout–drink. The gym kept him pumped, but the booze had put big bags under his eyes: thirty-five going on fifty.

Stella showed him the dead face of Jimmy Stone: the photo she had shown to Ferdie and Mack and Billy. He said, 'It's been round.'

'What has?'

'That someone topped Jimmy Stone.'

'And the word is?'

'He hired on, you know? Worked here and there, whatever was going. Nothing special recently. It's a puzzle.'

'Enemies?'

'Yeah, well, he was a bit of a prick, Jimmy Stone. Bit of a wanker. People didn't really use him for top jobs. He drove for a firm a couple of times, but they didn't use him again.'

'Why not?'

'Last time was a wages van. Jimmy forgot to change the plates on the car. Also, he went up the back of a fucking Routemaster on the getaway run.' Mick laughed. 'Everyone's yelling and screaming and slapping his head. Went all the way to the switch car with the front banged up and smoking.' He made it sound just as if he'd been there.

'Which firm?'

Mick shook his head. 'Too late. The money's back in circulation.'

'I'm sure. Which firm?'

'I can't.'

Which meant, I'm still connected and there's more in progress. Stella felt as if she were behind the lines.

'So . . . enemies.'

'Nah. Not really. People marked him down as a prat, but nothing to get him topped.'

'I heard he used to go about with some hoolies.'

'Oh, yeah. He was up for that.'

'Who are they?'

'Depends.'

'On what?'

'Well, you have club sides, then you've got England. Club sides ruck each other, know what I mean? But if it's a trip, some foreign club, you'll find all sorts going. Guys from different clubs. In England you're Chelsea or Leeds or Liverpool. In Germany or Greece, you're all English.'

'Which club did Jimmy support?'

'I don't think he gave a toss about football. He fancied a ruck, though. Used to go to the England away games. And he liked to go out on the hunt.'

'Hunting what?' Stella asked; but she already knew the answer.

'Pakis, niggers, illegals, beggars. You're not fussy, are you?'

'Illegals?'

'Come in the back of a truck or a container lorry. Unload in some lay-by up from Dover.'

'How can you recognize them?'

Mick laughed. 'You can tell.' He picked up his empty glass and looked at it. Stella put some money on the table and he left for the bar. American football had given way to boxing, two sluggers cheek to cheek, their arms entwined, until one broke the embrace and hooked his man under the heart. I've known relationships like that, Stella thought. Mick stood directly under the screen, waving Stella's ten-pound note at the barman.

You're not fussy, are you . . .?

You can tell . . .

Not 'you', Stella realized, but 'me'. Mick was talking about himself. When he came back, she said, 'You and Jimmy Stone, then, out on a hunt.'

Mick was taking the top off his beer. He shook his head without taking glass from lip.

'You and Jimmy Stone and a bunch of hoolies.'

'Never.'

'I could have a look back through the incident book,' she said. 'The last half-dozen racist assaults on your patch. See if we can put you at the scene.'

'Yeah? How?'

'Witness statements, forensics. We could send a few young coppers down to your gaff, see what we can turn up.'

He was pretty sure she wouldn't do that. Fairly sure. He drank off the shot of Southern Comfort and it steadied him down.

'Someone called Raymond,' she said. 'Know him?'

'I know a geezer called Raymond, yeah.'

'Big friend of Jimmy Stone.'

'Yeah.'

'Raymond what?'

'What?'

'His last name.'

'Who the fuck knows?'

'He likes to go hunting, does he?'

'Yeah.'

Mick was trading minimal information now and Stella knew that she'd made a mistake. If chissies are invisible friends, they don't exist if you're not thinking about them. Don't ask about their own lives, their own secrets. That's not the deal. The deal is that they sit in the confessional of the pub or the closed car and confess the sins of other people. *Other* people.

Stella set about warming Mick up from cold again. She said, 'Jimmy Stone and Raymond, that's all I need to know.'

'Okay.'

'You know our arrangement, Mick.'

'Sure, yeah.'

'I just need to know about Jimmy. Jimmy's as far as it goes.'

'I don't know his last name – Raymond except they call him Fetcher.'

'But you know where I could find him.'

'There are a few places on Harefield he goes. Bit of dealing. Bit of gambling. Not at weekends, though. Weekends, you go clubbing, don't you?'

'Jimmy must have had other friends.'

'Hoolies. They're all your friends, aren't they? All mates.'

And so they are, once you've gone up against the Krauts in Dortmund or the Turks in Istanbul; once you've stood in a comradely circle, kicking shit skittles out of some nigger-Paki-illegal.

'But Raymond and Jimmy were close.'

'Seemed to be.'

'Describe him to me.'

'My height, black hair, wears an earring.'

'Short hair?'

'About a two cut.'

'Something more.'

Mick thought for a moment. 'Got a long nose, dead straight, doesn't go in here.' He touched the bridge of his own nose.

'Why do they call him Fetcher?'

'He's good at making a score. Got contacts. Send him out for something, he fetches it back to you.'

'What?'

'Whatever you want. Brown, uppers, dope.'

'Give me a call next time you're all going to be in some shebeen on Harefield.'

Mick looked worried. 'I can't be there if you lot come in mob-handed. Everyone'll be carrying. Either I get charged – and I'm not having that – or it's just me who doesn't, which gets me killed.'

'Okay, don't be there. Just phone.'

'The only one not there when the bust goes down?' Mick shook his head. 'Just as bad. Just as dead.'

'Look, one way or another, I've got to have this guy. You can give me an address if you like.'

Mick laughed. 'I don't know where he lives, for Christ's sake.'

'Not on Harefield . . .'

'Nah.'

'So if we're going to take him, it has to be when he's at the shebeen. Think of a way. Call me.'

The door opened and a couple of girls came in off the street, not sports fans but they needed shelter. The cloud ceiling had dropped to rooftop level once more and the streets were wet, vehicles going past in a hiss of spray. Stella folded some banknotes and put them under Mick's shot glass.

'He had a picture of Reggie Kray in his coffin.'

'Who? Jimmy Stone?' Stella pretended not to know.

'Yeah.' Mick pocketed the money. 'Open coffin, like, and Reggie laid out in his Sunday blue. Big respect.'

The apartment Ivo Perić was renting had a washing machine, but Perić was a little shaky on the mechanics of wash programmes and spin cycles. He put in everything he'd been wearing except the leather coat, poured powder on top and set the machine for 'Cottons/90°', then he examined the coat for stains, taking a kitchen sponge to dark patches round the cuffs. They mopped up nicely; leather was good like that.

He had slept until noon. Now he made coffee and poured himself a whisky to go with it. There wasn't much whisky in the bottle because he had come home from the towpath the previous night and got drunk very fast. He drank down the leftovers as a defence against the black bile and skewed vision of a hangover. Depth charges were going off in his skull, but it was nothing. As hangovers go? – nothing.

The booze set him up. He could feel a niggle of hunger and remembered his Golden Fry takeaway bag broken open on the road. Then remembered the chase and the way a long vibration had gone from the point of contact right to his shoulder when the driftwood club stopped short against the first man's head.

Hangover? *There's* a hangover.

Then he remembered how the last van man had looked up at him, head yanked back, as the blade went across his eyes.

Now you see me. Now you don't.

He got some food out of the fridge: eggs, bacon, bread. He thought back through the towpath action and the memory made his muscles twitch, so that he fumbled an egg, juggled and almost lost it. He closed his eyes to see things better, and laughed.

You don't know where I am, do you? You can't hear me coming, can you? Fieldcraft. Just like Bosnia.

He thought further back, and the laughter shrank to a tight smile. Oh, Blondie, Blondie, Blondie. If only you were here with me now, what I'd do to you, how you'd squeal.

He cooked and made a phone call while he was eating. He gave a code name and got one back.

'How are things with you?'

Perić forked in some eggs. 'Fine. Boring. What will happen?'

'We don't know yet. There's a meeting soon.'

'Why meet with these pigs? Why not just –'

'I know . . . It's business. It's money. We don't want a war unless it's necessary.'

'We're good at war.'

'We're good at business. Listen, you're set up, right?'

'Sure.'

'So if it comes to that, if there's no other way, you're in place.'

'I'm in place. I'm in a two-room box with a fucking big gun and a fucking big bomb and nothing to do.'

'Watch TV. Phone for a girl.'

'It's my life: TV and a girl and a pizza to go.'

'Sounds like heaven to me.'

'Fuck your mother.'

The other man laughed. A clear line, he could have been in the next room. He said, 'A decision soon. Until then, keep to yourself.' A pause, then: 'Nothing of the man you killed . . .?'

'What?' Perić was startled. How could the caller know about the van men? Then he realized that the question referred to Jimmy Stone. 'The police? Nothing. I think he's a mystery to them.'

'Good. Be a mystery yourself.'

Perić put down the phone and finished his meal with the remainder of the whisky. If only you knew, he thought. He wondered how many people had seen him on the run, making for the river. Plenty. But most would have already decided to forget they were there. Also it was dark; dark and raining. If ten people came forward, the police would have ten different descriptions.

After he'd finished on the towpath, after the job was done, he'd jogged all the way down to Putney Bridge and climbed the railings into Bishop's Park, then cut through backstreets to his door. His leather coat was slick with rain, blood splashes wouldn't have shown; and like everyone else he walked head down against the wind.

He watched an afternoon movie, then checked the

washing machine. His clothes were free of bloodstains, but had shrunk a full size.

'Tell me about him,' Anne Beaumont said. 'About John Delaney.'

'He's a journalist.'

'You make it sound like "He's a vulture".'

'You can usually find them waddling round a kill. A child abducted and slaughtered, bodies buried in a cellar. There's the press, flap-flap, gobble-gobble.'

'You've seen this.'

'Oh, yes.'

'And he makes you angry for that reason . . .'

'Who said he makes me angry?'

'You did. Though not in so many words.'

'Ah . . . The all-seeing eye of the therapist.'

Stella was in an armchair next to a bookcase. It was deep enough for her to tuck her legs up. Sometimes she'd go to sleep in it, then wake up and give her dream to Anne newly minted. There were surprisingly few shrink-texts on the shelves; the books seemed to be mostly gardening and cookery.

Anne was looking out of the window at the blur of early evening lights through the rain. 'It's never going to stop,' she said. 'The whole world is dissolving.' Her hair shelved across her cheek. She had a longish face and a small mouth that curved erotically when she smiled. The shirt-and-skirt combination she often wore softened her figure but couldn't hide it. Stella wondered what it was like to go with a woman: how it went – the give and take.

'If I'm angry,' Stella said, 'it's not with him.'

Anne turned back from the window and smiled. 'At least that came from you.'

'He wants a story, that's all.'

'He's asked you to go to dinner with him – didn't you say that?'

'He's flirting. He wants the inside track.'

'What does George think?'

Stella was silent on that one.

'How many dead-baby dreams this week?' Anne asked. It was unusually direct.

Stella said, 'He knows something I don't know. And he knows things I do know that he shouldn't know.'

'Which means?'

'First, that he's got a source unknown to me and therefore unknown to my colleagues. Second, that someone from the squad is talking to him.'

'How does that make you feel?'

'Jesus, is Delaney's deep throat a factor in my analysis?'

'Everything that affects you is a factor in your analysis.'

'I don't know what I feel about it,' Stella said. 'Betrayed?'

'By Delaney.'

'No, of course not; by whoever's talking to him.'

'But Delaney's bound up with betrayal,' Anne observed. She was talking about George: talking about something Stella hadn't yet admitted to herself.

'Three,' Stella said. 'Three dead-baby dreams, since you ask. But I also had a dream about gentle creatures on a pebble beach.'

Anne smiled and accepted the diversion. 'What sort of creatures?'

'I don't know. Zoo creatures. Not Barbary apes.'

'Where was the beach?'

'Somewhere . . . I went as a child, I think.'

'What happened in the dream?'

'Not much. I mean, I can't remember much. It was a good dream. I was on the beach, there was the sea, sunlight on the waves, I think, and the animals.'

'Gentle animals.'

'Yes.'

'Soft animals.'

'Yes,' Stella said, then, 'Oh! –' and her hand went to her mouth. She looked at Anne with tears in her eyes. 'Nursery animals . . .'

Anne nodded, her eyebrows raised very slightly.

Stella shook her head. 'No,' she said. 'No, that's out of the question.'

'It was a good dream. Felt good, you said that.'

Stella shook her head mutely, appalled at the way her feelings had circled round to sandbag her. She put a hand over her eyes and tears dripped from between her fingers.

'Never,' she said. 'I'll never be pregnant again, never.'

She said the same to George as he was putting shirts in a suitcase that lay open on the bed. Next to it was his portfolio, next to that his laptop, then his cell phone and charger, then an all-country power-plug adaptor. He wasn't naturally methodical, but the Seattle commissions meant a lot.

He paused, carrying a shirt in both hands like an offering. 'I know that, Stell. You told me that.'

'You think I'll change my mind.'

'I don't think anything. I hope you will.'

'I won't.'

'Okay.'

'That's what I wanted to say. I won't change my mind.'

'Okay.'

'I thought you ought to know.'

'Okay,' he said, then put the shirt down and went to her and held her while she cried.

John Delaney was getting dressed to go out. He was wearing black jeans, a black roll-neck and a light cotton zipper jacket. And a body wire that he'd bought at a shop in South Audley Street, where they sold everything from a briefcase that filmed you to a phone that stole your deepest secrets.

He drove through the Gate and along Ladbroke Grove until he hit the Harrow Road. There were five girls working the crossroads, standing a little way back from each corner of the intersection and waiting for the punters to cruise up. They would lean over, straight-legged, and put their hands up against the car's roof, breasts pushing forward in crop-tops, little skirts riding up at the back, as if they were already braced for business. They moved from place to place during the evening, avoiding the occasional police patrols, but never away from home turf: the pimps patrolled more often than the cops.

Punters liked to stop in the dark spots just along the Harrow Road, a funeral parlour in one direction, a church in the other. Pause, set a price, pick up. There were places to park. The girls dropped their heads and got down to it, or they worked away with their hands like cooks with a whisk. Then back to the crossroads and the four-way possibilities.

It was conveyor-belt business. Fast flesh.

Zuhra Hadžić saw Delaney's Peugeot as he came up to the lights. She crossed the road and walked away in the direction of Kilburn, paddling through the neon flood from kebab-and-curry places that the girls called 'the strip'. When the lights changed, Delaney drove across, passed her, then pulled over and lowered the near-side window. Zuhra looked in.

'Soon I will say, "Here is regular man".'

Her English wasn't great, but few of the men she encountered wanted to make conversation.

Delaney said, 'Get in.'

She was tall and slim, and her black hair was cut in a bob. Delicate olive skin that looked pale under the neon, high Slavic cheekbones, a wide mouth. Only the darkness round her eyes spoiled her good looks; that, and a little scar that puckered the skin at the point of her jaw. She was dressed in whore's street-wear: a red plastic blouson over a spaghetti-strap top; when she sat down, her skirt almost disappeared.

'Same as other times. For fifteen minutes in car is twenty pounds.' She seemed apologetic.

'That's fine,' Delaney said. 'That's not a problem.'

Zuhra stared out of the window, arms folded across her breasts, one shoulder leaning against the glass. Suddenly, she looked mortally tired.

At the next set of lights, Delaney turned right, heading for the dark, quiet side streets off the strip.

15

Sometimes you can see things coming at you. You might get a feeling, like the onset of a chill or that sudden unease when you sense someone moving up behind your back. It's leery and it makes you jittery, but at least you have an idea that things are about to take a turn for the worse; a notion of darkness gathering.

But sometimes you don't see a thing.

The nightlife on the Harefield Estate was rich and varied. There might be a dogfight in one of the lock-ups or some bare-knuckle on waste ground between the blocks. There would be high-ante gambling in a dozen or more apartments, along with some high-risk drinking. Drug deals were the estate's commercial regulator – it's the economy, *stupid!* – but any night of the week you could find people making a career in gun deals or credit card deals or car deals. There were brothels in every block and crack factories, too. And you couldn't talk about insiders and outsiders because if you came home to find your door kicked in and your sound system gone, it was just as likely to have been your next-door neighbour as anyone else.

The kids were most active. The kids were *hyper*. Cocaine was their drug of choice and cars were their recreation. Not their own cars, of course. The cars they drove at night were dead metal by the morning. The law called it 'twoccing': taking without the owner's consent.

Beamer and Stanley had other names, given names, but street-names worked better for them. Beamer liked BMWs. All in all, he'd take any performance car that presented itself, but a BMW brought a special smile to his face. Stanley carried a Stanley knife. There's nothing too oblique about street-names.

That night Beamer passed up a Golf GTi and a Ford Focus before he found the 528i sitting in a side street near Fulham Broadway. Twoccers are mechanics, too; the boys were in and pulling away into the Broadway inside three minutes: Beamer and Stanley in the front and Linda in the back.

Linda was along for the ride. Linda had the coke.

Beamer took it easy along the Fulham Palace Road, and easy along Shepherd's Bush Road, then opened up on the slip road to the Westway. Once they hit the three-lane breeze that led to the M40, he pushed it to eighty, weaving between horn blasts, tailgating fast-lane dawdlers; even so, they were looking over their shoulders for a red-stripe. A chase would be fantastic, sure, but not until they'd had the best of the car.

After a few miles, they came up on to the motorway – the blacktop, the *track*. Beamer took them halfway to Oxford with his foot hard down, getting a hundred and ten, a hundred and twenty, Stanley and Linda whooping and yelling as he scorched the family estates, the dinky jeeps, the low-fuel minis.

They came off at the Chiltern cut and found a lay-by. It was a country darkness and no moon, so they left the vanity lights on while Linda tapped three lines on to her make-up mirror and the boys got into the back. Everyone did a line, then everyone did two more. Linda wiggled out of her underwear and went arse-up for the driver, then arse-up for the driver's friend. When he got back behind the wheel, Beamer was seeing things very clearly. Crystal clear.

There's a disused lorry park alongside a disused machine shop in the hinterland of Harlesden. Twoccers go there to do some drag. You can put on the handbrake, select top, then fifteen guys hang on to your rear bumper while you rev hard, until the back end of the car disappears in a cloud of tyre-smoke. When they let go, you almost hit G-forces.

Back off the M-way, Beamer, Stanley and Linda spent an hour or so taking the 528i way past its limits on the lorry park tarmac. The engine-and-wheel noise was the sound of precision engineering under torture. They could be heard several streets away, but no one was going to lift the phone. They got down over the last of Linda's stash, then decided to dump the car somewhere off their patch. Torch it maybe, that would be cool.

.They hit ninety on the slip road down to Holland Park Avenue, then took the outside lane up to Notting Hill Gate. Beamer was looking for trouble; looking for the cops; looking for a chase to end the night. They came over the crest at the top of the avenue, made a tight S between a cab and a flat-bed truck, and took out two guys who were crossing the road on a red light.

The two men had been at a stag party. One was the best-man-to-be; he never made the wedding because he was in ITC with two broken legs, a broken arm, several broken ribs and a ruptured spleen. His coma lasted eight days. He was lucky because in the split second before impact, he'd sensed something; he'd looked up and seen it coming.

The other man was DC Paul Lester of AMIP-5. He hadn't seen a thing.

It was four-thirty a.m. A little crowd of nightbirds gathered: shift workers on the way home; early-starters beginning their day. A young woman in high heels and a poncho got down on her knees to give Paul Lester mouth-to-mouth, sweeping her hair back with one hand to keep it off his face.

The 528i had fishtailed wildly, then handbrake-turned into Pembridge Road. After that, anybody's guess. The young woman in heels kept going until the ambulance arrived, but it was like kissing stone.

By the time DC Lester had been taken to A&E at St Mary's, pronounced DOA, papered and tagged and transferred to the morgue, it was seven o'clock. They knew who he was from the MasterCard in his billfold, but he had worn his Nicole Fahri to the stag and hadn't wanted to bulk out the pockets, so his warrant card was at home, along with his spare plastic and his organizer. His mobile phone was still showing a signal: a triumph for hardware technology. Lester was the software, here; *too* soft, too prone to damage. A charge nurse in A&E pressed the OK button and watched Paul's home number pop up on the LCD display.

He thought he'd leave that call to the cops.

*

Stella was in early. She had driven George to an early check-in at Heathrow, picked up coffee and a toasted sandwich at a deli in the Gate, and gone straight to work.

First in, she thought, then heard the sound of bees swarming in one of the upstairs rooms. For a moment, she thought the sound might be coming from inside her own head, but when she listened inwardly, the tinnitus was the same constant whine, like a steel thread being drawn over a metal edge. She went out into the small lobby, tracking the noise, and knew by the fluctuation in tone that it was an electric razor. She checked the rooms and found a long night's detritus in Sorley's office: polystyrene burger box, crumpled Budvar cans, a two-pack ashtray. The DI had pulled a chair in from the outer office and set it in front of his desk chair to make a leg-rest. Stella realized that he must have slept sitting up.

She went to her desk and started the paperwork, head lowered, but she tracked his footsteps as he came downstairs and heard him pause when he saw her. As he passed, he said, 'You're early,' then crossed to his office and slammed the door. A few minutes later he reappeared, took a couple of steps into the room, then stopped short. Stella looked at him and shrugged: *It's nothing to me*, but Sorley was carrying the night-crap, the cans, the McDonald's box, the saucer full of butts, as if it were evidence that they ought not to ignore.

He said, 'I'm trying to work out what to do.'

That was when the call came in about Paul Lester.

The uniforms hadn't used the home number on Lester's mobile. They did some basic checking which led straight to AMIP-5. Sorley called the station officer at Notting

Hill, which was only a minute or so faster than crossing the road to talk to him. The SO told Sorley everything they had to hand on the incident and said, 'No, it's fine. Your officer – you do it.'

Stella took Andy Greegan because Andy and Paul had worked as a team – scene-of-crime officer, exhibits officer. They had sat at back-to-back desks and tossed packets of Marlboro Light to and fro.

As they got out of the car, Andy asked, 'Name. What's her name?'

'Cheryl,' Stella told him.

'Cheryl.' He said it under his breath as if he might be tested on it later. 'Cheryl, Cheryl, Cheryl.'

It was a new house on a small private development in North Kensington, just on the border of the badlands. Each 'unit' had its little driveway, its ten-foot strip of grass, its up-and-over garage. They were ringing the doorbell when she pulled up into the drive alongside them: back from the school run and the trip to the supermarket, irritated with Paul, perhaps, for having seen the stag out to the bitter end. He would have gone straight to work, his stomach churning, his headache like rocks in a box. He would phone any time now.

She stared at them. Even when Stella started towards her, Cheryl didn't get out of the car or wind down the window, but her eyes clouded and her mouth twisted as if she had just bitten on something sour.

Stella reached the driver's door and stood there, waiting. Cheryl lowered her head on to the steering wheel, eyes tight closed, and wouldn't come out.

*

People got on with what they had to do. Stella tried John Delaney on his home number and got his message. Then she tried him on his mobile and got him.

'The mystery man,' Stella said, 'you know who he is. So you said.'

'I thought you hadn't heard me.'

'What made you think that?'

'Your eyes rolled up and you fell into my arms. It's happened before.'

'I want to talk to you, Delaney.'

'I'm finishing a piece. Cult suicide, crooked clergy –'

'Or I could send a car and two large, ill-tempered cops.'

He suggested they meet at the Sun in Splendour, which told Stella that Delaney was probably local.

The wind had shifted. The weather people had promised a day's respite and so it was: blue sky, hot sun, just a few puddles left in potholes. Summer had a few days to run and Portobello was full of tourists with money to spend. The antique shops had spilled their stock out on to the pavement along with the browsers, the rubber-neckers, the hucksters, the well-heeled tourists and the pickpockets. There were tables set out for the cappuccino-and-baguette crowd. Further down Kensington Park Road the pavement tables had pink tablecloths and anemones in a vase for the Ladies Who Lunch.

Stella said, 'I heard you, all right, and I want to know how. How you know. But first I want to hear whether you really *do* know.'

'A man called Jimmy Stone. Bit of a crook. Clearly nothing to do with the God-fearing Deevers.'

'Okay. And you knew some while before you told me, didn't you?'

'Did I?'

'You were carrying a folder with lists of murderabilia items. You got them off the internet.'

'Ah . . .'

'Which means that someone in my squad is talking to you.'

'Does it?'

'How else?'

'How else? A dozen ways. I could've hacked into your computer. Simpler than that, I could have been sitting with a paper and a beer while a couple of off-duty coppers talked the case through.'

'I don't think so.'

'Think what you like.'

Stella felt a little rush of anger. She said, 'I'm the police, you bastard.'

'And I'm the press.'

They were sitting in a booth, drinking but not eating. Stella had said no when he'd offered her the bar menu; having lunch together would have seemed too cooperative, too intimate. This was business.

As if to give the lie to that thought, he asked: 'Have you heard about your test?'

'A couple of days.'

'Lots of luck.'

'Why did you call me?'

'I'm writing a piece –'

'You told me.'

'No, not the religious crazies. That's almost done. This is about another sort of victim. The girls that are smuggled in from Eastern Europe. They come expecting to get a job as a waitress or a cleaner and wind up in the meat market. They come from countries where "police" means "illegal arrest, torture and death", so they tend not to turn up at the local nick asking for help. They're sold like cattle, kept prisoner, forced to give the kind of service that other whores refuse and beaten if they step out of line.'

Stella knew as much about the skin trade as any copper not actually serving in Vice. She said, 'What's your angle, Delaney? Serial compassion?'

'It's the kind of piece I write,' he told her. 'Wrongful arrest and false imprisonment are also on the list, along with unreliable evidence and confessions extracted under duress.'

'Nothing personal, then.'

He smiled. 'I'm having another drink. Let me get you one.'

'I just need to know what you know and how you know it. After that, I'll decide whether or not to arrest you.'

'I need a deal.'

'No deals.'

Delaney went to the bar and fetched another round. When he returned, he said: 'It's not for me.'

Stella sighed. 'Look, Delaney, you're not in a position to –'

'I've got some information about Jimmy Stone. I'm not sure whether it will help, but I know it's something you don't know –'

'– because someone's updating you on the investigation –'

'– I'm not admitting that. Look, I'm a journalist, we go to prison to protect our sources, didn't you know that?'

'Could be your next stop.'

'The information came from someone you'll want to talk to. I need to protect that person. It's not complicated.'

'I can't give that sort of a guarantee.'

'Jesus Christ,' Delaney gave a little laugh. 'Of course you can. You have informants, you have a witness protection programme, you give amnesty to villains who tell you where the body's buried, it happens all the time. I'm not asking for much, I just want this person helped.'

'You'll have to tell me more. I can't say yes to just anything.'

'She's illegal.'

'One of the girls you mentioned a moment ago?'

'Yes.'

'Where is she from?'

'Bosnia.'

Stella picked up her untouched drink and took a sip. 'And what you want . . . really want . . . is a story.'

'I'm writing the story anyway.'

'With unauthorized police help.'

Delaney shrugged. 'I'm writing it. I haven't published it. No one's been compromised.'

'You know what she knows. So you're withholding information. That's very, very thin ice.'

'You *think* I know. You can't *prove* I know.'

'What's her name?'

'Not yet,' he said.

'Fuck it, Delaney. I wish you wouldn't keep behaving as if you had any leeway here. If I ask for her name and you refuse to tell me, that's a criminal offence; don't you get it?'

He held out his hands, palms down and close together, as if waiting for her to snap on the handcuffs.

Stella sighed an angry sigh. 'She has information about Jimmy Stone, yes?'

'He worked on and off for the guys who run her.'

'And who are they?'

'I need that deal.'

'Does she know who killed Jimmy?' She paused. A thought struck her. 'Do *you* know?'

'If I did, I'd tell you.'

'Yeah? In return for what?'

Delaney was suddenly angry. 'It's not for me. This isn't for me. I could have kept quiet and written my story and the hell with her having unprotected sex thirty times a day and the hell with you still relying on house-to-house to give you some sort of a lead on Jimmy Stone.'

'I'll have to talk to my DI.'

'If that's how you want to do it.' Delaney got up. He said, 'Call me any time.'

Such clarity, such perfect timing, such skill behind the wheel. In the small hours of that same morning, Beamer gunning the car along Westbourne Grove, then up towards the park and pulling over soft and easy in Moscow Road.

Linda saying, 'You hit them. You hit those guys,' sounding excited, unable to stop laughing. 'Christ, they went up in the fucking air.'

Stanley finding a newspaper in a garbage can, then rolling it up and shoving it into the petrol tank to soak before throwing it on to the back seat and flipping his Zippo.

Some early bird reported the fire. By the time the owner had been traced and taken to the scene in a red stripe, the fire brigade had doused the interior. It was still smoking; water was running over the sills.

The guy who owned the 528i was a City trader who had bought it just three days before, demo model, top of the range, only eight thousand on the clock. He was bug-eyed with misery. 'My car,' he said. 'Oh, Jesus fucking Christ, look at it.'

The driver of the red stripe told him that the vehicle was being impounded by the police for forensic testing since it had been involved in a hit-and-run incident in which one man had died and another had been seriously injured.

'It's a tragedy,' the City man said, watching as his car was winched up on to the back of a low-loader. 'Look at it. Will you fucking *look* at it!'

Delaney drove past the scorch patch on the Moscow Road and through the park to Kensington Gore.

He thought, It's a gamble with this Stella Mooney. He thought she'd strike a deal, but he wasn't sure. He thought she might be unhappy in some complicated way.

Every time he saw her, she shook him up. He knew the feeling and knew he ought to avoid it, but that wasn't easy.

It had started to follow him around.

16

Mick Armitage aka Jesse, aka the tattooed man, took a five-minute cab ride to Notting Hill, then walked up Campden Hill to the Windsor Castle. It was a small pub with an open fire and wooden floors; it liked to pretend it was in the country. By the time he'd drunk enough to make him unsteady, the place was full and the bar staff were moving fast, trying to keep track of the banknotes being waved at them. Mick was waving his money along with the rest. Directly behind him, a man in a Benetton polo shirt was fanning Mick's ear with a twenty.

Mick raised a rumpus about not being served. He swore at the barmaid and got a hard stare from one of the guys working alongside her. He paid for his drink and laughed in the guy's face as he turned away, putting his shoulder hard into the chest of Benetton Man, who told him to be careful, for fuck's sake. Without giving a warning blink, Mick brought his pint glass round in a hard arc and took Benetton Man just under the ear: a short fight and a bloody one.

It was a five-minute cab ride for Mick, but only a two-minute journey for the patrol car. They had cuffed Mick and put him in the back when a four-man back-up team arrived, annoyed because the action was over.

One of the cops gestured towards Mick. 'No problem: it was just him. Glassed some poor bastard. There's an ambulance on the way.'

The back-up man peered in through the patrol-car window, where Mick sat with a serene, out-of-focus look about him. On the way to the nick, he asked for DS Stella Mooney. He kept asking for her while they booked him, charged him, took care of his personal possessions and walked him down to the cells. He wouldn't give them his name and address.

'DS Stella Mooney,' he said as the cell door closed in his face.

Things to do while your lover is away . . .

You can drink the bottle instead of splitting it. You can watch anything on TV: absolutely anything at all. You can phone for a tandoori. You can call a few friends and discover that they're busy being half a couple. You can take an unread book to bed and set it aside unopened while you help yourself to an orgasm then drift off to sleep with the lights burning.

You can dream your dead-babies dream and wake in stark horror with no one to tell. But that's the way of things even when he's lying there next to you.

Stella got up and made tea. There was a solid pain in her chest and she could feel a headache building from the wine. She wanted to cry for her own dead baby, the one she had bled on the way south from Wester Ross, the one she had secretly named, but the grief was as hard and locked as a logjam. That's what was paining her; that's what was backed up beside her heart.

At that time in the morning it was *World Cup Snowboarding*, *News 24*, *AMA Supercross* or re-runs of *Wish You Were Here*. Stella stared at the screen without registering the images. After half an hour, she fell asleep where she sat.

The phone woke her. Six-thirty a.m. in London is ten-thirty p.m. in Seattle and she guessed that George had made a mess of the time difference, but when she lifted the phone she got a story that concerned a prisoner in charge and his last-thing-at-night, first-thing-in-the-morning demands to see DS Stella Mooney. The night shift had told him to shut up; he was taking a risk with their patience and better nature. But they had passed the request on to the day shift, who heard it again from Mick.

It took them a while to ID Stella. When they realized she was part of AMIP-5 and currently investigating the murder of Jimmy Stone, they decided it might be important to let her know that the prisoner had been asking for her since his arrest the previous evening.

He was eating breakfast, so she talked with him in his cell. She had to paper him for that: a form to say she was taking responsibility; another when she left. For a man with his record looking at a charge of GBH, Mick seemed remarkably chipper, forking up his egg and bacon and sausage and a slice.

He said, 'I'll be on remand, right?'

'If you refuse to give your address,' Stella said, 'they've got nowhere to bail you to. See what your brief has to say.'

'I'm not calling a brief just yet.'

'Or giving your address.'

'No.' He filled his mouth with egg and lifted his tea mug to his lip while he chewed.

'Then a very irritated magistrate is likely to remand you to Brixton. Is that what you want?'

Mick spoke round his mouthful. 'That's right.'

Stella waited to be told why, but Mick just grinned. She said, 'They tell me you glassed some guy in a pub on Campden Hill.'

'I did.'

'And what – you're going to make it self-defence?'

Mick laughed. 'Yeah. That'd do.'

'Why did you ask to see me, Mick?'

'It's for you, isn't it?'

'What?'

'He didn't do nothing, the geezer in the pub. I was looking for an excuse.'

Stella could feel something taking shape; something that felt horribly like a plan. Mick was giving her a knowing sideways glance.

'Thursday,' he said. 'They'll be there.' He gave Stella an address on Harefield. 'They'll be there and I'll be banged up.' As if she might have missed the point, he said, 'Fetcher, right? Otherwise known as Raymond.'

Stella stared at him. 'If I'm going to nick Raymond, you need to cover your arse.' Mick nodded, smiling. 'And the best possible place for you to be when the bust goes down, and not make them suspicious, is in a cell.'

Mick nodded again; his smile broadened. 'Clever, right?'

'You didn't think he might be upset at all?'

'Who?'

'The guy you glassed. The guy needing fifteen stitches and a pint of blood.'

Mick shrugged. 'I don't suppose he was best pleased.

Just . . . you know . . . he was in the right place at the right time.'

'I wonder if that's the way he sees it.'

'Yeah . . .' Mick laughed. 'So a week on remand, then out.'

Stella wasn't sure whether Mick was giving her the game plan or issuing an instruction.

'You'd better tell me exactly what you expect me to do.'

Mick took the remark at face value. 'Have a word. You need a result. I need to protect myself. Assisting the police, right? Just make it a ruck in a boozer. He hit me, I hit him . . . Forgot I was holding the glass. Few hours' community service – I can get ringer in for that.'

'Community service? They're likely to want you for GBH. And you've got serious form.'

For the first time a little spasm of doubt registered in Mick's expression: a twitch of the eye, a tiny downturn of the mouth.

'This is the deal,' he said. 'This is how I get you what you want.' The Judas window on the door slapped back and forth: someone making sure that everything was as it should be. Mick banged the heel of his hand on the concrete-slab bed. 'This is *police* work, right?'

Stella shook her head: not denial so much as disbelief. 'Jesus Christ, Armitage, you amaze me. You open someone's face with a pint pot and you want the police to say you were doing us a favour. Have I got that right?'

'Yes – doing *you* a favour.' And he repeated the Harefield address, just in case she was too stupid to make the connection.

Stella got up and rang Mick's panic bell. After a moment she rang again.

'So?' Mick asked.

Stella kept her back turned to him.

'So?'

She said, 'I'll do what I can.'

Your pseudonymous chum, your little helper, your invisible friend.

Stella signed Mick off and gave the form to the custody sergeant. She said, 'I know who he is, but I don't know where he lives. Sorry.'

The sergeant shrugged. 'Bloody great stash, probably. The grapevine will let his mates know where he is, they'll go in and clean house, then he'll give us an address and get bail. Bastard paperwork.'

When she got back to AMIP-5 there was a new face at Paul Lester's desk.

'Leon Pritchett,' he said, and shook hands. Pritchett was thin and bald at thirty; he had smooth skin and a wrinkle-free brow. Put him in a tousled wig and you'd take ten years off. Stella noticed that the hand he shook with had fingers that carried a nicotine blemish. If he eats Snickers and salt-and-vinegar crisps, she thought, he should fit in just fine.

She knocked on Sorley's door. He was on the phone, but he beckoned her in; the call wasn't business; something about a second-hand car. She told him about Mick Armitage, referring to him as Jesse. Sorley looked at her, stranded between tears and laughter.

'He saw it as a piece of police work?'

'Tactical, more or less.'

'What do you want?'

'It's a fairly long-standing relationship.'

'Useful?'

'Yeah, sometimes. Possibly this time.'

'He thinks he's going to walk, does he?'

'After a week on remand: thereby taking him out of the frame when we pop over to Harefield.'

'Which you intend to do.'

'Jimmy Stone didn't die in a hoolie brawl or because he ripped off someone's stash. He was done by a professional. Which means he was involved in something, knew about something, stumbled on something . . . I don't know . . . unusual. Unusual for Jimmy. We've continued to trawl the murderabilia site without really getting anywhere. The only serious lead is this Raymond. Jimmy didn't have that many friends. Who is Raymond? Who are his connections? How to find out? Only one way. Ask him.'

Sorley nodded. 'All right. I'll talk to SO19. It's bloody short notice; they'll need a couple of days to suss the place. Let me have the paperwork.'

'What about my chis?'

'He can't walk, Stella. See sense.'

'But we can do something . . .'

'I expect so.' Sorley gestured towards the outer office. 'There's a new guy in. Pritchard'

'Pritchett. We met. He seems okay.'

'Comes recommended. Sue Chapman's brought him up to speed.'

'Good.'

'There'll be a whip-round for a wreath or whatever. And a presence at the funeral.'

'You?'

'Sure. You too. As many as can get away.'

Sorley was spinning out the conversation, looking for a way to get something said. He gestured at the phone. 'Guy with a car to sell. Ford Fiesta. Sounds okay.'

Because he was finding it difficult, Stella took the lead. 'Not a family motor.'

'No.' He gave a sour little smile. 'No, that's right.' He picked up a pencil from the desk and started to turn it top-to-tail one-handed. 'I'll find a room or something. I'm not sure what you do. But just now I'm using the office.'

Stella had worked with Sorley on half a dozen occasions. Each case has its personal connections. For as long as it lasts, the team is a closed community, people confide in each other, grow temporarily fond of each other. There's a shared intimacy of jokes and problems and junk food. Then you move on and three months later you're having trouble remembering the names. Stella knew about Sorley, knew about the wife and the three kids, the house in Perivale, the family holidays, the mother whose bills he paid; she knew about him, but she didn't know him.

'There's no way things could work out?' she asked.

'It doesn't look that way.' His face said, Ask me why.

'Lousy luck,' Stella said.

After a pause, Sorley said: 'Between us, okay?'

'Sure, of course; between us.'

The moment for 'why' had passed. To paper over the cracks, Sorley asked, 'What does he want – Jesse?'

'Community service.'

Sorley laughed. 'And some poor bastard fronts for him, am I right? Someone else Snowcems the old folks' home.'

'That's the way he sees it.'

'It's another planet, isn't it?' Sorley observed. 'If only they knew.' He meant the punters, the public, the rate-payers. The people who thought in straight lines.

She left the office without asking him about the Bosnian girl looking for a new life. One deal at a time.

She went to her desk and dialled Delaney's mobile. He came on immediately.

'What does your friend want?'

'Papers,' Delaney said. 'Simple as that. Papers mean freedom.'

'Okay,' she said. 'I'll do everything I can –'

'No,' he cut her off, 'no, I don't think so. No IOUs. This has to be watertight.'

'Who do you think I am, Delaney? The Home Secretary?'

'No, but I think you can talk to someone who can talk to someone who can talk to him. Get back to me when that's happened.'

'Here's how it works – and you know this, you *know* this – I can make some headway when I've got a reason. A solid reason. When I can say that she helped us, has *already* helped us, and we've had a good result out of that. She needs to put something in the bank.'

'You didn't say this before.'

'You were doing most of the talking,' Stella said.

'This is from your boss, is it? Your DI?'

'That's right.'

The lie came smoothly. You can be foxy, Delaney; well, so can I. Foxy lady.

'I'll talk to her.'

'Good. Tell her this: I'm not Immigration. I'm not interested in her status or the status of any of her friends. Our meeting will be off the record, okay? She doesn't have anything to fear from me. I just want to hear what she's got to say. When it comes to papers, I can't guarantee that because it's not in my remit, but I can put in a word. I can use influence. If it turns out that she's been of material help in solving a serious crime, then it's bound to assist her case.'

In my remit, she thought. *Assist her case*. Weasel words. Officialese. She wondered whether Delaney would tune into it and find the lie.

'She's scared,' Delaney said.

'She doesn't have to be.'

'She's turning thirty tricks a day. She tried to run away and she's got the scars to prove it. Between a rock and a hard place: that's how she sees things. The pimps are the rock. The hard place, that's you. The police.'

'Tell her it's not like that here.'

'Tell her yourself.'

They made a date for the following night: if the girl agreed, if she'd come. Delaney nominated a rendezvous and gave Stella the registration number of his car. She hung up and started to make a few notes for Alun Ward: general stuff about murderabilia contacts who had proved useless, about the house-to-house that yielded next to nothing, about the unconnected death of Paul Lester. She mentioned Mick Armitage as an ongoing source, but only in passing, calling him Jesse, a minimal presence in the report and with not much to say for himself.

Although she and a dozen armed officers would be visiting the Harefield shebeen in three days' time, she held that piece of information back in the interests of departmental security. Hot news gets everywhere.

A call came through from her doctor. He said, 'You're clear.'

'Sorry?' She'd heard but she wanted to hear again.

'You're clear. The ape wasn't rabid.'

'Good. Great, that's great.'

'They took their time. Really, you should have been having precautionary treatment, just in case. Bit late in the day if the news had been bad.'

'How come no one suggested it?'

'Good question. Anyway, you're okay. You're fine. How do you feel?'

'Wonderful,' Stella said. 'What do you think?'

17

The river was pocked with rain, dragging its garbage on a midday ebb tide. Wherever the flow thinned and the river bed shelved up, the water left its detritus. Alongside Queen's Wharf, on the Putney–Hammersmith stretch, there was driftwood, dock-floats, plastic bottles, a beer crate, hanks of rope, the legs and lower torso of a woman.

The first people to see it paid it no mind; they thought it must be the separated section of a shopfront mannequin. Then someone stopped on the paved towpath to look more closely and saw that gulls were hacking at the thigh-flesh. The remains had been washed into the wire cage of a supermarket chariot and it didn't take long for the scene of crime team to name her Trolley Dolly.

She had been sawn in half at the waist and there was no sign of the rest of her.

'A long way downstream,' Sam Burgess suggested. 'Or buried in a wood, or shoved down a drain, or minced.'

Sam's little kingdom of slabs and sinks, of jars and trays and sluices, was lit by halogen and today the music was *Rosenkavalier*. Beside Sam stood a man in his early forties with a sweep of dark, greying hair and a deep beard-shadow. He was a stone overweight but tall, so he carried it lightly, and his fingers under the pale, talc-dusted latex gloves were long and nimble.

Walter Reinhardt was a pathologist from one of

London's best teaching hospitals and he was on call for cases like this. He could build a theory from a hint, a person from a set of clues. They pored over the human fragment together, Sam playing the role of assistant and note-taker.

What they got was little enough. She was in her twenties. She was a natural blonde. Anal and vaginal swabs revealed nascent blow-fly maggot activity, though the little necrophagists were more plentiful in the anal swabs.

'Which means she beached arse-up,' Reinhardt observed in a satisfied tone, 'as the SOC photos show.'

The pupal development of the earliest maggots suggested she had been in the water somewhere between twelve and twenty hours. The superficial damage was the result of collision with floating objects and predation by fish and gulls. There was no sign of wounding or attack.

'Apart from the fact,' Reinhardt mentioned, 'that someone used a meat saw to separate her top from her bottom.'

Despite the immersion, there was evidence of recent sexual activity. Her toenails were painted a deep, dark red, and the cosmetic company could have used the slab-shots to push their trademark, Sta-fast Colourways, were it not for the livid grey-green puckered skin of the model. The part of her body available to Sam and Reinhardt had no distinguishing features: no tattoos or birthmarks. Her navel wasn't pierced and nor (a more exotic thought) were her labia.

'Someone's been careful,' Reinhardt told Sam. 'It's like trying to guess the jigsaw picture when all you've got is a piece of sky.'

'We've got the wrong half,' Sam observed. 'We need the hands.'

'They'll have harvested the fingers,' Reinhardt told him. 'The fingers come off with pruning shears. They know enough to destroy the fingers. If anything's been minced, they'll have minced the fingers.'

Reinhardt dictated a few more notes, but drew few conclusions, except to suggest that the investigating officers might want to consider that the dead woman had worked as a prostitute.

'Where do you get that from?' Sam wondered.

Reinhardt pointed at the little pout of the pubis. For the first time, Sam registered how surreal, how obscene, the part-corpse looked: slightly parted legs, a bit of a belly, and the focal point of the genitalia; as if that *were* the point, as if she were the brutal personification of a sexist joke: the Business End, Solo Snatch, the Perfect Wife. Reinhardt was indicating the pubic hair, which was shaved to a close-cropped, narrow strip.

'Does that mean –?' Sam paused. 'No . . . Women do that, don't they? Women who aren't prostitutes?'

'You move in exotic circles,' Reinhardt said, and smiled to see Sam blush.

An AMIP team was assigned to the case. They would post flyers asking for help; given the nature of the find there would be an immediate appeal on *Crimewatch*; missing persons would be contacted; there would be checks on the city's abattoirs and they might interview butchers with erring wives and bad tempers – but no one really expected to find out who or why, not with only half a corpse to rely on.

Without fingerprints, without a face, Trolley Dolly was cold cuts.

Delaney had given Zuhra a mobile phone; she had zipped it into the inside pocket of her red plastic blouson. It was like a false friend, waiting to betray her. She kept it switched off unless she was making a call, as she was now, standing in the doorway of a Box Clever store, knocking her thigh with her fist in high frustration and waiting for Delaney to pick up.

Stella had been right in guessing that Delaney was local. He lived in a small apartment in Pembridge Square, with everything in its place, just the way Delaney liked it. Desk on one side of the main room, a small dining table under the window that looked out to the square, a TV and sound system on corner shelves, the fourth wall taken up by a long, low sofa. A galley kitchen was separated from the rest by a worktop and bar stools. The second bedroom was his office.

In the days when Delaney used to fly out to report on some war or another for some paper or another, he would leave the apartment looking like a show-home. It wasn't a passion for tidiness so much as superstition: a welcome home waiting for the survivor. If everything was in its place – books dead-on, pictures dead level – all would be well. Now he didn't run those war-zone risks. Now he could leave home without things being pin-perfect.

He picked up Zuhra's call as he was driving the back route through the Saints. She sounded anxious, her accent thick.

'Don't come,' she told him.

'I'm on my way. The detective is on her way.'

'Is too difficult.'

'She thinks she can help you.'

'No. Too much problem.' The fear in her voice was loud and clear.

'What's happened?' he asked. 'Has something happened?'

Zuhra had her back half-turned to the street. One way, an eye out for her pimp; the other way, an eye on the rental store's ten slimline flat-screen, top-of-the-range TVs, all showing news footage of Queen's Wharf – the police presence, a scrap of interview with the man who dialled triple nine, the forensic team in their white coveralls, white hoods, white gloves, stalking the foreshore like ghost dancers.

She had heard the news earlier. She had read the front page of the *Standard*. She knew about Trolley Dolly.

'Another night,' she told Delaney.

A night when this girl's death wasn't there as an example to them all, when the pimps weren't giving them a sideways look and a sharky smile that meant: Get cute? Get *that*. A night when it wasn't so strong an imagining: the body braced on a table and someone leaning over with a snaggle-toothed saw, the flesh parting, the *grate-grate-grate* as he went between the vertebrae.

Delaney knew that Stella Mooney was going to be there against her better judgement and, he suspected, without having put things on record – without an okay, without the *paperwork*.

'It has to be now,' Delaney told Zuhra, and switched off his phone.

Stella drove up to the crossroads and pulled into the nearside lane where traffic was moving more slowly: she wanted to watch the girls at work. She came to the front of the queue with perfect timing as the lights changed to red. It was raining. They were selling sex in the rain.

There seemed to be some sort of radar, some sexual sonar, that operated between the whores and the cars. A driver would slow, almost imperceptibly, and a girl would start to walk towards the point on the pavement where, given the rate of deceleration, the car would eventually stop. Then it was lean in, hoist your arse, drop your shoulder, state your price.

She watched them in their flimsy reds and golds, their satin and leather; tits shoved up and out by underwired bras, the lacy ribbing of stay-up stockings in full view beneath Lycra minis.

What does it take? she thought. What in God's name does it take?

The backstreets had closed down: the blank breathlessness of empty theatres. Except here and there, in cars parked furthest from the street lights, little sideshows were in progress; little psychodramas. Each had a common plot, the meeting of strangers.

Stella parked and walked past the crooked silhouettes: one person bowing to another; someone using a mortar and pestle. Delaney's car stood on the corner as if ready for a fast getaway. She got in beside him and said, 'She didn't show?'

Delaney half-turned in his seat: a gesture. Stella turned also and saw Zuhra Hadžić low in the rear seat, almost horizontal, her eyes fixed on her. When Stella said hello,

Zuhra merely dropped her gaze. Delaney took them back down the Harrow Road and half a mile off-territory.

Zuhra said, 'I can be fifteen minutes. Is five minutes gone.'

Stella showed her the 'Jimmy Stone is dead' picture and Zuhra nodded.

'You know him?'

'Jimmy.'

'How do you know him?'

'He fuck me.' It was a pretty straightforward answer.

'He was a client?'

'No. He work for Tanners. I was freebie.' Zuhra was glancing up and down the street, hoping not to see familiar faces.

The Tanners, Stella thought, turning up again like something on the sole of her shoe. Paul Lester hadn't found a connection, but here it was.

'Stevie Tanner,' she suggested.

Zuhra gave her a look that was surprise and fear mingled. 'Yes, Stevie.'

'Stevie runs you?'

'Yes, Stevie.'

'What did Jimmy do for him?'

'Make errands, watch girls sometimes.'

'Watch the girls . . .'

'We are on street. Someone watches to see if we get trouble, some punter with bad attitude maybe. Also to see we keep working.' Reminding herself of her schedule, she glanced at her watch. Stella wondered whether it might be whore's standard issue, an all-plastic, gas-station timepiece, dividing the night into fifteen-minute segments; pick up, jack off, get back.

Stella put the picture of Jimmy Stone back in her bag. 'This man was murdered.'

Zuhra nodded as if in agreement. 'Good.'

'You didn't like him . . .'

Zuhra looked at her full-on and Stella saw her clear for the first time, the smooth olive skin, the perfect cheekbones, the deep, dark eyes. The rip along her jawline that made the flesh ruche up in an ugly little snarl.

'He was dogshit,' Zuhra informed her. 'He was always there for freebie. Always. Sometimes me, sometimes other girl.'

'So he was your minder.'

'If I am in street. Not if I am in house.'

'Sorry?'

'Some are street girls, some are girls in house. Brothel. Sometimes we are one place, sometimes other.'

'Where is it? The brothel?'

'For me? Paddington. There are others.' Zuhra beat a little drum rhythm on the seat back. She said, 'I need papers, missis. With papers I can go.'

'Stella. My name's Stella. Where will you go – home?' She noticed how Zuhra's mouth turned down, a bitter arc, when she said the word 'home'.

'What else do you know about Jimmy Stone?' The real question, the let's-do-business question.

'Nothing. Too much.'

The response fooled Stella into thinking Zuhra was being coy. 'You want something from me. It's a two-way street.'

Zuhra's laugh was low and humourless. 'Nothing of his secrets. Too much about what he likes to do with girls.'

Delaney felt the small hairs stir on his forearms and wondered what that was about.

'Ever see anyone else with him?'

'Stevie Tanner. Also one time he bring friend of his.'

'Who did? Jimmy?'

'Jimmy. Yes.'

'Raymond? Was the friend a man called Raymond?'

'No. This man is called Fetcher.'

Hello Raymond. Hello Fetcher. I'm looking forward to meeting you.

'What did Fetcher do?'

'Fuck some girl. That's why Jimmy bring him: for freebie – you are my friend, look what I got, you want some?'

Merchandise. They were just merchandise. Just product.

Zuhra thought of the girl in the river. Half of her in the river. She was from the Ukraine, but Zuhra couldn't remember her name. Tanya? Olga? Separated from herself.

'I must go,' Zuhra said. 'Now. Don't wait.' She was talking to Delaney.

'Can we talk again?' Stella asked.

'Papers,' Zuhra said.

'I'll be working on it.'

'Work hard.'

Delaney let Stella off first: it had to look as though Zuhra was being dropped back on site by her punter, cash in hand and ready for the next. Zuhra was edgy about the time, so Stella got out on the main road close to the side-street junction where she'd parked her car. Delaney made a fast U-turn.

What do you wear to hobnob with a whore? Stella had decided on jeans, DKNY T-shirt, a three-quarter-length black satin coat. Maybe it was the coat that provoked the man in the late-registration Volvo to cruise past and pull over. Stella noticed and laughed under her breath. Her warrant card was in the hip pocket of her jeans and she undid the buttons on her coat to give easy access. A glance at her ID was going to take the edge off his appetite.

The window came down as she drew level. Her intention was to lean in, let him commit himself, then give him the bad news. She'd ask for evidence of identity: his driving licence or credit card, then copy it into her notebook. She wouldn't use it, but this was one customer who was going to have a whole row of sleepless nights.

It was her intention, but it wasn't what she did.

She stopped and turned towards the car, bracing her hands against the roof. She cocked her hip as if that's what she always did. When she stooped, her breasts felt heavy against the T-shirt.

'Are you doing business?'

There was a child-seat in the back, along with the domestic jumble that people take into their cars. This was Family Man.

She gave him a list, as if it were the list she always gave.

'Full sex, no rubber.'

She gave him a price, as if it were the price she always gave.

He made a counter offer.

Stella said, 'Okay.'

She was trembling, but she knew it wasn't fear, because she had the warrant card in her pocket; and it wasn't some sort of perverse excitement, because she would sooner have eaten razor blades than got anywhere near this sicko husband-and-father. She was seeing things from Zuhra's point of view – the strange car, the nameless man, her own body up for sale. And because she did have her warrant card, because she felt safe with Family Man, because this was a sad creep who didn't know what he'd got himself into, she could push it as far as she wanted. She could play the whore without whoring. Maybe get into the car. Maybe take his money. Maybe even let him see what he was going to be missing: just a glimpse, just a whiff. It was power.

'Get in.'

Stella looked at him and smiled. 'You don't do it for me. Sorry.' She pushed back from the window and continued up the road. She wanted to laugh out loud. What'll you do now, Family Man? Go home and give your wife the benefit?

Car tyres in the rain made a series of harsh whispers, much like the sound behind her: the rustle of his clothes, the rush of movement as he came up to her. She only had time to half turn and step back a pace before his punch caught her solidly on the shoulder. He'd aimed his fist at her head, but the body-blow was enough. She went back on her heels, stumbled and fell.

As she was falling – when she should have been yelling, 'Police officer, *police officer!*' – she was thinking, Shit, no, if I go down I'm in trouble. If I go down, I'm dead.

He got in a good kick that took her high on the arm, then he was gone. Stella got on to her hands and knees, then looked up and saw Delaney moving Family Man back towards his car with a series of hard shoves, the arm going in and out like a piston, the heel of the hand striking Family Man's chest just below the throat. She could hear Delaney talking, but not what he said, his voice low and threatening, offering advice you wouldn't want to ignore. He stood at the kerbside until the Volvo pulled away, then walked back to where Stella was standing, clutching her bicep and muttering under her breath.

'What?' Delaney asked.

'His licence plate number,' Stella said, and repeated it once more, slowly, so that it was committed to memory. 'Uniform can have it. Kerb-crawling. We'll see how the little woman at home likes that.'

Delaney looked at her. 'So he just jumped out of the car and whacked you . . .'

'Not exactly, no.'

'He pulled over. He thought you were a tom. Nice looker in black satin. A sudden surge in the groin; sudden rush of blood to the brain.' He was putting the story together in the way that amused him most.

She rubbed her arm. She'd had enough of violent men, apes, grinning journalists.

'I'll drive you to your car.'

'I can walk.'

'Did he hurt you?'

'No.'

'Your arm.'

'It's fine.'

'Get in, for Christ's sake.'

★

He pulled up just behind her car, watched her drive off, then followed her home. She parked and got out, slamming the door hard, then walked over and stooped as he wound down the nearside window, her arms braced against the roof, her hip cocked.

He said, 'I meant to suggest a drink.'

'Did you?'

'We need to talk, don't we? About Zuhra.'

'Okay,' she said, and got into his car for the third time that night.

The pub was an island of noise in a quiet Kensington square. Delaney and Stella sat by the open door because the rain had stopped and there was a scent off the flowers that grew in barrels and hanging baskets. Some pubs had flowers, some had broken glass; it was the same postcode.

Stella lifted the vodka slowly, her third, paused with it at the fat of her lip, then drank half. She felt good immediately and recognized that as a bad sign.

As if it had suddenly occurred to him, Delaney said, 'You pulled him.'

'What?'

'That punter. You let him think you were on the game.'

'You're a journalist,' she said, 'you're schooled to think bad thoughts.'

'You turned him on, then you turned him off.'

'Nasty wormy thoughts.'

'You wanted to see what it felt like.'

Stella laughed and finished her drink, then went to the bar to order another round, unnerved that he should have read her so easily and so well. She came back with their drinks and started talking as soon as she sat down.

'What you heard – what she told us – it's not for publication, I hope you understand that.'

'Who says?'

'A D-notice, if necessary.' She thought her voice sounded a little muzzy.

'Am I likely to publish this story piecemeal? Of course not. When there's a full story to write, I'll write it.' He downed his drink and pulled the fresh one towards him. 'Apart from which, nothing at all gets written until Zuhra's out of danger.'

'That matters to you . . .'

'Of course it matters. And now I come to think of it, you're more of a danger to her than me –' he raised his eyebrows as if inviting agreement – 'you and your "No guarantees, I'll do what I can, official channels apply" . . .'

'I know what they go through,' she said. 'I know they're prisoners and I know they have to do things other prostitutes won't do. I know it better than you.' Suddenly, she was angry. 'I can imagine, Delaney. I can imagine, what it's like to have some creep with body odour like sewage come on to your tits. I can imagine it a hell of a lot better than you.'

Delaney held his hands up: No contest. He said, 'There's a Thai restaurant just round the corner, or a pasta-pizza place in the next street.'

Stella drank her vodka and stood up. Yes, she definitely felt good; and yes, that was bad.

They had some wine with their meal and Stella drank most of it; somehow it failed to leave its mark, but the vodka she ordered with coffee did the trick.

'What did you think, Delaney – that if you kept turning up in the pub at the right time I'd finally suggest we go home to bed?'

'It seemed like a subtle and original ruse.'

'Designed to wear me down.'

'Persistence was part of the plan.'

Being out in the rain had emphasized the slight curl in his hair; it was nicely tousled, as if he'd tried to get it to look that way. His mouth was a good shape for kissing. Stella shook her head as if to rid it of such thoughts; Delaney wasn't sure what that meant.

He said, 'Fetcher . . . Isn't that what she called him – Jimmy Stone's friend?'

Stella was watching his expression. How much do you know? How much has someone already told you? 'Fetcher, yes.'

'So he's on the list?'

'Definitely.'

'One of Stevie Tanner's people, you reckon?'

He's fishing, she thought. He doesn't know about Mick Armitage; he doesn't know about Raymond; he doesn't know that SO19 are on a two-day recce over at Harefield. Whoever was talking to him has gone underground.

'Tanner's, possibly, or just a friend. Who knows?'

'Here's an idea. Organize a deal for Zuhra, a deal that makes her safe, then get her off the street, keep her from harm. That way there are no fifteen-minute deadlines, no pimps to be afraid of. She can talk, you can listen.'

'You feel something for her, Delaney?'

'Sympathy.'

Out in the street, the drink hit her. She stumbled against him and he held on to her arm until they reached the car. He opened the door for her and she felt her way into the passenger's seat as if she were blind, then went to sleep before he had started the engine.

She remembered some stairs and the door to his apartment, but didn't really come to until he put on some music and handed her a mug of coffee. The music was downbeat, breathy jazz and the coffee was too hot to drink. He sat down next to her and without first working out how best to do it, she leaned across and kissed him.

A feeling went through her like light through water.

He held her in his arms, but didn't return the kiss. She let her head settle on his chest and heard the slow syncopation of his heartbeat and the jazz coming from a long way off.

She woke at three a.m. in bed and fully clothed. Before she could get up, he was entering the room and crossing towards her, the light from the hallway making him seem unnaturally tall. She seemed to hear the echo of her own cry and realized that she was weeping. He knelt on the bed and held her until, finally, she pushed him away and leaned back against the pillows. She was still slightly drunk, and the memory of the dream was strong – full of colour and sound and herself there, solidly *there*, standing in the hall and looking up at the blameless feet, her shout of protest ringing on the air.

'What is it?' he asked; and that simple question was enough.

She told him about the Bonnelli children and the three o'clock dream as if he had a right to know. Told him about her own lost child and how, in the dream, there were three little bodies, not two, hanging from the banister.

She told him everything and then she slept.

18

Funerals in the rain work well: everything damped down, raindrops mingling with tears, the *hush-hush-hush* of the downpour like a calming voice to the bereaved.

Cheryl Lester followed her husband's coffin to the graveside, bringing with her three children under ten. AMIP-5 were a long way down the line of mourners, Stella alongside Pete Harriman, the others paired off in the same way and trying not to walk in step. It occurred to Stella to wonder why it wasn't a cremation; so little space in London, graveyards stripped of their dead so that the developers could move in.

The priest was wearing a slicker and boots, and his Bible came with a customized plastic cover. The coffin was mounted on a little wheeled trolley. The undertaker's men brought it up to the apron of astro turf, then got busy with straps. Someone held an umbrella over Cheryl's head; her children stood close to her and she moved her hands, nervously, over their heads, as if numbering them one by one.

Man that is born of woman . . .

The undertaker's men took the strain on each end of the straps as the coffin went down, rocking slightly, and out of sight.

'Oh, Christ,' Stella said. 'Oh, no.'

It was involuntary, but she said it so loudly that she turned heads and Pete Harriman put an arm round her

shoulder, briefly, as if to lend strength. Cheryl Lester
looked across the grave to where Stella was standing,
and her eyes asked a question.

*What? Why do you care so much? What makes you call
him back?*

Stella lowered her head. She might have been saying
a little prayer. But in fact she was thinking back to her
evening with John Delaney, her realization that suddenly
he wasn't any longer a step ahead of the game, didn't
know about Armitage or Raymond or the raid that SO19
had designated 'Operation Raindance'.

Whoever was talking to him has gone underground.

The priest cast down some nuggets of mud that rattled
the lid of the coffin, ashes to ashes, dust to dust, and led
Cheryl by the arm to the very lip of the grave to say,
Look: all is well. All is well.

In the small hours you can see the lights of the city's
insomniacs; they bloom like nightflowers.

There were times when Ivo Perić could almost hear
the bomb-blasts, almost feel the whicker of bullets in the
air, almost see people falling as he advanced, the Street
Sweeper bucking in his hands. He liked it up close, liked
to be close in, liked to be able to see what he killed. In
Srebrenica he had reaped them like fields of harvest
wheat, sheaves of men going down as he walked towards
them. Women and children, too, though some of the
women they saved, just for a while. The fields were thick
with bodies; later JCBs had arrived to plough them back
into the earth.

These memories sustained him through his nights of
boredom.

Earlier that same evening, he had received his daily phone call. A different voice this time, which asked, 'How is it with you?'

'I'm a little crazy.'

'Don't go crazy. Get drunk. Have a woman.'

'You are describing my life.'

'Sounds great.'

'Fuck your mother.'

'Listen . . . not long now.'

'How long?'

'There's a meeting this week.'

'When this week?'

'Calm down.'

'I'm fine. Don't tell me to calm down, because I'm fine. Just give me something to do or bring me home.'

'Soon. We'll know soon.'

Perić walked to and fro in his room, casting a fluctuating shadow on the thin curtains. Hour after hour, he dwelt on the smell of cordite, the noise as you went into the thick of them, cutting a swathe; and, later, after nightfall, you and the others in a bar, still in your work clothes, badges and berets, smoke stain and bloodstain, a bottle and a girl for everyone and fires burning across the town.

The memories consoled him. A man could go a lifetime without having such luck.

Cheryl Lester sat on the floor in her children's bedroom in the glow of a revolving night-light and watched them as they slept. She was holding a glass of gin. She'd been drinking most of the day, but she felt pretty steady, which was bad because she wanted to be numb. The night-light was dolphins leaping, and she watched it go round. In a moment, she would get back to business; and there was a lot of business to be done: the mortgage, insurances, loose ends.

His clothes could go to a charity shop; she'd put his motorcycle up for sale. But she wasn't sure what to do about the mementos he'd kept: a few love letters, a brochure from a seaside hotel, the photo of them both on a beach that they must have asked some passer-by to take.

She wondered who she was, the girl in the photo, the girl who had written the letters. She wondered how Paul had managed to steal the time and how he had managed to find the money.

Stella was making a late call. She'd been phoning most of the night but only picking up his message. When she woke, she called again. Three a.m. A good time to find him in.

'You were paying Paul Lester for information.'

'Who?'

'Fuck off, Delaney. You had a deal with him: strictly cash, I'd guess.'

'I have many sources. I always pay them well and I never reveal their identities. It's the same for you, I expect.'

'It's illegal, what you were doing.'

'Are you sure?'

'Offering bribes to a police officer? Are you kidding me?'

'I didn't bribe anyone.'

'Sure, okay, stick to that, stand on that. But if I find anything that links you to Paul Lester, note, tape, cheque, phone number, any fucking thing at all, I'll definitely hit you with it.'

He said, 'I've got your watch.'

'You got –'

'Your wristwatch. You left it.'

'Keep it,' she said.

'Why are you angry with me, Stella?'

Because of what you told me? Because of what I know about this time of the night and bad dreams?

'You're a sleazebag,' she said. 'You're a journalist. I forgot that for a moment; silly me.'

She hung up and called George's hotel in Seattle. He lifted the phone on the first ring.

'You're there . . .'

'Early night,' he said. 'The clients are happy, the deal's in the bag, just some details to clear up; papers to sign.'

'What are you doing?'

'Watching TV.'

'What's on?'

He laughed. 'I don't know. Some show.'

'Hurry home,' Stella told him. 'I miss you.'

19

The SO19 inspector was called Stuart Lawson. He was a tall man, so tall that it was noticeable even though he was sitting down. Stella was sitting three seats away so she wouldn't have to look up all the time. Lawson and Stella were sharing a people carrier close to one of the Harefield approach roads. He'd been through this many times before, but there was a fidget to his voice.

It was twelve-ten a.m. and reports from the surveillance team told them that the apartment was full of people and music. Half an hour earlier, a pizza-delivery guy had turned up with a tower of boxes. There hadn't been time or opportunity to put in a camera probe, but it was a fair bet that booze and drugs were also on the menu.

'We've recorded quite a lot of activity over the last two days, people in and out, we're assuming that's normal. Difficult to know how many at any given time, but my tactical adviser is working on half a dozen, so with your lot in there, that could have risen to fifteen or twenty. It's not an easy venue in surveillance terms. In surveillance terms, it's a fucking nightmare. One unit surrounded by other units – tough to get it right – the coming and going. Not easy to get close. Fortunately, there are some vacant units. We're in a vacant unit. The assumption is that there will be weapons on site, so we'll go in hard. High-risk assessment. I don't want anyone from your outfit near the place until we've secured. When we've secured, I'll give you the nod.'

Blue on blue, that's what SO19 worried about. Blue on blue is why they secured before letting anyone near; it's why they tried to keep guns away from detectives. Blue on blue is a cop shooting a cop in error: it happens; and the best way to avoid it is keep amateurs off the scene, especially amateurs in plain clothes.

If possible, they would have a dummy run at a similar venue. Operation Raindance hadn't given time for that, but Harefield had been raided before, and the tactical adviser had spoken to the TSG inspector. The Raindance surveillance team had already colour-coded the apartment: white, black, red, blue – that's front, back, right, left. No good yelling *Go right*, or *Get round the back*, with people coming at the place from different directions and at night. Everyone was wired and miked. Before they went in, the team would communicate only with clicks: a coded system that had to be learned and learned well.

All this had to be papered: the equipment, the operation, the intent, the expectations. Reports on everything. And when it was over: more reports.

'Jesus Christ, the paperwork on this.' Lawson had just finished talking to the tactical adviser on a two-way radio. 'We're lacking a video man,' he said to Stella, 'but he's on his way. I don't want to move before two a.m. if possible. Best to wait till later so that everyone's asleep in bed and there are no innocent parties about, but I don't suppose your lot intend to stay the night.'

The video man would provide filmic evidence as back-up for the paperwork – to show that everything was done by the book. Because people's privacy was being invaded: the privacy of pushers and gun dealers and all-round bad bastards.

The firearms team would have been briefed, but just so far. They would know what kind of premises they were going into, what kind of numbers they were dealing with. In the hours before Operation Raindance got under way, the officers would have been told to switch their mobile phones off and talk to no one about the job. Bad news travels faster than good news and this raid was going to be very bad news for some.

Stella said, 'There's a guy in there called Raymond. His nickname is Fetcher. He's my particular interest. I'd like him in one piece.'

Lawson looked at her, glancing down from somewhere near the vehicle's roof. 'We'll do what we have to. The intention is never to discharge a weapon unless it's unavoidable. All in all, I'd sooner call them out – zero contact. But since this is nominally a drugs raid, we don't want a kilo or two of coke going down the pan. Any luck and they'll be shitting themselves when we go in. It's a fine art, rapid entry.'

Two hours later, he took another call to say that things were set. The video man was there, ambulances were waiting in side streets and two local hospital A&E rooms had been put on alert. The ambulances and the hospitals would be separately designated for police and villains: never the twain. The area had been sterilized: nothing in or out.

'Okay,' Lawson said to Stella, 'I'll let you know,' and pulled back the sliding door on the people carrier.

*

They went like shadows on shadows, until everyone was in place: white side, black side, red side, blue side. There wasn't much chance of suspects leaving side and back since the apartment was on the first floor, but such a thing had been seen before. The stonework beneath the window next to the front door had been marked with a large, red arrow – *this* window, guys; don't miss. In through the door was obvious, simple and direct, so that's what they would do.

Click-click to say move up. *Click* to say we're set. *Click-click-click* to say go.

It went like this.

One: CS gas in through the arrowed window.

Two: stun grenades in. Flash-*bang!*

Three: the Hatton-gun blew the hinges off the front door.

Four: the hydraulic enforcer flattened the woodwork.

Five: they were in, running hard through the hall, one going right, one left, the rest down the middle to the main room.

And they were yelling, all of them yelling like crazy men: *Police! Police! Get on the floor! Get down on the floor!*

Everyone did just that: they got down on the floor. No one tried to run, no one showed a weapon. The only two people who didn't do exactly what they were told were in one of the bedrooms, bare-arsed when the officer kicked his way into the room, and locked on to each other. The woman had her legs up over the man's shoulders; the man was rigid in all areas. The woman looked up at the cop in his baseball cap and boiler suit, but what she saw mostly was the MP5 rapid-fire, red-dot-sighted weapon he was pointing at her. She seemed oddly calm about that. Her eyes were wide and unfocused, and she was smiling a hazy smile.

After a long moment, the man levered himself off her and, without looking over his shoulder, went crabwise to the floor. The woman stayed belly up on the bed. She said, 'That's good; I thought he'd died of fright.'

By the time Stella got to the scene, there was a helicopter with a floodlight overhead and a fair-sized audience out on the walkways. Handlers with sniffer-dogs were quartering the flat and coming up roses everywhere they tried. She walked over the flattened door and down to the main room. There were twelve people face down and cuffed, including the lovers, who were still naked. Stella crouched down to look at the faces of the men, looking for black hair – about a number-two cut – looking for an earring, and a nose with no bridge.

The lover stared back at her wide-eyed, as if he were sending a psychic message. He was a perfect match.

Stella said, 'Hello, Raymond. Nice to see you again. Everything went down brilliantly, didn't it? Thanks a million.'

Raymond sat in an interview room, mute as a stone statue. Pete Harriman's cigarette packet was open on the table. Raymond took a cigarette and leaned forward to catch the flame of Harriman's lighter: his only gesture, his only betrayal of need.

'You know why I said that, Raymond.' Each of Stella's words carried a little plume of secondary inhalation; a low layer of smoke lapped the room like early-morning mist. 'I said it to make sure you can't go back to them. They think we're old friends. They think you shopped them. So you might as well do just that. But before you talk to the drugs squad, there are some things I'd like to know. First among them is who killed Jimmy Stone and why.'

Raymond passed a hand over his eyes and sighed heavily. He seemed to be weighing things up. Finally, he shook his head more in resignation than anger, and said, 'You'd better call DS Alun Ward at SO10.'

But Alun Ward was already on the way.

They made a tight triangle, Sorley, Stella, Ward, in the almost empty upstairs room that AMIP-5 used for meetings. A desk, a phone, three office chairs on wheels. Ward was so angry that his chair nudged back and forth as he spoke, as if he were looking for a kick-start in a roller-derby.

'My DI's going to be asking for a full inquiry,' he said. 'You were supposed to report back. I told you we had a man undercover, I told you Jimmy Stone was a factor in that. Report back, that was the idea. That was the *requirement*. If you had told me you'd been tipped off about Raymond, I'd've told you to stay away. I'd've told you he was Diver. Do you know how long it's taken to set this up? To get him in there? To have him trusted? He was getting information on hoolie activity all over the country. All over Europe. We were coordinating this with police forces in five British cities, and specialist squads in Germany, France, Belgium, Holland, Greece, Turkey, *Jesus!*'

Ward stopped talking, but he didn't take his eyes off

Stella. She said, 'If you had been a little more free with information, it wouldn't have happened.'

'No! You were supposed –'

'Have you got a paperwork problem, DS Ward? I have. How many reports do you write a day? How many do you think I write? My reports were sent to you on a regular basis. An officer called Susan Chapman would have forwarded them. Are you saying I didn't include every detail of every action taken by this squad? You're right. Are you saying I didn't advise you of every passing thought, every idea, every lead that might or might not be followed up? Right again.'

Ward shook his head angrily. 'It's not a question of half-ideas, half-thoughts, is it? This was a major SO19 operation. And I told you from the start that need-to-know wasn't an option. It never is when someone's undercover and at risk. That's why it was down to you to tell me what was going on.'

'You had your necessary secrets,' Stella said, 'and we had ours. Operation Raindance was like all SO19 ops. High-level security. It's more than probable that the officers didn't hear about the target until the last minute: after the phones were switched off and the body-armour put on. I don't dictate SO19 policy.'

Sorley thought she was doing pretty well for someone hip deep in shit. *We* had *our* secrets. *SO19 policy.* She was putting up a good deflection shield. But if the SO10 command leader really had asked for an internal investigation, it was going to be difficult to keep her out of trouble.

'He's hopelessly compromised,' Ward said. 'They think he's a chis. There's no way back in. He'd be dead inside an hour.'

Sorley got up and made for the door. 'I'll phone your DI,' he said. 'There's obviously some sorting out to be done.'

'Not in our squad,' Ward snapped.

Sorley hesitated for a fraction of a second, almost going up on tiptoe, then continued towards the door, closing it with a *click-snap* that offered Ward a hint: don't push.

There was a silence. Stella held Ward's gaze: *Yes?*

He said, 'You stupid fucking bitch.'

She got up. 'There's a pub,' she told him, 'just across the road.'

The pre-lunch quiet, Ward with a Budvar, Stella with a tomato juice, Worcester, tabasco, and just maybe a vodka.

'When they went into the flat, your man Raymond was fucking a woman who was later discovered to be a prostitute; also discovered to be stoned shitless.'

'Yeah?' Ward shrugged and gave a half-laugh. 'Maybe he was off-duty.'

Stella laughed along with him. She said, 'Let me tell you what I know about Raymond. His nickname was Fetcher. Why? Because if you wanted to score, old Fetcher would oblige. He'd pop out to the sweetie shop and pretty soon he'd fetch some back – anything, whatever you wanted, brown, speed, skunk; hey, all you had to do was pay the going rate.'

'If you're –'

Stella raised her voice slightly to close Ward down. 'Raymond was one of the few friends Jimmy Stone had. Why? Well, Jimmy was good cover, I expect, but he was also a way into areas where Raymond needed access.

Jimmy Stone worked part-time for the Tanners. Heard of them? Yes . . . Jimmy worked mostly for Stevie Tanner. One of the things Jimmy liked to do for Stevie was pick up on the girls that work the kerbs: make sure they were time-effective, therefore cost-effective. You know? The fifteen-minute trick. Jimmy liked this job because there were perks: free fucks and blow jobs. Raymond used to go along when Jimmy was on street patrol, because he liked that, too; he liked the freebies. The point here –'

'If you're undercover, you have to live the life,' Ward said. 'You're a dealer? You deal. It's the only way to stay trusted and stay alive. You can get nicked and strip-searched and given a bit of a smack in the cells by cops who don't know anything about you except you're a lowlife bastard, but you don't say a word. You wait for police bail, get back on the street, behave the same way as before. Some of our guys have even done time: not serious stuff, obviously, but a few months. It's part of the job; part of the cover. Until some ditsy bitch decides to –'

'– the point here is that Raymond wasn't in as a drugs dealer and he wasn't in as a whore-minder, he was in as a hoolie. If I've got it right, his job was to infiltrate certain BNP shitehawks who like to stamp on the faces of people in the wrong teamshirts. You said it yourself – that you were working with police in other cities, other countries. If I hadn't taken an interest in Raymond, who would ever have known that he was dealing drugs? Who would ever have asked where he got them and how much money he made from the sales?'

Ward had finished his beer. He pushed the glass aside as if clearing space between himself and Stella. 'In our job, you do whatever you have to do to maintain cover.'

Stella nodded as if she'd expected the remark. She said, 'Bullshit. When our lines crossed – yours and mine – you started to get very edgy: late-night calls from the pub, a lot of bollocks about your DI warning me off. Raymond was in to do one job and he was doing another. He was freelancing and the fact that he was in deep cover gave him the opportunity. Where did he get the stuff from? Easy. He got it from you; and you got it from seizures made by the drugs squad, so there's someone back along the line, maybe a couple of someones, who also ought to be nailed.' To make the point, she said, 'Nailed. Not given a bit of a talking to. Nailed.'

'You'll get nowhere with this,' Ward said.

'No? I bet I can. I bet I can get a *long* way.'

'What do you want?'

'I want whoever murdered Jimmy Stone. That's the crime written up on the whiteboard in my squad room. That's my day-to-day stuff. That's the file I want closed. So I need a short while with Raymond.'

'He's being pulled out for debriefing.'

'Leave him with me for a day.'

'It's not my decision.'

'Make a recommendation. spirit of cooperation, damage already done so might as well . . . You know how it goes.'

Ward went to the bar and came back with a drink for himself. 'What's the deal?'

'Who mentioned a deal?'

'Please don't bugger me about, DS Mooney, because I'm sick to fucking death of you as it is.'

'I'm not interested in you, Ward, and I'm not interested

217

in your friend Raymond. I'm interested in closing the Jimmy Stone case.'

'No reports on this?'

'Has to work both ways. I say nothing about you, Raymond and dealing; you withdraw your report on any flaws in my liaison with SO10.'

Ward drank his drink, got up and walked out of the pub. That was a yes.

20

Now that Raymond had stopped being either Fetcher or Diver, he had moved from the MDF-and-glue place he'd been renting in Harlesden and was back at home: a second-floor flat in a Fulham terrace with clever paint combinations and a kitchen that had clearly been equipped by a woman. Stella went to the bathroom and found exfoliating body wash, skin lotion and pantyliners.

Raymond told her he preferred 'Ray'.

'Sounds too friendly,' Stella observed.

'Isn't this friendly?' He indicated the coffee he'd made, then enlarged the gesture to take in his living room. Here we are, he seemed to say, sitting in my place, drinking my coffee, talking cop to cop.

Blue on blue.

'It's a truce,' Stella said, 'nothing more. That's why I'm here alone.'

Raymond said, 'Oh, well, fuck you then. What do you want to know?'

'Who killed Jimmy Stone. That's all. Who and why.'

'No idea. Next question.'

'You're going to have to do better than that.'

'If I don't know, how can I tell you?'

'Don't piss me off, Raymond. I'm easily pissed off.'

'Jimmy was an odd-job man. He worked for the Tanners, you know that; he ran a little business in keep-sakes for sickos, you know that too.'

Stella nodded and waited for Raymond to continue while he waited for her to respond; and a sudden thought slipped into the silence: something that hadn't occurred to Stella before.

'You helped him out there as well, didn't you? He had autopsy reports and scene-of-crime photos.'

Raymond picked up his coffee and looked away, as if something fascinating had suddenly happened in the cut of sky framed by the window. 'You want to know who killed Jimmy? Between the Tanners and his murderabilia customers and the people who just didn't like Jimmy Stone?' Raymond shrugged. 'Well, hey . . . Hell of a list.'

'No,' Stella said, 'too general. Jimmy was killed by someone who knows a lot about how to kill people.'

'Always nice to get the attention of an expert.'

'Does your wife know you go with prostitutes?'

'Oh, please . . .' Raymond held his hands up and laughed in what seemed genuine amusement. 'Please, I'm doing my best.'

'No kidding? Does she?'

'Girlfriend.'

'Girlfriend. Does she?'

'I don't know,' he said. Meaning, I don't know who killed Jimmy Stone. 'If I did, I'd tell you.'

'Let's talk about the girls.'

'For Christ's sake . . .' He affected a weary tone, but there was an unmistakable hint of concern.

'Not your relationship with the girls,' Stella said, 'the girls themselves. I'm looking for the person who killed Jimmy Stone. That's what all this is about. There are no murderabilia leads, so I'm left with the Tanners, who are pretty good candidates because Jimmy was in with them, ran errands for them, must have known things about them, and they don't think killing someone is that big a deal. When he worked for them, specifically for Stevie Tanner, Jimmy was a street-minder. So let's talk about the girls.'

'Well, you know, some are home-grown but a lot come in from Russia, Romania, Bosnia. Lots from Bosnia. Stevie had them on the streets and in houses but strictly confined to his patch. A turf war involving prossies is a messy business: too easy to damage the merchandise. No one wants a blow job from a face full of scar tissue.'

Terrific, thought Stella. I'm glad you shared that with me. And so sensitively put. She asked, 'Who brings them in?'

'The Bosnians? Okay, well, they're run mostly by an outfit in Serbia: in Belgrade. You know how it works: promises, promises . . .'

Promises of work permits, of visas, of jobs as waitresses, short-order cooks, cleaners, hotel skivvies, the opportunity to earn money, send money home, save for a future far from the memories of war zones and rape camps and mass graves. The girls are given free passage in return for an IOU promising to repay the 'travel agents' and their 'employers' in Britain.

They think this is legally binding; that they'll be held to it by the police.

They think the police are their enemies.

They think the police are also fresh back from the war zones, the rape camps, the mass graves.

They come to Britain in the holds of boats, in the luggage compartments of Eurostar, in container lorries crammed with vegetables and fruit and livestock. They are the livestock. When they arrive they are imprisoned, terrorized, beaten and raped. They travelled across Europe to get away from terror and beatings and rape, and here it is again, all of it, waiting at their destination. They are in the rape camp. It's a backstreet terraced house or it's an endless parade of cars parked up in the dark.

They're high-yield, fast-turnover product. Fifteen minutes max, and top dollar because they're providing services that are tough to find elsewhere: the stuff that other whores won't touch, stuff that brings risk of pain or disease or death.

Kamikaze sex.

There's wastage, of course, but there's also a plentiful supply of 'replacement units'. If they get chippy, hey, just saw them in half and heave them into the Thames.

'Did Jimmy talk to you about the girls – about the Tanners' operation?'

'Not really. I knew. I know about that stuff.'

Of course you do, you bastard. You know all about it. But that didn't stop you. Stella had left her coffee untouched. It would have been like sleeping in his sheets.

She said, 'I mean about their methods in particular.'

Raymond shrugged. 'You mean import–export.' Stella nodded. 'They come in trucks, mostly. Stevie Tanner used to fly out to Belgrade from time to time, but the Serbs organized things their end. Jimmy told me there was some aggro between Stevie and the Serbs; needed to be sorted out.'

'What was it about?'

'The usual: who got what. The Serbs could see that

the real money-spinning end of the operation was over here. They exported the girls and got paid a flat fee. The Tanners put them to work and made money on a continuing basis. For the Serbs it was a bit like selling the goose that lays the golden eggs.' Raymond sensed there was a pun hidden somewhere in his remark and laughed loudly.

'Did Stevie sort it? Did he solve the problem?'

'Last I heard, they were negotiating.'

'When did you hear that?'

'Week ago? Ten days?'

'Heard it from Jimmy . . .'

'From Jimmy, yeah.'

'More like ten days, then.'

Raymond nodded. 'Okay.'

'So let's get this clear: Jimmy knew about these negotiations. He knew about the problems between the Tanners and the Belgrade end.'

'Seemed to.'

'Knew a lot? A little? Why are you making me drag this out of you, Raymond? We're supposed to be laying down the basis of a deal.'

'He seemed to know a fair amount, yes.'

'But he wasn't Stevie Tanner's best pal, was he?'

'No.'

'He was a little man, a gopher, a part-timer.'

'So how did he know as much as he knew?'

'That's right, Raymond. Thank you for helping me out. How did he know?'

'You think he got it from one of the girls . . .?'

'You'd have to make it a possibility, wouldn't you?'

Raymond shrugged. 'I don't know. I mean, I really

don't know, okay? My interest in Jimmy was his hoolie connections, his Nazi connections, a few email contacts on his murderabilia website. Through Jimmy, I was making contacts, getting information about where the next ruck would be and how it would be set up. He had a loose mouth, yeah, but if he didn't say much about Tanner business, I suppose it might have been because I didn't ask him. It wasn't my area of operations.'

'Apart from fucking the girls.'

'Apart from that.' Raymond grinned winningly.

'Apart from dealing drugs.'

Raymond was silent on that one.

'What's her name?' Stella asked. 'Your girlfriend.'

'Paige.'

'What does she do?'

'Beautician. Why?'

'I like to get a picture.'

Andy Greegan put on his jacket and stopped behind Stella's chair on his way to the squad-room door. He said, 'Do you fancy a drink?'

'I do. But I think I'll get this finished.'

'It's late.'

Stella lifted her arm to look at her watch, but there was only the pale outline of a watch against a faint tan. 'Not,' she observed, 'too late for a drink.'

'Never too late for that. Are you sure?'

'Sure.' She indicated the pile on her desk. 'Paperwork.'

'Yeah. Shit. Paperwork.' He leaned forward to see what she was writing. He read *Raymond . . . illegal immigrants . . . sex workers . . . drugs for profit, without informing . . .* 'You think he fessed up everything?'

'I do, yeah. I think the stuff he got from Jimmy Stone about the girls and about the Tanners' problems with the Serbs was all side-of-the-mouth stuff, you know? All incidental. Things Jimmy talked about when he wasn't talking about hoolies.'

'He was really doing all that, was he? Raymond, I mean? Dealing drugs from the cupboard, raping the girls?'

'I didn't say he raped them.'

'He didn't pay them, did he?'

Stella looked at him. 'Good point.'

'So next we look at the Tanners.'

'Sounds right to me.'

'Heavy hitters.'

'They are, yes. Also slimeballs.'

'Are you all right?' he asked.

Stella had a finger in either ear and was shaking forcibly. 'I've got this noise . . . A ringing in the ears. It's driving me crazy.'

'Angel voices . . .'

'Fuck off, DC Greegan.'

'It'll go.'

'No, it won't. That's the point. It's there all the time.'

'Ear wax.'

'No, it's not.'

'Tiredness, then.'

'No, it's not.'

Greegan shrugged and buttoned his jacket, then glanced at the window, reamed by lines of rain. 'When's George back?'

'A couple of days.'

'That's good. No one should sleep alone.'

*

At eight-thirty, just as Stella was finishing her report, Mike Sorley came in with a Domino pizza box and a store bag that clinked. He pulled up short when he saw her, then put his shopping down on Leon Pritchett's desk. The desk where Paul Lester used to sit.

'He's doing well,' Sorley said. 'The new man.'

Stella nodded in agreement. 'Fine. People seem to like him.'

'I've spoken to the DI at SO10. Guy called Ryder.'

'Not best pleased,' Stella guessed.

'He's going to ask for a full inquiry. Seems to want blood.'

'My blood.'

Sorley was lighting a cigarette. He coughed a laugh through the smoke. 'Your name certainly came up.'

Of course, Stella thought. Of course Ward couldn't keep his end of the deal. If someone under deep cover gets exposed, people are going to want to know how. Ward might not have pointed directly at me, but it was my operation that caused the problem. Ryder has to push for an inquiry to cover his own arse.

Sorley delved into the wine store bag and brought out a bottle of Fair Valley red and a corkscrew.

'Did you buy it?' Stella asked. 'The Fiesta?'

'It's in the car park.' He pulled the cork and fetched a couple of plastic cups from the water cooler. 'I've got a flat, off the Uxbridge Road. It's okay: a studio flat. Not my area of London, really, but it's close to the office.' He poured wine and opened the pizza box. 'Small place. Not much of a kitchen, but then I'm not much of a cook. You like American Hot?'

He pulled a chair over to Stella's desk and they tore

off a pie-slice each. She said, 'What happened?', not really wanting to know, because she was pretty sure she'd be hearing the old story about coppers being married to their jobs, lonely evenings in front of the TV, coping with the kids when he came to the office at the weekend, the way that murder squad work was relentless, and that AMIP officers were always on call, always on the case.

Sorley said, 'It's been happening for a while, but, just lately, worse. We have a row, voices get raised, it all gets a bit out of hand.'

'You hit her.'

'She hits me.'

'Sorry?'

'She loses her temper and hits me. Punches me: goes for the face. Pulls my hair out. Puts her hands round my throat. Picks up a knife.' He took a big mouthful of wine and picked up the bottle to refill his cup. 'I'm frightened.'

'Of her?'

'Of myself. She starts, but I don't do anything. Hold on to her arms, perhaps. Leave the house. But one day – I told her this – one day I will. I'll punch her lights out. Just keep punching. Go on punching her till I can't lift my fist. Because I don't really know why she thinks she's got the right to do that – to go at me; to *attack* me. I told her: they talk about a red mist, don't they? One day will be red-mist day. And I don't want that to happen. So I've moved out.'

'You came close,' Stella guessed.

'Yeah, that's right. I came close. She threw a mug of coffee at me and I came very close.'

'She'll ask you to go back,' Stella told him. 'She'll say things will change.'

'She already has – asked me to go back; nothing about change though.'

'Will you?'

'I miss the kids, I miss the house, I miss the furniture, I miss the fucking carpets, for Christ's sake. The other night I woke up in the night for a piss and went out of my front door into the hall without knowing what I was doing.'

'Because that's where the bathroom is at home.'

'Stupid, isn't it? We're creatures of habit.'

He looked lost, Stella thought. He looked like a man finding his way in the dark in a strange house. Suddenly she didn't want any more of Sorley's pizza or his bad news. She felt bad news of her own might be on the way. She put her report in front of him.

'What's this?' Sorley spoke through a mouthful of American Hot.

'My report. Alun Ward – Raymond – hoolies. Let DI Ryder have it. You might find he'll go quiet on the inquiry.'

'What were they up to?'

'My opinion? Dealing confiscated drugs. Raymond was also using prostitutes run by the Tanner family. Effectively, it was rape, though I doubt any of the girls would want to give evidence in court. I don't think they were the only people involved in the drugs business, but they were at the sharp end.'

'You talked to Raymond?'

'I did, yes.'

'He was helpful?'

'He was.'

'Why? You do a deal with him?'

'That's right.'

'But you're handing in this report anyway, and you want it forwarded to DI Ryder.'

'Yes.'

'And DS Ward and this Raymond are likely to be badly fucked over, in addition to the fact that you wrecked their deep-cover operation.'

'They're bent,' she said. 'Fucked over's too good for them.'

Sorley smiled and shook his head. 'Whatever . . .' He picked up the report and weighed it in his hand. 'There's a lot of it.'

Stella gave a mock sigh. 'Yeah. *Paperwork.*'

Delaney opened the door to her, but didn't step aside. He leaned up against the jamb, holding her watch in his hand.

Stella was wearing her denim jacket, jeans, no make-up, hair pulled back in a ponytail. She looked as if she had just got out of bed, which was true. She'd gone home and taken a hot shower, feeling the water loosening her limbs. Tired, she'd thought. It's good: I'm really tired. She had put out the light and lain in the dark for ten minutes. Then called him.

He said, 'I know. I know why you're angry with me.'

She put a hand on his chest and pushed him back, then walked past him into the living room. When he caught up with her, she turned and kissed him on the mouth.

'I live with someone, have done for five years, more or less. It's very likely that we'll get married.'

'Okay.'

'There are things he doesn't know about me. The

things I told you about, the dream, the fact that I'm seeing a shrink.'

'What? You think I'm going to track him down and tell him?'

A little rush of adrenalin dizzied her. She hadn't thought of it. 'Would you do that?'

'For Christ's *sake*. Of course not.'

'I don't know why I told you that stuff. I don't know what possessed me.'

Good name for it, Delaney thought. Possession. The child who goes everywhere with you; the child you carry round.

'Maybe you told me because I don't matter.'

'Yes,' she said. 'It must be that.'

He moved to return her kiss, but she sat down and covered her face with her hands. He put the watch down and crouched in front of her, touching her shoulder, moving a skein of hair.

She looked out at him through the lattice-work of her fingers. 'Look, I'd love a drink. Have you got some wine open, or something?'

'You like vodka.'

'I've been drinking wine.'

He fetched a bottle from the wine rack and drew the cork. 'He's away, is he? Your partner.'

'Yes. What made you –'

'You stayed out all night; it didn't seem to matter.'

'I love him.'

'I bet you do.'

He poured the wine and handed her a glass.

'I just . . . I came to ask you . . . What I told you, it's so . . . *personal*, it's so *private*, do you understand?' She tried to think of something that would let him know how frightened she felt. 'It lives in my heart.' She felt foolish as soon as she'd said it.

'Who did you think I might tell?'

'Anyone. I don't know. It would make a good story, wouldn't it?'

'I told you once: I don't do that kind of work.'

Stella sipped her wine and looked round the flat as if seeing it for the first time: which was almost the case. Everywhere, things tidy, things in order, things neatly arranged; the whole flat said *Fear of chaos*.

She remembered something: Delaney talking about crooked evangelists and the sudden start he had given when she'd said, 'It sounds personal.' Almost before she could properly form the thought, she said, 'Have you got a wife somewhere, Delaney?'

'Divorced,' he said, looking at her in surprise. 'She lives in America.'

'And is she a happy-clappy soul who gives her worldly possessions to God and her body to the man who brings a message from the Lord?'

He didn't reply for a moment. Finally, he said, 'Why ask if you know?'

'I don't know. Didn't.'

'You've been checking: looking for ammunition of your own.'

'Not so. It may surprise you, but sometimes deduction is ninety per cent intuition.'

'You didn't come for the watch. What did you come for?'

'I need to see Zuhra Hadžić again.' It was the truth, but not the whole truth.

'She's in danger every time you do that.'

'It's important.'

'Why?'

'I can't tell you.'

'Yes, you can. Remember, I know a lot already.'

Stella shrugged. 'I'm pretty sure Jimmy Stone was killed because of his connection with the Tanners. Specifically with Stevie Tanner and the girls that come in from former Yugoslavia. I don't know why. Maybe Zuhra knows: without knowing she knows. Use any of this, I'll have you arrested.'

'You just kissed me,' he said. 'Now you're threatening me.'

'Will you set it up? Same deal as last time.'

'Do what I suggested. Get her immunity from prosecution, get her a visa, get her off the street and put her in a safe place. That way she can talk to you for longer than it takes to turn a trick, and without running the risk of being seen.'

'I'm looking at that. People have to be asked. It's not easy.' But she wasn't looking at it, hadn't asked, and she wasn't sure why. Maybe because it wasn't her case: she just needed to get whatever information Zuhra could give and move on. Maybe it was too much like hard work; like paperwork.

'They watch her all the time?' she asked.

'You were there. She had fifteen minutes, maximum.'

'When does she sleep? She must sleep.'

'They're in prison. They have jailers. Even when they're on the street, there's an invisible rope on them. It's called fear.'

'Ask her,' Stella said. 'See what she says.'

'In the meantime, you'll keep trying – for her papers.'

'Sure. Of course.' She picked up her watch and put it on. 'It's late.'

'What do you want from me?' he asked.

'You're my contact with Zuhra Hadžić.'

'Sure. Why did you kiss me?'

'I don't know. I don't know why I did that.'

The rain had lifted for the moment. Stella could even see a couple of stars above the dull orange wash of the London night sky.

She got into the car and drove, but didn't go home because suddenly home was the last place she wanted to be, among her things and George's things. You surround yourself with *things* and call it a life.

Up on the elevated section of the Westway, she could look across to the bulk of tower blocks, their landing lights, the lights of windows rising in grids to the sky. All those lives packed in; five hundred little psychodramas, top to bottom, nose to tail.

In the streets around Paddington Green, girls were working the kerbs. They braced themselves against the car roofs, cocked a hip and looked in on the next punter, Family Man, perhaps, or Axe Man for all they knew. A hard night ahead, Stella thought. A hard night of jerking and sucking and humping.

She cruised through like a visitor to a safari park, watching them at close quarters, their leopardskin crop-tops, their feather boas, the gaudy exotica.

*

Keep driving, keep moving, don't stop. London streets are never empty. Keep driving and you have to concentrate. Stop and you have time to think.

She was still driving when dawn nudged a green-gold tint into the sky, then sheeted the river in the same colour. The sun was up for almost an hour before a cluster of ragged clouds came in, backed by a westerly wind, and the sky filled and the rain began.

21

There's never a good time to die, but six-thirty in the morning has to be one of the worst. The sounds of things starting up, the city waking up, a new day dawning that you'll never live to see. It's not good to die in a windowless cellar. It's not good to die with a hangover beating your brain and all your sins in place.

Frank Turner was a man of no importance and his death wasn't going to affect many people. Well, no one really; except Frank, of course. Frank was going to hate it. He hated it already, because even though it hadn't happened yet, even though the moment hadn't come, he knew it was on its way. He'd been waiting for it ever since they picked him up at half-past four that morning, betting the last of his cash in a bootleg casino on the Soho–Chinatown divide. He'd made a break for it once they'd got him on to the street, but they'd had two cars and five men, and anyway Frank had been drunk, so he hadn't got far.

Three men with him, two in the following car; Frank sat between a big-built guy in a bow-tie and a short, bald guy in a snappy grey double-breasted suit: the clubs and bars they'd been touring all had dress codes. The men taped his hands and feet and put something with sledge-hammer bass on the CD system, then worked on him round the ribs and heart for a while, using metal fists and a short steel bar. This was to soften him up and shut him up. Bow-tie Man dragged Frank's head down to his chest to muffle his screams, then reached round and cracked his kneecaps with the steel. Run once, you don't run a second time. Frank was sitting on a security sheet in case of accidents, and they had a bag for him to throw up into.

You wouldn't say that Bow-tie Man and Snappy Suit Man hated their work; it paid well and it was regular; but you'd have to allow it was *hard* work: searching, running, catching, beating. You put in a lot of effort. Bow-tie Man continued to hold Frank's head to his chest as if he were consoling and comforting.

'Frank,' he said, 'Frank, Frank, Frankie . . . you silly cunt.'

And he was right. Frank Turner worked for a number of London's businessmen. Sometimes, though not often, the business in question was straight; mostly, though, he worked for people like the Tanner family. He was a negotiator: special needs dictate special skills. Frank knew how to knock at the front door but come in the back; how to deadlock a deal with all the advantage on the inside. It was about feel, about talent, like judging the angle on the eight-ball or knowing when to bet the pot. Nothing silly about that; but Bow-tie Man was right because Frank had been commissioned recently by the Tanners and he'd been skimming. Frank had been taking some off the top. And, yes, that *was* silly.

Now Frank was sitting on a wooden ladderback chair in the cement-floor basement of a house in Stonebridge. The Tanners had a piece of Stonebridge and the Yardies had the rest. The lines of demarcation were tightly drawn;

there were routes in and routes out. Frank had skimmed a few of his clients, but he knew it was the Tanners who had pulled him because of the route they had taken, and because Bow-tie Man and his friends were white.

Frank was having trouble breathing through his nose because the metal fists had caused some internal problems and when his mouth filled with blood, as it had from time to time, he'd snorted some of it down his nose and things in there were crusty. All in all, Frank was a mess. His shirtfront was streaked red, his jacket sleeve was torn away at the shoulder and his trousers were wet with piss; a little puddle had gathered on the thick plastic sheeting under his chair. The sheeting covered the entire floor and continued up to waist height on the walls. There was a builder's toolbag in a far corner, together with some overalls, a button-through navy-twill storeman's coat and a roll of dark green garden-waste bin liners. Bow-tie Man, Snappy Suit Man and the three others stood round like workmen on their tea break.

The basement was whitewashed and the whitewash looked fresh. Apart from the chair and the builder's equipment it was empty Neon strips lit the place. The ceiling was a network of waterpipes and wires.

Truly, it was no place to die.

Stevie Tanner came in like a man with better things to do. He was broad across the shoulders and a little paunchy, fleshy-faced, his dark hair glistening with gel. He was talking as he entered: bad-tempered and brusque. It was clear that Stevie was not a morning person.

'Fucking time to be getting up . . .'

He was taking a handgun out of the inside pocket of

his jacket: a Smith & Wesson Sigma .380, configured for a southpaw. It was a light gun, some would say a ladies' gun, but the point was that it didn't spoil the cut of Stevie's jacket.

'I haven't even eaten yet. Have you eaten yet . . .?'

He didn't seem to be talking to anyone in particular. Snappy Suit Man had collected the storeman's coat and moved round behind Frank, though Frank had eyes only for Stevie as he strode towards him, his feet making odd crumpling noises on the plastic sheeting. To compensate for the lightness of his weapon, Stevie always loaded with Starfire rounds, hollowpoints guaranteed to mushroom on impact.

'And it's fucking raining,' Stevie said to no one in particular. He didn't even seem to be looking at Frank. 'Fucking raining *again*. Call this a summer?'

He walked behind Frank, pulling the slide on the Sigma. 'Soon as I get a break, I'm gone. Somewhere hot by the sea.'

Snappy Suit Man helped Stevie on with the storeman's coat and Stevie shot Frank once in the back of the head and again through the heart, taking a moment to aim carefully between the rails of the chair. He stripped off the coat and dropped it on the floor. The hollowpoints leave spatter and spray. Bow-tie Man and the other three had already pulled on overalls; they were unpacking the builder's bag and pulling bin liners off the roll. One of the three removed a chainsaw from the bag and cranked it up, then pulled on a pair of clear-plastic safety goggles. Two untied Frank from the chair and stripped him. At first, the saw was deafening in the confined space; then the pitch softened as the teeth began to bite. No one was likely to hear it and complain, since the Tanners owned the houses on either side.

Stevie Tanner went upstairs, still grumbling, and through the front door to the street where an S-class Merc was waiting, a driver at the wheel, the engine still running. He got in and slammed the door.

'Back home,' he instructed. 'All I've had inside me this morning is a coffee.' He peered out of the tinted window.

After a minute he said, '*Fucking* rain.'

No one from any of the AMIP squads was going to be troubled by the death of Frank Turner. No one was going to report him missing or worry about his disappearance. He wasn't going to turn up in the river as half a person, nor were handy portions of him going to be dug up by someone's pet dog in the New Forest. There would be no corpse, no *corpus delicti*, no person or persons unknown, no clues, no case.

Frank wasn't even history. The Tanners knew how to do that. They knew how to make somebody a nobody.

Still driving in a circle, but vaguely heading for the AMIP-5 squad room, Stella was passed by Stevie Tanner's car on Western Avenue. It cut across two lanes at a set of lights, nudging her out of position and gunning through on amber. Stella palmed the horn, but there was no sign of life behind the one-way glass; it could have been a remote-control car programmed for aggressive driving.

Traffic had built up on the western approach roads and she spent an hour and a quarter in tailbacks. She got into the office without sleep, make-up or a change of clothes. Sue Chapman looked at her, but said nothing.

Sorley came to his door and beckoned her in. He had hidden the evidence from the night before, but there was still a faint whiff of pizza in the air. Stella shut the door, but didn't sit down.

'I've sent your report to SO10, but I also put in a call to DI Ryder: just to put him in the picture before a copy gets as far as the SIO.' There wasn't a senior investigating officer in the country who would fail to act on such a report and Geoff Meakin would be quicker than most.

'What did Ryder say?'

'He wants blood.'

'Whose?'

'Everyone's.'

'Including mine.'

'He wants it. I've told him he can't have it.'

'Thanks, boss.'

'It's not because you found them out, it's because you fucked up his hoolie operation.'

'He'd sooner have had Raymond and Alun Ward dealing drugs and the hoolies in the bag, is that what he's saying?'

'Of course. Who wouldn't? All that hard work, all that budget, all that paperwork.'

'What will he do?'

'I'm not sure. Suspend and investigate is my guess. After that, it's out of his hands.'

'They're a liability, bent coppers. They make everyone's job more difficult.' She thought of Paul Lester lobbing cigarettes across to Andy Greegan or coming into the squad room with a box of pastries.

'I know that.' There was an edge to Sorley's tone. 'What about the Tanners?'

'We need to talk to CID, we need to talk to Vice. We need to talk to chissies. I'll dole out the jobs and see what we've got in a few days.'

'I'm being asked questions about budget,' Sorley said. 'We're twelve days into the investigation.'

Any murder inquiry that goes longer than a fortnight without significant progress is growing weaker by the day. Pretty soon, the cutbacks begin: staff, resources, office space, but mostly personnel.

'The bits and pieces are to hand,' Stella said. 'Jimmy, a professional killer, the working girls, the Tanners. It's just a matter of finding the links.'

'People talk about the good old days,' Sorley said. 'Ronnie and Reggie, loyalty to the firm, you could go out in Bethnal Green and leave your door unlocked, they only topped each other . . . It can't have been like that, can it? But these Tanners, they're like generals in a war. If you're not in their army, you must be the enemy. They don't mind who they kill. There's a story in CID that they took out this guy who decided to ringfence a bit of their territory. Just a few streets, he wanted. But, you know, any sign of weakness The Tanners never got named for it, but it's certain they hired the guys who did him. They found him out on the Scrubs. These guys – they'd taken him somewhere and skinned him alive.'

Stella called a meeting and distributed tasks. She also mentioned the problem with budget. Then, as a grace note, she told them the story that Sorley had just told her: a man lying out on the Scrubs, stripped to the raw. A word to the wise.

Pete Harriman said, 'There's your answer. Let the bastards kill each other. *That's* cost-effective.'

Sue Chapman was logging reports. She said, 'You look like a hard case.' She meant the denim jacket, the hair scraped back, the naked face.

'You logged my report on DC Lester . . .'

'I did, yes.'

'I never showed it to Mike Sorley.'

'Oh, okay.'

'It's just theory. There's no real evidence for it.'

'No? We could find some, I expect. If he was getting a bung, there'd be some sign of it. Bank deposits that can't be explained, a savings account, even a John Doe account. Leave a decent interval, then pop round and go through his stuff. Ask his wife: if there's spare cash floating about, she'll have found it.'

'Let's leave it,' Stella said.

'What do you want me to do?'

'What is it: floppy disk and hard copy?'

'Yeah.'

'Bin it. And take the file off the computer.'

'He was bent, Stella.'

'Was bent. Is dead.'

'What about this journo – the one you think was putting in the bung?'

'No,' Stella said. 'Just bin it. Bin the lot.'

Delaney was making scrambled eggs and coffee when Zuhra Hadžić called him. Phone calls were one-way traffic because if any of her minders found it, the phone was a definite passport to pain.

'How is it with my papers?'

'She wants to talk some more.'

'Okay. How is it with my papers?'

'She wants longer. Not in the car with a fifteen-minute deadline.'

'Oh, good. Perhaps then I ask will it be okay if I go to police station for a while. I bet Gerry will think this is fine.' Gerry was a Tanner family minder, he organized things on Zuhra's stretch of the street.

'This is a good time for you. It must be, or you wouldn't be able to phone me.'

'Mornings, yes. I am in bathroom.'

'How long do you get?'

'Not easy to say.'

'Roughly.'

'What?'

'Approximately.'

'What?'

'About how long? An estimate.'

'In the mornings, a couple of hours maybe, but I cannot leave.'

'He's there with you Gerry?'

'No. But he comes back I don't know when. Soon, maybe.'

'Could you say you're ill? You have to go to the doctor?'

'Ill with what?'

'Say you've got a dose – the clap or something.'

Zuhra laughed. 'You think they care? Keep working, keep working . . . Anyway, even if they say yes, someone will take me and wait.'

'So trust me. Trust me when I tell you about the police. Ask for refugee status.'

'Yes, I know about refugee camp in England. This is prison and for money you have banknote with Mickey Mouse. I wait for papers.'

'And while you wait, you turn thirty tricks a day.'

'I wait.'

'You can't think of a way? It can be any day, any time. We'll provide a safe place to talk and make sure you get back fast.'

'Only way is to leave before men get here.' She was talking about the minders, the stand-in pimps. 'Then maybe I get back before they come. If yes, that's good. If no, I make some story where I have been.'

'What will happen – if you get back late?'

'What do you think?'

'They'll hurt you.'

'Of course.'

'Okay, listen, don't do it. We'll keep to the car and fifteen minutes.'

'You think she will get my papers?'

'I think she'll try.'

'You think she will get them?'

'I don't know, Zuhra, and that's the truth.'

'You trust her? She is *police.*'

'I can't tell you what to do.' There was a long pause. Delaney said, 'Hello?'

'Not police building. I don't go there.'

'Give me a pick-up point. We could drive round.'

'No. People can see.'

'We could go to my flat.'

'Wherever,' Zuhra said. She gave him an address in Hammersmith. 'By the end of this street is cinema. Take me from there at eight o'clock in morning.'

'Make it earlier if you want.'

'No. There are more girls here. They mustn't think where am I going. I can say I must get food or coffee or something.'

'This is tomorrow.'

'Not tomorrow. I have to think of best way to do it. I will call you maybe in two days.'

'Listen, Zuhra, you don't have to do this.'

'Tell her where are my fucking papers.'

Community service has its hidden benefits. You can do some rough gardening in a children's home, with the possibility of a brisk trade in uppers and weed, or you might get graffiti removal, which provides a good opportunity for sussing which houses belong to people who work all day. There's always a scam. Which is why Mick Armitage, the skin artist also known as Jesse, was able to sit over a beer and a Southern Comfort while some sixteen-year-old ringer took tags off street furniture on the million-pound side of Holland Park Avenue.

Stella gave him the touchstones, one by one: Jimmy, street girls, the Tanner family, an import-export business in Belgrade.

He said, 'I can't ask, but I can listen.'

'How much use is that?'

'I can go at it from the side.'

'What?'

'You know . . . hints.'

'Heavy hints.'

'No, listen, Stella, this is the Tanner family we're talking about. They took a man off and skinned him. Left him out on –'

'The Scrubs, I know.' The Tanners' skinned man was becoming an urban myth.

'You think the Tanners killed Jimmy?'

'Or had him killed . . . I don't know.'

From time to time, Mick looked over his shoulder, or scanned the bar. He seemed edgy. 'They generally do their own work. Stevie'll turn out for a wet job any time.'

'So I've heard.'

'But Jimmy was never in it at that level; turf wars or takeovers or heavy business like that. If you made a league table, Jimmy would be Accrington Stanley. So how come Jimmy winds up dead?'

'If I find out why,' Stella observed, 'I find out who.' A thought struck her. 'The Tanners. Where do I look for them?'

'Hugo has got a house over by Holland Park. They meet there, mostly.'

'I don't want to doorstep them, Mick. Where do they go when they go out?'

'The Cross Keys. Or the John Peel.'

He was looking round again, a quick left-and-right, then a glance over his shoulder. A pretty girl walked in; pretty, but too much of everything: too much hair, too much make-up, too much underwiring. Mick's eyes followed her all the way to the bar and lingered while she ordered her drink.

Finally, he said, 'It went down okay . . .?' He meant Operation Raindance.

'Fine.'

'They're all banged up on remand, yeah?'

'That's right. You don't have to worry.'

'I was in Brixton, I'm not worried.' But he was. 'Fetcher was there.'

'That's right.'

'And he did the business, yeah?'

'Mick, I got what I went for. You're not in the frame. It's okay. Relax.'

'Maybe we shouldn't meet here. Find a new place. Or get me on the mobile.'

'I don't do business on the phone,' Stella said. 'Better to talk things through over a drink.'

'Yeah . . .' Mick nodded and gave Stella the name of another pub on the edge of the turf. He was thinking of the skinned man and how long he would have taken to die.

Stella left first. She went straight across the road to a café and sat at a table just back from the window.

Mick emerged fifteen minutes later. With him was the pretty girl who had too much of everything. They walked to a small silver VW convertible and the girl got into the driver's seat, leaning over to kiss Mick as she started the car. Stella tried to see Mick in that light, Mick in bed, Mick the lover. Somehow the image wouldn't stick. She made a note of the car's licence plate number.

Why are you jumpy, Mick? You were safely behind bars when the Hatton-gun blew the hinges off and they went in screaming like crazy men. What's happened to make you afraid?

'But you didn't sleep with him?' Anne Beaumont asked.

'When I woke up . . . when I was having the dream, he came in from the other room. He might have made a bed up on the couch, I don't remember.'

'And you told him about the dream? About the dream and why you dream it?'

'Yes.'

'And you told him that one of the dead babies is yours?'

'Yes.'

'And you told him about me?'

'Yes.'

'But you've never told George about any of these things.'

Stella picked at a loose piece of skin above the quick: went a little too deep, and it stung and brought a smudge of blood. She remembered Henry Deever scouring his thumb with his nail, the way he made a noise like a kite in the wind when he jumped.

'How does that make you feel?' Anne asked.

'Guilty, mean-minded, traitorous. Is that the answer you were looking for?'

'Do you think you'll tell George, now?'

'George isn't here. Isn't in London.'

'When he gets back?'

'Are shrinks supposed to ask all these questions? Sounds a bit judgemental to me.'

'I'm curious,' Anne said, 'and I'm not a conventional shrink. I *engage*.' She said it with a hollow intensity designed to make Stella laugh. 'Did you want to sleep with him?'

'I was drunk.'

'Yes. Did you want to?'

Analysis isn't like confession, Stella thought. With analysis, God isn't listening.

'Yes,' she said, 'I did. I still do.'

When Stella walked into the John Peel, Denis and Stevie Tanner were the first two people she saw. There was a long bar raised on a three-step dais: leather stools, mirrors, a bronzed boy who was fast with a cocktail shaker. She ordered a drink and sat halfway down the bar, giving herself two views of Denis Tanner's table: direct if she leaned an arm on the bar and looked outward, reflected in the bar mirror if she turned her back.

She ticked the Tanners off, like a teacher calling the register. Denis, paunchy, a bit of wattle round the neck. Next to him was a blonde with perfect roots and a cleavage gone crêpey from too much sun: Carrie, his wife. A man in his thirties, fleshy round the face, dark hair with a touch of gel, suit with a touch of class: this was Stevie. Next to him was a younger woman, attractive and anxious to show it. Her colour job might have convinced you that she was a natural blonde if it hadn't been for the eyebrows, but her jewellery was real and so was her interest in Stevie. The other couple didn't register with Stella, but the woman was pretty and thin and blonde. Stella wondered whether all gangsters have blonde women. Maybe they came with the job.

She watched them laughing and drinking and spending their money. They're a species apart, she thought. They think that none of it applies to them – the rules that govern most people's lives, the lines that shouldn't be crossed, the laws that protect and control. They have their own rules and the trick about those rules is that they only advantage the Tanners. The loaded-dice rules. The marked-card rules.

The Tanner family sold drugs and guns and girls, and hurt people who made life difficult for them. Killed people who made life difficult for them. It was a way of life. They wouldn't have understood the nine-to-five, the tax bill, the family car; that stuff exists in the world occupied by Straight Man, an odd creature who speaks in a soft voice and has never developed a taste for blood.

The women were laughing because Denis had told a joke. The men looked like they'd heard it before. The waiter brought wine and Denis made a show of sniffing and tasting and nodding. While the waiter poured and people read their menus, Stevie's blonde took his hand and did something with it under the table. From the position of his arm, its slight movement, Stella could tell he was following her lead, but he kept his head turned from her as if this would disguise what was happening. He glanced across to the bar and caught Stella's gaze in the mirror. She held his eyes a beat or two longer than she should have and he frowned.

She paid attention to her drink, finishing it and signalling to the barman, trying to seem preoccupied, but when her eye found the mirror again, he was standing behind her, his fleshy face creased by an expression that asked, What? What is it? Then came a moment of recognition.

'DS Mooney,' he said. 'Stella Mooney, of Harefield.'

As she turned – because there was no other way to react – he stepped aside and asked the barman for cigarettes, a poor excuse for coming to the bar, but then he didn't need one.

'You went over. You joined the opposition.'

He stripped the cellophane from the pack and leaned across to drop it into an ashtray, coming close to Stella, almost touching. As he moved back, he let his hand drift in front of her face, the same hand that the blonde had moved under the table, then paused, holding his index finger under her nose. She gave a little jump, but he steadied her by putting his other hand in the small of her back; steadied her and held her in place. The bone of his finger was hard against her septum.

'Recognize that smell?' he asked, 'You *cunt*.'

He patted her on the back and smiled at her in the mirror, then turned and went to his table. Stella sipped her drink, waiting for the heat in her cheeks to fade.

When she raised her head again, it was the blonde's eyes in the mirror, a look to shatter glass.

22

Sue Chapman had printed off hard copy of a slew of reports and picked out certain remarks in yellow highlighter.

> Information is that the Tanners sometimes
> lay off options in Chinatown. They have ten
> plus legitimate businesses, all of which
> make money. These include a part-share in a
> casino and an executive car company. The
> brothers have form, but only one of the sons
> has ever been nicked: Maurice's GBH.

DS Harriman talking to a chis

> The Tanners have been investigated by the
> Inland Revenue twice and five times by VAT.
> Whoever keeps their books is a clever
> bastard. They have a villa on the coast near
> Alicante. Maurice Tanner has served eleven
> months, three weeks of a three-year
> sentence for GBH and is expected to be
> released on parole any minute. He's kept his
> head down and done his time. It's known that
> the Tanners have interests abroad, but the
> who what and where is unclear.

DC Greegan, information taken from CID records

> Maurice Tanner is serving a sentence for
> GBH. He's been having a pleasant stay:
> people know when to show respect. It's
> known that the men in the family have
> specialist areas (guns, Denis; girls,
> Stevie; drugs, Maurice and Hugo) but they
> can cover for one another if the need
> arises. Denis has a wife and a girlfriend.
> Hugo has a wife and a girlfriend. Maurice
> has a wife, three children and several
> girlfriends: nice one. Stevie is divorced,
> plays the field, and has a nasty temper. Well,
> they all have nasty tempers, but Stevie's
> is full metal jacket.

DC Sheppard, talking to a chis

> The Tanners seem to have loose arrangements
> with other criminal gangs, especially in
> west London, though they sometimes do
> business in Chinatown. Nothing has ever
> been proved against them. There are
> theories about this: coppers taking bungs
> is one, but it seems to have more to do with
> a network of odd job men and part-timers
> with a high turnover factor. Everything is
> at arm's length from the Tanners. Added to
> that, the briefs they hire are top of the
> range. One son is doing time. Expected to be
> out soon. Girls, guns and drugs, but
> everyone seems to know that. We can guess at
> the points of origin of the guns and the
> drugs without being sure, but the girls are
> mostly from Eastern Europe.

DC Pritchett, chis plus colleagues in CID

*

Stella was leafing through the reports at the bar, her drink untouched, when Delaney turned up. She said, 'You're late.'

'Traffic. Does it matter?'

'Yes. It matters because I have to get home.'

'He's coming back: your . . . partner.'

'Already back, I expect.'

'What's his name?'

Stella hesitated. 'George.'

'Why am I here?' Delaney asked.

'I wanted to see you.' She paused, then looked away. 'I had to see you.' She shuffled the reports into a pile and shoved them into her briefcase, but made no move to leave, although she wanted to. 'I'll call you.'

'Why?'

She didn't answer, so he said, 'Maybe I'll call you.'

'No. Don't do that.'

He pictured her on the phone, George nearby as she half-turned, lowered her voice, spoke in fragments – all the tell-tale signs. He asked, 'Where's your car?'

They walked down the street together, close enough to touch. When they got to her car, he waited for her to pop the electronic key, then opened the door and handed her in. She sat with the key in her hand.

'Go home to George,' he said, hoping it was a clever move.

They drank a bottle of champagne to celebrate, then went to a neighbourhood restaurant. George was full of his trip. Just for tonight he was the deal broker, the hustler. He told her stories about Seattle and the people there, and made her laugh. The food was good and the wine wonderful. Stella told herself she was exactly where she wanted to be.

They went home and made love. Even when they had finished, Stella held on to him as if she were drowning.

Mick Armitage walked out of the pub and straight into the upswing of a baseball bat. Some sound or something half-glimpsed told him it was coming, but he only had time to get an arm halfway to his face. The blow broke his wrist, which meant he didn't take the full force to the head, so he stayed up, but he was knock-kneed and going nowhere.

There were three guys and they did a good job. They didn't really judge how hard they hit him or how many times or whether what they were doing would kill him; it wasn't an issue. The issue was pain. The issue was *damage*.

They worked on Mick until someone in the street – there were plenty of people in the street – started yelling at them that he was calling the police. He yelled it from a good distance. Then a woman started screaming, and when the driver of a Saab stopped to watch, another car tailgated him in a shower of broken headlights, after which fifteen or twenty people piled out of the pub and the pavement started to get so crowded that there wasn't really enough room to swing your bat. And then the whole thing, the whole event, started to become unmanageable, what with the yelling and screaming and jostling and horns blowing as the traffic backed up behind the crash.

Mick was laid out, misshapen and bloody but still

breathing. The paramedics put him in a neck-brace and looked about for anyone who might be with him, anyone who could tell them whether Mick had allergies or epilepsy or diabetes. Or, if things went the other way, whether he carried a donor card.

The girl who had too much of everything watched from a distance.

She was still keeping her distance next morning when Stella arrived at the hospital.

The cloud ceiling seemed particularly low over the car park, low enough to trap smells from the kitchen and the incinerator. Stella bought a ticket, then walked between rows of cars towards the reception doors. The girl was sitting in her little silver VW using the vanity mirror to apply lip gloss and liner, with the rest of her gear lined up on the ledge above the dash: blusher, mascara, eye-shadow, eyeliner. Glamour Girl with her glamour gear. She didn't notice Stella's long look because she had eyes only for herself.

Mick was out of ITC and conscious, but the medics were going to keep him for quite a time; there was a danger of thrombosis, to say nothing of the head-to-toe breakages. He seemed dazed from the painkillers, his face half-empty, but there was a lost look in his eye that had nothing to do with narcosis.

Stella said, 'How did they know?'

Mick's head was held in a steel skullcap. He was bare to the waist and the parts of him that weren't bandaged or tattooed were beetroot and black, his nose out of true, spiky stitches lacing his brow and the line of his jaw. On one side of his chest, a samurai warrior flourished a slightly buckled sword, and the death's head centrepiece was a touch lopsided.

Stella remembered hoolies and Paki hunts and wondered just how sorry she should feel.

'Know? About you? They didn't.' His voice came in a hissing whisper and he spoke out of the side of his mouth like a confidant, because the teeth in his lower right jaw had shifted some way. The words came in little manageable groups. Between each group he moved his mouth, like a cow on the cud, and his throat jerked. Stella didn't want to think about what he was swallowing.

She cast round for another explanation. 'The Tanners . . .?'

'Nah. It was them. Off Harefield. For sure.'

'They knew you'd grassed.'

'Yeah.'

'But they don't know why.'

'Yeah, *they* do.' He paused and worked his mouth as if trying to find a less painful way. 'You don't.'

Mick was in a side ward close to the nurses' station, the 'at risk' location. A charge nurse came in with a full syringe in a papier-mâché kidney bowl and some medicine cups. He shot Stella a glance – *later, okay?* – and she walked through the open door and down the corridor to the hospital's fast-food café. Glamour Girl was a little closer now, in from the car park but not all the way. She thumbed coins into the drinks machine and walked with her coffee to a table by a window that let on to the pay-and-display, as if being able to see her car from there might reassure her.

Stella bought a bottle of water and sat down three tables away. Glamour Girl hadn't provided herself with a paper or a magazine; her gaze went only as far as the lip of her table. She sipped her coffee, leaving a blood-red half moon on the cup.

The charge nurse had manhandled Mick into a more upright position and put some pillows to his back.

Stella said, 'What is it I don't know?'

'You wanted Fetcher.' He paused, gathering himself for the next word-group. 'There was something. I wanted too.' Stella waited. 'Guy called Bassie.'

She thought back through the Operation Raindance paperwork. Those who weren't Raymond hadn't interested her much, dealers and dopeheads, someone else's business. A guy called Bassie . . . She half-remembered.

'Bassie had a neat. Business going. Cheap booze. Bootleg, yeah? Some brand. Some home-brew.' Mick looked as if he'd gone almost as far as he could go. He added, 'Poteen.'

'He supplied the estate,' Stella guessed.

'Yeah, but. Not just.'

'Shebeens.'

Mick nodded, then stopped short: nodding was a grave mistake. He swallowed mightily. 'Every place.'

'It was a takeover,' Stella said. 'A one-man smash-and-grab.'

'Yeah.' A noise came from Mick's mouth, ugly and wet. He was laughing. 'Bassie banged up. Me in. Like Flynn. Sweet.' The gargle-laugh came again,

'Who's the girl?' Stella asked. 'All tits and hair, waiting for me to get clear.'

Mick said, 'Can you. Help her?'

'She's involved?'

'She needs. Help.'

'Was this a double takeover, Mick? Bassie's business and Bassie's girl?'

Mick's eyes closed for a moment. When he opened them, they held a little less light than before. He said, 'I got. One thing. For you. Tanners.'

He swallowed and gave a great shudder.

'Talking to a geezer. Been doing stuff. For Stevie. Told me. There's a meeting. People flying in.'

'From Belgrade?'

'Yeah. Meeting. Sort things out.'

'When?'

'Soon.'

'What day?' Mick closed his eyes, a weary Don't know. 'Okay, I'll work with soon. What's on the agenda?'

'Who runs. Things here.'

'Who runs the girls . . .'

'Yeah.'

'Where did this come from?'

'Nah . . .'

'Who told you, Mick?'

'Fucking look. At me. Do I want. More?'

Mick's eyes were duller, now, the whites like tinfoil, the pupils shrunk to black dots. The charge nurse came in and added something to the notes hanging at the foot of the bed, then nodded Stella towards the door.

'He'll sleep for quite a while. You can come back.'

'I don't need to. An officer will take a statement.' Which will say mugged by person or persons, Stella thought. Another jot on the street-crime statistics.

Mick's head rolled sideways, livid against the white of pillows.

*

Glamour Girl had gone back to her car. She was sitting with her hands on the steering wheel as if the car might be about to drive off with her. Stella opened the passenger door and got in, reaching across to grab the girl's arm as she went for a fast exit.

'You're not going home without seeing him, are you?'

'Seeing who?'

Stella smiled. 'He said you need help.'

'Did he?' Glamour Girl looked away out of the side window, her teeth catching her lip. 'We got the timing wrong, that was all.' She was trembling, her hair moving as if caught by the faintest breeze. She dug a packet of cigarettes and a tiny gold lighter out of her bag. 'We went too fucking soon.'

'Why not wait?'

'It was me,' she said. 'I thought if we left it, we might lose it.'

'Someone's always looking for the main chance,' Stella observed. 'They might have thought Mick was a bit quick off the mark, but what made them think he'd shopped them?'

'It was me,' she said again. 'I should have stayed clear. Bassie had his suspicions about me, but he didn't know for sure. Didn't know who it was. Suddenly, he's banged up and Mick's got the business and me. If I'd kept out of it . . .' She exhaled a long plume of smoke that spread across the windscreen.

'Why didn't you?'

'I just wanted to be with him. Couldn't wait.' Glamour Girl was crying, little black tracks taking her cream-and-pink face back to the skin. 'You know?'

Stella thought she did know, yes. 'What do you want?' she asked.

'A million quid would be a start. Got a million quid?' Stella smiled, shaking her head. 'Or else take me back a couple of days and I'll do it all different.'

'It's GBH at least. Possibly attempted murder. If we put a case together, will you testify? There's a witness-protection programme that –'

Glamour Girl was laughing through the tears. 'Listen, there's a difference between a good hiding and a bullet in your brain.'

'What will you do?'

Glamour Girl pulled round in her seat and looked at Stella, as if getting a clear view of her for the first time. 'What's it to you?' Stella shrugged. 'Because he's your chis, is that it?'

'Yes.'

The girl wound down her window and lobbed her cigarette out. A great ebb-tide of smoke poured through into the cool air. 'I don't know,' she said. 'I don't know what the fuck I'll do.'

Stella told Mike Sorley that she needed some surveillance at Heathrow and suggested that SO12 might like to help out. Special Branch had a permanent station at the airport, alongside Customs and Immigration. Sorley made a phone call and discovered that Stella's reputation had gone before her.

'They're a bit wary.'

'I just want some surveillance pictures of people getting off flights from Belgrade over the next few days. They don't even have to come out from behind their two-way glass. They're not being wary, are they? No. What I'm hearing is special ops solidarity.'

Sorley's eyes swivelled away from hers and Stella knew she was right. The women-haters, the beefy boys and their all-for-one-one-for-all.

'Stupid tart, is that what you're hearing? Stupid bitch, stupid cow, stupid mare?'

'Look, Stella –'

'Needs a good seeing-to, ha-ha?'

'You dropped in unannounced –'

'Trust a cunt to force a cock-up, ha-ha?'

'Stella, shut up –'

'Because I've heard it all before. I've been hearing it for years, if you're a woman in the police force you hear it a lot.'

Sorley waited to see if there was more. Then he said, 'Look, you barged in on a well-established undercover operation and fucked it up. Okay, these guys were at it; doing some on the side. But that's beside the point –'

'No, it's not –'

'– when it comes to leaving an officer out in the open.'

'Do you think that?'

'It's the way people see things.'

'Yes, sure, I know. But do *you* think that?'

Sorley slapped the palms of both hands down on his desk – *stop!* There was a long silence in the room. They could hear each other breathing.

He said, 'I'll try. I'll ask Customs. People travelling from the former Yugoslavia – they keep tabs; they've got a vested interest.'

'Thanks,' Stella said. 'Thank you very much.' As she was leaving, she added, 'Sir.'

*

A new set of snaps had gone up in the AMIP-5 squad room: the Tanner brothers, the Tanner sons including the absentee Maurice, the Tanner women, plus front and side elevations of a big house near Holland Park. Among the old snaps was a newspaper cut-out of an ape. It wasn't a Barbary ape, it was an orang-utan, but it was wearing a silly smile and that was good enough. A speech-bubble said, 'I love you, DS Mooney.'

Someone had made a chart with critical-path analysis arrows. Everything started with Jimmy Stone and proliferated, like a family tree. The Deevers, Mack, Ferdie, Billy Whizz, Raymond, now the Tanners.

The only name that wasn't there, the only face, was John Delaney's.

He called at about seven-thirty, when Stella was standing at the fish counter in the supermarket. Because cops have to eat.

'Zuhra just phoned. She says tomorrow morning.' He gave her the place and time. 'She's taking a great risk.'

Tuna, because George likes tuna.

A man in a white mesh trilby cut two steaks, slapped them on the scale and gave her the price.

She said, 'Okay, that's fine.' The remark worked for Delaney and for the tuna.

'It's fine that she's taking a risk?'

'It's fine for tomorrow at eight.' She took the package and walked towards the cheese counter.

'How are her papers coming along?'

'We'll get there.'

'You think so.'

'You know I can't promise.'

The woman at the cheese counter looked at her enquiringly. She was used to busy people. Stella pointed at what she wanted.

Roquefort –

'Stella, let's meet.'

'You'll be there tomorrow, won't you?'

'I mean tonight. Now. Let's meet now.'

Brie –

'I don't think so. I mean, I can't.'

'I need to see you.'

I just wanted to be with him. She remembered the way Glamour Girl's mascara tracks had made a mazy path to her chin. *Couldn't wait. You know?*

'It isn't possible.'

'Okay. All right. But when?'

And a strong Cheddar –

'I'm not sure, Delaney.'

'Soon . . .'

'Yes, soon.'

– because George likes Cheddar.

She drove to Delaney's flat and sat outside for ten minutes. Tuna and salad and cheese: nothing to spoil or go cold. She went to the door and put her finger on the bell, but without ever intending to ring it. When she turned, he was coming along the street towards her. Of course he was: that's the way risk works.

She thought it odd how she recognized things: the pile of mail on the hall table, the polished banister, the turn of the stair, a narrow window with a stained-glass poppy. He opened a bottle of wine and put out some olives, and it was really no stranger than being in her own kitchen, the day's work done, time for a drink and some conversation. He handed her a set of keys and she took them without saying a word.

'Will you pick me up, or shall I meet you there?'

'You shouldn't be there at all.'

'If she sees a car full of cops, she'll leg it. Be serious.'

'It's a police operation.'

'Deputize me.'

Stella laughed. 'How long will we have?'

'An hour, I should think. She'll ask about her papers.'

'And I'll tell her I'm on the case.'

'Will you?' He poured two glasses of white wine. 'Are you?'

'Yes.' This was no time to start talking about the FO and government policies on immigration.

'There's no chance . . .' he broke off, looking at her across the top of his wine glass.

'Of what?'

'Of you deciding to hang on to her? You wouldn't do that . . .'

'I ought to. She's a crucial witness in a murder investigation and more than likely to go missing at any time.'

Stella shook her head. 'No. Listen, you have to trust me.'

'*She* has to trust you.'

'Yes.'

He took her glass away and put his arms round her. She said, 'It's all right,' meaning yes, it's time, let's go to bed, that's what I want; but he just held her for a while and then let her go.

'Overtime,' Stella told George.

They unpacked the fish and the cheeses together and

George opened a bottle of wine. Stella put out some olives. She could have been in Delaney's flat: the wine, the olives, the domestic arrangements.

'We don't need the money,' George observed, 'not with my deals coming through.' He was talking about overtime.

'That's your money.'

'It's our money.'

'Sure, of course, I appreciate that; I just like to have . . . you know, for clothes and so on. My own.'

'It's still our money. Your money and my money. Our money.' He smiled and put his arms round her.

'Yeah. Listen, it's my job and the job has to get done. The work's there whether I want it or not.'

George's hands went to the small of her back, then down over her flanks to cup and squeeze.

She said, 'Do you want to eat now, or later?'

He laughed. 'Meaning you're hungry.'

'I am.'

He fetched a griddle pan from the cupboard and set it on a burner, then splashed in some olive oil. 'Sure,' he said, 'why not? – we've got all night.'

The drum of rain on the windows, the muffled roar of 747s on the approach run.

George was a good lover; he knew what to do and when to do it. They had a routine for this, just as they had a routine for most things.

Stella turned him on his back, so she could straddle him. So she could see him that much better.

23

Some mornings, Ivo Perić would wake late and stay in bed until noon, drifting in and out of dreams: scenes of blood, scenes of triumph. There was one dream that recurred. He was riding a lion and carrying his gun, the Street Sweeper. The lion's bulk moved under him; he could feel its heat and its heartbeat. A mob on all sides, a multitude of voices and faces. He fired, swinging the gun left and right like a hose, and a path opened up for them.

Other mornings he woke early, feeling edgy and oddly dissatisfied. On such mornings he would go for a hard run, maybe five miles. He liked to run that stretch of towpath where he'd jumped Van Man and his friends. It cheered him up slightly to replay the event, the timing, the element of surprise, the look on Van Man's face as Perić dragged his hair back and cut him.

After the run, after the technicolour flashback, he'd shower and walk down the main street to a Starbucks for coffee and a pastry. It wasn't a good thing to do because you get recognized, you become a regular and people can ID you later, but he'd stopped caring about that. He was bored. He wanted a green light on the job and a plane home.

The counter-man recognized him and said hello. Perić nodded and took his coffee and croissant to one of the fixed stools by the window. He liked to watch the people go by. Someone at a table recognized him and said good morning. Someone at a window stool recognized him and smiled.

Zuhra Hadžić recognized him as she passed on her way to meet Stella and Delaney.

She stopped in the street, as if she had suddenly run into a wall, and stared at the man sitting in Starbucks' window, sipping his coffee as if that's what mass murderers were entitled to do. As if Ivo Perić doing something that simple, that human, wouldn't cause suns to collide and the world to shift on its axis.

People bumped her and told her to get the hell out of the way. And that's what she wanted to do – get out of the way, out of harm's way, but she was locked. Perić put down his coffee and took a bite from his croissant, then looked up, chewing. In the fraction of a second that it took him to raise his eyes and see Zuhra, she had run a short film in her head.

A burning house. Bodies on the ground. A young woman being dragged away, screaming, by men in paramilitary uniform. Others laughing as they drink plum brandy and throw more burning brands in through the windows of the house.

Zuhra watching from hiding.

A man with a gun, a big gun, emerging from the burning building, bringing with him a woman in her forties, an old woman, an old man, a ten-year-old boy. These people are Zuhra's mother, her grandmother, her grandfather, her brother. The young woman they are dragging away to rape is her sister. Her father is not there, because the men have hamstrung him and left him in the burning house. He is not there, but Zuhra can hear his screams. The man with the big gun is this same man sitting in the Starbucks window now, with his 'continental breakfast'. The same face, but not laughing the way he was laughing then.

Her mother is naked. They are done with her. She can barely stand. The man lets her fall to the ground. He takes out a handgun and kicks Zuhra's grandmother to her knees. Zuhra's grandfather throws himself at the man, so he dies first: three bullets. Her grandmother simply kneels and it only takes one.

The man takes her brother by his hair to where her mother is lying. He reaches round to his belt, comes up with a hunting knife, holds the boy so he is facing his mother, and cuts his throat.

Zuhra can see it and she can hear it. Despite the shouts and the laughter and the crackle-roar of the fire, she can hear everything. How it is to burn alive; what noise a child makes when you draw the knife across; what cries a mother utters when she sees such a thing.

The man drops her brother and kneels down to her mother, as if to say: See? See? He shows her the pistol, then he shoots her with it and walks away. He is walking directly to where Zuhra is hiding – a store barn twenty metres from the house. Then he seems to change his mind and peels off to follow the other men. Zuhra's sister can be heard. She can still be heard. Zuhra is shaking so hard that she is bruising herself where she is pressed against the slatted wood of the barn.

Last night she had stayed with a friend, then she had come home. At first there was nothing to see, nothing to cause alarm, except, perhaps, for the odd silence and the fact that there was *no one outside. It was a farm, and the work was outside. She was passing the barn when she heard the screaming and saw the first lick of flame curl up out of a window.*

He walks towards her, then he peels off. He is laughing, but there's no one for him to share the laughter with. He doesn't seem to need to. He's laughing for his own benefit. Zuhra looks at his laughing face, narrow and hard with those strangely prominent blue eyes, and knows that she'll see it for ever.

And there it was, staring back at her from Starbucks' window as Perić registered the expression of rank horror on her face, the look of hatred and revulsion; and though he'd never seen this girl before, he knew what that look must mean.

She watched him as he got down from his stool, watched him as he crossed the coffee bar and came through the door, watched as he came towards her, his hand out like an old friend, then her scream froze him for a second, froze those around her, and somehow liberated Zuhra into action. She turned and ran back the way she had come, shouldering people aside, getting off the pavement where the crowds were thick and running in the road, in the face of cars, horns sounding, a motorcycle weaving round her and mounting the pavement, people yelling, Zuhra outpacing him, going out of sight as she turned a corner, crossed a road, found an alley, found an underpass going down to the river.

Perić came round the same corner at a dead run, but there were too many choices: this side of the street or that, the alley, any one of twenty High Street stores. People were looking at him, asking themselves why he was chasing that girl, why she had screamed. Someone was using a mobile phone. Perić jogged across the road and went into a shopping mall. He made a half-circle and walked out of an exit further down the street, then immediately took a side road.

Stella was standing outside the cinema looking lost, like someone drastically early for a blind date. After a while, she walked back to her car, pulling up short for a moment because a man striding past, but looking over his shoulder, baulked her. He was wearing a leather coat that was a decade out of date, and he seemed to be short of breath.

Delaney said, 'Eight-thirty.'

'You're not the only one with a watch. What do you think?'

'She's lost her nerve or got caught.'

'Or just couldn't get out.'

'Yes, or that.'

'Is there any way we can get in touch with her?'

'I have to wait for her to call me.'

'When will I see you again?'

'Whenever you like.' He looked out of the car at the people passing by, all of them innocent until proven guilty. 'Is this what it's like, then? A stake-out?'

'Stake-out?' She grinned. 'No, you have to have cold coffee and bacon sandwiches and a fat cop with halitosis telling you more than you need to know about why England can't find a left-sided player.'

He reached out and touched her hair, only briefly. She said, 'I can't keep her a secret for ever. Her name's going to come out.'

'Why?'

'I'm just an ordinary copper. I can bend rules, but I can't make up new ones.'

'Pretend you're her. Think what that must be like.'

Stella started the car. It had rained all night, but now the skies were clear and summer was back for a day.

Zuhra stopped running after ten minutes. She sat on a bench looking on to the river and waited so see whether she would faint. Slowly, the dizziness receded, along with the nausea. Not the fear; that stayed.

Too late to go back, now. Pretty soon, Gerry and the rest of the street-minders would be at the house asking for her. She took the mobile phone out of her pocket. John Delaney and the police. The police. That man and others like him had called themselves 'The Police'. She had no passport, no visa. She was an illegal immigrant working as a prostitute.

The woman with Delaney had said, 'My name's Stella,' as if she might prove a friend, but then everyone had a given name, even the police, even that man with his coffee and his pastry, and his sins that seemed to weigh on him lighter than a feather.

She put the phone back in her pocket. He was here in London, that man. Should she stay or run?

24

Every meeting has its protocols. Neutral ground was an issue, and while it was true that the members of one group were in a foreign country, at least the talking could be done somewhere other than Denis Tanner's house. The Serbs had insisted on this. Stevie had booked the private dining room at the John Peel.

The agenda was simple: one item only, no matters arising. The numbers were even: on one side, Denis and Stevie Tanner and a minder; on the other, a spokesman called Savo, an interpreter called Jovan and a minder. The minders sat at a table apart. The Tanners, father and son, and the Serbs, sat either side of a roomy table that had been laid for dinner.

That was another protocol: lavish hospitality. They started with champagne cocktails and then ordered some good wine. The dishes that came and went were smoked salmon, Whitstable oysters, crab, prosciutto, grilled crayfish, rack of lamb, poulet, sea bass, osso bucco. They had cheese and dessert and bitter chocolate with their coffee, and everyone lit a cigar to smoke with their brandies.

Jovan was working overtime, because Savo spoke to him in Serbian and the Tanners spoke to him in English.

Savo pulled on his cigar and took a big, rich lungful of smoke. He said, 'Kaži im da odjebu.'

Jovan smiled at Stevie but spoke to Denis Tanner. He had decided that Denis would be making the final

273

decision. 'He asks how much flexibility is in your position.'

What Savo had actually said was, 'Tell them to fuck off.'

Denis laughed. 'That's easy. None. It's our patch, we run it. You get a good price for every unit of merchandise delivered. No, not a good price, *top* price. Am I going to let you come in and run things on our turf? It's our turf, that's the point. Ours.' Denis glanced over at Savo. 'Would he do that? Would he let me come over your way and start pulling all the bloody levers?'

Jovan turned to Savo. 'I on tebi kaže da odjebeš.' *And he says fuck off back to you.*

Savo sighed. He said, 'Nastavi da pričaš.' *Keep talking.*

'Here is where we stand: top price for the girls is one thing, but our problem is the money stops with that payment. This is like selling to a man a printing press from which he can make as much money as he likes. There is no sense in it. We must keep finding fresh product and sell for one-off payment. You may keep using that same product over and over and taking money each time.'

Denis laughed affably. A little closer and he might have patted Jovan on the shoulder. 'It's the way of things, mate. It's how things are. What's your solution?'

'Try to make a fair deal, perhaps.'

'You've got one. Best deal in London for that kind of product.' Denis dropped his voice, suddenly confidential, as if he were talking to a third party. 'Look, Jovan, what are you going to do? Ask him. What's he going to do? Blockade me? Cross me off his customer list? This is the pussy market we're talking about, not rough diamonds.

It's coming in from Russia, Thailand, China, all parts of Africa. There are wars all over the fucking shop and every place there's a war there are refugees and everywhere you find refugees, my old mate, you'll find girls for sale. It's a gash glut, Jovan. It's a snatch mountain.'

Stevie laughed at the idea. He was drunk and the laugh was loud and sounded insulting. The minders looked at the table for four, then at each other.

'Nema šanse.' *It's hopeless.* Jovan made a tiny gesture with an upturned palm.

'Pokušaj ponovo,' Savo replied. *Try again. Keep trying.*

Delaney spent three hours touring the pick-up sites he knew of, but didn't see Zuhra. In truth, he hadn't expected to.

He stopped for a girl and drove out towards Scrubs Lane. He gave her twice the rate and asked if she knew Zuhra Haždić. She didn't. She'd never heard of her. She said it as if she had her hand on a Bible in a court of law.

'Do you want something?' she asked, meaning sex.

'No.'

'You have to take me back.' You *have* to. On the return journey, she said, 'You're not police.'

'No.'

'Stay away,' she said, getting out of the car. 'Stay the fuck away. It's good advice.'

They were still smoking and drinking brandy at one o'clock in the morning, but the talking had become a little one-sided.

There comes a moment when you pass through drunkenness into a kind of dazed sobriety; when you've smoked so much that there's nothing to do but keep smoking. The room was lapped in waves of blue; they bellied in the heat from the lights and drifted back down, shifting in little flurries when someone spoke or waved an arm for emphasis.

Jovan was seeking a compromise. He'd been seeking it for more than an hour with Savo watching him, heavy-eyed, only the weight of booze holding his anger down.

'We don't ask to control the girls once they are here.'

'No? I thought that was what you wanted. That's what we've been discussing, isn't it? You on site; on our turf.'

'We can see that an arrangement must be reached.'

'We've got one already. Bloody good arrangement. You ship the tarts, we give you cash.'

'There must be something more for us. Something that allows us . . . what is it called? Residuals.'

'What?'

'A percentage of your gross.'

Denis sighed and poured himself a brandy, then poured one for Savo. He appeared to be thinking. He said, 'What percentage?'

Stevie heard this through a booze haze, but he heard it, and his head came up. Savo heard it too, but only the tone of voice, though he saw Stevie's reaction and looked at once towards Jovan. He asked, 'What?'

'Napredujemo. Sada je sve samo pitanje vremena.' *A breakthrough. Now it is just a matter of time.*

They talked long into the night, then they shook hands and went their separate ways. The Serbs had missed their plane, but Denis Tanner was on the case. He would personally reserve rooms for them at the airport hotel and re-book their flight. The minders opened car doors.

They were wearing heavy stubble and looked glassy-eyed with tiredness, but their jackets were still buttoned.

The car carrying the Tanners, father and son, whispered down into Ladbroke Grove. The first hint of dawn showed a red-yellow glow as the silhouettes of rooftops and streetlamps came clear and sharp-edged.

Stevie said, 'Fifteen per cent?'

'Yeah.' Denis reached into the seat pocket in front of him and found a hip flask of whisky. A freshener; something to get the heart started. 'I got sick of talking to him. It wasn't going nowhere.'

'We're going to lob over fifteen per cent?'

'No.'

'What, then?'

'We'll top the bastard. He can have a hundred per cent of that.'

The dawn light held up and brightened until halfway through the morning, when the clouds came down like a trapdoor and the temperature dropped. Stella was in Sorley's office playing a truth game that involved Sorley getting only as much as he needed to know· which was enough to make him shake his head in sadness and anger.

'She's an illegal.'

'From Bosnia.'

'She's a material witness.' Stella took that to be rhetorical. 'And you had her, but now you've lost her.'

'I thought I'd get more out of her if I put her on a long leash.'

'And who do you report to? Me, isn't it? So where's the paperwork on this?'

'It would have been wrong,' Stella said, 'to pull her in.'

'In your judgement.'

'If you translate "police" from her language to ours, you get "murderous bastard". I didn't think she'd see cops as her friends.'

'You being an exception.'

'That was the idea. I thought she would talk to a friend.'

'Not if she's bunked off.'

'I'll find her.'

'Yes, you will. Make it soon.'

'If I find her . . . I need some leeway.'

'Meaning?'

'To deal with it myself.'

'Not arrest her.'

'That's right.'

'Give me a good reason.'

'One way, she'll be useful. The other way, she'll be deaf and dumb.'

'Jesus . . .' Sorley shook his head. 'It depends . . .'

'On what?'

'Circumstances.'

'Okay,' Stella said, 'I'll take that as a yes.'

Sorley turned to a report on his desk: a fresh issue. 'One way and another, you're asking for a lot. Especially this.'

'It's just surveillance.'

Stella was sure that the alliance between the Tanner family and the Belgrade connection was getting ragged; Mick Armitage had said as much. Things being shaken up, things coming loose – it was all to the good. She wanted to know if the Tanners seemed rattled, wanted to know where they went and who they saw; for that, she needed surveillance.

'There are four in the Tanner family,' Sorley said. 'One's in nick, so we don't have to worry about him, but keeping in touch with the other three – that would be a costly business. You need a minimum of two cars for each of their vehicles, you need to work shifts round the clock, you need lots of overtime, lots of manpower, lots of paperwork. The SIO isn't offering to increase my budget, he's asking me to find ways of cutting it.'

'I know there's a link between the Tanners and Jimmy Stone's death.'

'You think. You *want* there to be. Okay, find it. And find this –'

'Zuhra Hadžić.'

'– right. But don't ask for more than I can give. That covers money and tolerance.' As she was leaving, he said, 'By the way, I got Customs for you. They're filming passengers on incoming flights from all parts of Serbia.' She paused to thank him, but he held up a hand. 'Keeping secrets from SO10 is one thing, Stella. Keeping them from me is another.'

She gave Steve Sheppard the task of scanning the Customs and Excise videos. The others were going over old ground. Pete Harriman was talking to Billy Whizz in an interview room at Wandsworth nick; Leon Pritchett was coordinating a 'did you see?' campaign; Andy Greegan was off AMIP secondment for a week and back with CID. You could hear the wheels slowing.

Sue Chapman was still learning about the people who

liked murderabilia. From time to time, she crossed over on to other websites to see if the market was freshening. She discovered that there were pictures of Trolley Dolly on offer: Trolley Dolly at the scene; Trolley Dolly on the slab. A sample snap could be downloaded, a tease, a loss-leader. She stared at the pale legs, the little pubic pout. Someone's offcut. A bearded homunculus.

Sue watched Stella as she walked through. *Are you ill or tired or what?*

He opened some wine; she had brought taco chips. A little home from home. Family business.

'Why?' Delaney asked. 'Why did you tell Sorley about her?'

'I told you I might have to.'

'I don't get it.'

'You went looking for her. Any luck?'

'No. You know that.'

'Exactly. I can't just let her go. I can't ignore her. If she doesn't turn up, if she doesn't phone you, I'm going to have to try to find her. For that, I need to call on other departments, other resources. I can't do that without warning. I didn't write a report and Sorley didn't ask for one, which means she's off the record for the moment.' He drank some wine, refusing to meet her eye. 'I'm a cop, Delaney. Didn't you know that?'

'What else is happening?'

She told him about having the Tanner family watched and about Customs videoing through two-way mirrors. She didn't tell him that she intended to look for Zuhra herself.

They finished the bottle and ate the tacos and she left.

It's worse, she thought. These early evening trysts, this being a couple, even though, even though no promises are made. It's worse than adultery.

She sat in the car and lied to George over the phone. *Overtime*, she said. *Paperwork.*

25

Girls in Lycra, girls in fun furs, girls in crop-tops. Girls in thigh boots, girls in fishnets, girls in blonde wigs. Girls in red stilettos, girls in skirts tight as bandages. Just cruise by and take your pick.

This was where they had found Zuhra the first time. Not the crowds and action of the West End, not the worst of the west London badlands. The punters were mostly Joe Normal. Joe on his way home, Stella thought; Joe pulling over for one of those early-evening trysts. In the daytime, kids went to school here; people picked up groceries and their laundry.

She parked in a side street and walked back. She was wearing black jeans, a black denim blouson and sneakers. She looked like a passer-by. The pimps and street-minders saw her and watched her, but didn't pick her as a poacher. She saw them, too. There seemed more of them than usual, more cars parked with their nearside wheels up on the pavement, more men in zipper jackets and earrings, more movement in the corner of her eye. There was a sense of menace in the air; menace and tension.

At night, the main strip was loud and bright. Stella walked up from the crossroads past fast-food places, bars and shopfronts. The girls were on the move, too, but strolling, waiting for the next Ford Mondeo, the next Vauxhall Vectra. Zuhra wasn't among them. Stella reached the end of the strip, went into a late-night grocery store and bought some milk and cigarettes, then walked down on the other side of the street.

No Zuhra.

She took the risk of making the circuit again, immediately, playing to a script where she had forgotten something crucial from the grocer's. Olives and taco chips, she decided. She made a loop, carrying her 7-Eleven bag like a passport. She saw girls and she saw Joes, but there was no one called Zuhra doing business. In the window of the TV rental shop, seven screens were showing silent passion, silent warfare. In dumb-play, sex looked like first aid and violence looked like dance.

That was what Stella saw as she came down the side street towards her car: something like a dance, a waltz, perhaps, with the two silhouettes swaying slightly and seeming to be joined at the hip. Then the voices started and things were suddenly ugly. The man's arm rose and fell and he called her *Shit!* called her *Slag!* She backed off, one hand extended, and asked him to please, *please*, come and get some of what she wanted to give him. What the woman was saying made sense when Stella saw light catch the blade she was holding.

As Stella crossed the street towards them, the man moved in, kicking at the girl's knife-hand. He missed, but caught her high on the thigh; she screamed at him and hopped back, still waving the knife. Stella could see the expression on the man's face, his lips drawn back like a dog's: Family Man gone feral. As she came up to them, the girl saw her and was distracted, which gave the man an advantage. He stepped in and grabbed her wrist, then reached for her throat.

Stella said, 'Police.' The man didn't seem to hear her,

so she said it again, taking hold of his arm at the same time. He turned and Stella anticipated the punch, swivelling sideways then back. He'd opened himself up, put himself off balance. Stella moved in and backhanded him across the throat. He put both hands to the place and bent forward, rasping and gagging as if he had a fishbone in his gullet.

Stella took out her warrant card and, when he'd recovered a little, showed it to him in the light from a streetlamp. He walked away and got into his car. Stella followed him and rapped on the glass. When he wound down the window, she braced her hands on the roof, cocked a hip and leaned in. There were tapes on the back seat: *Humpty Dumpty Rhymes* and *The Wheels on the Bus*.

'Stay there. You might have charges to answer.'

'She had the knife.'

'Really?' Stella said. 'I didn't see a knife.'

She walked back to the girl and asked her what she wanted to do, though she had already predicted the answer. *Nothing. It didn't happen.*

What the girl actually said was: 'Cut his dick off, but that's maybe against law.' She had a strong accent, but her grasp of English was good.

Stella went back to the car. She said, 'Go home. I've got your registration number. I'll probably be calling to have a word with you and your wife.'

The girl was hiking back up the street at a fast rate. Stella caught her up. She said, 'You'd better give me the knife.'

'If I didn't have knife, I would have a different shape face.'

'You don't want to kill someone.'

'That's what you think.'

'He attacked you? What for?'

'He want anal. I don't give anal.'

They reached the junction with the main strip. Stella realized the girl was heading for a pub.

'Don't you have to get back?' Stella asked. 'Fifteen-minute trick?'

The girl stopped a moment and looked at Stella. 'Sure. Also I have to have drink. You really police?' She started walking again, spike-heels tap-tap-tapping. She was wearing silver Lycra and a nylon mink.

'Police, yes.'

'Jesus Christ. You Vice?'

'No. I'm looking –'

The girl shoved through the pub door and walked through thick drifts of cigarette smoke to the bar and ordered a vodka. When she turned, Stella was behind her, signalling to the barman for another of the same. She paid for both, scooped them up and took them to a table. The girl sat with her and claimed her drink.

'– I'm looking for a girl called Zuhra. Zuhra Hadžić.'

'I don't know.'

'From Bosnia.'

'Sure. I can tell from name.'

'You never met her . . .?'

'No.'

'Are you from there?'

'From Russia. I am Katya.' The name was an after-thought; as if she had suddenly decided to be herself.

'You work for the Tanner family. For Stevie Tanner.'

'Who?' When Stella smiled at her response, Katya spread her hands: *So what do you want me to say?* She drank half her vodka down in one and glanced at her watch.

'Lots of minders on the street,' Stella said. 'What's wrong?' Katya shrugged, but Stella knew she was acting. 'Someone expecting trouble?'

'Why do you ask me? Ask them.'

Stella took a card out of her wallet and passed it to Katya, who snatched it and shoved it into a pocket in the fake fur. '*Jesus.*' She glanced round anxiously. 'You give me *police* card?'

'If you hear anything about Zuhra Haždić, call me.'

'Sure.'

'Or if you need something. If you need help.'

'Sure.'

'Leave the knife at home.'

'Sure.'

Stella glanced round the pub. There were girls who looked like Katya and there were men who looked like bastards and there were a few civilians, but no one who looked like DS Stella Mooney. She said, 'Don't all whores give anal?' It was genuine curiosity.

Katya looked at her a moment before speaking. She said, 'I am not whore, I am engineer. Back in my country – engineer.' She drank off the rest of her vodka. 'I am engineer who don't give anal.'

26

You see a 747 taking off and you wonder how. You think of three hundred people at thirty thousand feet, watching small-screen TV and eating lemon chicken, and it doesn't seem possible.

Jovan turned from the window of the airport hotel as the jet eased slowly into the sky; he liked watching planes take off better than he liked watching the adult movie channel. Savo and the minder preferred to watch the girls with their big, solid breasts and their tight pubic strips going down on their backs, going down on their hands and knees, going down on their co-stars. At just that moment, two girls were doing things to each other while a man did things to each of them in turn.

Savo was watching with half an eye; he and Jovan were talking about the meeting, patting themselves on the back, calling themselves *tough hombres* – that was how they said it in London. *Tough hombres.*

Savo went to the mini-bar and helped himself to whisky and chocolate and nuts; he sat cross-legged on the bed and expressed a firm preference for the girl on top. The minder sat motionless in an armchair, staring intently at the screen as if he'd signed up for an Open University course in oral studies.

They were feeling good. Sure, they had missed their plane because the negotiation with the Tanners had lasted so long, but that was fine because they had got what they wanted. Denis Tanner had re-booked them on a flight that left early next morning, and that was fine too because it gave them the opportunity to watch an adult double bill and order room service.

The trick about an old trick is to make sure that there are no mistakes. Old tricks are fine because you know they work, but since they've been used before they linger in the mind and the slightest error can cause suspicion.

The men working for Denis Tanner had room 309. The Serbs were in 310. Tanner's men were using a basic but effective listening device, just an amplifier with a sensitive diaphragm held up against the wall, but it was more than enough; hotel walls aren't built for privacy. One of the men was a professional: he was called Suitcase because he came with a Globetrotter case on wheels that carried his equipment. He was a big man, muscly, but had a small head for such broad shoulders; to offset this, he wore his hair long. The man with the listening device was a specialist, too, in his own way; he spoke Serbian. Some people he worked with called him Ian, because they didn't know any better. His name was Yannis. He was small and wiry, like a bantamweight.

The two men had met for the first time a couple of hours ago and driven straight to the hotel. They had insisted on changing rooms twice before settling on 309: not difficult clients, just choosy. The first thing Suitcase did when they got into their room was order room service. Yannis listened at the wall. After twenty minutes, he heard Jovan come into the room. The conversation went to and fro; the TV came on.

'The boss-man and the negotiator are there. Someone's put on the blue movie.'

'What about the minder?'

'Where else would he be?'

'Not good enough. Can you place him in the room?'

'No. But where else would he be?'

Suitcase shook his head. 'I need you to place him
there. Keep listening.' He opened his Globetrotter and
took out a Heckler & Koch USP 12 with a threaded
barrel and fitted a Blackhawk silencer. The H&K was
carrying Whisperload sub-sonic bullets to make the risk
of noise even smaller, but to compensate for the loss of
velocity, the rounds were hollowpoint to make the
damage greater.

Yannis listened for another ten minutes, switching
hands and position from time to time. Then he heard
the room service order go in: three steaks, three bottles
of wine. The minder said he wanted his steak rare.

'They're all in there. They just ordered from room
service.'

Suitcase glanced at their own room-service trolley
standing by the door – the old trick. It had taken twenty-
five minutes to arrive. He put the TV on and settled
down to watch fifteen minutes of Lick-Bitch, or whatever
it was called. Cock-Jock.

Jovan went to and fro between the window and one of
the two armchairs, between the slow, gracious heft of the
planes and the bang-slam on the screen. He wanted to
go back to his own room – Savo and the minder were
together, he was just down the corridor – but the food
was coming to Savo's room and, in any case, Savo liked

him to be there to deal with any translation problems. Maybe the steaks were well-done; maybe there was only one bottle of wine. Jovan wanted to phone his girl in Belgrade. He wanted to put the adult movie on his own TV and watch it while he talked to her.

The food arrived and Jovan motioned to the waiter to leave the trolley in the lobby, but the man wheeled it in and past the bed, masking the TV screen for a moment. Savo and the minder leaned first this way, then that: a girl was tonguing her way down the hairless chest of some stud, now his lower ribs, now his belly.

Jovan walked across to the waiter intending to give him a tip. They stood face to face, each with his hand extended and, at first, it was all moment-by-moment.

A thud, as if something had fallen off the trolley.

The girl straddling the man, her eyes rolling up in ersatz ecstasy, her back arched.

Jovan still in the act of falling as the minder noticed that something was happening in the room.

Suitcase turning, the H&K still half-hidden under the table napkin.

Then things came in more of a rush: Savo leaping off the bed, going for the door, the minder taking two hollowpoints to the left chest that knocked a fist-sized crater out of his back, Jovan still with a trace of life in him getting up on his elbows; Suitcase noticing this and putting a fast one into the back of Jovan's head before catching Savo in the lobby with a round that ripped into his lower back, then two more on top of each other – *phat! phat!* – to the left back and the neck.

You need to be close with a silencer, which is why, with Savo, it took three.

Suitcase looked round. It was a mess. It was always a mess. There was no way to get to the door with clean shoes, so he took them off, together with his socks, and walked barefoot through the blood and brain and flecks of flesh. The bathroom was off the lobby. He went in and rinsed his feet in the bidet, then put his shoes and socks back on. He wasn't worried about leaving DNA, because you always left DNA, but in the slew and sludge of the room, it would be difficult to isolate. In any case, Suitcase had never been arrested for a crime, because he carried no allegiances and didn't stay in one place for long. A keyword for the assassin – relocate.

He returned to his room and repacked his Globetrotter. Before Suitcase had wheeled the room-service trolley into room 310, Yannis had pilfered a BLT and a bowl of fries; now he sat on the bed watching a movie and dipping into the bowl.

Suitcase joined him for long enough to share the sandwich, then they went down to the desk and checked out. It was quite usual: people from first class and club using the hotel for a few hours before their plane was due rather than sit in the departure lounge.

At the airport, they separated. Yannis got the tube into town. Suitcase caught a plane to Moscow. Moscow was a seller's market.

Death brings its own stillness to a room; most often, it brings a heavy silence, too, but the girls were still gasping and squealing, the studs still grunting and gurning. A mobile phone started to ring: Savo's; then it stopped and Jovan's began; after a moment, the minder's started up, then Savo's again; all three: different tones, different tunes. For ten minutes, the phones rang on in series like a musical canon, then they stopped. Not long afterwards, the movie stopped.

A proper silence settled.

27

Unlike the occupants of room 310, Ivo Perić picked up his phone on the second ring. He had been asleep, but woke quickly. He'd been sleeping more and more over the past few days. He wanted to find that girl, the one who had stared at him, but reckoned the odds and saw that they weren't in his favour. In a city of twelve million people, what kind of luck was it that brought her close enough to see him, but not close enough to be caught? He knew that runs of luck can go either way and thought it better to stay off the streets; but caution meant boredom and the only way to deal with that was the old routine: booze, a girl some nights, and sleep.

'Well,' the phone voice said, 'it's time. Get ready.'

Perić laughed out loud. He climbed out of bed and teased the curtain aside. It was raining: a light drizzle that the wind carried back and forth in drifts.

'I am ready. I have been ready for three weeks.'

'Good. No problems your end?'

Van Man and his friends; the girl who stared. Say nothing about them. Perić didn't want to be recalled now the hit was in sight. 'No problems.'

'That is good.'

'So negotiations broke down.'

'Negotiations seemed to go well. Then everything was . . . cancelled.'

'Cancelled?'

'In blood.'

Perić hissed through his teeth. 'I always thought it would come to this.' Hoped it would come to this, he meant. 'What happened?'

'They are all dead. All three.'

'Fuck your mother.'

'Exactly.'

'I shall enjoy this.'

'Ivo . . .'

'It's why I'm here.' He meant in London, but he might just as well have meant 'Here on earth'.

Room 310 was silent no longer. The video man and the stills man were seeking angles, members of the forensic team in their all-whites were stepping a mazy path through the gore; the exhibits officer was logging items, the doctor was instructing paramedics who were breaking out gurneys and body-bags. It wasn't Stella's team but Stella was there, along with Pete Harriman and a guy called Gary Peters, who worked for Customs and Excise. Peters had tight curly hair with a strongly defined widow's peak. As the paramedics started to lift the bodies, he turned away, screwing up his face.

'We snapped this lot coming in the day before yesterday –'

Stella was holding some prints taken from video footage that Steve Sheppard had singled out. It was the minder who gave the game away; Jovan and Savo could have been any kind of import–export execs, but you can't hide a bench-press torso in a grey suit, and even in the grainy-blurry shots Stella held, the minder's jacket seemed to be about to pop its seams.

'– they seemed likely,' Peters concluded.

Harriman was talking to the exhibits officer which reminded Stella to ask him, 'Anything on them?'

'Plane tickets. The usual. Except this one was carrying a gun.' Harriman held up a Yugoslav Crvena Zastava 7mm automatic that had been bagged and labelled.

'He didn't bring it in with him,' Peters said. 'I'll guarantee you that. And he'd've dumped it before going through to airside.'

Blood on the walls, blood-soak in the beige carpet, a fine mist of blood gone hard on the TV screen. The whole room seemed splashed and streaked. A forensic officer was collecting skull fragments, piecing and matching like an archaeologist with pot-shards.

'Reckon they're yours?' Peters asked.

'Looks like it,' Stella said. 'The minder, the gun. The fact that someone killed them.'

The officer in charge took her out into the corridor. He said, 'They're not yours. They're mine.'

DI Dave Lennox, paunchy and bald, in a plain grey suit that carried nicotine in the very weave. Little whiffs of halitosis made Stella take a step backwards. Hard-working cops, cops who stay up all night, have a problem with personal hygiene.

'That's right,' Stella agreed. 'But they're tied in to me. They're part of a case I'm working on.'

'Which means what? You're going to give me a result?' A notch on the gun, he meant, a gold star on the paperwork and with minimum effort.

'You think I've got a cast-iron theory about who did this? No.' Stella lied with a straight face and a clear blue eye. This sort of confusion was a real problem: one case

295

blurring into another. If Lennox learned what she knew about the connection to the Tanner family, he might try to shoulder her aside. My corpses, my villains.

'But you've got some kind of a theory?'

'My victim's called Jimmy Stone. So far it's person or persons unknown. There might be a connection with the Serbian mafia, but it's just a whisper. If I get more, you'll be the first to hear.'

Lennox lit one cigarette from the butt of another and exhaled: smoke with an underpinning of bad breath. 'We can work together on this, right?' Meaning, you tell me what you know and I'll keep myself to myself.

'Sure,' Stella said. 'Two-way traffic.'

Mike Sorley was leaving for the day. He looked cheerful with his big bag of goodies from Habitat furnishings: a lampshade and some scatter cushions. He said, 'I'm getting the hang of this. Visiting rights established, top-of-the-stove cooking, the sports channel.'

And you've met someone, Stella thought. She handed him a report and he tucked it into the Habitat bag. 'There's a DI Lennox,' she said, 'who needs a bit of guidance from you.'

Suddenly, Sorley looked a little less happy. 'What kind of guidance?'

'Guidance in the wrong direction. Our Serbs are now his Serbs.'

'These are the bodies at the airport hotel.'

'Those bodies, yes.'

'You think they came in for a meeting with the Tanners. A dispute with the Tanners.'

'I think it. I don't know it.'

'Your chis told you as much.'

'Only that some Serbs had arranged a meeting with the Tanners –'

'A meeting about Stevie's whores. Who runs them.'

'– but was it *these* Serbs?' Stella stood aside to let Sorley get to the door, then followed him as he walked through the empty outer office. 'If Lennox thinks the Tanners are involved, our lines are going to get tangled. Two outfits watching them, two outfits chasing the same leads.'

'So how long do you intend to keep him in the dark?'

'If we nail the Tanners, and if they did kill these guys, *have* them killed, then we solve Lennox's problem, don't we?'

'You want me to speak to his SIO. Get the airport killings put down to us.'

'On the grounds that we're halfway there.'

'Halfway?'

'More than halfway.'

'Okay,' Sorley said. 'It makes sense to me.' Smiling a sunny smile again.

Stella and Delaney kissed like friends: light contact, no hands. They drank wine and she told him more than he was entitled to know: about herself, about the carnage in room 310.

'You think Stevie Tanner killed them.'

'No. But I think he arranged it. Or one of the Tanner brothers did.'

'The minder – the guy who caught everyone's attention on the customs video – you say he was carrying a gun.'

'He was.'

297

'But he didn't bring it in with him.'

'Through the detectors? Impossible. Some guns are mostly plastic and you stand something of a chance with them, but this was nickel-plated.'

'So where did he get it?'

'Plenty of Serbs in London.'

He said, 'Are we just going to go on like this? How do you feel about it? Are you going to say something to George?'

'I don't know,' she said – an answer to everything.

Anne Beaumont asked her the same set of questions and got the same answer. This was after Stella had walked into her room and cried without pause for ten minutes.

Anne said, 'This is different. I haven't seen you like this before.'

'You've seen me cry.'

'Yes. This is different.'

'You think I'm in trouble.'

'In trouble. In crisis. Yes, I do.'

'No,' Stella said, 'I'm okay. I'm fine.' But she could feel the cracks opening.

'Is there any way you can take a break?'

'A break?' Stella laughed. 'You mean – what? – time off, a holiday?'

'I mean time to think.'

'Jesus Christ,' Stella said, 'the last thing I want to have to do is think. Think about what? Whether I fuck up my life? Whether I dump a good relationship for a passing fancy? Whether I've got the right to just wake up one morning and decide to change everything for everyone?'

London has more cars than it has road. Stella had

parked two streets away and her hair was dripping rain-water. Rainwater and tears falling into her lap.

'Of course you have the right,' Anne told her. 'Everyone has the right. If you want to change your life . . .' She broke off, because something had occurred to her. 'You're in love with him,' she said, 'don't you think?'

Stella spoke from behind her hands. 'Don't be fucking silly.'

They both knew who 'he' was. Not George.

Stella was the last appointment of the day. An hour by the clock, no more no less, except crisis doesn't have a timetable, so they kept talking. Anne put on a table lamp and Stella shifted to keep out of the light.

'There are street girls and girls in houses. It's a tread-mill. They catch everything going because they have unprotected sex – that's the selling point. They get beaten up and raped and terrorized, but they think the police would be a worse option, so they're stuck. They're slaves.' She paused. 'John's writing an article about it.'

'So his heart's in the right place.'

Stella said, 'They're all somebody's daughter.'

A silence fell in the room that someone had to break. 'It was a girl,' Anne said. 'I'm right, aren't I? Your baby was a girl.'

Stella got up and found her coat and walked back to her car through the rain.

28

A t first it had been fifteen-minute tricks because that was the trade Zuhra knew best. After a couple of days, though, a punter had asked her to go home with him. They'd agreed a price. Zuhra knew it was a risk, but she was cold and wet and business had been slow. Now she took what came: fast jobs, slow jobs; fist jobs, blow jobs. The idea was to make lots of money and try to make a connection that could get her some papers: she knew that in a free market everything was for sale; it was the democratic way. At least, now, her money was her own.

She was living in a squat and working the Bayswater Road and Queensway. The squat was fine and she paid her way, but she knew she would have to move on soon; she made people edgy. A working whore: a disease factory.

She walked the kerb for a while, but the rain was bad for business. She looked over her shoulder a lot: not for punters, they would find her; no, she was looking for something she knew she might not see until it was too late. You could spot the cop cars easily enough, and the punters' cars were obvious if you knew what to look for, but a car driven by Stevie Tanner, or one of Stevie's little helpers, might look like anything, might come from anywhere. She didn't want to see the inside of that car.

She got picked up by the park; a Cherokee: she had

to step up a long way in her fanny-wrap skirt and her high heels. She directed the guy to a certain street, but he asked her what she charged for the night.

'The night . . .?'

'Yes.'

'Go to your place?'

'That's right. How much for that?'

'You mean the night and go home tomorrow?'

'Yeah.'

She named him a price and he nodded. He asked her about a couple of things, things he liked to do, and asked if that would be okay. Zuhra told him it would be fine.

Do what you want. Kill me. I don't care

He lived in Hampstead, well off-turf, and Zuhra was grateful for that. She was grateful for the ride in the big jeep and grateful for the view of London from the hill: the lights and towers. She thought she might pretend she was on a little trip, going somewhere nice with someone she had only just met, but liked a lot.

He put some music on and poured some wine and asked her if she'd like to take a shower. She knew she had to say yes, because that was one of the things he'd asked for. His apartment was large and almost luxurious, but showed no sign of having a torture chamber, a dissecting room or a disposal chute. She took her clothes off and ran the shower and got in. He watched her for a while as she soaped herself, then got in with her. It was fine. He didn't hurt her and he didn't call her names or spit on her.

He soaped her body and she soaped his. He kissed her when he fucked her.

*

Stella sat at the kitchen table with a whisky and listened to the wind in the wires. Except the sound was in her head, in her head between her ears. She saw the tinnitus as a thin silver line stretched between her eardrums and carrying her thoughts in code. She considered that if they weren't such bad thoughts, the noise might fade a little.

It had been the worst dream of all time; she could barely manage to tell herself about it. Not that things in the dream were so different from usual, but they were clear, so achingly *clear*; and the horror was in the detail.

She needed someone to listen: not to that awful detail, but just to listen while she spoke about anything. Not Anne Beaumont. It was three a.m. for one thing; also Anne was getting close with her guesswork: too close even for a shrink. No, *especially* for a shrink. George was asleep, but she could wake him, she knew, and he would be endlessly kind. She was beginning to think of George as the kindest man in the world.

She dialled and Delaney picked up on the fifth ring. He listened on into the night, Stella's voice not much more than a hum, the low tone of the conspirator.

Zuhra woke to the sound of birdsong. The bed she was in was so big that she didn't have to touch him unless she wanted to, but she wanted to. He woke and smiled as though he knew her; he made love to her and said sweet things, then he went back to sleep while she watched the early-morning dusk grow thinner.

When he woke again, he looked panicked to find that it was broad day. She thought he might want to get into the shower again, but he shook his head and yanked the sheets off the bed, bundling them into a pillowcase.

Zuhra stood naked in the middle of the room, feeling stupid. His wife's clutter was everywhere: dressing table, closet, bedside table. He threw her clothes at her. *'For Christ's sake . . .'*

Five minutes later, she was on the street.

George was clearing Stella's glass and the whisky bottle when she made it downstairs next morning. Her mobile phone still lay on the table next to a half-eaten sandwich.

He said, 'This overtime seems to be taking its toll.'

'It's my overtime,' she told him, turning away, 'my choice, okay? My problem.'

He looked at her, then tossed the glass into the sink, where it broke. 'Of course,' he said, 'you're absolutely right, and fuck you.'

It was quite something for the kindest man in the world.

29

Mike Sorley was still looking as if he had a new purpose in life. A closer shave, a pressed shirt, and he was down to two packs a day.

'I've got our Serbs back,' he told Stella, 'for the time being. No one likes it except you and me. I've also arranged for a tax inquiry on the Tanners. They won't find anything, but it's an opportunity. Oh, and DC Greegan is back on the strength.'

'All of which means . . .'

'I've told the SIO that we're almost there.'

'Why did you do that?'

'Because we're running out of time and you keep asking me to spend money I haven't got. It was the only way to get some more of both.'

Stella hoped that she might meet the woman that Sorley had found. She wanted to thank her.

The man from the Inland Revenue was called Tony Brett: dark suit, striped tie, a hint of cologne – the real thing making a real assessment. He had taken the train up from the south coast that morning. Pete Harriman and Leon Pritchett went along as taxman's assistants. They sat on an outsized sofa in a large, airy room that Hugo Tanner liked to call his den. On the other side of a three-foot-square glass coffee table, on a matching sofa, sat Hugo Tanner and two accountants.

Brett and the accountants spoke in tax-patois, enemies on common ground. Hugo Tanner sat back on the sofa and pulled on a cigar, giving the appearance of a man with nothing to fear, which pretty much summed up his position.

Harriman took notes. Pritchett held an impressive-looking folder full of figures that might as well have been in cipher. At a certain point, he asked to go to the lavatory. On his way there, he bugged the drawing room; on the way back, he bugged the kitchen. Later, Harriman went into another room to make a call and bugged the phone. Before they left, Pritchett placed a basic adhesive bug on the underside framework of the sofa they were sitting on.

While his accountants put away their folders and laptops and Psion organizers, Hugo Tanner shook hands all round and smiled a beneficent smile. He clapped Tony Brett on the back and told him to take care. They had been out of the house for five minutes when Hugo walked to the bottom of his very large garden and made a call on his mobile phone. He mentioned that he'd had a visit from the Revenue and suspected that they had taken their snooping a bit further than usual. Although he was wrong about the personnel, the effect of his phone call was the same. The man he was talking to would take half an hour to get there and five minutes to sweep each room.

Harriman dropped Pritchett at the squad room, then drove Brett back to his train station. He asked, 'What do they squirrel away in any given year? Ball-park figure.'

'Four million, five . . . We're not sure.'

'And nothing's traceable to them?'.

'Nothing illegal. They declare income from a couple of legit casinos and limited investments. That's all. We know how it's done. The problem lies in proving that they're doing it.'

'I'm definitely in the wrong job,' Harriman observed. Then, 'If you know how it's done –'

'– why don't I do it myself?'

Harriman shrugged.

'Good idea,' Brett said. 'I never thought of it.'

Andy Greegan sat with the two desk clerks from the airport hotel while they went through mug shots that seemed to fit the physical characteristics of the two men who had checked into room 309. After they had finished, the room-service waiter looked too, as did the duty manager.

They wouldn't have found Suitcase if they'd searched for a week, because he wasn't there.

They all saw Yannis, but didn't pick him out. He was just a face in the crowd.

Denis, Hugo and Stevie Tanner were in Hugo's newly swept den, each with a VSOP and a Romeo y Julieta. They were still gangsters, but for just now they were *businessmen*-gangsters, with their brandies and cigars and formal agenda. There was only one item to be discussed: the sense of unease, the sense of menace that Stella had noticed on the street that evening when she'd encountered Katya. The sense of unease had a name: it was called Dawson. More accurately, it was Dawson and Vickers, but Tony Dawson was the man you spoke to if you had a problem, and the Tanner family did have a problem. For a month or so they had been negotiating with Dawson about trespass.

Tony Dawson and Dougie Vickers ran a business in Kilburn. For the most part, they dealt in cars. Their garages and sales rooms were on the cusp of being legitimate. Of course, they were happy to sell on vehicles that had 'modified' papers, or where the clock had been moved back fifty thousand miles, and they were specialists in what the trade referred to as 'bent metal' – cars that had been in major accidents, cars that had been written off, cars that might even be three different vehicles welded together. When you bought bent metal from Dawson and Vickers, all you saw was the paint job.

Their real business, though, where the serious money came in, was car theft. No danger of them stealing your family runaround, of course. They lifted top cars for top people: orders already placed, customers already nominated. They could have a Bentley or a Roller, a Jag or a Lexus, nicked, re-sprayed, re-papered and out of the country before the owner woke to an empty garage the next morning.

The Tanners had a reason for being interested in this operation. A fair number of the cars Dawson and Vickers wanted were parked in the rich areas of their patch. The fastest route to Kilburn was through Kensal Green and Kensal Rise. Just recently, Dawson and Vickers had received record orders and were harvesting cars at such a rate that even the cops were impressed. Impressed and annoyed. Which meant that police activity had increased; which made the girls jumpy and the minders jumpy and the Tanners jumpy.

That morning, Denis Tanner had gone a mile or two north to talk to Tony Dawson again. Tony had given him a drink, listened to what he had to say, then told him to fuck off. Stevie was eager to solve the Dawson–Vickers problem himself, but even he could see that the Tanners were going to need an unbreakable alibi.

Hugo was holding a cordless phone, looking at his brother, and waiting for agreement. He said, 'Sooner the better, right?'

'This week,' Denis suggested.

'If they can do it. If they're not booked up.'

'Where will we be?' Stevie asked.

'Anywhere visible. There's a mid-week match, isn't there?'

Stevie downed his brandy and got up for a refill. 'Fucking Tony Dawson. Fuck him.'

'They will,' Denis assured him. 'They'll fuck him, all right.'

'So I make the call?' asked Hugo.

'Yeah, sure. Fuck it. Call them. Give them the job.'

Hugo thumbed the buttons. He was calling some professional problem solvers, people who would take the weight, people who would shoulder the burden; and because problems can happen anywhere, these men were mobile; they would travel. The only place where they didn't operate was Glasgow, because they came from Glasgow. That aside, they would go anywhere, though most of their business seemed to be done in the south. They would finish the job, then catch the sleeper home.

They were known as the Boys on the Night Train.

★

Hugo made the call. Like all good businessmen, he was prepared to negotiate on the matter of cash. They fixed on a date that suited everyone: Wednesday, the day of the match.

His next call was to Yannis, because the boys on the night train would need someone with local knowledge: someone to point the finger. Yannis was freelance, so not directly traceable to the Tanners. The only people who worked for the Tanners on anything like a regular basis were the minders who watched the girls, and even they were part of a workforce that changed month by month. It meant that everyone was expendable, everyone replaceable.

Yannis said sure, he was free on Wednesday.

30

Maybe it was the clothing she wore: same as last time. She had thought to wear the black satin coat, but then remembered how the punter who attacked her had decided satin was whore's-wear.

Maybe it was the route she took: same as last time.

This was deliberate, since Stella reasoned that if her jeans and sneakers had made her anonymous before, they would do the same now; and if she lived in the neighbourhood, why wouldn't she brave the rain and go to the all-nite for milk and cigarettes?

Or maybe it was the way she looked at the girls, looked at the cars hissing by in the wet. Whatever it was made a difference, because this time one of the street-minders picked her out.

She came back on the other side of the road with her 7-Eleven bag: same as last time.

It started to rain more heavily and she turned up her collar. She was thinking about Zuhra, thinking about how solving Jimmy Stone's murder might depend on what the girl could tell her about Jimmy's connection to Stevie Tanner. She was thinking budget and paper-work.

When the car cruised up behind her and slowed, she didn't bother to turn. He must be stopping for someone else: who would pull over for a girl with a 7-Eleven bag? Something hit her, as if she had been violently jostled.

For a moment, she thought that the car might have mounted the pavement and nudged her; then she was pulled backwards, and when she opened her mouth to yell, the arm that was encircling her waist tightened, hard, taking her breath away.

The back of her head connected with the doorframe, and then she was inside and the car was moving. She heard a metallic shunt as the locks went down in unison. There were just two men, the driver and the guy in the back with her. He was wearing a tracksuit over a gym T-shirt and a pair of New Balance sneakers: Action Man. In the half-dark of the car, he raised his finger to his lips and smiled. Stella couldn't decide whether to be glad about the fact that her warrant card was in the satin coat she had decided not to wear.

She was dazed and sick from the blow to the head. Action Man started to unbutton her denim blouson and, when she pushed his hands away, stopped just long enough to slap her face, lightly. He pulled her arms free and went through the pockets of the jacket, finding a money clip with thirty pounds in it, her car keys and her mobile phone. He slapped the side pockets of her jeans, then helped her to roll on her side while he slapped the back pockets harder than he needed to tell that they were empty. He held her arms out sideways and left them there while he patted her down from neck to rump, then under her arms and over her breasts. He took his time with that.

The 7-Eleven bag was on the floor of the car. She said, 'What do you want with me? You think I'm a street girl? No. Look – I was shopping.' She said it with a breathlessness and open fear that were genuine, but all he did was raise his hand as if to slap her again, then lower it when she stopped speaking. He worked his way through the phone book listings on her mobile, but there was nothing as obvious as Detective Constable Harriman or Area Major Investigation Pool Headquarters. From somewhere down the strip there came a chorus of horns as someone went through the junction on red.

While Action Man was holding it, the phone rang. He looked at the LCD display which read 'unidentified number', then took a snub .22 from an ankle holster and opened his mouth, like a mother setting an example to the child she was spoon-feeding. Stella knew what he wanted. The barrel nudged her lips and rested on her bottom teeth. She drew her tongue back from the tang of metal. Action Man pressed OK and put the phone to his ear.

Delaney said, 'Stella? Hello, Stella?' Then came a pause, then the connection was broken.

Action Man cocked the gun, just for fun. He said, 'Hello, Stella.'

Life is a system of choices and people make the wrong ones all the time.

Tell them I'm a cop and maybe they'd have to kill me anyway. They're already guilty of kidnapping and assault. Don't tell them and the result could be exactly the same. Why do they want me? Who do they think I am?

They were on the strip in bad traffic. Thank God for London tailbacks. Maybe someone had been rear-ended coming out of the junction, because this snarl-up was serious. The lights were green, but no one was moving. Action Man said, 'Traffic shit . . .' He tossed the phone down on the seat and put the gun back in the ankle holster; who needed a gun for a street girl with bad manners?

Am I easier to kill if I'm a cop? Easier if I'm a freelance hooker looking for business in the wrong street? Easier if I'm someone out to buy cigarettes and milk, someone who doesn't matter?

It was oddly quiet, apart from the dull double-swipe of the wipers. The car slid up towards the lights as they went red. The girls were still working the kerbs, trying to decide which drivers were looking for action and which were just part of the jam. Stella thought she saw Katya leaning down to the window of a green Renault.

Here's another problem: say I'm a detective and Stevie Tanner will know we're on his patch. He'll know we're looking for something. Not the usual clear-ups by the vice squad. They're just pay-and-play. He'll start to check the back-catalogue and that could include Jimmy Stone. He'll be prepared; he'll be ready.

The lights changed and something seemed to loosen up down the line, because suddenly drivers were out of first gear and the traffic was moving at a trickle. Stella could see the junction and cars travelling fast on the crossroad. She thought she had maybe thirty seconds. She spent ten of those rehearsing what she was going to do next, thinking through the moves.

Get it wrong and there's no way back.

She leaned over and put her head on her knees, then made little gulping sounds like someone swallowing against an obstruction. Action Man said, 'Oh, shit. Hey . . . don't throw up, okay? Don't do that.' He grabbed her arm to straighten her up. She turned with him, turned towards him, and put out a hand as if to fend him off, but the hand was travelling faster and harder than he'd thought, and the fingers were forked.

Stella missed the left eye but connected with the right, her finger pointing as she'd been taught.

As if you want to go right through. As if you want to scrape the back of his skull.

He screamed and put both hands to the place and jerked back, because no one who's taken that sort of a jab to the eye can do anything else. Stella was going for the ankle holster, but Action Man was kicking out with the pain. The driver turned in his seat and grabbed Stella by the hair. She half-stood to get leverage and brought the side of her clenched fist round into his face.

It was awkward and clumsy and farcical. Action Man with his hands to his face, blood from his wrecked eye seeping from under his fingers. The driver with one hand on the wheel trying to haul Stella into the front of the car. Stella pounding at his face back-handed. All this stopped when the car side-swiped a heavily wired town jeep going in the opposite direction. Stella fell sideways, landing on Action Man then rolling away fast. The driver rose in his seat and connected with the roof of the car, a blow that seemed to compact his neck by three vertebrae.

Stella levered up the door lock. She heard Action Man say, ' . . . *can't see* . . .', then stepped out of the car as four guys started across from the jeep, all doors open, aftershock bass pounding the street. She walked down towards the junction, jostling people who had stopped to watch, and realized that somehow she was carrying her phone and the 7-Eleven bag. She could hear horns and people yelling. Someone spoke to her, but she just

314

kept walking as if all she needed was cigarettes and milk.

And to make a phone call.

There are tests you can run, party games almost, to determine what you want. What you really want.

The house is on fire: you grab something as you run from the flames: what is it?

You're in trouble and you need a refuge: where is it?

You're scared and lost and you need someone to help you through: who is it?

John Delaney poured Stella a whisky. He said, 'Did you really expect to find her?'

'Why not? She has to live. Most whores go home, didn't you know that? Most go back to whoever protects them. Whoever feeds off them. Battered wives do the same.' She laughed. 'It's a chick thing.'

She was very pale and the Scotch did nothing to bring colour back to her cheeks.

She said, 'It's stupid. I feel stupid. SO10 are good at this kind of thing. They train for it. I know I'm in a dangerous job; I just don't expect it to happen.'

'You were out on a limb: no one put you there.'

'I thought I might see her. She's my lead. She's my hot connection.'

'You could trawl the streets for her: send her description round, give a photofit to the patrol cars.'

'That way I have to make it official. Have to do the paperwork. Zuhra becomes an illegal immigrant. I thought that's what you were anxious to avoid.'

'I am. It's interesting to discover that you're avoiding it too.'

'If she's caught, other agencies are involved. I want her to myself. Exclusive. She might be able to give me the link between Jimmy Stone and Stevie Tanner. That's the agenda. Fuck immigration.'

'Look,' he said, 'it's possible she's dead. You must have thought of that.'

She held her glass out for a refill and he took it wordlessly. It was close to ten o'clock and she thought she would have to make a phone call pretty soon. She would have to call George, who these days seemed to know less and less about her life.

'We could go to bed together if you like. I thought that's what you wanted. I thought that's why you started following me around.'

He had gone to the fridge for ice. Now he handed her the glass, half-full, and she set it aside. He said, 'Let's not talk about that.'

She walked over to him and put her arms round his neck. She was shivering and the sensation ran through him like the faintest of seismic shocks. He put his hands on her shoulders, then drew her in and held her, feeling her cheek against his, cold as glass and carrying a faint dew of sweat.

She said, 'I don't care what happens.'

While Stella was walking the strip in her black jeans and sneakers looking for Zuhra, Zuhra was working the lower end of Queensway, with nowhere to sleep that night, needing to raise the money for a meal, a room in a DHSS hotel and, she thought, maybe a rock of crack to take the edge off. Things were slow and the cops were doing a loop, coming up behind the punters' cars as they slowed and giving a tap on the siren, *whoooop*, letting the red/blue lights run up and down the roof-bar.

Zuhra went into a pub and ordered a drink.

If you're selling you have to advertise. Zuhra was wearing her work clothes, micro-skirt, lamé crop-top, stiletto boots, fake fur. The barman took her money and turned away, but most other men looked up or looked round, even those who'd had their backs to her, as if the same sudden thought had surprised all of them. The women knew she was there, but they didn't look at her.

She had left the squat because no one wanted her there, though they had never said as much. Also it was a place of bad dreams. Each night she saw her sister screaming; her mother half-dead, watching as the man brought his knife to her son's throat. She would fight against sleep until her body was shaking with the need and her eyes were burning; then came the moment when she walked towards the house and heard the first sounds, saw the first lick of flame, all so real, so *close*. Zuhra had got by on two or three hours of sleep each night and she was close to hallucinating. Those terrible images, that loop-tape, stood just on the edge of consciousness, waiting to become part of a waking dream-life, and that would be unbearable. No one could live through that. She drank her drink and wanted more, wanted something stronger and better, a taste of oblivion.

When she got back to the street, someone had followed her from the bar and now he fell into step beside her, the better to do business. They stopped in a doorway while he found the money and she put it in the zipper pocket of her fake fur, then asked him where his car was. He told her he didn't have one. They walked for five minutes to find a place; it was a narrow alley at the back of a row of shops and away from streetlights; he pushed aside some garbage bins like someone opening a door on to darkness.

He was a hefty guy, his head shaved, his ears plugged by studs and rings. He wanted to touch her, so she stood there patiently like an animal being examined by a vet. He wanted her to touch him, so she tugged and stroked for a while, looking straight into his face but seeing nothing. Then he turned her and braced her against the alley wall like someone rigging a piece of machinery, and she was glad to have her back to him.

It was cold in the alley and the rain funnelled in. He was buckling his belt as she turned, hobbled by her underwear, and he hit her once, hard, enough to knock her back against the wall, then reached in towards her zip pocket. When she struggled, he hit her again and she went down, legs splayed, her mouth and nose running red. He had the money in his fist, balled up ready to hit her even harder if she got up, but she didn't. She stayed there, long after he had gone, sitting bare-arsed in a puddle of trash and rainwater, feeling the throb and grate of her broken nose-bone, thinking that this was what she'd always expected; this was what she deserved.

She walked through the rain down to Hammersmith and through the Broadway until she came out on to the bridge. She wondered whether death by drowning was an option for strong swimmers. Wouldn't they automatically swim, just *swim*, wouldn't instinct take over? Not that this was going to be a problem for Zuhra, because she couldn't swim a stroke.

She had heard it was a gentle way to die. Gentler, anyway, than a bullet to the back of the head. Gentler than a knife sawing at your throat. Those images circled in the air like malevolent birds: their cries were her father's screams. Rainfall on the river was smoke as it rose from the house. She saw everything plain; she saw Perić's face as he walked towards her hiding place.

It would be good to die, she thought, but not yet. She took out the mobile phone that Delaney had given her. Although she had barely used it, the battery was very low. Enough for one call, perhaps.

31

Stella walked naked from the shower into the bedroom. The claw marks on her neck had faded to pale pink, but the bites on her back had kept their sickle shapes and were still rimmed with purple. Her body was firm, her breasts high and rounded, thighs smooth, arse sitting pretty; maybe a little extra weight around the hips that gave a small pout to her belly: erotic, even if she didn't think so. Any man would have thought himself lucky.

George watched as she pulled on a T-shirt, then got into bed and sat cross-legged under the duvet with a pile of reports in front of her. They were living in a land of permanent truce and he wasn't sure why, or how they had got there.

He said, 'What's happening?'

She said, 'We've hit a wall.'

She thought they were talking about the Jimmy Stone case; he thought they were talking about their relationship. Then she said, 'Hence all the overtime,' and he saw what she meant.

'What happens if . . . nothing happens?' he asked.

'The money stops and we run out of time.'

'Case closed.'

'Yes.'

'How long have you got?'

'Not long.' She was flicking through the reports, talking to him but not looking at him. He moved closer to her and slipped his hand under the T-shirt to rub her back. The scar tissue was lumpy under his fingertips. Stella continued to read but the words didn't register.

If I had made love with John Delaney tonight – what would I do now? What would I feel?

George's hand moved across her ribcage to the underside of her breasts.

Would I let this happen? Would I enjoy it? Will I now?

The reports slithered to the floor as her legs parted. George moved on her slowly and gently, his face in her hair. Her mobile rang, but she ignored it.

When Delaney got to the bridge, Zuhra wasn't there. He stared down into the water as if he might see her face, illuminated by the bridge lights for a moment, then brimming, then gone. On the north side there were houses and pubs and boat-stores. A few dedicated drinkers were leaving the nearest pub; a man was walking his dog; someone came up fast on a bike and disappeared under the far end of the bridge. On the south side, the towpath was dark apart from a single soft glow between trees at the curve of the river.

He parked and started towards that light. The rain had faded and a warm wind was funnelling along the river and shaking the trees. He went ankle-deep in puddles and once skated along on a mud-slick waving his arms to keep a balance. The light came and went with the contour of the path. He knew what it was.

They were tucked into a little horseshoe clearing behind the trees that bordered the main path, four of them sitting round the fire on sacks and broken cardboard boxes: the city's outcasts living on the fringe, on the edge of things. Delaney stood a few feet back from the circle and waited until one of them half-turned and stared at him. It was dark under the tree canopy. The wind tossed the flames of the fire and shadows flashed in the clearing.

A plane went over, low, following the course of the river, then there was a backwash of silence. The one who had turned to look got up and walked towards him.

'I am here,' she said.

He took her into the bathroom, where he bathed the blood from her face and put some antiseptic on the cut to her mouth, then she stripped where she stood and got into the shower. When she emerged, he handed her a drink which she swallowed in one, holding the glass out for more. He sat her down and tested the swelling on her nose with his fingertips: the merest touch. She winced and pulled back.

'It's broken,' he said.

'I know this.'

'It needs to be set.'

'A private clinic maybe? Where your royal people go?'

'Is there anything you need?'

'Food, more whisky, drugs. You have any drugs?'

'No.'

'It is a shame.'

He made pasta with sauce from a can and put a ready-made salad into a bowl, then sat with her while she ate. She smoked and drank whisky between mouthfuls as if she were keeping several appetites at bay.

'I'm glad,' he told her, 'that you didn't kill yourself.'

'Why?'

'Just . . . glad.'

She looked at him. 'That is very polite.'

He smiled. 'Okay, I'm sorry. Why didn't you?'

'The water was moving quickly. You could see shapes. It looked very nice.' She paused, looking for a better word. 'Looked like sleep was underneath.'

'And so . . .?'

She told him about coming home that day when there was silence round the farm, no one working, then the first lick of fire and the screaming. And the rest. She told him about the man who had used the knife and the gun with such calm delight, whose face she had seen so clearly as he walked towards the store-barn where she was hiding. She spoke about the morning when she was on her way to meet him and Stella and happened to glance sideways at the window of a branch of Starbucks where people were drinking their morning coffee.

'He saw me and he knew. It was in my face. I ran away and I thought just to stay hidden, to make money if I could, maybe find someone who gets me the papers I need. Then I thought, maybe it is best to die. Everybody else is dead. Then another thought – this man – he can be found if he is here. Will someone help me find him?'

'Who?'

'This Stella. From the police.'

Stella woke at three and remembered the unanswered call on her mobile. She picked up the phone and dialled for her messages. Delaney's voice said, 'Zuhra's here. She's at my flat.'

Stella opened the bedroom door and switched on the hall light so that she could see well enough to gather some clothes. George shifted in his sleep, turning towards her. She paused, then picked up her shoes and sidled through the door.

She left a note on the kitchen table and closed the front door by degrees. George heard the final click. He heard her car door slam and the engine start. He waited until she had driven off, then switched the light on and got out of bed. Downstairs, he found the note, then poured himself a drink and took it into the living room.

TV was *Judge Judy* or *Snowboard World Cup*. He watched without seeing. This small-hours existence was a life anyone could lead.

Stella let herself in and found them asleep together, he leaning back into the corner of the sofa, she lying half on top of him, face-up. His breath was lifting a strand of her hair. She closed the door hard and they woke.

They talked for an hour, then Zuhra went into the bedroom and fell asleep again. They had talked about the man in Starbucks and about what had happened to her family in Bosnia. They had talked about Stevie Tanner. Zuhra had known Jimmy and she knew Stevie, but, apart from the fact that Jimmy had sometimes hired on as a minder, she didn't know much.

'Stevie Tanner, this is the man who makes the money. He owns the girls. He holds the agreements they make to repay their travel costs. Ten, twelve thousand pounds. This they can never do. So they must work for Stevie Tanner. Also they are in fear. But he is not down on the street. He is not the one who does the beating of girls who run. If he killed Jimmy, I don't know. Maybe they had row or something.'

She had paused, then said, 'You will find him?' She had meant Ivo Perić.

Delaney said, 'She trusts you. She's decided to trust you.'

'Okay,' Stella said, 'that's fine. Except there doesn't seem to be a damn thing she can give me that will put Stevie Tanner and Jimmy Stone together.'

'She's linked Tanner to the illegal girls – these so-called contracts.'

Stella laughed. 'Jesus, Delaney, you're the guy writing the article. Can't you see: Tanner's built a brick wall between himself and the street girls. They work as free-lances; the contracts mean nothing. It's only the girls who don't know that. They might get picked up and fined sometimes, or the minders pay the bill. If you clear an area, they shift a couple of streets. If you take one batch of girls off the street for a few days, others arrive, same stretch of kerb, same prices, same country of origin most probably. No one talks because no one wants to die. I know what Stevie Tanner does, Vice know, you know. If you want to finger him in your newspaper story, fine, go ahead. It might wreck his reputation among your readers, but it won't put him in jail.'

'What about this guy she saw in Starbucks?'

'Yeah,' Stella nodded. 'A Serb. The Belgrade connection? I don't know . . .'

There was a touch of grey in the sky and a touch of orange; you could hear birdsong along with the dawn traffic. Stella's eyes felt grainy. She wondered if George's smell was still on her.

'There are some photographs I want her to see.'

'Can she see them here?' Delaney asked. 'Not at the nick?'

'You think I'm going to arrest her?'

'No, I don't. But I think she comes from a place where you go into police stations and don't come out. I think what happened to her must have been pretty much unendurable: I don't see how you get through it, how you stay sane. Then you hand some bastard all your money, and when you make it to the land of fucking promise you're so traumatized, so in fear of authority, so terrified of a beating, that scumbags like Stevie Tanner can put you to turning four tricks an hour every waking moment.'

'Listen – don't you think I feel for her? You're talking to a woman.'

'I'm talking to a *police*woman.'

He wished he hadn't said it, but too late, too late.

Stella pulled the parking ticket off her windscreen and drove the mile to AMIP-5 in a record twenty minutes. It gave her enough time to make an audiotape for Sue Chapman to transcribe: an update for Sorley on Zuhra and the man in Starbucks. A postscript marked for Sorley's eyes only said: *You promised to give me leeway with Zuhra Hadžić. I still need it. I'd like this report to be confined to AMIP-5 officers.*

Leon Pritchett wasn't at his desk, but he was a good exhibits officer and his filing was meticulous. Stella took out the morgue photos of the three Serbs and slipped them into a brown ten-by-eight envelope. She felt suddenly dizzy and a thread of bile rose in her gullet: the effect of the blow to the head as she was being pulled into the minders' car, perhaps; or the effect of Zuhra Haždić's story.

She got a glass of water from the cooler and sat at her desk. Either people were on a break or she'd wandered on to the *Marie Celeste*. Pete Harriman came in and glanced across as if surprised to see her.

'Sorley was looking for you.'

'Okay. Tell him I'll be back.'

'They found the bugs.'

'What?' It took her a moment to connect.

'Either they sweep on a regular basis, or they swept because we'd been in. Hugo Tanner's place – they found the bugs.'

'That's terrific,' Stella said. 'Now they know we're interested.'

'No. They think we were the Revenue.'

'You think that's what they think. What does Sorley want?'

Harriman shrugged, then glanced round the office. 'This is beginning to look like an unsolved. Jimmy Stone was a small-time lowlife. People are beginning to wonder whether he's worth the bother.'

'He's not. The Tanners are.'

'Is it a war,' Harriman wondered, 'or a vendetta?'

Stella ignored him. 'We've got the airport bodies,' she said. 'It's all part of the same problem. Who's chasing that?'

'Greegan and Sheppard. One at the embassy looking at visa applications, one tracing people who were guests at the hotel that day.'

'They were here for a meeting with the Tanners. They wanted to up the ante: maybe even try to run the girls

327

themselves. We know that. The Tanners had them killed.'

'I believe you. Where's the evidence?'

Like everyone, it seemed, Andy Greegan was out of the office, so Stella called him on his mobile to tell him that she needed him and his laptop. She hesitated for a moment, then gave him Delaney's address.

Harriman gave her a sideways look and asked if she wanted to share it with him: whatever it was. She showed him the audiotape, then put it on Sue Chapman's desk with a Post-it note.

'Read this,' she said, 'then let Sorley have it. And tell Sheppard to stop making a meal of it. And ask Leon Pritchett where the fuck he was when I needed him.'

When Stella got back to the flat, Delaney was out. Zuhra was lying on the sofa watching daytime TV and eating fruit. The fruit bowl was on the table in front of her as if she needed to keep a supply to hand. Delaney's Scotch was there for just the same reason. Stella opened the brown envelope and put several photos down on the table. Sam Burgess had made a good job of cleaning the men up and making them look a little more like themselves. He'd even managed to jigsaw Jovan, who had taken a head shot.

Zuhra set her apple aside and picked up her drink. She stared at the three faces, dead faces, her free hand shifting the photos, rearranging them, as if to cast them in a better light.

'I don't know these two.' She meant Jovan and the bodyguard. 'I know him. He is Savo Branković.'

'How do you know him?'

'He made arrangements for me. He tells me that I will have visa and permit, that I will work in a hotel cleaning rooms, then maybe later I will be waitress. It is easy to get here by truck and boat. Fifteen thousand Deutschmarks.' She looked at the half-closed eyes, the slack jaw. 'I am glad that he is dead. Good news. How did he die?'

'Someone shot him.'

'Who?'

Stella shrugged. 'Not sure.'

'Stevie Tanner?'

Stella hesitated. In her mind's eye there was a little drama in which Zuhra took fright, ran away, hit the street again, was picked up by Stevie Tanner, suffered great pain, told him everything she'd learned.

She said, 'We don't know.'

It was just before noon and Zuhra was drunk on Delaney's whisky, though her speech was steady and her eyes seemed clear

Stella said, 'I have to go now, but Delaney will be back soon.'

'Where is he?'

'I don't know, but he'll be back.'

'After they had gone,' Zuhra said, 'I buried my family. I buried my grandparents and my mother and my brother and my sister. They had cut her.' She made a sweeping gesture that went from her ribs on one side, curved down to her groin, then rose again. 'My father I could not bury until the fire had stopped and the house had cooled. I waited that day and that night and half the next day. There were burnt chairs and burnt wood from the roof –' She paused and looked to Stella for the word.

'Rafters.'

'Okay, rafters, and the same from the floor and there was my father, but all looked the same, like burnt wood. Except his head.' She tilted the bottle and filled her glass. 'I buried them all, but I said no prayers.'

Stella stood by the window and looked out. She said, 'I have to go.' Zuhra's face was a misty reflection in the glass.

'That man,' Zuhra said, 'he sits in a café drinking his coffee and eating *pecivo* like there is nothing to fear. Like he is ordinary man.'

Stella watched sunlight picking out raindrops on the glass. Zuhra lifted the bottle once more. Only now, after the fifth drink, was there a slur to her voice.

'Except his head . . .'

32

'The hand-to-hand was in Dobrinja, but for the farm boys in the hills it was a turkey-shoot. Every crossroads had its warning painted up somewhere: *Snajper.* They could pick their pick: this person from a water-queue, that person from a group running across the road. It was target-practice. They'd've hit more, but they were pissed from breakfast time. Every target was selected, nothing random. All in all, it was incredibly personal. When they were shelling, they could look down at the city blocks, the hotels, the libraries, the apartment buildings and say, "Let's do that one. Or that one. Or that one over there."'

Tim Ross had been in Sarajevo throughout the siege, apart from a few trips home to get back in touch with his sanity. He and Delaney had found a pub close to where Ross lived. He had just returned from Israel: a life of small wars.

'We reported what we saw. Three years . . . An entire city under siege and Her Majesty's Government did fuck all, the bastards, except fanny about, tell lies and look for advantage – who to do deals with, who'd be left standing.'

Wherever they are, wherever they go, journalists build up networks: people they can call on, people who know where the bodies are buried. Ross wrote a name and telephone number on the back of one of his business cards.

'Go slow,' he said. 'Some of these guys shouldn't be here, if you know what I mean. Shouldn't be here and can't go home.'

Delaney took the card. He said, 'What's it like out there these days?' He meant the front line.

Ross grinned. 'You miss it.'

'The fuck I do.'

'You loved it. Sitting in some hotel bar with the local hooch and the local girlies, watching tracer rounds coming in, everyone living off their nerves.'

'You mean you.' But Delaney remembered those nights . . . those days of driving the jeep over back-country roads towards wherever you saw smoke or heard gunfire.

'No, you're right,' Ross told him. 'Get a wife, do the garden, put on a little weight.' He paused for effect. 'Wait to die.'

Andy Greegan set up his laptop and colour printer on Delaney's kitchen table and asked Zuhra for a colour.

She said brown.

He asked for a style.

She pulled her hair back sharply from her forehead.

He asked for a shape.

She said, 'Like this,' and held the palms of her hands close together.

He asked for a number.

'Thirty-five,' she said, 'maybe forty.'

He asked for another colour.

She said blue.

He selected and dragged, putting all that together, and she looked at the face on the screen.

'Not brown like that,' she told him. 'Lighter.'

He chose something between brown and blond.

'And not this nose. The nose is sharp but not so long. And the mouth not so thin.'

Greegan blocked and dragged. Zuhra looked again. It was no one she recognized.

'The eyes are . . .' She didn't know the word, so she drew in the air with her finger. 'They stick out.'

'Bulbous,' Stella said.

'What?'

'Bulbous.'

Zuhra laughed; it seemed a ridiculous word.

Greegan picked out a new pair of eyes. He asked about the eyebrows and the chin and the broadness of the forehead and they worked on those aspects for a while. Then they went back to the shape of the face, the cheeks, the jawline. Zuhra still didn't like the hair; it wasn't as full as Greegan had made it, and there was no widow's peak. And there was a continuing problem with the nose and the eyes. Particularly the eyes.

They took a break for coffee, then went back to it. After a while, the eyes came right, then the nose. Greegan painted some stubble on the cheeks and chin. Stella noticed the tension in Zuhra's gaze as the man emerged.

She asked for a little more eyebrow and a little less chin. Greegan made those changes and a silence settled in the room. Zuhra stared at the face unblinking, though there were tears on her cheeks and her mouth had found an ugly shape.

'This is him,' she said. And spat on the screen, trembling.

*

333

The mid-week match was an international qualifier and the hoolies had dressed for the occasion. Dressed down. Most of them were stripped to the waist, but carried their scarves and club shirts in their hands. They wore nose rings and lip studs, eyebrow hoops and tongue bars. Their faces were painted in tribal colours and their tattoos told the same story: a union flag with a fist in the middle, with a dagger in the middle, with a swastika in the middle. They chanted and clapped their hands to the rhythm of the chant, like warriors beating their shields with their spears. In truth, they didn't really know what they wanted or hoped for or hated, but they knew it came with blood.

Denis, Hugo and Stevie Tanner got out of their XJS at the gate, deliberately blocking the road. A police officer on horseback waved a riot baton at the car and told them to move it. The Tanners gave him a hard look, then Stevie leaned down and nodded to the driver. Hugo smiled at the copper and gave a friendly wave of the hand: Don't worry, we're out of here . . . But they stayed still long enough to be sure that the surveillance camera had them all nicely framed.

They sat in the west stand, where they always sat, among people they knew. Twenty people, maybe thirty. They bought drinks for the row. They cheered and swore and yelled advice.

The hoolies were a red, white and blue phalanx behind the goal. They sang war-songs and held their scarves aloft like banners.

Yannis had provided a people carrier that held seven men: two-three-two. The three was a tight fit, because the boys on the night train were broad across the chest. The carrier had one-way windows; you might have thought it was taking celebrities to a tinseltown rave.

There was a battle-plan for this and it involved classic infiltration techniques. They always travelled separately or in twos. They ignored each other when they got to the mainline London station. Some took the tube, some the bus; no one took a cab; and they regrouped at an agreed spot fairly close to the strike point. In this case, a side street just off the Uxbridge Road. Yannis was driving the carrier. One of the boys on the night train was carrying a small, boxy leather case of the sort airline pilots use. He put this under his feet as they swung down to Shepherd's Bush roundabout.

Dawson and Vickers. They had two calls to make. Vickers was first. He lived in a new development in north Kensington and Yannis was there with the boys on the night train because he had spent some time making himself familiar with the geography and with the routines of Dougie Vickers and Tony Dawson. It was a difficult operation, because the boys couldn't take one man without taking the other, but they weren't going to be found together. Dougie was going to be at home, because it seemed he was always at home. He had a state-of-the-art DVD set-up and a new girl, and he liked to order in. Tony would be at the pub. The timing was critical, because they had to take both men while the football match was still in progress.

Yannis stopped the carrier on the opposite side of the road to Dougie's house and some fifty feet back. It was almost eight-thirty and still light, but it was a quiet road, the sort of place Dougie Vickers had always wanted to live: trees, smart conversions, a long line of late-registration cars. The boys dipped into the pilot's bag and came up with a weapon apiece: all silenced, all rapid-shot.

When the street was empty, three of them walked up to the house like guests to a party and rang the bell. No ski masks, no haste; it didn't take much skill because if you ring someone's doorbell, they usually answer, and you put one of the boys out front, one to either side, and whoever answers the door, you shoot that person first, but you don't stop there because the idea is to keep the thing contained, to keep it bottled.

The boy out front smiled at the pretty woman as she opened the door and shot her before she could speak. There might have been something about his face, something she could read there, because her mouth had opened wide as if she might be about to yell, rather than ask him what he wanted. He shot her once through the chest, and she gave a sharp cough, then sat down hard, arms and legs straight out like a doll's. He stepped into the hall, putting a second bullet into the top of her head as he went. The two back-up boys came in after him and closed the door. The first slug had moved her a step or two back along the hall, so there was no obstruction and the whole thing was over in eight seconds.

They found Dougie watching a big-screen DVD with a friend and shot them both where they sat. The friend saw them first, but had no time to get up. Dougie caught his reaction and turned in his chair, which was all he had time to do. The boys shot Dougie and Dougie's friend a total of fifteen times because the angles were all wrong and these guys had their backs to the action. There

336

was a pause after the disabling shots had gone in, and secondary shots to the chest; then they topped each man off with a bullet to the back of the head.

Yannis had brought the carrier up so that it was directly opposite the house and one of the boys who had stayed in the vehicle got out to survey the street. When the front door opened, he nodded and held up a hand. The other three ambled across the road and climbed aboard. No one spoke, but one of them laughed as if he were remembering a good joke.

Tony Dawson was more of a problem, but only in logistics. One theory was wait for him to leave the pub and then do him. This wasn't going to work, because he had to die while the Tanners were at the match. Another theory was wait for him to go to the lavatory, follow him in, catch him with his cock in his hand. This would work, but it meant that one person, at least, had to be in the pub for an extended period. Sure, they could work a rota system, but there was still an unreasonably high chance of someone being able to give a description later. So they decided to steam the place. They'd done it before and it worked, but, more than that, it was a real eye-opener. It was a *blast*.

One went in and took a fix on where Tony Dawson was sitting: at a booth with two women and another man. A surplus of three: you could call them the anonymous dead. He got back into the people carrier and described the layout to the other boys, then they crossed the road, went into the pub and, without breaking their stride, shot everything to shit including Tony Dawson.

Three of them took chunks out of the walls and ceiling

while people ran or hit the floor, the other three poured funnel-fire into the booth. Tony died with a glass in his hand and an unfinished sentence on his lips. The three with him died. Two people in the booth directly behind him also died. Seven were wounded.

The noise was deafening and then it was over. This one had taken twelve seconds, from start to finish. Yannis had the carrier at the kerb. The boys piled in and he made a fast U-turn. They put their guns back into the pilot's bag, then, like chimps grooming, checked each other for wet stuff. Then they passed round an aerosol can of deodorant and each unbuttoned his shirt just enough to be able to get a couple of good squirts under the armpits and round the chest. Under the sweet odour of the spray lay the sharp tang of cordite.

Yannis drove the carrier back to the pick-up point: a side-street cul-de-sac. He seemed calm, though he was fizzy with adrenalin. He asked them what it had been like, but no one replied, not even when he pressed them, not even when he tried to encourage them with a couple of jokey remarks. He told them about the hit at the airport hotel, making a good story of it, but they kept their silence.

They slid the doors open as soon as he parked. The last man out shot Yannis twice in the back and once in the head. 'No witnesses' was part of the deal they had agreed with Hugo Tanner.

Cops and journos have a good deal in common: their secret informants, their inside knowledge, their way of standing outside the law. Also they do a lot of business in pubs.

Tim Ross's contact was Goran No-name. Just Goran, he said. Delaney bought him a drink and they sat together at the corner table of a vast, shabby pub in the hinterland of Maida Vale. It was early and they were the only customers. There was loop-tape music, two fruit machines that played their own frantic tunes and, at the far end of the room, a stage hung with rippling fairy lights. On the stage was a drum kit. The whole place could have been an example of installation art, including the two men in the corner, one sipping his drink and waiting while the other stared at a colour print of a man with fair hair, pushed back, a narrow face and slightly bulbous eyes.

Goran laid the print back on the table with considerable care. He said, 'He is in London?'

'That's right.'

Goran spoke softly, like a man used to subterfuge. 'You have business with him?'

'Sort of.' Goran raised an eyebrow. 'On behalf of a friend,' Delaney said.

'I think perhaps your friend is no friend of this man '

'You're right.'

They were going through an oblique process of elimination. In Goran's world, everyone had a story, but no one was obliged to tell it.

'Okay,' Goran said. 'Okay . . .' He got up and went to the bar for two more drinks, waving aside Delaney's offer to pay. When he returned, it was with another question: 'Police also . . . They want him?'

'Yes.'

'Not for war crimes?'

'No.'

Goran nodded. 'I, too, would like to meet this man. Perhaps you will find him first and let me know.'

'I can't do that.'

'You are working with the police.'

'In a way.'

'In a way is not *yes*. In a way is *I make the rules.*'

'All right,' Delaney said, 'put it like this. If you give me information about where to find this man, I shall hand it over to the police. My guarantee to you is I won't say where it came from.'

'You protect your sources . . .' Goran gave the ghost of a smile.

'That's right.'

'Democracy is a wonderful thing.'

'That doesn't stop you looking for him if you want to – now you know he's here.'

'I do not have the resources of the police.'

'Which is why you should leave it to them.'

'Okay . . . Okay . . .' Goran's voice was almost a whisper, but his eyes were glittering with anger. 'This man should die.' A pause, then: 'I don't know where he is. If I knew, he would be dead. Or I would be dead.'

'So,' Delaney said, 'who is he?'

'Ivo Perić.' Goran grimaced, then took a sip of his drink and washed the liquor round his mouth. 'You have heard of a man called Zeljko Raznatović?'

'No.'

'His other name is Arkan.'

'Yes,' Delaney said, 'I've heard of him.' Arkan and his 'Tigers' were a group of paramilitaries, the worst of them, the most brutal, the most voracious. During the Bosnian war, these men woke each day with nothing much on their minds but rape and murder. Nothing on their minds but fun. 'He's dead.'

'Yes, he is dead. The world is a lighter place. But his men are not dead.'

'This man . . . Perić . . .'

'He was with Arkan.'

Delaney told him what had happened at the farm: Zuhra's story.

'I do not know about this particular case, but, yes, I do know it because it happened all the time and everywhere.'

He fell silent for a moment, seeming to concentrate on the flicker and flash of a fruit machine: its sunken pirate ship, its gold doubloons.

'Like many of the mass murderers from our war, Perić has a new profession now. After the Second World War, many Nazis got their old jobs back, or found new opportunities. Those who were SS, those who ran concentration camps: industry was waiting for them, a new world to be built. Werner von Braun goes to America and becomes rich scientist and TV personality.' Goran smiled and shook his head. 'Do you ever ask yourself how these things happen? It is a mystery. The human heart is a mystery.'

'Money, isn't it?' Delaney offered. 'It all comes down to money and expediency.'

'Yes . . .' Goran nodded. 'Money is the greatest mystery.'

'What is it, this man's new profession?'

'Ah . . . In some ways, not so new. He kills people.' Goran laughed. 'For money. He is assassin. Some say it was he who killed Arkan.'

The loop-tape was soupy ballads, 'Moon River' too

loud and too long. The fruit machines played electronic scales. A man came out from the back and moved the drum kit a few inches to the left: the curator, perhaps, re-siting the exhibits.

'If Perić is in London,' Goran said, 'he is here to kill someone. I guarantee.'

Everything seemed satisfactory. Dawson and Vickers closed down for good; the Tanners secure on CCTV tapes and surrounded by witnesses; the match ending in a three–nil victory for the home side; hoolies crammed into pubs the length of the King's Road singing songs of violence and patriotic gore; the boys on the night train actually on the night train and bound for home.

Just one glitch, one fly in the ointment. Yannis wasn't dead. He had two bullets in his back and one in his head, but he wasn't dead.

After the boys on the night train had left, Yannis had stirred. He'd been unconscious for three minutes and bleeding heavily. He couldn't move, but he could see. The impact of the bullets had thrown him off to one side, so that he was lodged half-upright against the driver's door. His peripheral vision had closed down, as if he were looking through a mask with tiny holes for the eyes, but his head was cocked sideways and he could see the ignition key.

He was lying on his right hand and there was no possibility of freeing it because his torso was dead; his body was dead. Just his eyes were alive, his eyes, his mind and a small part of his left hand. He reached out, letting his fingers fall against the key. That was enough for a while. If he looked down, he could see blood splashes from his chest hitting the same spot on his thigh, one every three or four seconds. He knew that there had been blood flow from his head because he could taste it, but it had dried on his cheek along with a little slurry of bone and tissue.

Three times he tried to turn the key, but his fingers fell away. The fourth time, he attempted to lurch forward to lend his hand impetus. There was no movement in him, but it might have been that the thought of it gave him added strength because the key turned. While that strength remained, he flopped his hand against the indicator stalk. Just that – a motionless vehicle with darkened windows, parked up with its left indicator flashing.

It was ten minutes before a man passing by noticed and thought to worry about the battery. He tried the door and found it unlocked. When he opened it, Yannis fell out into his arms, sending his rescuer to the ground. They lay there a moment, Yannis staring up at the darkening sky while the man struggled out from under, whimpering with shock.

The paramedics had him as a certain DOA, but Yannis didn't die. He was refusing to die. When he slipped into a coma, he was entering a twilit world where the not-quite-dead live; the not-dead-yet; the undead.

The police, knowing a gangland hit when they saw one, put an officer outside his room and admitted that they were playing a waiting game. Because Tony Dawson and Dougie Vickers had been murdered the same day, the AMIP squad handling the case made Yannis their special responsibility. No one made the connection with the airport killings. Why would they?

33

Since Zuhra had moved in, Delaney's flat had become almost neutral territory. It was eleven a.m. Delaney and Stella sat on bar stools either side of his kitchen work-counter and drank coffee and talked about her like anxious parents.

'She's sleeping,' Delaney said. 'She sleeps all the time.' He had given up his spare room to her: his office. The sofa bed was permanently down and the room in darkness most of the day. 'It's restorative,' he added. 'She's healing herself, don't you think?'

'Or depressive,' Stella said. 'People who are depressed sleep a lot.' She paused. 'You can't cure yourself of what she's been through, can you? There isn't a cure for that.'

'Not a cure, no. You might find a way of dealing with it, perhaps.'

Stella shrugged. 'I don't think so.'

An insight touched him. 'You know about this.' She didn't answer. 'After the case where the children . . . where she hanged the children . . . the sister . . .'

'Bonnelli,' Stella said.

'After you lost your child.'

'It wasn't the same as being in a fucking war.'

'I don't say it was. I'm talking about sleep equals depression. That's how you know.'

'Yes, all right. That's how I know. I went to bed with the intention of never getting up.'

'Why did you – get up?'

'Sometimes I wonder.' As if to show that it wasn't a flippant remark, she added, 'I can't remember.' She picked up the computer graphic of Ivo Perić and stared at it. 'Have you told her his name?'

'Yes.'

'What reaction?'

'I think it made things better and worse. Better to have a name for the devil, worse because it gives him an identity: a personality. As if he had a life outside the murder of her family.'

'Which, of course, he does. A purpose, anyway.'

They had spent the last hour talking it through. Stella had arrived at the flat and Delaney had told her about his meeting with Goran No-name, and they had reached a conclusion almost at once. They'd kept worrying at alternatives in case they were wrong, but there were no alternatives, not really.

'The Tanners are importing girls from the former Yugoslavia. The girls are supplied by the Belgrade branch of the Serbian mafia or whatever they like to call themselves –' this was Delaney going through it one more time – 'who think they deserve a lot more of the action. They fix up a meeting with the Tanners but know full well that they might get stiffed. They do get stiffed: terminally. So it's Plan B.'

Stella nodded. 'Perić would have been put in earlier, so he was in place if needed. A sleeper. He's here to kill someone if things go wrong. They have. So I imagine he's already been given an instruction to go ahead.'

'The Tanners,' Delaney said.

'Maybe one of them: to show class. To issue a warning. Stevie, perhaps; he runs the girls.'

'Maybe all of them.'

'Maybe.'

'Because I don't see the murder of Stevie bringing the others back to the negotiating table.'

'Who knows. Gangland business – it's realpolitik. Whatever works.' Stella was already framing the report in her head. She would be asking Sorley for more money, more time, but now she had a good reason.

'What about Jimmy Stone?' Delaney asked. 'You're putting him down to Perić, right?'

'It makes sense. There's a two-way link. Jimmy worked for the Tanners, but he was a chancer. Perić would have needed someone who could give him information about his targets. Knowledge is power. Perić makes a friend of Jimmy, gives him money, too, I expect. Jimmy's talking, Perić is listening; this goes on for a couple of weeks until Perić hears something crucial, something that gives him the opportunity he'll need if he gets instructions to do the job.'

'What?'

'Exactly. What? I don't know. The other thing I don't know is when Perić is likely to make the hit. The negotiators are dead; I'm surprised it hasn't already happened.'

Zuhra came into the room, looked round and left. She could have been sleepwalking. Stella thought that it was almost possible to see the dreams circling the girl's head.

'What's going to happen to her?' Delaney wasn't so much asking a question as seeking a promise.

'You're looking after her,' Stella said. 'She'll be fine, won't she?'

She kissed him goodbye and he kissed her back.

Pete Harriman and Steve Sheppard organized a limited house-to-house in the streets close to where Jimmy Stone and the Deevers had been found dead. Stella went to see Mary Callaghan. Like the officers working the area, she was showing the computer-fit of Ivo Perić.

Mary said, 'I thought that was all over and done with.' She meant murder and undeclared rents, but mostly undeclared rents.

'Oh, no,' Stella said. 'These things stay on record for a long time. For ever . . .'

Mary looked at the likeness of Perić and said she'd never seen him. Stella was pretty certain that Mary thought it the safest thing to say.

Harriman and Sheppard had better luck: two positives and a maybe, all from close neighbours. One of the positives was from the man who lived in the flat below Jimmy Stone's. He'd seen Jimmy and Perić together a number of times. 'Couple of drunks,' he said, 'falling up the stairs, laughing. No consideration. I told them . . . bloody noise.' He pointed to the computer-fit of Perić. 'He raised a hand to me. Bastard.' Harriman could see the memory of fear in the man's face.

Mike Sorley looked at the reports – of the house-to-house, and of Delaney's meeting with Goran No-name, which, in the telling, had become Stella's meeting with Goran No-name. He said, 'How in hell do you expect to keep this girl –' he shuffled paper – 'Zuhra out of the picture if she can ID your assassin?'

'I don't. What I want is something in exchange for her testimony – when the time comes. I don't see how Immigration can refuse.'

'No? They can refuse anything. What will you do about the Tanners?'

'Do about them . . .?'

'You're pretty sure that one of them at least is about to be murdered by a professional assassin. You wouldn't think of warning them at all?'

'I've no hard evidence.'

Sorley smiled. 'So they're bait.'

'It's all guesswork, boss, isn't it?'

'If you want it to be.'

'But I think we ought to keep an eye on them. If I'm right, then where they go, Ivo Perić is likely to follow.'

'We tried bugging them. It was money down the drain.'

'Their movements, at least. If we can't get them on tape, at least we can know where they go and what they do.'

Sorley looked dubious. 'For a limited period,' he warned. 'Jesus . . . cash and paperwork, cash and paperwork.' He made a note. Reading upside down, Stella deciphered it as: *One week, tops.* 'So you've put Jimmy Stone down to this guy.'

Stella nodded. 'First it was conjecture, then it was fact. The house-to-house puts Perić with Jimmy at Jimmy's bedsitter. Perić would have made contact with people who could give him some inside track on the Tanners, and his most obvious route is through the girls, and Jimmy was a street-minder, so he adopted Jimmy. Good tactics.'

'Why did Jimmy have to die?'

'Perić got what he wanted and Jimmy was known to have a loose mouth. He's safer dead. Professional tidying.' To back her theory, she added, 'Apart from anything else, the method makes it Perić.'

'The probe.'

'Yes. Very professional.'

'So we have a prime suspect.'

'Yes.'

'And what about evidence? Got much of that?'

'There were prints all over Jimmy Stone's bedsit. There'll be DNA. We can speak of motive and opportunity. Eyewitnesses put him with Jimmy close to the time of the murder. Then there's whatever we'll find when we arrest the man – the murder weapon, Rohypnol, maybe . . .'

Sorley nodded. 'So not much, then. Nothing solid.'

Stella could see that he was right. To change the subject she asked, 'How's your new life?'

'Working out.'

'What's her name?' Stella asked.

'Whose name?' Sorley picked up the reports and started doing sums in his head. As Stella was leaving, he said, 'Valerie.'

Luck isn't a lady, isn't fickle or elusive or capricious; luck is a system. It relies on averages and percentages. No luck recently? Well, it simply means that it's not your turn. It'll come. The only problem is, it might come too late.

Stella Mooney's luck turned when a punter on the strip decided to fuck and run. The girl in the car with him happened to be Katya. When the guy had tried to take his money back and kick her on to the street empty-handed, she'd pulled her knife, and when he'd started slapping her, she'd cut him across his hands so badly that you could see the finger bones.

The driver had got out of the car and run down the road, waving his arms and screaming. If Katya had been thinking, she would have run in the opposite direction; as it was, she'd had enough of this guy with his beer gut and his bad breath, enough of the way he shoved her face down into the back seat of his car while he rammed into her and swore at her; she'd had enough of him and all the others like him, and now she'd started cutting him she thought she'd like to keep going.

Two officers in a red-stripe picked them up, the punter whirling and yelling, spinning blood from his finger-ends, Katya coming after him like the avenging angel. The coppers administered first aid until an ambulance arrived, then loaded Katya into the car. A small crowd had collected. Katya saw her minder across the street, his face like stone.

Stella and George had declared a truce, but only in the sense that a truce reminds you of conflict past and conflict yet to come. As the phone went, Stella was telling George a lie that went something like *the case, progress, result, cash, paperwork.* As she was speaking, she knew she couldn't do this much longer.

George took the call and handed the phone to Stella without speaking. The duty sergeant at Paddington nick told her that they were holding a young woman on a malicious wounding charge and had found Stella's card in her bag, a dainty rhinestone item that also held a dozen condoms, a tube of spermicidal cream, a pack of Benson & Hedges, a lipstick and a wad of tissues. The card had been tucked into a tiny pouch compartment next to a photograph of an old woman.

'Well, she is not old,' Katya told Stella. 'This is my mother. She is forty-eight.' Stella was looking at a lined face and grey hair. The mouth was trying to smile but the eyes were having none of it. 'Russia is terrific place since we got democracy,' Katya observed. 'Moscow is great city now. You can buy anything you want; all you need is money.' She laughed. 'Free market. What does that sound like to you? Market where things are free?'

Stella on one side of a table, Katya on the other, nothing between them but Katya's pack of B&H that was feeding a non-stop habit.

'The man you cut is having a blood transfusion.'

'Oh yeah? I hear English blood is full of hepatitis and cow disease.'

'He went into shock.' *And more people die of shock* . . .

'Fuck him,' Katya said, 'and fuck his mother.' She was close to tears. 'I need a deal.'

'A what?'

'I can't go back. What I did is worst thing. Bring police to the strip, cut a punter. Know what you get for this? Sawn in two pieces and put in river.'

Trolley Dolly.

'You know about her?'

'Sure, of course. Everyone knows about her.'

'No, I mean you know who she was.'

'Olga. I just know that name.'

'She worked the strip?'

'Oh, yes.'

'Who killed her?'

'Would have been Stevie Tanner.'

Stella paused. She wasn't part of the investigating team here, so her talk with Katya was by permission. Anything she learned would have to be passed on. Verbal first, then paperwork. She thought, I ought to have a tape on this, but it wasn't that kind of an interview and, anyway, she didn't want to give Katya time to think, time to reconsider.

'You know that? You know it was Stevie Tanner?' Stella held her breath.

'Sure.'

'How do you know?'

'Who else would it be?'

Stella nodded and half-smiled. She felt let down. 'I bet you're right. But you don't know, do you? You couldn't prove it to me?'

'I will say to a judge if you want. I need papers, now. I can't go back on the street.'

'You won't be on the street, Katya. There's a malicious wounding charge.'

'I go to prison?'

'Maybe. I'm not sure.'

Katya heard what lay behind her hesitancy. 'I go back to Russia?'

'Yeah, well . . . That's usually the way.'

'I die here, I die there.' Katya shrugged. Suddenly her face was awash with tears. 'What difference . . .'

'Why would you die in Russia?'

'I stole money from some people. How do you think I pay to come to England? To my wonderful new job in nightclub with new clothes and new friends and new life?' She laughed without mirth and Stella could see her mother in her. 'I say what you like. About Stevie Tanner? I say whatever you tell me.'

'We don't work that way.'

Katya gave a shout of laughter. 'You are police, yes? Every police work that way.'

'Even if I said yes,' Stella told her, 'there would have to be proof. Did you see Stevie kill Olga? Can you give us a scene of crime?'

Katya took another B&H from the pack but didn't light it. She lowered her forehead to the table, very slowly, and stayed like that, eyes closed, arms hanging at her sides. No one spoke. Stella got up and walked to the door, but an afterthought took her back. She found the computer graphic of Ivo Perić in her pocket and held it out.

'Do you know who this is?'

Katya opened her eyes and looked at the picture. She was almost too weary to be surprised. 'Oh, yes,' she said. 'This is bastard who likes to put bag on your head.'

Stella was oddly shocked that the flat should be so close to where she lived, as if by being there, in her neighbourhood, Perić had made things personal.

Katya had given them the address. SO19 had looked at the place for a day and concluded that the ground floor flat was occupied by an elderly couple and the first floor by two girls who left for work at eight and came home at six. Perić was gone. Like Suitcase, he knew the keyword for the assassin – relocate.

Stella and Pete Harriman spoke to the old couple and showed them the computer-fit. They had seen him now and then. He was a considerate neighbour, quiet and unobtrusive, even though he seemed to be at home most of the time. Was he out of work? they wondered. They thought he was probably Italian, or French.

The girls would be happy to help, they said, but hadn't known him because he'd moved out before they moved in. They were a little less happy when Stella sent in a forensics squad who took the place to pieces. The girls had been living in the flat for a week or more, so the DNA was thoroughly corrupted, but the smudges of gun oil were enough to tell Stella that she was standing in the flat where her prime suspect had once lived. The Semtex, in its greased wrapping, had left no trace.

'Which means what, in your opinion?' Sorley asked. He was referring to the gun oil.

'Which means his job is to let the Tanners know they can't fuck with the Belgrade mafia.'

'He'll hit one of the family . . .'

'Stevie is my guess.'

'You're sure about this?'

'I'm not sure about anything. But why else is he here?'

'And you're convinced he *is* still here?'

'You mean, in the country?'

'Yes.'

'Why wouldn't he be?'

'He was living in a flat in West Kensington. You found the place. He'd gone.'

'He's got a job to do. He's here.'

*

He's here, she thought. You're here, aren't you? You're somewhere in the city, probably somewhere close, somewhere nearby, because people get attached to a certain district: they know the geography, they know the shops and the cafés, they know how to work the transport system from there.

So where are you?

She was sitting in traffic on her way to an appointment with Anne Beaumont. The computer graphic of Perić's face was on the passenger seat. There he was, in the car with her, not saying much, witnessing one of the legendary London tailbacks.

You're a mean-looking bastard. You look every inch a killer to me.

Zuhra's story came back to her in jagged fragments, the mother naked and too torn up to stand; the grandfather trying to protect his wife; the brother with the knife at his throat; the screams of the sister; the screams of the father. Each little tableau had Perić somehow at its centre, both director and principal actor, but he wore the two-dimensional face of the computer-fit, its enhanced colour, its lines of assembly, its fixed stare.

What does it take to be like you? What blackness in the soul, what joy in pain?

Stella was right about the geography. Perić had relocated to a cheap hotel in Shepherd's Bush Road, the Acropolis, of all unlikely names, uncomfortable but completely anonymous, and, anyway, he wouldn't be there for long. She inched past his window as traffic filtered through towards the Goldhawk Road. She was fifty feet away from him, looking at tail-lights blurred by rain while he sat at a table with the tools of his trade before him: the Semtex, the Street Sweeper, the Militech 11mm back-up.

He liked the smell of the gun oil, muddy and slightly sweet; he liked the solid weight of the Semtex. He liked the feel of the guns, the way the mechanism on the twelve-gauge slid and locked, the way the magnum lay balanced on his palm.

There were other smells and sensations that lingered in his memory. The way a gun bucks and hammers in your hand; the smell of smoke; the smell of fear. He had felt alive, then, all senses primed. The war had made him more himself.

He put the guns and the Semtex away and stripped to put on a pair of shorts, a T-shirt and some sneakers. He felt angry, but had no focus for his anger; he felt violent but had no target; he needed a run to take the edge off his appetites.

He locked his room and went downstairs to the street. As he jogged across the road, Stella edged forward another car's length. If she had looked in her rear-view mirror, she might have caught a glimpse of him, weaving between vehicles, then turning his back and lengthening his stride as he made for Holland Park.

'You knew them because they used to be your friends. They were your neighbours and your friends. It wasn't as if they were strangers in the night. You knew them because this man's daughter had married your cousin, or this woman's husband was your father's workmate. People you see in the street, at the market, people you ride with on the bus. From your town, your village, your street.'

This was for Delaney's article. He was taping Zuhra. She was sitting with her back to him because she found it easier to speak if she had no one in view. Her voice was even and soft.

'They would come to your door to ask maybe do you have some herbs or sugar, they have run out. In the street you see them. You might stop for talk about this and that – you laugh, tell jokes against the government, ask where does the money go to . . . the sort of things people always talk. Then one day they knock at your door and when you open it they kill you. They go into your house and rape your wife and your daughter and then they cut their throats. The old people they stick like pigs. They take out all the men and boys and they dig pits and line them up by the pits and shoot them all. Shoot them all.'

Zuhra wasn't weeping and she wasn't showing anger or hatred. Her face was expressionless, like a note on one level, like white on white.

'Who are they?' she asked. 'Who are these people who one day are your friends and the next day come to torture you and kill you?'

The tape turned in silence because Delaney had no answer.

There were two big vases full of flowers in Anne Beaumont's consulting room. For some reason they made Stella uneasy. Something to do with her intimacies and confessions being muddled with everyday living. Except everyday living was exactly the issue: where to live every day, and who with.

'I've decided to leave George,' she said, and the remark surprised her, since it was the first she'd heard of it.

357

'To be with John Delaney.'

'No, to be on my own. Not with either of them. Somewhere that's no man's land.'

'You mean no *man's* land . . .?'

'Exactly.' Stella liked this: making it up as she went along. 'My own space. Then decide what to do.'

'Will you tell George about Delaney?'

'Are you supposed to ask me that sort of question?'

'Not really.'

'I won't tell him,' Stella said. 'Not at first, anyway.'

'It's the first thing he'll ask you.'

'What?'

'If there's someone else. He's bound to.'

'I'll lie.'

'You're happy with that . . .'

'Totally happy. Utterly happy, yes. Very happy with that, thank you.'

Anne laughed. 'Okay. What about Delaney?'

'How do you mean?'

'What will you tell Delaney?'

'Nothing. It's none of his fucking business.'

Anne could hear the raggedness in Stella's voice. She said, 'You're approaching a crisis, you know that, don't you? We call this a crisis: it's a technical term.'

Stella looked round the room as if she might see it coming. She asked, 'What does it mean – to sleep all the time? To just go to bed and sleep the day away.'

'Is this you?'

'No.'

'It's you, isn't it?'

'No, I promise. Someone I'm involved with professionally. A woman.'

'She's suffered a trauma . . .'

'Bosnia,' Stella said. 'She's Bosnian. Her family died. She saw it happen.'

'If it were you,' Anne said, 'wouldn't you find it easier to be asleep?'

'I guess so.' Stella paused. 'Apart from the dreams. She must have dreams.'

'Difficult to avoid them,' Anne conceded.

Stella didn't speak for a while. Then she said, 'Why the flowers?'

'It's my birthday.'

Stella put her head in her hands. She said, 'I'm really going to do it.'

Delaney rewound the final tape and listened to it from start to finish. In all, Zuhra had spoken for two hours, then she had gone back to bed.

Stella used her key like any home-coming wife. Delaney opened wine and laid out some snacks in accordance with their little evening ritual: a sacrament of sorts. He played her part of the first tape and the air was thick with images. He hadn't shaved that day and when he kissed her, she felt the scrape of his bristles on her jaw and neck. When he kissed her and, for the first time, put a hand to her breast.

Later that same evening, George was going into the bathroom as she was coming out, one of those chance meetings. He asked her if she was all right and she told him she was fine, if a bit tired what with all the overtime.

A little badge of red on her neck.

34

'They fucked up,' Stevie Tanner said. 'Pure and simple. They let us down.'

His father shrugged. 'They put two in his back and one in his head. How fucking certain do you need to be?'

'They fucked up.'

'They're a good firm,' Denis said. 'They don't make mistakes.'

'They just fucking made one.'

'In the round. They don't make mistakes in the round.'

'In the fucking round? What the fuck's that?'

'Mostly. Mostly they don't make mistakes.'

'Jesus Christ. Jesus fucking *Christ.* I don't care if they make one fucking mistake every millennium, they made one and it's one too many.'

'They've been in touch,' Denis said.

'Yeah? What did they say?'

'Offered a rebate.'

'A rebate? A *rebate?*' Stevie held his hands out and looked round, appealing to an invisible audience. 'Oh, well, that's all right, then. That's fucking handsome. That makes all the fucking difference.'

The boys on the night train had been a decision made by Hugo and Denis. They'd used them before. It had been a management decision, but *old* management. Now Stevie and his father were involved in a pissing contest that Stevie wanted to win. At the back of his mind – time for new management.

They were sitting in the kitchen at Hugo's house, where they always met. Hugo opened some beers and switched on the oven. They would have pizzas and beer for lunch. Pizza was manageable because only two procedures were involved: unwrapping and heating. More than two procedures constituted cooking. He said, 'The man's in a coma. He's got a bullet in his fucking brain. Calm down.'

'People come out of comas. They emerge. Ever heard that – *emerge*? It's what they do.'

'Sometimes,' Denis said.

'Sometimes is too fucking often for me.' Stevie took a swallow of beer, then grimaced and looked at the label. Nothing was to his liking, least of all Yannis-the-Undead. 'He's a fucking time bomb.'

'So what do you want to do?' Denis asked. 'Let's hear it.'

'Years go by, and they still emerge.'

'Right. You're right. So let's have your solution, shall we?'

'Top him. It's obvious.'

'Oh, yeah, right, why didn't I think of that?' Denis shook his head in amazement. 'You don't think the filth will be up for that? You don't think they'll be expecting someone to come round with a shooter and do the business? Nah, you're right. Why not pop over there and do him now? We'll keep your beer cold.'

'It can be done.'

Hugo was ripping clingfilm off the pizzas. He said, 'You see it in films, don't you? Some geezer dresses up

361

as a doctor, or someone turns up with a bunch of flowers and a damp hanky.' He laughed. 'I don't think so, Stevie, mate.'

'Look,' Denis said, 'it's in his brain. The fucking bullet's in his brain. Suppose he does come round – he won't know shit. He won't know who the fuck *he* is, let alone remember what happened. Don't you get it? His brain's mashed up.'

'He's going to die,' Hugo said. 'He'll never say a fucking word; not a word.'

'You think so?' Stevie asked. 'I think he'll emerge. Then we're all fucked.'

'Just keep your head down,' Hugo advised. 'They've got seven dead up in north Ken and they're looking for candidates. Stay in a few nights. Rent some videos. Help yourself to something out of stock.'

Over the next few days, Stevie did all those things and a few more. By 'something out of stock' Hugo meant the girls. Stevie ordered them up two at a time in case of disappointment; he played pool with side bets starting at five hundred; he got on to the internet and looked at gun sites and attack-dog sites; he got drunk, which was bad for his pool game and very bad for the girls.

His only trips out were to the John Peel restaurant and to Wandsworth Prison. Pete Harriman reported this to Stella. It was all he had to report.

'He went to see his brother,' Harriman told her. 'It's a regular visit. The prison staff know him.'

'Very caring,' Stella said. 'Remind me. What's his name – the brother?'

'Maurice.'

'How much longer has he got to do?'

'Not long, boss. I could find out for sure.' Harriman was lighting a cigarette with a cigarette. He said, 'I spoke to the DS who's looking at the north Ken job. They're treating all the deaths as one incident.'

'So would I.'

'They like the Tanners for it.'

'Just the Tanners?'

'Well, there are three or four firms who were looking to increase operations in the area.'

'You mean on that turf or specifically in the business of car export?'

'Both.'

'They've looked at the Tanners, have they? Where they were at the time and so forth?'

'Not spoken to them, obviously. Don't want to do too much too soon; but they've got totally impeccable alibis. They were at Stamford Bridge – any number of people to speak for them, to say nothing of CCTV footage.'

'Very convenient,' Stella observed. 'Are we getting in their way?' She meant the other investigating team.

'That's why I was talking to the DS. No, we're okay so long as we keep each other informed. They know we've got the Tanners under surveillance. If we report to them, it saves them the bother.'

'And it comes out of our budget,' Stella said. 'Okay, stay with them. Don't get close, don't get seen. I've got enough trouble with crossed lines.'

Sorley's report on the SO10 inquiry was under a pile of other stuff she didn't want to read.

'Did he eat alone at the John Peel, or did he have company?'

'He didn't eat. He went in for ten minutes, then came out again.'

'What time of day was this?'

Harriman looked at his notes. 'Eleven.'

'In the morning.'

'Yeah.'

'Did you talk to the manager?'

'No, boss. We're keeping our distance, aren't we. Stevie Tanner's a regular there. Him and the rest of the family. Ask questions and they'd get to hear about it.'

'Type it all up for me,' she said, then leaned forward, resting her elbows on the desk, and put her hands over her ears.

'Are you okay?'

'I've got this non-stop ringing in my ears and it's driving me nuts. It's there all the time. It's there waiting for me when I wake up.'

'Tinnitus,' Harriman said. 'My uncle had tinnitus.'

'Did he ever get rid of it?'

'Yeah, eventually. He took an overdose.'

They were doing lots of things to Yannis just to keep him alive. The A&E consultant had handed him over to ITC with a shrug that meant, 'A flatliner – any minute – your problem,' but Yannis was holding on. Every hour, the prognosis was a little better, though no one could say whether he would ever swim up from the black depths of coma. Whether he would *emerge*.

At some point, they would operate to remove the two bullets still lodged in his body, one just behind his shoulder blade, the other in his skull. The third had gone straight through, piercing and collapsing a lung. Yannis wasn't dead, but he was a hell of a mess.

The investigating team knew who he was – Yannis Stamas – and knew he had form, but they couldn't come close to working out why he'd been shot. The notion of Yannis as a tour guide for some hitmen was too obscure. A DC with a bright idea pulled Yannis's mug shot from the files and ran a computer check on it. The only recent match was a series of witness statements that included descriptions of a man who, with A.N. Other, had booked into the airport hotel and taken room 309. These cross-references were faxed over to AMIP-5, where Stella Mooney was writing a letter to George to tell him why she was leaving.

Sue Chapman handed Stella the fax.

Stella said, 'I hope this guy wakes up. I hope he wakes up with enough brain left to point a finger at the Tanners.'

She sat on a stool in Delaney's flat and used his kitchen work-counter as a desk. There were pieces of A4 paper laid out on which she had written certain critical facts with arrows linking them. There was an arrow going from Jimmy Stone to Ivo Perić, an arrow from Perić to Stevie Tanner, an arrow from Stevie to Savo Branković, an arrow from Branković to Yannis. She inked over the Perić–Stevie arrow to make it stand out. Then she inked over the Jimmy–Perić arrow.

'Jimmy had some information about the Tanners. That's why Perić made a friend of Jimmy, then killed him. Yannis and a person unknown popped the Serb contingent when they tried to keep the girls to themselves. Now Perić has to respond in kind. So what was it that Jimmy gave to Perić that makes his job easier?'

'A gun?' Delaney was sitting in an armchair with his laptop balanced on a board that went across the arms of the chair. He would get his work room back when Zuhra stopped sleeping.

Stella looked across at him. There they were: she with her homework, Delaney with his, a drink apiece, a picture of domestic contentment.

This is bizarre, she thought. This is seriously weird.

'He's already got a gun.'

'So Jimmy gave him a means. An opportunity.'

'Yes, that's what I think.'

Delaney pushed the board aside and walked over to where she sat to top up her glass. They were drinking Sauvignon Blanc because she preferred its tart, gooseberry taste to the buttery smoothness of Chardonnay. They had a store of little domestic intimacies like that, but had never seen each other naked.

The letter to George was in her pocket. It said everything and nothing. *I need space.* The usual old stuff.

While Stella briefed them, the AMIP-5 squad picnicked: crisps, pastries, chocolate and coffee: comfort-junk, and not an apple in sight. A cumulo-nimbus of cigarette smoke drifted beneath the ceiling.

'What it amounts to,' Andy Greegan observed, 'is using the Tanners as bait. The trouble with that is keeping tabs on all of them – not easy.'

'Not easy and expensive,' Sorley added. He was standing in the door of his office, neither in nor out: it was Stella's briefing, but he was there to do mental maths.

'There's another issue,' Stella said. She was raising a concern of Sorley's. 'If we think these men are in danger, especially Stevie Tanner, should we warn them?'

There was a pause before Steve Sheppard said what they were all thinking: 'Why not wait till he's popped Stevie, then nab him? Good result.'

Harriman said, 'What evidence is there that Perić is here to kill Stevie Tanner?'

Stella said, 'Logic dictates.'

'What evidence, though?'

'None.'

'Then we're not obliged to warn anyone about anything.'

'So it's surveillance work, mostly,' Stella told them. 'We're waiting for our prime suspect to put in an appearance.'

They talked for a while about the tactics and apparatus of surveillance work, which seemed to revolve around cars, mobile-phone black spots, on-road hand-overs and map references for Burger King. When the meeting broke up, Stella asked Leon Pritchett to unlock the exhibits room.

Pritchett was a good exhibits officer: every bit as good as Paul Lester had been and less likely to take backhanders from chippy journos. His shelves were neat and labelled.

'What are you looking for?'

'I don't know,' Stella said. 'A link.'

She spent an hour sifting through Jimmy's cache of murderabilia, the lists, the gruesome items themselves, the catalogue. She booted up his computer and searched the website and his WP entries, making notes for the purpose of elimination.

She instigated searches under 'Tanner' and 'Perić' and 'Zuhra Hadžić', and then under 'Stevie' and 'Denis' and 'Hugo' and 'Serb' and 'Belgrade'.

She looked under 'Branković' and 'Savo' and then under 'Forte' and 'John Peel' and 'Starbucks' in case Jimmy had regular venues where he met either Stevie or Perić.

She tried 'Raymond' and 'Yannis Stamas' and 'Dougie Vickers' and 'Tony Dawson'.

At a loss, she tried relevant London districts and postal codes, then 'Mick Armitage' as himself and as 'Jesse'. She tried a dozen other long shots and drew a series of blanks.

She leafed through Jimmy's notebook and started making anagrams out of the names of horses, as if Jimmy would have been smart enough to think of such a thing. She stared at the entry 'JP' with its future date and remembered thinking, when she'd first seen it, that a future was something Jimmy had left behind.

The date was two days hence. Stella entered it on the computer, but nothing came up. She glanced at the notes she'd been making; a series of possibilities and subsequent deletions. Then she blinked; her hand gave a little jump, as though she had been nudged and she went back to the squad room, moving quickly.

'JP'. *The John Peel*.

Pete Harriman's report documenting Stevie's recent trips was on her desk. She glanced at it, found the place and read for a few seconds. 'Where's Harriman?' she asked.

Sue Chapman answered without looking up from her keyboard. 'Just left.'

Stella ran out to the car park and stood in front of Harriman's car just as he was about to drive through the gates. He wound down a window and leaned out.

'You said Stevie Tanner was in the John Peel for about ten minutes.'

'That's right, boss.'

'Did you find out when Maurice Tanner is due for release?'

'I did, yeah. It's the day after tomorrow. Why?'

'I expect there'll be a welcome-home party, don't you?'

Harriman shrugged. 'There usually is.' He switched off the ignition as Stella came round to his window.

'You're Perić. You want to catch Stevie Tanner away from home, in the street, off guard, his mind on other things.'

Harriman looked at her. 'Going into the John Peel.'

'Gift in hand, girl on arm, smile on face.'

'It sounds right to me. What made you think of it?'

'Jimmy Stone. Jimmy made me think of it.'

Stella hadn't lost her Harefield Estate accent, it had simply softened; if you're a resident, it stays sharp – both the tone and the argot – but only someone who lived there could tell whether or not you have perfect pitch. When she called the John Peel, she thickened it a little for good measure.

'I'm calling for Mr Tanner.'

'Oh, yes?' It was a woman's voice; she sounded pre-occupied.

'It's about the party.'

'I spoke to him about that. Everything's ready.'

'I want to make sure we've got the numbers right. Stevie's a bit vague when it comes to numbers, yeah?'

Female solidarity. Men? Keep them out of the kitchen.

'Eighty-five, he told me. Sixteen children.'

'Okay, that's it, yeah. And we're starting at eight.'

'Seven-thirty.'

'Did Stevie say seven-thirty?'

'He did.'

'So seven-thirty. Buffet, yeah?'

'You've got the whole restaurant. Buffet serving, but enough covers for eighty-five.'

'That's it,' Stella said. 'That's great.' She was about to hang up.

'I told Mr Tanner he ought to have some fish.'

'What?'

'On the menu. Some fish. For those who like it. Not everyone wants a chunk of meat these days. BSE, swine fever, foot and mouth, E-coli.' She sounded like a vegetarian with a grudge.

'You're right.'

'I like a bit of fish.'

'Yeah . . .'

'It's very traditional, what he's chosen. We like the chance to expand. Let the chef have a bit of a free hand.'

'Best to keep it the way it is,' Stella told her.

The woman sighed. 'Oh, well,' she said, 'I suppose the prawn cocktail is fish of a sort.'

*

Stella made an audio tape setting out times and tactics and left it on Sue Chapman's desk.

> This man will be armed. My theory is that he
> will attempt to assassinate one or all of the
> Tanner family at the welcome home party for
> Maurice Tanner which is being held at the
> John Peel restaurant.
>
> Firearms will be issued to officers.
>
> Officers will communicate on an open line.
> After a positive identification is made, an
> arrest will be made.
>
> We have the element of surprise. All things
> being equal, we should be able to make the
> arrest effectively without weapons being
> used.
>
> The suspect might have to be taken in a
> public place. Be aware at all times that
> members of the public will be present.
>
> There will be a full briefing at 1800 hours
> tomorrow.

She left a note on Sorley's desk.

> Have read DI Ryder's report asking for a full
> inquiry. As we know, his officers were
> selling drugs from stock to their criminal
> contacts. They might say that this was part
> of their cover, but they never reported it,
> so far as I'm aware, and never
> requisitioned. Also, they kept the money.
> We can do a deal, or go for mutually assured
> destruction. His choice - and yours. I
> would suggest that we've got the advantage:
> I was lax; they were dealing scag.

The letter to George was still in her pocket, a little bomb on a short fuse.

I need space. Try to understand.   Love . . .

35

Zuhra had woken, but her features were still blurred and softened by sleep. It seemed to Stella that she was looking at a face underwater. She asked, 'Is that all right? You'll do it?'

Zuhra nodded.

Stella glanced at Delaney as if to ask whether he thought Zuhra had understood what was wanted of her. He shifted slightly in his seat so that he was facing Zuhra directly and said, 'He won't see you. You'll be in a van, okay? – a car with windows only in the back.'

'A van, yes,' Zuhra said.

The cops call it a 'nondy' – nondescript vehicle. It might have a trader's name on it or just a coating of dust.

'We need to be sure, Zuhra. We've got the computer-fit you gave us, but you're the only person who can really identify Perić.'

Delaney turned to Stella. 'Where? Where do you expect to find him?'

Stella shook her head. 'I can't tell you that. I can't give anyone operational details.' She looked back to Zuhra. 'It *will* be safe. *You* will be safe.'

'Yes?' Zuhra asked. Then: 'It doesn't matter.'

'It matters to me,' Stella told her.

Zuhra was holding a glass of whisky. When she was awake, she drank. If Delaney asked her what she wanted, she would reply, 'A drink,' and if he asked her what kind of a drink she would say, 'Something strong,' as if 'strong' were the only useful definition.

She asked, 'After you have arrest him, what will happen?'

'He'll be charged, kept in prison, sent to trial. If he's found guilty, he'll stay in prison.'

'What will be the charge?'

'Murder.'

'Whose murder?'

'A man called Jimmy Stone.'

'You have good proof of this?'

Stella remembered Mike Sorley's remark: So not much, then. Nothing solid. 'Trust me,' she said.

Zuhra laughed. 'Yes, I trust you because I must. But in Bosnia, during the war, *police* is not a good word. You are police.'

Stella remembered the moment when she had stood at the top of the stairs that led down to Sam Burgess's underworld and made that instinctive connection between the halogen-and-steel brutalism of Sam's domain and the manner of Jimmy Stone's death.

She thought of the way the term 'Secret Police' had arisen in her mind.

'I have proof,' Zuhra said. 'This man is war criminal. He must be punished for that. For my family.'

'One way or another,' Stella said. But behind the remark was a tinge of anxiety.

This bastard's mine.

'What do you say to him?' Delaney asked. 'What do you tell him?'

'The police work all hours. He knows that.'

'The reason I ask,' he said, 'is that I can't do this much longer.'

'I know.'

'He sounds like a nice guy.'

'He is a nice guy.'

'Jesus . . .' Delaney washed his face with his hands. 'I wish . . .' He broke off and took a drink, and abandoned the remark altogether. 'I'm writing her story. It started out as a piece about the street girls from Bosnia and Russia and Africa, but now it's become Zuhra's story. When she's clear and free, I want to publish it.'

Stella could hear something behind what he was saying: the journalist's voice. She remembered his persistence, the way he'd held on so tenaciously to the Deevers when he was chasing cults and the slick crooks who preyed on the devout. She remembered that he had been paying Paul Lester for information.

You corrupted one of my officers. You behaved just like any red-top weasel.

It was a good reason for leaving now, going home to George, telling him that the job was slowing down and the overtime was drying up. Pretty soon, this case would be over and she would be back to normal duties. Maybe they could get away together for a couple of days, talk things through, take life easy.

A loyal thought, a sensible thought. She glanced over at Delaney, sitting cross-legged on the sofa, barefoot, wearing blue jeans and a plain white T-shirt and looking like everything Stella had ever wanted.

She said, 'Back off, okay?'

'Look, who gave you Perić in the first place? Who got you the name?'

'And I'm grateful. But you're not getting anywhere near this. It's a police operation.'

'I reported from war zones.'

Stella laughed. 'Jesus, what are you saying? You want to be on the scene with gun and camera?'

'If you knew where he was, you'd take him tonight. As it is, though, you want Zuhra for tomorrow night . . .' He was reading the signs. 'You're using a surveillance vehicle, which means you'll be parked on the street. So . . . tomorrow night, Perić is going somewhere, meeting someone, there's some kind of – what? – event, and you know what it is and where it is and you expect him to be there.'

'I expect him, I don't expect you.'

'It'll be a public place. Other people will be there. Why not me?'

'They'll be there by accident.'

'I'll stay out of the way. Whatever you tell me to do, I'll do.'

'Jesus *Christ*, Delaney, will you stop it?'

There was genuine anger in her voice. He held up both hands. 'Okay. All right. Tell me about it afterwards.'

'I'll tell you what I can when I can.'

'Good enough,' he lied.

After Stella had left, Delaney went to his work room. The door was partly open. Zuhra was sitting up in bed with her glass of whisky, which was fuller than when Delaney had last seen it; he noticed the bottle on the floor within arm's reach.

376

He sat next to her and she shifted her legs to give him more room. He said, 'You only have to do this if you want to.'

'I want to.'

'Okay. She'll look after you. If she says you'll be safe, then you will be.'

'Yes,' Zuhra said. 'It doesn't matter if it is safe. Safe is not –' She paused and frowned, looking for the words, then remembered and smiled. 'It is neither here nor there.' She said it with a laugh: such an odd phrase. 'Safe is neither here nor there.'

'You'll get your papers, Zuhra, I promise. I'll help you. Find you a job. You can stay here as long as you like.' She was dark-eyed with sleep and pale as death. He wanted to make her more promises than she needed. A glut of promises.

'What will you do – you and Stella Mooney?'

'Do?'

'She is married to another person, am I right?'

'More or less.'

'More or less. Neither here nor there.' Zuhra laughed again. 'What will you do?'

'I don't know. We haven't talked about it. Nothing, I expect.'

'Yes? Is that what you expect?'

He nodded. Zuhra took a big swallow of the Scotch and shuddered. It was just what she wanted, except she wanted a little more. After a moment or two, her eyelids fluttered closed, then opened briefly.

'If it is neither here nor there,' she asked, 'where is it?'

*

Ivo Perić had gone from heavy stubble to a beard in just a few days. He liked the look of it; also it made him feel a little safer. That girl was a danger to him. He wished he could find her again, a second chance encounter, and take a little time to ask her who she had told about him, what she had said. To make her talk, then put her out of harm's way.

No one knows where I am or why I'm here, he told himself reassuringly. A day. Just a day. He would leave by boat, then take trains across France and Italy.

The Acropolis was noisy and dirty, a stopover for refugees and the homeless. It was like living in limbo, which was exactly where he wanted to be. He took a tepid shower in the plastic-sheeted cubicle in the corner of his room, then changed his clothes and walked to an Indian restaurant in Hammersmith. He liked to order the hot dishes and take the fire off his tongue with cold beer. He sat at a table by the window so he could watch the street life, the boys in little warrior-bands, the girls with their bare legs and their navel rings. They made him hungry.

Later he went to a club where the lights were hard and fast, like a fire-fight, and the music had a bass-beat that could shift your viscera. He was a little drunk by this time, and laughing to himself. He danced alone, in the thick of things, holding a bottle of beer, liking it when he was shoved this way and that by the press of bodies.

At the bar, he was picked up by a working girl who had a room just around the corner. She didn't want to put the bag on her head to begin with, but he showed her how much money he had to spend and spoke to her quietly, one hand on her shoulder, close to her neck.

378

She stood in the middle of the room, stripped and hooded.

No eyes to cry, no mouth to plead.

Delaney woke from a dream of loss and went to the kitchen to get water. He looked in on Zuhra as he passed. She was sleeping with the curtains drawn back. In the light from the street, he could see the tear-tracks on her cheeks.

He made coffee and sat on a stool to drink it, knowing it was a mistake: the caffeine would keep him awake for an hour or more. It's easy to know what to do, he thought, in a situation like this. Look at the past, take it from experience – you get over people. You think the way you're feeling will live with you for ever, but it doesn't. You think that a certain face will always compel you, but it won't.

He thought all these thoughts, then he thought of Stella Mooney and there was no way round her, no way of getting past her. Easy to know what to do, impossible to do it. There were certain signs that couldn't be ignored: he missed her as soon as she left the room; she interrupted his thoughts; most of all, he hadn't bothered to count the cost.

He sipped his coffee and listened to the city's night sounds: engines, distant music, sudden laughter.

You can lie trembling next to someone who loves you and wonder how in hell you came to this and what in hell you're going to do next.

You can reflect how appropriate the term 'in hell' seems.

You can make plans for a future that involves a place you don't recognize and someone whose face you can't quite see.

You can devise the ways and means of treachery.

You can defeat your dreams by being awake at three a.m., but you can't stop asking yourself the wrong questions.

Stella listened to the noise in her head, shrill and unrelenting, a cacophony of voices, too distant to be understood.

36

Cops know how to follow a car without being picked up. There are procedures; there's cop know-how. But the manuals don't say much about the idea of someone following the cops.

Stella used her key to Delaney's flat and found Zuhra waiting for her. She was wearing her own sneakers but Delaney's clothes – chinos, a T-shirt, a blue linen overshirt, the chinos cinched in with a belt, the shirt with its sleeves rolled back to the wrist. She had lived in her own clothes much too long and Delaney didn't own a washing machine.

It was two hours before Stella expected any guests to be arriving at the John Peel. They would park up and sit tight. The nondy was stocked with food and drink, though you had to be sparing on the drink. Stella asked Zuhra if she would mind going to the bathroom before they left. Then she went herself. Long stake-outs without being able to take a piss were the staple of police jokes, especially where women were concerned. Men could piss in a bottle.

When the van started up towards Notting Hill Gate, Delaney pulled away from the kerb. Because Stella knew his car, he'd taken the precaution of hiring something: a Vauxhall for anonymity. On the seat next to him was a camera, a Canon EOS, because it was the right piece of equipment for the job: self-focusing, compact, easy to load. He'd used it before in places where pointing a long lens would have drawn fire.

His reasons for wanting to be there at all were a mixture of instinct, selfishness and virtue. The people who had preyed on Zuhra – the Belgrade connection, the Tanners, most of all Ivo Perić – the world had to meet them and know them for what they were. But he was a journalist and it was in his blood to want the story and want it exclusively. He had no idea where he was going or what his chances were, but whatever came his way, he'd take that. The research was done, Zuhra's story was on tape; this was the endgame, now; this was the last call.

Driving towards wherever you saw smoke or heard gunfire.

When the van turned off Ladbroke Grove and stopped, Delaney drove to the next junction, took a series of left turns until he got back to the main road, then found a parking place some thirty yards back. He was screened from the van by half a dozen cars, but he knew that Stella and Zuhra wouldn't be there alone. Someone was watching the traffic and would have seen him drive up and park. He looked down the street, checking the options. He could see four pubs, two restaurants and a sushi bar that, in this neighbourhood, was dangerously close to being out of its depth. Not the sushi bar, he thought. And not the pub that was pretending to be an American diner with its stainless steel trim, its name picked out in pink and green neon. That left five possibilities at his end of the street alone.

He took an A–Z from the door pocket and made a

show of finding a map reference. A big panel van drew up in front of one of the restaurants, bringing the street down to one lane thanks to a blue Audi parked slap in front of the place, just where the van wanted to be. There were three men in the cab. The driver watched while the other two opened the doors and began to offload the components of a sound system while cars backed up and hooted. The John Peel, Delaney noted: someone was having a private party. The driver turned and looked at the cars, then lit a cigarette, taking his time. King of the Road. He walked across to the pub nearest to where Delaney sat, looking like a man with a thirst.

Delaney counted to twenty, then went in and ordered a drink. The driver was leaning on the bar, reading a paper. Delaney nudged in next to him. He asked, 'Is that your van, offloading to the John Peel?'

So here was a motorist with a problem: one of the horn-hooters. The driver took half a step backwards, giving himself room to swing his fist.

'Do you need me to move my car?' Delaney asked. 'The Audi.'

The driver relaxed and shook his head. 'Don't bother, mate. They'll be done soon enough. I'm just in here for a swift one.'

'It's a party, is it?'

'Yeah. They do them all the time. Soundblast Audio.'

'Looked like a big set-up.'

'Yeah? I wouldn't know.'

'Some kid's birthday,' Delaney suggested. 'Parents with more money than sense.'

'Probably, yeah.'

'A christening or a wedding or something . . .'
'Could be. Who knows? I'm just the driver.'

Ten minutes later, Pete Harriman and Steve Sheppard came into the pub. Delaney had installed himself by the window that looked on to the street. He could see the John Peel, but he couldn't see the nondy: he'd got half the action. He glanced across as Harriman and Sheppard ordered drinks, but they meant as little to him as he did to them. The pub was getting crowded and when the two cops moved away from the bar, they were hidden by other drinkers.

Harriman looked at every face in the pub twice. He said, 'He's not here.'

'No, he's not,' Sheppard agreed.

'What time is it?'

'Six-thirty.'

'Overtime,' Harriman said.

'I've only been married six weeks,' Sheppard said, 'overtime's a mixed blessing.'

They had watched the sound system being carried into the restaurant. 'Drinks,' Harriman observed, 'then a four-course meal, then some pillock makes a speech welcoming Maurice back to a life of crime, then they get stuck into the brandies, then the fucking disco starts up. It's going to be a long night.'

'Unless he pops Stevie before they get to the starter.'

'Nah . . . He'll let them get some booze down: think about it. Slower to see it coming, slower to react.'

Sheppard drank the last of his mineral water. 'He could be anywhere,' he said. 'He could be at home with a nice drink and a video, keeping an eye on the clock.'

*

'When you see him,' Stella said, 'just tell me. Tell me as fast as you can. I'll be getting out –' she nodded towards the doors of the van – 'don't come with me. As soon as you tell me you've seen him – as soon as you've pointed him out – I'll give a signal and he'll be arrested, okay? Surrounded, subdued and arrested.' It sounded as if she were rehearsing the event for her own benefit, ticking items off a checklist.

They had seen the sound system go in and had watched every move. Maybe that's the way Perić would do it – go in as a sound technician. Maybe he'd get by as a guest: eighty-five people, after all. Maybe he'd just walk in and start shooting.

Someone had put a packet of food in the van. Stella ate half a sandwich and took a swallow of water. Zuhra held her hand up, palm out: No thanks.

'Are you all right?' Stella asked.

'I am all right, yes.' She certainly looked calm. In fact, Stella thought, she looked more than calm. Dead inside.

They watched as the Tanners arrived at seven-forty-five. People had been going in for about twenty minutes. You couldn't see the heavy men on the door, but they would be there to keep out the freeloaders, the chancers, the hobos and the hoolies.

Denis, Hugo, Stevie and now Maurice, each man with his wife except Stevie, who had found a blonde with an all-over tan, most of which was entirely visible. They were dressed for a gangsters' night out, Issy Miyake, Versace, Donna Karan, the women wearing little halters and yokes of precious stones.

They had arrived in four cars travelling in convoy.

Zuhra watched them without blinking. Stevie turned face-on to the van – saying something to his brother – and Stella said, 'That's Stevie . . .' talking to herself.

Zuhra said, 'Yes. Stevie.'

'You met him?'

'One time. When I am first here. After the boat and the lorry. I am thinking, Here is the man who is my freedom. Here is the man who gives me papers and a job and a new life.' She paused. 'It was new life, sure enough.'

'What happened?'

'He tell me what I must do, I tell him no, he beat me. Then he tell me I owe him money and must pay or he send me to police. Then he fuck me.'

After an hour, the rain set in. It was dusk and the streetlamps were coming on, sodium and raindrops making the street half-dissolve into lozenges of light. The neon sign in the theme pub sent pink and green streaks across the glass. People went by behind umbrellas or with their faces lowered against the wet.

Stella made a call to Pete Harriman. 'It's not easy to see from in here.'

There were eight policemen waiting to take Perić, AMIP-5 officers plus some on loan. Harriman said, 'We've got the computer-fit.'

'I know. Just remember it's a likeness. Pull the wrong guy and everything's over.'

Zuhra sat in a collapsible camp chair at the back of the van and peered out into the street. It was like looking through a smoked-glass kaleidoscope. Stella switched her phone off and sat down next to her.

After nine o'clock.
Where are you, you bastard? Don't let me down.

Homecomings. Jimmy Stone had given Perić a rundown
on homecomings.

'Being inside –' He had looked at Perić a moment.
'Ever done time?' Perić shook his head. 'It's not so much
what you've got, it's what you can't have. If it's someone
like Maurice Tanner doing a short stretch for GBH, well,
he can handle that, no problem. He can get what he
wants in the way of booze and drugs and conjugal visits.
What he can't do is leave. What he can't do is go where
he wants. The thing about being in prison, you can't be
yourself. You're you, in a sort of way, but you're the *in
prison* you. Know what I mean?'

Perić had shrugged. He didn't, but he needed the
details, so he was prepared to let Jimmy talk. The TV
was on, the sound low, and horses were being loaded
into the starting gate. Jimmy had glanced across at the
screen, to check his investment.

'So when you come out, it's like you come back to
being yourself. Everyone knows this – everyone who's
done time. Result? Big party. Like it was a birthday, yeah?
Get dressed up, invite your mates, have a bloody good
time.'

'People get drunk,' Perić suggested.

'Definitely.'

'Few drugs, maybe.'

'No question.'

'If it is like birthday, people take gifts.'

'With the Tanners, a token. A bottle of classy wine, a
box of cigars.'

They had been in Jimmy's bedsit eating a simple meal of carbo-and-high-fat delivered to your door and splitting a bottle of Southern Comfort that Perić had brought with him. Below them, unheard and unknown, Caroline, Joanna and Conrad Deever had been sitting in a little ring close by the racked body of the crucified Christ, talking about their own deaths and what awaited them on the other side – visions of gardens in sunlight and gentle seascapes in the land of good health.

Jimmy had taken out his notebook and given Perić the date, the time, and also the address of the John Peel. 'It's a favourite of theirs,' he'd said. 'They've had it booked for weeks.'

The starter had given a shout and the gates opened. The horses had seemed to emerge at the gallop, all drifting across to the firm ground near the rails.

'What if this brother is not released on that day?'

'He will be. Maurice knows how to do time. Head down, nose clean, mouth shut. No one's going to make life difficult for him. He's a Tanner, he gets respect.'

'You are sure about this?'

'It's the closest you'll get to them, believe me. It's the best I can do for you.'

Perić had nodded and got up to pour Jimmy another drink. On TV, the field had separated into maybes and no-chancers. Jimmy was watching hard, now, his money riding on a maybe. Perić put the Rohypnol in Jimmy's bourbon and handed him the glass.

After the race was over, after Jimmy had seen his money stroll in fifth, they had talked for a little longer. Perić took a roll of banknotes out of his pocket and Jimmy looked pleased to see it, at least that's what his silly grin and unfocused eyes had seemed to say. The grin had stayed in place as Perić leaned over and slid his hand under Jimmy's shirt, looking for the hollow tuck between the ribs. The instrument in his hand looked like an engine-oil dipstick, narrow, flat-bladed and about a foot long. He put it in position while Jimmy watched, still smiling, as if fascinated to see a professional at work.

Perić had given it the heel of his hand in order to break through, then went searching for a second or two until he found the place. Jimmy half-rose. He made a sound like a man who has just been given a bit of bad news: a gasp-groan. Then he sat back, wide-eyed.

Perić had withdrawn the steel softly, like a surgeon. He took back the roll of banknotes. If he'd gone a little further, he would have discovered Jimmy's six-hundred-pound wedge, but now he was eager to leave. Being in Jimmy's company, in Jimmy's building, put him at risk.

He switched off the television and paused to swallow what bourbon there was in his glass. Then he tidied up and wiped the place down before leaving.

Ten minutes later, Jimmy blinked and refocused. Maybe the dose of roofie hadn't been that large; maybe some strange sense of urgency had come upon him. He didn't know what he was feeling, but he knew it wasn't good. He got up and took a step towards the door, then another.

Dead man walking.

37

The room at the Acropolis was eight-by-ten with a double bed, a wardrobe, an armchair and a coffee table. The TV was bracketed to the wall, and to get round the room you had to sidle between the gimcrack furniture.

Perić sat in the armchair and watched something on television. There was always something on television: it was a way of not thinking while you waited for your life to catch up. On the coffee table was a gift-wrapped package about the size of a box of cigars.

He thought he'd give it an hour, maybe. At ten-thirty, surely, the party would have come down to lights and loud music and people drunk-dancing.

Delaney knew he ought to be drinking mineral water, and that's where he'd started, but the last three had been beers and now he'd ordered a Scotch to chase. Sitting in the window seat with the babble of talk and loop-tape music behind him, smoke hanging in blue banners, waiting for someone to arrive at the John Peel with a gun over his shoulder and carrying a placard that read 'Assassin'.

Like Harriman and the rest of the AMIP-5 team, Delaney had a colour print-out of Perić. He removed it from his pocket and held it down by his knees to take a covert glance. It was a face made of bits and pieces; the face of someone you would never expect to meet.

Perić dressed for the occasion. The suit, the linen shirt, the tie that he tied with a broad knot. The Militech 11mm was a temptation, but he couldn't afford to be patted down at the door.

He picked up the gift-wrapped package and went out into the street. It was raining, which usually meant taxis would go to ground, but a Citicab came along with its light on and pulled over at once.

Bilo mu je suđeno. *It was meant to be.*

Delaney was thinking the same thoughts as Perić: lights, music, dancing – who would know any better if I walked in and bopped in a corner? By this time it was four beers and two Scotches, and he was pretty sure that nothing was going to happen, so what difference?

I walk in, I get sussed, I'm a freeloader, or I'm someone who found the wrong party. A bouncer shows me the door. I apologize. Easy. If I don't get sussed, then I'm there if anything breaks.

He thought that's what he'd do. Definitely.

It occurred to him that he might be putting himself in a room where there'd be gunplay, but that didn't bother him too much because he was a little more than slightly drunk; and he thought he might have one more before he left his seat at the window and walked across the road to the lights and laughter.

Just slightly more than a little drunk, because that's just how he used to be on those days when he found himself driving towards wherever he saw smoke, wherever he heard gunfire.

Cabs carrying latecomers had been pulling up for the last hour or so. As the people got out, the cab would mask them from the nondy – and it was raining and the light was poor and Stella was beginning to think they might not be able to take Perić on the way in, which would mean taking him on the way out. That would be after one or more of the Tanner family had been killed. She had already written the report in her head and it didn't make good reading.

Perić stepped out of the Citicab, his coat collar up. He had already paid the driver, and it had been when he leaned forward to hand over the money that Zuhra had caught him in profile as she looked through the rain-spattered window of the van and into the rain-spattered window of the cab. Then he was out and walking into the John Peel while the cabbie separated fare from tip.

She said, 'Maybe that was him.'

Stella reached for her phone. 'The guy in the cab?'

'Maybe. He had beard. This is different.'

'So why do you think it was him?'

Zuhra shrugged. 'Looked like him.'

'But the beard . . .'

'Looked like him, okay? *Like* him.'

'Jesus Christ . . .' Stella peered into the street, as if hoping that the theme pub's neon script might carry a message for her: *Stella Mooney – that was your man!*

What she saw was John Delaney walking down the street and making straight for the John Peel.

*

It was easy. Just as easy for Delaney as it had been for Perić. He nodded at the bouncer on the door as if he'd been out for a breath of air. The bouncer nodded back. He was looking in at the party where the music was loud, the beer was cold and some pretty girls were dancing so hard they were falling out of their clothes.

Delaney bopped his way across the room, got a beer at the bar and looked round the room. There were twenty guys who could have been the Tanner family, and he couldn't see anyone who looked like Ivo Perić. He took out his camera and pretended to frame up a couple of shots. Some girls dancing in a circle waved for attention and, when he put the camera up to focus, they turned their backs on him, looking over their shoulders and wagging their backsides.

Delaney smiled and swigged his beer. He thought that Perić wouldn't turn up now. Another half-hour and it would be easy to forget why he was there . . . The music a little louder, the booze a little freer, the girls a little closer.

There was a table in the corner of the room where the presents had been laid. Perić set down his gift and walked away from the table taking a mazy route towards the door. He wanted it to look as if he were neither arriving nor leaving.

Without meaning to, a girl baulked him with her dancing; they knocked into one another. She looked him up and down, then laughed and stepped left and right to prevent him from getting past: the music had changed to something slower and she needed a partner. Blonde, slender but with some weight to her breasts, a bright red spaghetti-strap dress that touched her everywhere: she looked like the pick of the bunch.

Perić laughed back at her and held out his arms. Why not? He had all of five minutes. *Nema problema.*

Stella called Harriman. The stake-out was in cars, one other van, and also a shopfront currently up for rent. Harriman was in the darkened shopfront along with Steve Sheppard.

'A guy just got out of a taxi and went in. Did you see . . .?'

'Guy with a beard.'

'Yes.'

'No, I didn't see him. I mean, I saw him, but . . .'

'Okay.'

'You think that was Perić?'

'I don't know.'

'What does she say?' He meant Zuhra.

'She thinks maybe.'

'Oh, that's good. What do you want to do?'

'If we make our move and it's the wrong guy, we're fucked.'

'If you don't and it is, someone else is fucked. Could be *mortally* fucked.'

Stella looked towards the restaurant. Perić maybe, but Delaney for sure. This was going badly.

For the slow number, hot colours: red and yellow and deep blue spotlights chasing each other across the floor. The girl squirmed in Perić's arms. He slid his hand over her rump, then all the way round to her thigh and up into her crotch. She liked that. He held her off a fraction so that he could get to her breasts. The girl's hand slipped down between his legs a moment, then teasingly away.

Perić kissed her and said, 'Wait for me.'

She watched him as he walked across the floor. She thought he meant 'for a moment or two', but he was talking about eternity.

There was no one for Stella to ask except Zuhra. She said, 'What made you think it was Perić?'

'I don't know.'

'You saw his face.'

'From the side.'

'Not enough to recognize him.'

'No. It is dark, there was rain on the window, this man has a beard –'

'Christ, Zuhra, I know, I know all that. Something. There must have been something.'

'A feeling.'

'What kind of a feeling?'

'Like a dirty finger touched my heart.'

The remark took Stella's breath away. She lifted her phone to call Harriman, to send them in, when Zuhra said, 'Look. It is him.'

The bearded man was leaving the John Peel. He got into the blue Audi that was parked directly in front of the restaurant, and drove away.

Stella got out of the van and crossed the road to the restaurant. Through the window she could see the lights and hear the music. She could see people dancing, people laughing and drinking, a blonde in a bright red dress

leaning up against a pillar and waiting for her partner to
return.

No one dead. No one on the floor with blood puddling
round his head. No shocked faces, chaos, screams.

He went in and he came out again. Why?

Harriman appeared at her side. She said, 'He went in
and he came out again. Why?'

Harriman peered in through the window. 'Something
happened. He took a look and decided the odds were
against him. Bad set-up . . .' None of that sounded right
to him.

The music changed and the girl in the red dress crossed
towards the bar, looking left and right for her lost man.
The music was hard and fast and she wanted to show
him how she looked when she danced that way. From
outside in the street, the bassline was like a series of low-
level detonations.

Stella said, 'Christ, I know what this is. Clear the area.'

Once she had said that, Harriman knew too. He started
back up the street, yelling, dialling on his mobile phone.
Stella went into the John Peel at a dead run, her warrant
card held up to the man on the door. She crossed the
floor, knocking people aside, setting up an errant wave
of movement that went against the rhythm of the dance.
She reached the sound system and ripped out whatever
wires she could see. When the music died, and people
turned towards the silence, they saw Stella with her arms
in the air like a preacher.

She said, 'Police' and 'Bomb' in several combinations.
She looked round for Delaney, but couldn't find him. It
had already occurred to her that none of them might
make it.

*

It goes different ways for different people. Some stood still, waiting to be told more: that it was a joke, or what they should do next. Some looked round for their belongings, or started towards the coat check. Some knew exactly what she meant and went for the door at a flat-out run.

After that, everyone got the idea and the door was a funnel. Stella saw a woman kick through the crowd, turning a boy of about six aside with her hip and smacking his face into the door jamb. Stella scooped the boy up and shouldered through. Outside there were sirens and lights coming in from all directions. The AMIP-5 team were clearing the street. People were emptying out from nearby buildings in the same moment as others were crowding in from either end of the street, wanting a better view.

The nondy van had been moved down the street, but Zuhra was standing on the pavement looking like someone who has just woken from a dream. Stella handed the child to a uniformed copper and hurried across.

She said, 'Zuhra, you have to get back.'

Stella grabbed Zuhra's arm and, in the same moment, looked round to take stock. People were still clearing the restaurant and, as she turned, there was John Delaney, one in a crowd, emerging from the door.

She opened her mouth to yell at him and her words were wiped by the explosion: a full-blooded, near-unbearable fist of sound, like a thunderclap striking right beside your head. Stella and Zuhra were thrown against the window of the shopfront where Harriman and Sheppard had waited, the breath knocked from their lungs. Stella looked back towards the door of the John Peel and seemed to see Delaney at the very heart of a red, blossoming rose as the fireball bellied and spread. He was airborne, arms and legs flailing, then he was lying in the road, a dead weight.

She ran to him, looking right and left for the paramedics. Delaney and maybe fifteen others, all caught by the blast. Some were up on their hands and knees, or sitting in the wet, heads bowed like rag dolls; others were either unconscious or dead, it was difficult to tell. Delaney was spreadeagled, ready for the chalk outline. When Stella got to him, she put him in the recovery position and yelled for help. There were paramedics coming down the street from either end, sirens whooping and dying as more ambulances arrived.

Delaney shifted and got to his hands and knees. 'Don't move,' Stella told him.

'Jesus Christ, what was that?'

'It was a bomb. Don't move.'

'I'm moving because I can. I'm happy to move.' Apart from a cut above his eye, he looked normal. Everything had missed him: glass, masonry, brickwork. He looked normal, but he couldn't get up.

'You might have internal injuries, so stay the fuck still, and what do you think you were *doing*?'

'Doing?'

'Going in there. This was a police operation. You knew –' Between anger and fear, she couldn't find the words.

Delaney coughed and held his chest. He got off his hands and knees and lay down, his head on her thigh. 'Pretty good, huh? I followed you all the way.'

'Fuck you, Delaney. You're under arrest.' She was now angry enough to hit him.

'Did they die?'

The Tanners had been among the first out. They had grouped, found their own and made sure they were safe, then disappeared: not in the long black cars that had brought them. They knew enough to keep belly-down at a time like this. Whoever had tried to hit them might not be alone. Stella had seen them, before the blast, manoeuvring down the street, hands raised for taxis.

'No,' she said, 'he missed them.'

A paramedic team started to examine him. After a minute or two, when they had decided he was walking wounded, he was given a foil cape and led away. Stella watched him all the way to the ambulance and waited until the doors closed on him. She was crying. She realized she must have been crying all the time.

Andy Greegan had been responsible for the technics of the stake-out. He gave Stella his notes, which included the licence plates of vehicles parked in the street.

'Clever,' Stella said. 'Jesus, that was clever – parking a car directly in front of the restaurant sometime earlier. This guy really thinks ahead.'

Greegan had already put out an APB on the car. He and Stella were walking through a litter of glass and splintered wood, casualties still being stretchered past, ambulances coming in along with specialists from the bomb squad, a police helicopter clattering overhead.

'He's gone, though,' Greegan said. 'Long gone. He could be anywhere.'

*

Anywhere has to be somewhere. As Greegan was speaking, a call came in to say that two officers in a red-stripe had spotted the Audi parking on Shepherd's Bush Road. The driver had gone into one of the cheap hotels. He hadn't yet come out.

38

You could travel light, sure enough, but there were always details to be taken care of, and the success of a job depends on the details. There were people detailed to the clean-up operation. They had never met Perić, but they knew about him and knew what they had to do.

Perić made a phone call to a number in Earls Court. Someone would turn up after he had gone. The key to the Audi and the key to his room Perić would leave in the exhaust pipe of the car. The Audi would be returned; the room would be wiped down hard; the guns would disappear. Both guns and Semtex had been waiting for him in a suitcase at a left-luggage location when he'd first arrived in London. What remained of the money he'd been given for expenses – Jimmy's pay-off mostly – he put into a nylon money-belt with a plastic zip, and he strapped the belt under his shirt. His train and ferry tickets went into the button down pocket of his shirt.

He packed his clothes, folding neatly and layering with care, but there was tension in every gesture. He felt hungry but didn't want food. *Appetites* – there was time for a drink, but there wasn't time for a girl. He looked at his watch and calculated that he had twenty minutes before hiking to the tube. No taxis, now; it was time to lose himself in crowds, following a schedule that would allow him a little leeway, but wouldn't put him at the station or the ferry-port longer than necessary.

He poured a good shot of whisky and smelled it before he sipped it. All his thoughts were of movement, travel, home. It didn't occur to him to wonder how many people had died inside the John Peel. He sat down, glass in hand, and reached for the TV remote control. Everything was quiet. He switched the TV on and surfed through a gameshow, a movie, a wildlife programme, a garden makeover, then he switched off again, suddenly, his head lifted as if to a strange scent.

Everything was quiet.

He went to the window and looked out on a deserted street where there should have been traffic and people. Exactly opposite was another hotel; to its left a video-rental store, to its right a late-night café; both were empty. His view up the road to the right was obscured, but he could see away to the left where the road curved down towards Hammersmith Broadway: a bus went through and a couple of loose cars, then a red-stripe pulled across the road, sealing it. The last civilians safely off the scene.

He might have a few seconds or a few minutes. They would need to decide on tactics and they would need to find out which room he was in. Too late to go down the only staircase; too late to think of a back way out: they'd have covered that before clearing the road. He opened the wardrobe and took the guns out, the Street Sweeper and the Militech magnum, then went out on to the landing. His door faced another door: another room. Perić knocked and a man answered, in his fifties, olive skin and dark curly hair that made him Arab or Turk.

Perić showed him the gun and the man backed up, wide-eyed. They stood in the middle of the room while

Perić looked round for what he needed, then motioned to the man to sit down. He said, 'Don't worry. Nothing will happen. Stay quiet.'

The man sat while Perić brought two cushions from the armchair – two because they were thin – bunched them against the back of the man's head, then pushed the muzzle of the Militech into their folds and fired once. The man rocked forward, then back.

'Turk bastard,' Perić said.

He listened, but could hear nothing. Now he was in a different room, which would confuse them for a crucial moment or two. The dead man's window gave a slightly better view of the road, and Perić could see more vehicles arriving, figures deploying. He knew the battle-plan for this: sharpshooters on the outside, a group with rapid-fire weapons, gas and stun grenades on the inside; no way forward, no way back.

Only one chance here. I need a shield.

The figures Perić had seen deploying were SO19 officers. Stuart Lawson stood next to the partial cover given by an operations Land Rover and spoke to Andy Greegan.

'Where's DS Mooney?'

Greegan was staring up at the Acropolis Hotel. 'In there.'

'I hoped you weren't going to say that. Anyone else?'

'Two DCs, Harriman and Sheppard.'

'Wonderful,' Lawson observed. 'Are they armed?'

'Yes.'

'Give the filth a gun,' Lawson said, 'they think they're Mel-fucking-Gibson. We could have called him out. He's got nowhere to go.' He'd said this to Stella as they'd sat in the van on the Harefield approach road. 'No chance of that now.'

'She didn't know when you'd arrive,' Greegan pointed out.

'Then why not wait for him to walk out of the door?'

'That already happened once tonight. She lost him.'

They stood facing the door to Perić's room and took a moment to get set. Perić knew they were there by every step on the stair, by the sudden silence outside. He opened the dead man's door a fraction and there they were, one each side of the door, the third standing back and off to her right – out of line of a right-handed gun.

Perić stepped up behind Stella and put the Street Sweeper to her head: Harriman and Sheppard saw it as movement in the corner of the eye, but when they turned it was already too late.

Mistake. They had made a bad mistake. And their thoughts were the same as Lawson's: *Too late now.*

'This gun will take off her head and kill you too. Put down your weapons.'

Harriman and Sheppard lowered their guns to the floor, but didn't take their eyes off Perić.

'Tell them this. I have the woman. Next move – everyone out of this hotel. No one must be left. If I hear movements in this place, I will kill her. Slam the door to the street when you go out. If you do not clear the building, I will kill her. Next after that, I speak with someone who is senior man because now there will be a trade. Okay?'

He had Stella by the collar of her denim jacket, the twin barrels of the shotgun hard up against her skull.

404

Harriman and Sheppard went down the first few stairs; Perić talked to them as they descended, even though they were out of sight.

'Keep going. Clear the building. It is easy for her to die.'

Still holding the gun to Stella's head, he picked up the weapons that Harriman and Sheppard had dropped, and backed off into the room he'd emerged from: the room with the best view of the street. Stella saw the dead man in the chair and felt her legs start to go from under her. Perić held her up and walked her to the bed.

'Sit there,' he told her, then, immediately, 'No, wait.'

He patted her down, finding her handcuffs and her mobile phone. 'Now sit,' he said. He pulled her arms behind her back and cuffed her wrists, one either side of the bedrail, then went to the window. He knew what to do: one side of the window to look one way, then belly-down to the other side for a look in the opposite direction. The window was narrow so the angle of fire would be restricted. The curtain worked on a cord-pull. He closed it both sides then walked round the room to check where his shadow fell. He tugged the coverlet off the bed, pulling it from under Stella, then laid it on the floor to show him where his line of demarcation lay. Beyond that his shadow would strike the curtain.

Stella looked at the dead man slumped back in the chair, the front of his cranium a dark crater. His jaw had gone lopsided and his left eye lay on his cheek. The long, elliptical spillage of blood that went from his thighs to the floor was thickening and forming a crust.

Perić was holding Stella's mobile phone. He said, 'What is your name?'

'DS Mooney.'

'First name.'

'Stella.'

'Okay, Stella. You and me together.'

He smiled at her over the body of the man he had killed. Stella remembered the story Zuhra had told her, this man at the centre of things. This very man.

'Just you and me.'

From around them and below them came the first sounds of people leaving the hotel. Footsteps only, no one was talking.

Delaney sat in A&E still wearing his foil cape while the trauma team worked on people who were more seriously hurt.

'Keep the cape on,' the charge nurse had told him, 'and keep warm, and let me know if you start to feel strange. More people die of shock . . .' He'd left the rest unsaid.

I feel strange, all right. I feel like a man who's gone to sleep in his own bed and woken up in a foreign country.

He went outside into the rain and stood by the double doors to make a call on his mobile. His call was answered, but no one spoke at first.

'Stella . . .?'

Perić said, 'She is okay. She is not dead. You can make a deal with me? Let's talk.'

39

He phoned five news desks before he found someone who had the siege as a breaking story. The area was gridlocked for a mile in all directions, so he left his taxi in Royal Crescent and walked. His press card got him through as far as the police lines – a slantwise view of the Acropolis and the curtained window – and he stood there looking up along with everyone else, as if the arc lights out in the street might dim and the curtains go up on the show. After a moment, he thought to ask for the officer in charge. He didn't get Lawson, he got Harriman.

'Just to be sure – you know he's using her mobile.'

'We know. How do you?'

'I called her. He answered.'

'You called her?'

'I'm a journalist,' Delaney said. 'A friend.'

Harriman looked at the tape dressing on the cut above Delaney's eye. 'Is there anything else you can tell us?'

'No. I just made the call and this guy answered.'

'And you found us – how?'

'I'm a journalist,' Delaney said again. 'What's happening now?'

'We're waiting to find out,' Harriman said, and ducked back under the police tape.

Delaney could feel a headache nagging to begin and he was shivering slightly, although the wind that backed the rain was warm.

*

The bed was at the rear of the room and to one side. Perić sat cross-legged facing Stella and nudged the underside of her chin with the barrel of the Militech.

'What you think, Stella? You think we'll make it?'

'Tell them what you want. They'll give it to you.'

'That's nice.'

She felt dizzy. She was trying to breathe slowly and think straight. There were some basic rules for this kind of thing.

Don't antagonize. Don't show hostility. Don't argue. Don't talk too much. Don't panic. Make yourself known to your captor as a human being – show your feelings without showing fear. Try to reason with your captor, but don't deride him or suggest his position is hopeless: remember, you're the hostage, he needs that sense of power. Do what you're asked to do unless it puts you in clear danger. Do not resist violence. Don't negotiate, leave that to the negotiator.

Where is the fucking negotiator?

'You think we get what we want?' Perić asked. 'You think they will be sensible?'

'You want to get clear. I want to get clear. They want me to get clear. It all adds up.'

'Good,' he said. 'Because if they get tricky with us, I shoot your tits off.' He laughed and reached out and covered first one breast, then the other, with his free hand. 'A shame.'

She looked away to avoid his eyes and saw the dead man's broken head, his eye out on a string.

Perić said, 'Wait.'

He walked behind his coverlet-guideline to the door and went out. For a moment, Stella thought he had another plan, a way out, something no one else could have thought of; then he was back, carrying the bottle of Southern Comfort. He uncorked it and took a long drink.

She thought he looked pretty wild without the booze to help him.

The negotiator came on five minutes after that. Perić spoke the word 'Yes' four or five times, then held the phone to Stella's ear.

'DS Mooney . . . Stella . . . it's Matthew Lippman.'

Stella remembered his fat frame going upstairs ahead of her, the attic room, Henry Deever going past her with a sound like a kite in the wind.

'Matthew . . .'

'I'm going to ask for proof of life on a ten-minute basis, okay? Every ten minutes I get to speak to you or we assume you're dead. That's a given. He has to deal with that.'

'Okay.'

'Just so you know. Every ten minutes. That aside, we're going to find a way to give him what he wants. You can tell him that.'

'Okay.'

'Stay calm. Everything's going to be fine.'

'Okay.'

'He'll get what he wants. It might just take a little while.'

'Okay.'

She knew that he was saying only what he would be happy for Perić to hear.

'Okay,' Lippman said. 'I'll talk to you in ten.'

She looked up at Perić and nodded. He put the phone back to his ear. 'You know this,' he said to Lippman, 'how this goes. Me too. You promise but you don't give. You try to figure out how far can I be pushed, how much time can you waste. There are gunmen lined up on the window looking for one chance. I know this. I know your job. It is to try to make me see that all is impossible, but things will be better if I send out DS Mooney and put down my gun and give it up. Okay. Hang on the line.' He laughed. 'Is that how you say it? Hang on the line?'

'I'm hanging on,' Lippman said.

Perić collected the Street Sweeper and went elbows-and-knees to the window, tapped the glass with the barrel to break it, looked out once to find a target, braced himself and kicked out twelve shots. Twelve shots, three seconds. People went down like corn flattening in the wind. The police vehicle Perić had chosen seemed simply to disintegrate as flames chased along the chassis, then the tank exploded and a small fireball lifted into the air along with glass and charred metal.

Delaney was one of those flat on the tarmac. He rolled over and stood up and looked towards the curtained window.

Stella in there.

He was shaking suddenly, like a man with a fever.

Perić went back to the phone and held it to his ear until Lippman came back on the line. It took a while. 'This is to tell you don't jerk me around.'

'We're happy to talk,' Lippman said. 'Let's talk.' He gave Perić a number to call: his own mobile phone.

'A car,' Perić said. 'We will come out, she will drive, that is all.'

'It'll take some time to organize.'

'Bullshit. You have cars out there. Give me one of those cars.'

'Sure, no problem. I have to talk to the man in charge, you know? I don't authorize that kind of thing. I don't give the orders.'

'Fuck your mother,' Perić said. 'I think I just kill her.' He hung up the phone and smiled at Stella. 'I think I just kill you.'

'He said he's going to kill her.'

'Is he?' Lawson asked.

'Not yet.'

'Will he?'

'Oh, sure.'

'What does he –'

'A car.'

'I don't think so.'

'He's a good negotiator.'

Lippman looked down the street to where firefighters were dealing with the burning vehicle. Paramedics were treating a number of injuries, most minor, though one was a severed artery; they were stretchering that man to an ambulance, a female paramedic keeping pace, one finger stuffed in the wound to hold back the blood.

'Jesus Christ,' Lawson said, 'you're supposed to be the good negotiator. I've never given up a car, never. Once they're mobile . . .'

'You can fix the car.'

'Usually means the hostage winds up dead. They get in, the car travels ten feet and packs up. Doesn't improve the guy's temper.'

'There are advantages.'

Lawson nodded. 'Yeah, advantages for us. My men prefer a car to a house, of course they do. More contained, the target is sitting down and can't move about. We can load a CS gas expellant that operates on remote control. No, sure, it's fine for us – it's bad for the hostage. Keep talking to him.'

'I know that.' Lippman sounded aggrieved. 'I know to keep talking. The trouble is, he knows that too.'

Perić touched her eyes with the gun, touched her breasts, touched her between the legs. He said, 'We will drive to the coast, take a boat, take a train, go to my country, you will serve me as a woman should.' He laughed loudly and took a drink from the bottle.

When the phone rang, he picked up and said, 'Send a bottle of whisky.'

'Okay,' Lippman said. 'Maybe you'd like some food.'

'Just whisky and the car.'

'We're trying to organize that.'

'Organize fast or maybe I toss a piece of her out the window.'

'That's not going to work,' Lippman said. 'For this to go well, she has to be alive and well and unhurt. That's the way of it. Let me speak to her.'

'I let you hear her squeal,' Perić said. Lippman hung up, making Perić smile. 'Tough,' he told Stella. 'He thinks he is tough.'

*

Lawson was talking to the man who owned the Acropolis Hotel. He learned something about the shape of the rooms and the position of the furniture. He learned that there was an air vent that ran across the blocked-up chimney and a hand-basin in each of the rooms. Lawson had already put the utilities on standby, now he asked for the water to be cut off: part of siege technique was to use anything that made the hostage-taker uncomfortable. CS gas through the air vent was a possibility they were exploring.

In the meantime, Lippman rang back.

'Proof of life,' he said. 'Let me talk to Stella.'

'Fuck your mother.'

'Let me talk to her.'

She came on sounding shaky. Lippman asked, 'Are you okay?'

'Yes.'

'He hurt you at all?'

'No.'

'Okay, hand me back.'

Perić said, 'How is my car?'

'You car is under discussion.'

'Bullshit under discussion.'

'We're getting there,' Lippman said. 'Listen, I want to put in a land line.'

'What?'

'The mobile won't hold out for ever. Also, it's not secure. I don't want anyone listening in to this, do you?'

Perić looked at the battery indicator on Stella's phone. It was showing one bar. He said, 'Just get car. We don't need to talk more.'

'Yes we do. I need proof of life. That's non-negotiable.'

'She is alive. You spoke.'

'Tell me what you want in the way of food. Food and drink.'

More technique – you send in food. The plate has a built-in audio-tap. It gives you the upper hand. Your man gets on the line and says, 'I'm going to kill her. I'm killing her, okay? You're holding out on me and she's fucking dead.' Maybe you hear the hostage crying, or pleading. But then you hear him say, 'I'm not going to kill you. It's cool. I'm just telling them that.' It gives you the advantage.

You put in a land line. Some brave man goes up the stairs with a phone on a long lead. The extension stops at the door. Then you give four feet of wire from the door of the room to the phone itself. Why? Because you know that, when you go in, if your man is still on the phone to the negotiator as he should be, he'll be four feet from the door. Knowing where to find him makes it easier to kill him.

'No food, no phone,' Perić said. 'Just get a car.'

Mike Sorley arrived ten minutes later, just as Lippman was getting his proof of life. He asked for a report.

'She's alive and, as far as I can tell, unharmed. She certainly hasn't given any indicators that suggest ill-treatment. He's volatile.' Lippman looked towards the burned-out police vehicle and Sorley followed his gaze. 'We're trying to get food in to them –'

'Audio-tap,' Sorley suggested.

Lippman nodded, '– and a land line, but he's having none of it. Just asks for the car.'

Sorley looked at Lawson, who said, 'I'm resisting that. I don't like that.'

'I know it's not the best option,' Sorley said, 'but if you give him nowhere to go, what then?'

Lawson shook his head. 'Tough to say. He's got some pretty awesome firepower up there. Some sort of rapid-fire shotgun.'

'If he comes out shooting,' Sorley said, 'he'll be using her as a shield.'

'It's likely.'

'She'd stand more chance if you give him the car.' When Lawson didn't reply, Sorley turned to Lippman. 'Your judgement, your call – how long before this blows up in our faces?'

'The problem here is this guy knows what he's doing. Worse than that, he knows what *I'm* doing. You can bet that's why he's saying no to the food and the phone. All that being so, there's not much to distract him with. We could turn off the electricity and leave him in the dark. That might make him angry, but it won't rattle him.'

'Jesus,' Sorley said, 'why do negotiators never give a straight answer?'

'Part of the training,' Lippman said. 'Basically, my job is to bore people shitless.' Then he said, 'Okay, the way things are at the moment, I can probably keep him talking for fifteen, maybe thirty minutes. After that, who knows?'

Sorley asked Lawson, 'What's going to change in fifteen minutes? You've got men deployed, you've got the street contained . . .'

'Nothing,' Lawson agreed.

'Will he come out?' Sorley was speaking to Lippman

again. 'Will he send her out? Is there the slightest chance?'

'No.'

'Give him the car. Tell him the car's on its way. Let's get this done with.'

40

The ghost in the machine: what is it? The soul, the ego, pure spirit? Stella looked at the dead man and saw just a shell. Whatever it had been that made him himself had left, emerging from that ragged hole in his head, wings beating for the sky. He could have been a waxwork in an exhibition of early surgical techniques, or something from the Black Museum.

Flies had come from somewhere, a little group of them massing on the ceiling. She remembered the clouds of flies in the room where Jimmy Stone and the Deevers had sat round in a ring.

Perić was juggling with the Militech, spinning it on the trigger-guard. He said, 'You think they are fucking us around, Stella? I think so. You think it takes so long to fetch a car? No, surely not.'

'They have to get authorization.'

'Who you think they ask – the fucking Queen of England?'

'It takes time.'

'Yeah? I don't have time.' He dialled the number Lippman had given him and said, 'Look up to the window,' then walked behind Stella to unlock the handcuffs and pull her to her feet. He recuffed her, hands behind her back, and guided her to the window, staying very close to her, pressing up against her so that you couldn't have told which profile was which.

Those with binoculars saw it, Stella felt it – the blade of the knife as it touched her throat just under the point of the jaw, the cutting edge cold and rough as Perić applied pressure. He leaned on her to keep her trapped, which gave him a free hand for the phone.

'You can see?'

'If you hurt her,' Lippman said, 'the deal's off.'

'No, no. If I *kill* her the deal's off, because then I have nothing to trade. If she is still alive, you make deal.'

'Put the knife down and we can talk.'

'No. Listen. For the next ten minutes, she is probably alive. Probably. I don't know because sometime in the next ten minutes, I will cut her throat. I have done this to people before and it is not a good way to die. First, you know it is coming, second, it hurts. If I do it slow, it hurts a lot, there is much trauma. Okay? You understand all this? In case not, I tell you again. From when I turn off this phone, I start looking at my watch. Sometime before ten minutes, I cut her throat. Maybe it is three minutes, maybe it is seven. Now tell me, where is the car?'

'On its way.'

'Oh, yes? On its way? How long, you think?'

'I'm not sure. Soon.'

'Yes, it had better be soon. It had better be before ten minutes.'

'Okay, look, let's put a time on this, let's agree a time, something reasonable.'

'Sure. What you want? Three or four hours, maybe? Tomorrow morning?'

'The important thing is to stay calm. The car's coming. Don't worry.'

'I am not worried. Stella, she is a little bit worried.'

'Let me speak to her.'

'For proof of life? You have proof of life, here she is, look.'

Perić moved his hand an inch, the slightest of gestures, and Stella leaped.

'You see?' Perić asked. 'I make a start. Just a little.'

Sorley lowered his binoculars. 'Jesus Christ, man, he's cut her. Give him the fucking car.'

'It's not here.'

'When will it be?'

'They're coming through on sirens, but the whole fucking area's gridlocked.'

'Give him a car. Give him any car. Give him my car.'

'The car we're waiting for is rigged with a disconnector. There wasn't time for the CS gas, but at least we can immobilize it.'

'You think he's bluffing, do you?' Lawson didn't reply. 'You think that DS Mooney will still be alive ten minutes from now?' He corrected himself. 'Eight minutes?'

Lawson spoke to Lippman. 'What's your vote?'

'Truth? I've lost control of this. He's switched the mobile off. I can't read him; I can't second guess him; I don't know what he's going to do.'

'Give him my car,' Sorley said.

Lawson shook his head. 'A few minutes more. They could be here. If he kills her, we take him out, he knows that.'

'You're saying he won't kill her?' Sorley asked.

'I'm saying I think it's unlikely.'

'Ever known it happen? Ever known a situation where the hostage *was* killed?'

Lawson was silent. He'd known a few.

The flies were a little coronet round the dead man's head. They lifted and circled and dropped down to feed and lay their eggs.

Perić lay on the bed next to Stella and took long swallows from the bottle of Southern Comfort. He said, 'Before war came, know what I was?'

'Tell me.' Stella was fighting a nausea of fear, trying to keep the shake out of her voice. The blood flow from her neck had dried, leaving a double trail that stained her collar and ran out of sight. It was itchy.

'I was many things. Truck driver, taxi man, painter for houses, barman . . . Then comes the war and I am soldier. Fighter. Some fighters you must train: some have talent. I have talent.'

'If you switch off the phone, how will they let you know the car is here?'

'There is no car.'

'Of course there is. They told you . . .'

'No, no, Stella. There is no car. They have decided – first you die, then I die. After ten minutes they will come in.' He had reloaded the shotgun and laid it ready on the floor by the bed. The Militech was tucked into his belt. 'After ten minutes, they will come in after me and you will be dead.'

'Switch it on.' Her mouth was dry and she felt cold, as if the temperature had suddenly dropped. 'Switch it on and they'll be there to tell you the car is ready.'

'You believe this?'

'It's there. It's down there waiting.'

He leaned across and touched the place where he'd cut her, then touched her hair, then her mouth. 'If I switch on and they do not call . . .?'

She couldn't speak.

He switched the phone on and it rang almost at once.

Lippman said, 'The car's here. It's here. Bring her out.'

One arm tight round her, the magnum just behind her ear, his head so close to hers that their silhouettes merged. The car was right in front of the house. They walked out like a couple dancing a strange front-to-back version of the tango, step-perfect. To the SO19 marksmen, they were a single target.

He had told her what to do. 'We will get in on the passenger side, together. You will sit on my lap. Then you will move over to the driver's seat and I will crouch down below the dashboard. Then you drive.'

He had a plan, but Lawson and Sorley had none. In the moment before Perić and Stella came out, Lawson had said, 'He'll let her drive him for a while, then he'll kill her anyway. Abandon the car. Steal another, or hijack a motorist. She's as good as dead now.'

'But she's not. She's not dead now.' It was the best Sorley could do.

Delaney had stopped breathing. He watched as Stella and Perić advanced on the car. He could feel in himself the impulse to movement, but hadn't the least idea what he could do except get her killed.

Perić pulled them up for a moment while he looked round, trying to pinpoint the danger zones. If they made a move and he had to kill her there and then, he wanted to know where they would come from, where the covering fire was located. But there wasn't the tension in the air that always precedes violence; it felt good, it felt as if he was in with a chance.

A few more steps, and Stella could reach down to open the passenger door; then they would be in and travelling. Twenty seconds, maybe less. There was an unnatural silence: just the rumble of a plane above the cloud, a blackbird fooled by the arc lights . . .

And then a woman's voice, shouting.

Zuhra's voice, as she came out of the crowd and walked towards the car, her eyes fixed on Perić , seeing no one but him, her body rigid with hatred.

Shouting the name of her village – *Remember?*

The name of her mother and her father – *Remember?*

The names of her grandparents – *Remember?*

The name of her brother, whose throat was cut – *Remember?*

The name of her sister, who was raped and slashed – *Remember?*

Not policemen with guns, not fire funnelling in from the rooftops, just this girl walking towards him, hands at her sides, head thrust forward, calling his crimes out to him. He saw her and knew her at once, half-turned towards her, his gun moving from Stella's head to line up on his accuser. And, in that moment, between his head and Stella's head, there appeared a thin slice of light as his profile came clear of hers.

One SO19 marksman had the benefit of that gap. The bullet took Perić just over the ear. Stella felt herself hurled forward, but it was just his body shoving her as he fell. She hit the car and sat down in the road, breathless. Zuhra was standing quite still, staring down at Perić's body.

Then everyone was moving, Delaney included. He would have got to her, would have held her, would have told her that it was fine, it was okay, it was all right, but someone else was there first, Stella with her arms wrapped round him and hanging on as if he were her last chance.

'It's fine,' George told her. 'It's okay, it's all right.'

41

There was a lot to do.

Stella went to hospital and stayed there for three hours, then George took her home. She wasn't speaking and she wasn't crying. Someone had returned her mobile phone to her, but the battery had given out.

She stripped and walked into the shower. She had to stay there a long time, because she was washing the hardening cap of Perić's blood and brain tissue out of her hair.

She walked round the house, unable to settle, and George went with her from room to room. She was drinking as she walked: half a tumbler of vodka over ice, but it wasn't going to help.

She opened the french window into their scrap of garden and took a small chair to the step and sat there, just out of reach of the rain.

When the morning light pushed up behind the rainclouds, she slept.

That same morning, Yannis Stamas opened his eyes. He could see and he could remember and he could talk. What he couldn't do was move.

DI Mike Sorley paid him a visit on that same afternoon, because there were a number of things that Yannis wanted to talk about and AMIP-5 took priority with the airport hotel killings. Dawson and Vickers would come later. Yannis was sitting up, though that wasn't something he could do alone. He could swivel his head and he could breathe and the medical staff were calling him lucky.

Sorley listened while Yannis talked. He mentioned the Tanners a lot. From time to time he paused and licked his lips and Sorley helped him to a sip of water from a bottle with a plastic straw. He knew that beneath the sheets there were tubes and containers that took away Yannis's waste.

For a while, he tried to feel sorry, but soon gave up.

Three days later, Stella sat at a table outside a café in Notting Hill. It was a day of sun and high white clouds, a light breeze turning the leaves of the roadside trees. The café was just down the street from John Delaney's flat.

She had got up early that morning and driven to keep her appointment with Anne Beaumont, then left her car and walked through the park. She had nothing to do for a week: Sorley had suggested she take that long. She didn't need a week. She needed the rest of her life, or else no time at all.

She ordered a glass of mineral water, then took three items out of her pocket: her mobile phone, the set of house keys Delaney had given her, the letter she had written to George. The letter was dog-eared now, and still unopened.

She put all three down on the table in front of her.

What will you do?
I don't know. Maybe nothing.

That's not possible, is it? You have to lie or not lie. Be here or be there.

Doesn't it tire you – always taking the whitewater route?

I'm a shrink. It's my job. You hope that if you don't do something, someone else will.

Maybe.

And then it won't be your fault.

I think our time's up, isn't it?

So whose fault will it be, Stella?

Isn't our time up?

The waitress brought her water, then started to set the tables for lunch. From where Stella was sitting she could see Delaney's window. The curtains were part-drawn.

She shuffled the items in front of her, moving them one over the other in sequence: find the lady. She lifted the glass to drink and sunlight flashed through the water, blinding her to everything.

Read on for a taste of

Nothing Like the Night

The new Stella Mooney novel from
David Lawrence

Published by Michael Joseph
in May 2003 at £9.99

Once she had been beautiful; now she was eight days
dead, her body slashed repeatedly.

At first, she's just Jane Doe of Notting Hill, then DS
Stella Mooney finds a suspect. But while he is in custody,
another body is discovered, butchered in the same way.

It seems that Stella and her team are looking for that
most dangerous of creatures: someone who kills to feed
a terrible appetite. In fact they are up against something
even more terrifying . . .

Although it was broad day, every light in the house was burning and Stella Mooney knew something dreadful had happened. The place cast a hard, pale glare like a lamp in sunshine. Her first move – any police officer's first move – was to call for back-up, but either she was in a black transmission spot or her mobile's battery was down. She walked up the path to the front door and the journey seemed to take an hour. The sound of the doorbell, when she rang it, was shocking: it struck through the dead silence in the house like a sudden shout. The front door had a frosted glass panel. There were shadows on the glass. Stella wanted to turn and leave. She wanted to hurry away and be somewhere else; be someone else; but her hand went to the letterbox and she pushed it up and stooped and peered in.

The children were hanging from the upstairs banister, three children in their nightclothes. She could see their legs in cartoon character pyjamas, she could see their feet, still and white. She was still carrying her phone and, somehow, she was able to dial without taking her eyes from that terrible sight, but as she pressed the buttons they flew off into the air like tiny birds, fluorescent blue and emitting little beeping cries.

Stella woke sitting upright. She was speaking on an indrawn breath, but had no idea of what she'd just said.

She drew her knees up against the sharp pain in her abdomen and wrapped her arms round, hugging herself, stifling the sounds of her own weeping. The man beside her was fast asleep and she didn't want to wake him; didn't want to tell him about the dream that was still snagged in the shadows round the room. If she closed her eyes the images were still there: pale feet as still as stone. Stella shuddered then caught her knees more tightly. A two-tone ARV siren started thinly somewhere down the North End Road, swelled as the police driver pushed things just past the limit, then tapered off into silence. A 747 rumbled down the Heathrow corridor.

Three babies. Dead babies. One of them mine.

Stella stretched her legs to the floor and lifted her weight off the bed as slowly as she could. A couple of floorboards creaked and the bedroom door closed with a click because there was a wind outside and the basement flat had windows that had warped and doors that showed a gap above the floor. Stella had to tug the door against the draught to close it. She went into the kitchen and poured herself a drink: it was vodka and she felt the need of it. In the basement area outside the window, sheets of newspaper and burger cartons were floating and flapping, caught by a tiny twister. As she watched, sipping her drink, a dustbin lid lifted off and smacked against the basement wall. She looked up and saw the dark shape of the street's only roadside tree seeming to furl and unfurl as the wind battered it. Clouds were travelling fast and when Stella lifted her gaze to beyond the treetop, she saw, in a cloud-break, that rarest of all London sights: a star.

The house blazing with lights was something new,

otherwise it had been the usual dream. A dead baby dream.

She ate the ice from her first drink, and went to the fridge for more, her glass in one hand, the uncapped vodka bottle in the other. She was loading and pouring when the door opened behind her and he came into the room carrying her mobile phone.

'It went off. Sorry.'

'It woke you up.' She dialled 'last call' and checked the number.

'Well, yes. It doesn't matter.' He swapped the pager for her drink, took a swallow, then handed it back. 'Are you going to call, or do you want me –' *To lie for you,* was the unspoken part of the sentence.

'No. I'll call in.'

She lifted the kitchen phone and dialled DI Sorley's mobile. He must have been waiting for the call, because the ringing tone lasted only a moment. She said, 'It's DS Mooney, boss.' Sorley gave her brief details and an address in Notting Hill Gate. 'I'll be twenty minutes,' she said. 'Scene of crime people?'

'I've got some regulars,' Sorley told her, 'officers we like to work with. We'll have a full team by the morning. Anyone you fancy?'

Stella asked for DC Pete Harriman and DC Andy Greegan. She wanted Sue Chapman, if possible, as co-ordinating officer.

Sorley said, 'Greegan's already there.'

A couple of miles away, the same damp wind was blowing across the headstones and broken pillars of Kensal Green cemetery, putting up a howl when it hit the granite edges, flattening the posies of silk flowers. A dog was going through, a brindle half-hound, lean and low-backed, padding along in the pre-dawn dark and seeming to look for something. It caught a scent and turned down between one of the aisles of stones until it came to the blocky shape of a mausoleum. The lock on the barred gate was broken and the gate stood open. The dog went in and immediately shapes stirred in the blackness; a low growling started up, coming from half a dozen throats. The pack rose and circled, as if it were one dog rather than ten.

At the centre of this movement was a boy of about ten. He woke, briefly, as the cool air reached him and the growling of the pack quickened his senses; then, as the incomer was accepted and the dogs settled once more, he fell back into sleep.

Stella found some wallpaper music on the radio and drove too fast through the West Kensington backstreets. There were lights shining in the Harefield Estate tower blocks: shebeens in operation, crack parties, all night fuckfests. The wind hammered the great, grey slabs like the sea at a cliff-face. She wondered whether the people who slept in the topmost flats of the tower blocks could feel the sway. She wondered when the whores ever slept.

She thought she would never get rid of the dreams. The dead baby dreams.

You could smell her before you could see her: Jane Doe several days dead, flat on her back, one arm folded across her abdomen, the other flung out so that it overhung the edge of the bed. You could see she was a woman, but that was about all because her body had gone through a number of changes: the warp and weft of death, the addition and subtraction. It was still possible to tell that someone had used a knife on her: the multiple cuts were easily visible even though the body had begun to weep; but the one that had killed her was obvious: a dark gape across her throat, like a slice taken out of a watermelon.

DC Andy Greegan had already done his work: organizing an uncorrupted path from the street to the body, putting the stills photographer and the video man to work. Everyone knew what to do. A forensics team was fine-combing the room, looking for any hint, any murmur of a clue: forensic tittle-tattle. Like them, like everyone there, Stella was dressed in a white disposable coverall. Forensic officers went silently from room to room like ghost-dancers shepherding the souls of the dead.

With the hood pulled over and tightened, DI Mike Sorley was a tubby snowman with a five o'clock shadow. Like others at the scene, he had smeared a gobbet of cream astringent under his nose and was making a conscious effort to breathe through his mouth. Jane Doe was in the bloat stage of decay and she smelled powerful. Sorley showed Stella a photograph in a decorated leather frame: a head and shoulders studio shot of a young woman. She was beautiful enough to turn heads; maybe to stop hearts; certainly to break them: almost perfectly even features, apart from the mouth which was too full to be perfect, though who would have complained? A long sweep of throat; a plunge neckline that showed the rise of her breasts.

'Is this her?' Stella asked.

'Must be.'

Death had changed Jane Doe: changed her dress-size and her complexion; changed the shape of her face and the light in her eye. You'd have to know her to be sure. You'd have to be a loved one.

'There are two bedrooms,' Sorley went on, 'both have got girls' stuff in them. In this room, the clothes fit someone her size. The other girl must be going on six feet tall.'

'Where is she?'

'The other girl? We don't know yet.'

'Names?'

'If we're right, the dead one's called Janis Parker. Her flatmate is Stephanie James. We've got bills, letters, credit cards and so forth. Her passport was in her handbag.'

'For both of them?'

'A couple of bills for Stephanie James. Otherwise, nothing. Wherever she is, her personal stuff's with her. Why not?'

'So, credit cards for Janis Parker,' Stella said. Then: 'Money? Jewellery?'

'Jewellery, yes. Not sure about money. No folding stuff in her wallet, but maybe she just hadn't been to the cashpoint recently.'

'Not robbery, then . . .'

'Doesn't look that way,' Sorley said, then shrugged. 'But I wouldn't want to second-guess it. This is only what forensics have found: top of the pile stuff. You'll need to turn the place over when they've finished.'

Stella and Sorley stepped apart as a forensic officer went between them with a fine-mesh net mounted on a telescopic aluminium pole. He was netting flies. In a fresh body, there's a rough rule of thumb for calculating the time of death: 98.6 degrees minus the rectal temperature divided by 1.5 equals the approximate number of hours since death occurred. Jane Doe was a long way from being fresh and the pathologist would have to rely on other evidence: the time maggots take to hatch and pupate would provide more figures in the raw arithmetic of death.

Stella noticed something about the photo and about the corpse. She went closer, trying to think of Jane Doe as nothing more than a puzzle to be solved. The flesh was marbled, red and black, and swollen with gases; two maggot masses were feeding on her, one around the wound in her throat, the other in her groin. And more inside, Stella knew, feeding and growing and getting ready to break out.

She crouched down beside the body to take a closer look at the wristwatch on the outflung arm, then got back to her feet and turned to look at Sorley, but he had gone. She found him in the living room, standing close to the wall in order to keep out of the way of members of the forensic team who were working floors and surfaces.

'I already looked,' he said. 'Yes, it's the same watch as in the photo. Rolex. Very nice. Just like everything else.' He looked round the room at the minimalist furniture, the wide screen TV, the Bang & Olufsen sound system, the Damien Hirst spot painting. He didn't mean very nice, he meant very expensive. The TV was on: *España Viva*. 'Close relative ID will let us know for sure,' Sorley said, 'but it's her. Janis Parker.'

'Who found her?'

'There's a uniform with a sour look on his face parked outside in a marked vehicle. They took the call.'

Stella nodded. 'Okay, boss, I'll talk to him.'

'You saw the cuts on her . . .'

'I did, yes. A frenzied attack,' she added, putting the phrase in quote marks.

'Let's hope so.'

Stella looked at him. 'Hope so?'

'Because if it wasn't that, then someone was playing with her.'